FOOL For You

STEFANIE K. STECK

This one is for those who feel like they are too much and not enough at the same time. I guarantee you—you are perfect the way you are.

Author's Note

Fool For You is a contemporary small-town romance that handles mature themes. It is intended for an 18+ audience. Though it is cracked door, mild spice, and sexual acts are implied, there are no explicit details. It deals with topics that have taken research, such as day to day life of a barrel racer, rodeo broadcaster, and rodeo travel. Even with research, creative liberties were taken. Content warnings are—parental neglect, narcissistic parent and misogyny in a rodeo/work setting. I hope I have handled these topics with care. Your mental health matters most, so please protect yourself. Thank you for choosing *Fool For You*. I hope you love reading it as much as I love writing it.

Hartwell Hills
RANCH
Lake
Lottie's River
Lachlan's House
Cow Pastures
Main Barn & Events
Horse Pasture
To Gardens
Bunkhouse
Stables & Indoor Arena
Garage
Rhett's Cabin
Main House
To Town

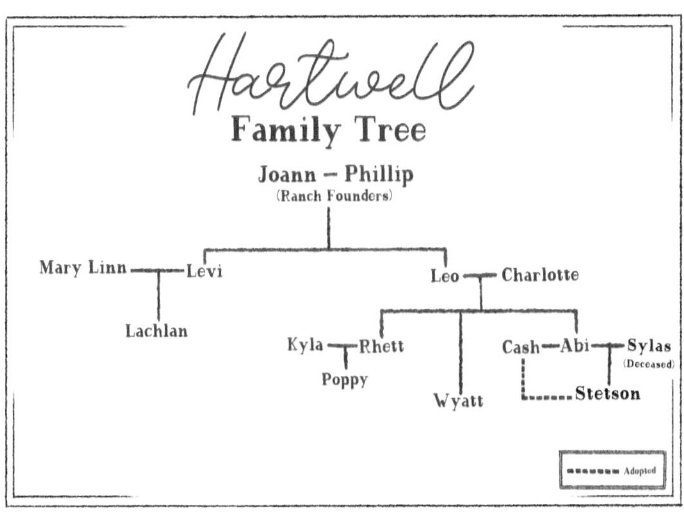

Hartwell
Family Tree
Joann — Phillip
(Ranch Founders)
Mary Linn — Levi
Lachlan
Leo — Charlotte
Kyla — Rhett
Poppy
Wyatt
Cash — Abi — Sylas
(Deceased)
Stetson
Adopted

PROLOGUE

Wyatt

THERE WAS NO DOUBT in my mind that Quinn Compton was the most beautiful girl I had ever laid eyes on. And I have seen—and been with—a lot of girls. But Quinn Compton, *man,* she blew them all out of the water. This barrel racer who had been spending all her time in my rodeo arena...there was something about her. And I wanted—no, *needed*—to find out what it was.

She was sitting at the opposite end of the bar top, a smile on her pretty lips as her laugh carried through the room. My brother, Rhett, and his wife had already made their way to the pool table. My overbearing cousin, Lachlan, was occupying himself with a solo game of darts. My sister was—well, I wasn't sure where she had gone off to. Scanning the room for Abi, I couldn't see her or Cash Callahan anywhere. Maybe it was for the better that my family wasn't around...I could get Quinn to talk to me then.

I had tried. Lord, had I tried. But she was making it hard. She would raise an eyebrow at me, roll her eyes, and heave a sigh of annoyance that forced her chest up in the air—which only distracted me more. But now with everyone out of my way...she was mine.

My mouth twitched as I watched her pull her drink to her lips, a smile escaping as she talked to Jason, the only bartender at the local joint in Alpine Ridge, The Steel. Quinn's brown hair was pulled into a tight ponytail, and her emerald eyes pulled me from my seat. I made it to her in record time, nothing in my line of sight but her.

Leaning against the bar top, cocking a hip as I crossed my ankles, I gave her a lopsided smirk—the same smirk I knew put so many others on their knees. Quinn's head turned slowly, her drink still lingering at her lush, kissable lips as she eyed me up and down. Her lips pursed as she swallowed, her eyebrows pinching in the cutest way.

"Quinn," I slipped her name from my lips, using the back of my fingers to run up and down the skin on her arm. "How long are we going to tiptoe around each other?"

Her eyes blinked, her face stoic and completely void. "I'm sorry, what?"

"Come on," I gave a laugh, stretching my neck, making sure to flash her some skin. I kept my hair short for a reason. The girls loved my neck. They would kiss and lick it every time. It was their weakness. "I see the way you look at me."

"The way"—she stammered, her finger pointing to her chest—"*I* look at *you*?" The same finger pointed at me.

A chuckle left my lungs. "I see it, I"—I raised my thumb to my bottom lip, rubbing a line down to my chin—"feel it."

"You feel it?" she repeated.

"Don't you?" I leaned in, my voice dropping so only she could hear me. She was so close to me, I could kiss her. All I had to do was—

She coughed. "No."

Quinn stood, taking a long drink of her beer before heading to join Rhett and Kyla at the pool table. Without missing a beat, Quinn picked up a pool cue, did a sexy little dance with Kyla, and then joined their game with ease.

She really was making this hard, wasn't she?

My family hustled around the arena to put our little makeshift rodeo together. I situated myself on the gate, locking the heels of my boots to the rail. Adjusting my baseball cap, I watched Cash—who was still hanging around, even though I'd rather he leave—sticking near my sister as they gathered everything for livestock rides. Lachlan was pulling in the calves, Rhett was leading horses to the chutes, and Stetson was rolling out the barrels with Quinn...

Quinn.

It had been less than twenty-four hours since she turned me down at The Steel, and since then, she had been taunting me. She would walk by me with a sway in her hips. She would flip her hair as she passed, her coconut scent filling the air around me. She would lick her lips, and her eyes—which still pulled me towards her—would meet mine.

Like I said. She was taunting me.

And it was working.

I couldn't keep my eyes off her.

There was just something about her...

"Compton." I hummed as she passed me for what felt like the tenth time. I had no idea what to say; I just needed her to look at me, needed her to *notice* me. "You belong on the dirt, don't you? Watching you ride..." I tsked my tongue.

"I mean..." she started, not letting me finish my sentence. "I'm a barrel racer, and I own two horses, so...yeah," her eyebrows pinched. "I belong on the dirt."

"You fit right in with the Hartwells. It's about time we make it official."

Oh, that was bad.

Play it cool, Hartwell.

"From here, it looks like everyone fits in but you." She tilted her head and gave me a puzzled expression. "Now, if you don't mind." She turned, her ass in those Wranglers the only thing I saw.

"Oh, I mind." I raised a brow and watched her walk away.

"Maybe"—she flipped around—"if you would get your ass off the gate and saddle a horse, I'd be more inclined to talk to you."

She passed me, each time teasing me more and more.

She had to know what she was doing to me.

Damn this woman.

She was going to be the death of me.

"So," I slipped my hands in my pockets as I walked up to Quinn.

It was done. She had been here for months, and she was officially finished using the arena.

The girl who had occupied my mind was leaving.

And I never got her.

"You're leaving."

Quinn glanced at me, those eyes still creating that magnetic pull, her hand still firm on her white horse's reins. "Yup."

"I take it you're coming back?" I took a step forward.

"Why would you assume that?" She raised a brow.

Frowning, I looked at Cash standing at her trailer. The man was moving here, most likely marrying my sister...he was Quinn's trainer...it made sense in my mind. Plus, I wanted to see her again. And again. And again. "Isn't Cash moving here?"

"And that would determine me coming back, why?" She stepped beside me, her horse's coat grazing my side.

"I mean, unless you're finding a new trainer—"

"I'm not."

"That means you have to be coming back here to train."

"Maybe he's coming to me?"

The horse's hoof hit the trailer with a clang, and she led him inside. I couldn't help but stare as her body moved. Her small waist, the curves in just the right places, as she bent and tied the lead to the hook. She flipped her long brown hair to the side, exposing her shoulders. Damn, she was sexy, but it was more than that. And I couldn't quite put my finger on it. She was feisty, determined, controlled, everything I wasn't. And I was intrigued. I wasn't ready to let her go just yet.

"Okay, Quinn," I sighed, trying to drop all demeanor that I *wanted* her. The normal pick-up lines weren't working anyway. It was time to up my game. "I know you're heading out, and I know you are going to a rodeo, but I'd really like to take you out. Let me buy you a drink at least—"

Quinn jumped from the trailer, her waves bouncing over her shoulder as her laugh filled the air, until her face turned serious as she put her hands on her hips. "No."

"Why not?" I took a step forward, almost trapping her by the edge of the trailer. Her horse whined, the echo filling the metal area. "I'm a good guy, Quinn, and I think if you gave me a decent shot, you'd see that."

Quinn's eyebrows rose, her forehead crinkling as she stared at me in complete disbelief. "A good guy?" she repeated.

"Yeah." I leaned forward, coming closer to her as I placed my arm right above her head, leaning on her trailer. "I have references if you'd like." I smiled down at her, loving how much shorter she was than me. I could pick her up and hoist her over my shoulder. I could hear her laugh now.

"Wyatt Hartwell, you are not a decent guy," she said sternly as her palm found my chest. She pushed hard, making me fumble back. "I know exactly what you are."

"And what's that?" I asked, my brow furrowing.

She heaved a sigh and straightened her back, and when her emerald eyes met mine, they were just as feisty as the rest of her. "You're a playboy who, rumor has it, is checking off the Miss Rodeos from every state. Call me a prude, but I'd rather not be with a man who has slept with fifty-plus women. You are handsome, I'll give you that, but you think you're irresistible. Let me tell you, you're not. You're childish—very childish—and Wyatt, that's a turn off. I do *not* want a man who doesn't have a speck of dirt on his jeans and"—she waved her arm up and down, gesturing to my pressed jeans—"you are more starch than man. And last, I've been here for weeks now, and all I've seen is your sister, brother, cousin, and Cash work their asses off while you sit on the sidelines and go to The Steel. Yet you call this *your* ranch. All you care about is who is keeping your bed warm and how soon you can announce at the NFR. Man up, Wyatt, get over yourself, and then maybe—" She scoffed. "Nah...not even then."

Then she turned, dirt flying around her boots, leaving me alone in the entrance to the stable.

What the *fuck* just happened?

ONE

Quinn

Eight Months Later

"I just don't understand why you're moving to Idaho of all places," my mother asked me, her voice carrying through the hallway as I packed everything I considered mine.

It wasn't a lot. My horses, Charming and Hook, were already at the stables, so I was using their trailer to get my things from Big Sky, Montana, to Alpine Ridge. So far, I had my bed, dresser, boxes full of random things, my extensive wardrobe, and my riding gear—all shoved in the back of the trailer. All that was left were the odds and ends to make my new place just that—mine. My toy horse collection from when I was little, books that have become a part of my personality, my turquoise jewelry and earrings, all the ribbons I'd won growing up, and photos of the many pageants I was forced to participate in. On second thought, those could stay. Mom would want to keep those. She could have them.

"Because." I sighed, passing the ribbons for a candle that was basically burnt to the bottom and placing it in the box. "That's where Cash is, and he's my trainer; it makes sense for me to call that home base."

"But this is home." She used her perfectly manicured finger to point at the floor.

I rolled my eyes. "And it always will be, but I'm traveling all over this year to make it to the NFR. It just makes sense to live where I train."

She folded her arms, her lips tightening. My mother, Helen Compton, was a former Miss Rodeo America, but she still lived and breathed that life. She was a coach and guide for the upcoming Miss Rodeo Montana's, getting them to the Miss Rodeo America pageant that took place in December during the National Finals Rodeo, the same place I was trying to get to. Her hair was still teased to perfection, the curls cascading down her shoulders with the perfect wings by her ears. All she needed was a hat with a crown and some fancy jewels, and you'd think she was still Miss Rodeo America. I loved my mother; she wanted the best for me, but for her...the best was following in her footsteps. She tried when I was a kid, but when I enjoyed the horsemanship portion more than anything and leaned that way in life, wanting nothing more than to compete—well, that wasn't what she wanted for me.

That was years ago. I was turning twenty-three this year, and if I was going to be one of the youngest barrel racers in the NFR this year, I needed focus. And let's face it, focus wasn't going to happen if I stayed in this room, staring at all these photos and ribbons.

I needed my own place, my own drive…and that was in Alpine Ridge.

"We haven't even met this man—" she began to argue.

"Yes, Mom, you have. He came here to watch me ride when I signed him, remember? Saddle bronc rider Cash Callahan? He's kinda hard to forget."

Cash and I had gotten closer than I was to my own mother in the year he'd taken me as a client. He actually seemed to care. When I injured my leg and hip last year, he was the one to stay with me and guide me through the healing process. He didn't even seem worried that his only client wasn't bringing in checks to pay him. Hell, he even paid for the use of the training arena. He stuck with me, and this year, he had more clients and even his own events to attend—but he still encouraged me to go for what I wanted. Cash Callahan was more than my trainer; he was my friend. He was family.

My mother straightened her back, her eyes looking towards the ceiling like she was trying to pluck a memory from the light bulb. "Oh yes," she finally sighed, dropping her chin. "I think I remember him, handsome man, Southern, older, right? It would be nice if he came around every now and then."

"Mom, he's my trainer, not my boyfriend." I reminded her, cringing at the thought. According to my mom, I should be in a serious relationship by now. She married my dad after she won America, at the ripe old age of twenty-two. "Trainers don't normally come to Sunday dinners."

"Neither do you." She raised a single brow, her voice lined with clear disdain. "It's been a while since you've joined your father and me for dinner."

How many eye rolls were considered too many? How many times had I rolled them so far?

"Mom," I sighed. "I'm normally traveling on the weekends."

"Yes, but you could come home. It's not like you're gone. Now you will be."

"Seven hours away is not 'gone,' mom."

"She has a point, Helen." My dad, the retired team roper Lance Compton, appeared in the hallway, his hands stuffed in his pants pockets as he peeked in the room. His gray hair was brushed back, his beard growing thicker, his emerald eyes that looked exactly like mine locked on me. He gave me a small smile, reassuring me that he was 'on my side.' "Seven hours isn't far; she's still in the same time zone."

"Lance." Mom turned, most likely shooting him a glare.

Where my mom was stern with me, my dad was gentle, but he always knew when to stay out of a conversation, and by the way his eyebrows shot up, this was one of those times. My mom would win whatever argument she was going to start.

He let out a puff of air. "Let me know if you need help, Pumpkin."

"I will, Dad, thanks." I gave him a wave before turning back to my mom. Her arms were still folded, her gaze still heavy on me.

Ignoring the ribbons that hung on my wall...again, I grabbed a stack of books that had been well-read, my comfort books. *Black Beauty, King of the Wind, The Black Stallion*—pretty much any book about a horse that came out when I was in middle school, I read it and loved it. I was *that* horse girl, and I was proud to say nothing had changed.

Mom's eyes followed my hands, locking on my ribbons. "You're not packing your ribbons?"

I didn't look up from the stack of books on the bottom of the box, instead concentrating on the cover of *Chosen by a Horse.* Finally—after what seemed like forever—I met her gaze.

"Come on, Mom." I slouched. "You'll appreciate those more than I do."

"Quinn, those are a huge part of your childhood."

"Exactly, my childhood." I grabbed the box, spinning on my heel to my bare bed. Setting the box on the bed, I moved to the next bookshelf. Framed photos of me and Hook during our first agility run, and then the day I bought Charming...all photos that friends of mine had taken. Hidden behind those were photos of a much younger me dressed to the nines with a sash across my chest, and a fake smile spread across my lips. I gingerly picked up the photos I wanted, ignoring the others. "I'm not a kid anymore," I continued. "You know I never really cared for that stuff."

With a huff, Mom stomped into my room. "You loved it." She moved the photo of me in a bright pink shirt forward, bringing it front and center on the bookcase. "I was proud of you."

"And you're not now?" I asked quietly, grabbing a few other photos.

The silence was deafening.

In order to make my mother proud, I would have had to do the exact same thing she did. Miss Rodeo Bozeman, Miss Rodeo Montana, and eventually, Miss Rodeo America. There was absolutely nothing wrong with that lifestyle. The Rodeo Queens did more than wave at the crowd, and I knew that. I saw what my mom did with those girls, but that wasn't me. I fell in love with the wind in my hair as the horse was running as fast as it could. I fell in love with the sharp turns as we took those barrels. I fell in love with competition. I fell in love with the rodeo in a different way than my mom did.

My last pageant was when I was thirteen, and I didn't even come in the top five. After that, I turned in my sashes and found a job at the local stables. I mucked stalls, I walked colicky horses, I filled water troughs and hauled hay—and when I made enough, I purchased my first horse, promptly naming him after one of my favorite TV show characters, Hook. Years later, I was able to get Charming from my own income and started to barrel race. I knew the first time Hook and I rounded all three barrels without knocking one down, that was my sport. That was what I was made to do. I signed up for my first rodeo, telling my mom I entered the pageant there just to get her to come. When I rounded barrels instead of taking a crown, she let me know she was disappointed. Her pride in me was gone.

She had never been to another one of my events since.

This was my thing. This was for me.

It didn't matter to me that she wasn't there; it wouldn't stop me from doing what I loved.

Folding up the box, I looked around my nearly empty room.

"I'll be leaving before lunch. I'll let you know when I'm there, okay?" I said softly.

"Quinn." Mom's lips tightened as she picked up the photo of me. "I just wanted the best for you."

"This is the best, Mom." I walked up next to her, taking the photo from her hands and placing it back on the bookshelf. "Maybe you can come to a rodeo and see for yourself?"

She inhaled. "I have a few girls going for Montana this year..."

Of course. She would go if one of the girls she was coaching were going to be there.

"Right, well..." I rubbed my thighs. "I have to keep packing."

A few hours later, I loaded the last of my boxes into the trailer, making sure everything was strapped down. I gave my dad a hug, a quick promise from him that he'd watch my location, before I gave my mom a tight smile and nod. She inhaled, but didn't return my smile. I climbed in my truck, buckled myself in, queued up my audiobook, and set out on my seven-hour drive to my new home—excitement filling my entire body the further I got away from my parents' house.

TWO

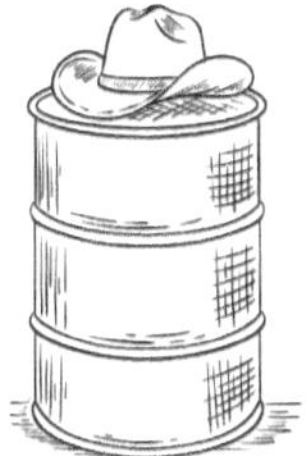

Wyatt

"Mmm," the gorgeous blonde next to me hummed, scooting closer, her skin soft and warm against me. "Good morning."

I mimicked her hum, giving her my signature sexy grin. Her fingers drummed on my pec before she pushed herself off, climbing from my bed. I could hear the faint taps of her feet across the hardwood floor as she took the few steps to the living room. The small apartment above the bunk house wasn't much, but it kept me out of the main house. Not that I didn't love my family—I'd just rather stay here. Especially with a naked woman walking around. Shifting, I took in the sight of—wait...what's her name?—as she bent over, grabbing my button-up shirt.

"Breakfast?" she cooed, looking over her shoulder.

I inhaled, scooching up on the bed a little, my head resting in my palm. "I'm not really a breakfast guy."

Whew...this was stereotypical.

Most of the time, I at least made the gal breakfast. I loved breakfast.

She twisted her lips. "Ah, come on, Wyatt. I'll make you French toast."

I raised a brow. "Do I have eggs?"

I could see her move in the kitchen; the apartment was that small. The studio was perfect for one person, two if they didn't stay long. The living room and bedroom blended into one, the kitchen having a small peninsula island large enough for one person to eat. The only two doors in the place led outside and to the bathroom. Home sweet home.

She opened the fridge. "Yep." She popped back up with a cheesy smile, holding the small basket of eggs that no doubt my sister, Abi, put in there a few days ago. She always made sure I had the basics. "French toast?"

"Sure," I breathed, pulling the blankets from my body and climbing from my bed. "I'll just take a quick shower."

She set the basket of eggs down, the cheesy smile vanishing as a sexy one replaced it. "Oh, in that case." Giving me a grin, she slowly unbuttoned my shirt, dropping it to the floor.

An hour later, fresh from the shower, I kissed the blonde as she stepped outside, my mouth pushing as she pulled. I stayed in the apartment, and she was finally out. We didn't even eat breakfast, and I still didn't know her name. I watched her car leave before I left the apartment, not even locking the door before going straight to the main house.

It was early still. There had to be some breakfast left.

And thank God I smelled coffee the second I opened the door.

"Abi?" I called, making my way into the kitchen, taking off my winter coat, and tossing it on the banister. Knowing my sister, she was there, probably still cooking or making another pot of coffee. She was always moving, always making sure everyone was taken care of.

When I walked under the threshold into the kitchen, I stopped, raising a brow to see my sister hunched over the counter, a rather large book open in front of her. Since my parents had retired, it was Abi, her son Stetson, and her fiancé Cash taking residence in the main house, and even though ranch hands still came in and out, it had become a quieter space. Which meant Abi could do something she wanted to do for a while, become a reader. Normally, I'd see her with AirPods in her ears as she moved, listening to her next audiobook, so seeing a book open in front of her was new.

Her brow was furrowed, her fist covered her lips, and she didn't even look up when I walked in. I let her read, obviously engrossed in whatever was happening, as I moved to get a mug. I filled it, grabbed the creamer, shut the fridge, grabbed a plate and some bacon, all while she read. She didn't even move once, and I wasn't being quiet.

"What'cha reading?" I asked, setting my plate down on the counter in front of her, causing a louder bang than I really intended.

She flinched, her eyes wide as she looked up at me. "How long have you been there?" she asked, taking a deep breath.

I raised my mug and pointed to my plate. "Long enough to get myself breakfast. Even said your name."

Giving me her annoyed sister glare, she sighed and looked down at her book. "You did not."

"I did. What'cha reading that has your attention so well?"

"*A Discovery of Witches,*" she responded as she placed the book-mark in between the pages and closed the book, its deep blue cover standing out against the marble. "It's getting good, and you just had to come in."

"Is it witch porn?" I asked, giving her a sly grin as I popped a piece of bacon in my mouth.

"What?" She stopped, dropping her arms as her brows furrowed.

"Isn't that what people are reading now? Smut?"

"Wyatt." She sighed, the disappointment apparent in her tone. "There is nothing wrong with smut; we've had this conversation."

"I'm just kidding." I gestured towards her book. "I've actually heard good things about it. They turned it into a show. Have you seen it? It's pretty good."

"Cash and I are going to watch it when I'm done." Abi turned away from me, opening the microwave to pull out her own coffee mug. I raised a brow and wondered how long it had been in there, or how many times she had to warm it up. "He's interested just from me telling him about it, but you know he doesn't read much."

"Where is Callahan?" I sat at the stool on the island, lifting my mug of liquid gold to my lips.

"Prepping the arena. He has clients today." Abi looked at her coffee mug, furrowed her brow, and went to the sink to empty the contents, pulling the carafe to refill her mug with a fresh drink. "A few barrel racers and a saddle bronc. He may ask you to keep time, that is, if you don't have any plans."

I nodded. "I have zero plans for today."

Abi took a long drink, her eyes not once leaving me. "Zero?" she parroted, her voice heavy from the hot coffee she just downed like it was orange juice.

Frowning, I shook my head, "None."

As much as I hated it, I had no plans for the foreseeable future, not since my last rodeo. And that was back in October of last year. My email and voicemail sat empty, proof I had seriously screwed up.

Abi narrowed her eyes slightly and nodded. "Okay, that's fine. I'm sure Lach can find something for you to do as well."

"Winter kinda lags on the ranch, sis."

"There's always something to do, Wyatt. I know you're not keen on ranch work—but when you say you have zero plans—"

"I'll help if they really need me." I looked up at her.

She was right, I didn't want to work on the ranch. I didn't want to own a huge percentage of it. I had five percent, and that was enough to eventually build a house on. I had no plans to ask for more, no plans to turn this into my entire life. This wasn't supposed to be my life. I'd been home for weeks, and I had managed to stay away from ranch chores, but my family had begun to get more ruthless, especially since I had only proven to them that I wasn't going back to work anytime soon—not by choice.

"I could put you on payroll at the stables? I could always use an extra hand, and you can get a check. I could get that set up now if you wanted?" She suggested scratching her hairline before running her fingers through her braid. Her engagement ring flashed in the light, reminding me my baby sis—even if it was just by three minutes—was getting married. My older brother, Rhett, was married with a kid. I was the only Hartwell with no future plans to settle down. And I was okay with that. When I didn't answer, she filled the void, "Maybe you should call Hawkins?"

Hawkins, a fellow rodeo announcer and friend, had been my only contact with the rodeo world since I managed to mess up my career. He'd been the one who kept me in the loop and tried to get me into jobs again, even putting my name in a few committees—but no such luck. Our texts and calls had fizzled once the prospect of my getting a job became low.

"What's Hawkins gonna do?" I asked, pushing myself up straight.

She shrugged her shoulder. "Get you a job, maybe?"

"He's trying," I grumbled, knowing he wasn't.

"Think he can try a little harder?" she urged, her eyes scrunching as she clenched her teeth.

My gaze met hers as I slouched. She was trying to be serious and get my ass in gear to get another job. Me? Serious? Nah. Plus, I really wanted the conversation to end. I raised a brow and grinned.

"What? You don't like me here? Sick of me already."

"You know that's not true."

"Oh, come on, Abi. I'm playing." I stood, grabbing my plate and empty mug. "I'll call him, but I doubt he'll have anything new. Most committees won't even consider my name."

Abi scoffed in annoyance. "I don't get it. The guy is fine."

"Well, when you knock out the head of one of the largest rodeo committees and everyone hears about it, no one wants you to announce at their rodeos. My name is no longer gonna help me."

We'd been over this. Again and again. I was so tired of talking about it. Hunching my shoulder, I raked my hand down my face.

"You're a good announcer. You have a finesse to you that no one really—"

"You think I don't know that?" I dropped my arm, frustration seeping out of me. Abi raised her eyebrows, biting her bottom lip.

Well *fuck*.

When I came home, basically a puppy with my tail between my legs, Abi was the only one I wanted to talk to. And I just struck a nerve.

"Sorry," I said softly, taking a step towards her to wrap my arm around her. She rested her head on my shoulder and let out a long exhale. "I'll be productive today."

Raising her chin, she met my gaze. "And what about Melanie?"

Melanie, was that her name?

Letting go of my sister, I returned to my seat. "I'll call her." I lied. I wasn't going to call her. I didn't even get her number.

She raised a single brow and dipped her chin. "Really?"

"Come on, Abi, you know with everything else, that's the only thing that hasn't changed," I muttered under my breath.

Just because rodeos weren't calling didn't mean my phone was silent. I still had the charm and charisma that seemed to attract the bunnies. At least that didn't fade with the hope I'd ever announce again.

I turned to Abi, leaning against the counter. She stood with her hip cocked, one eyebrow raised, and her arms folded. She had the mom thing down; even I was nervous for what she was going to say next.

"She's local, you know. She's going to expect more."

"No one ever expects more from me."

22   STEFANIE K STECK

"That's not true."

"Okay. Let me rephrase that: no girl ever expects more from me." I raised my mug, cheering myself, accepting that's just who I was.

"Ain't that the truth." A Southern drawl came into the kitchen, and with it, my soon-to-be brother-in-law. Cash Callahan removed his hat, his black hair untouched, as he made his way over to my sister, his hand slipping over her waist as his lips met her temple. "Why are we talking about Wyatt's love life?"

I raised a brow and tilted my head. "I wouldn't call it a love life," I muttered.

"Did you not see Melanie leave?" Abi looked at her fiancé, arching her back a little.

Cash raised his brow and gave a slight frown before shrugging his shoulder. "What's wrong with that?"

Thank you, Cash.

Hard to believe that six months ago, I couldn't stand this man after he all but vanished from our lives after Abi's husband—his best friend—died, hurting my sister in the process. Then here he was, marrying my sister and taking my side. Shortly after he moved to Hartwell Hills, Abi shoved a paintbrush in both of our hands and practically forced us to paint her stables. It took a week just being him and me, but thankfully, it broke the dam. He apologized for screwing up when Sylas died, I apologized for holding a grudge, and slowly, the man became a friend. Dare I say, a best friend?

Not that I would admit that aloud to Abi. She could think I still hated him.

"She's local. He never brings local girls back here." Abi raised her hand at me.

"He can bring whoever he wants here, as long as they stay in the apartment and Stetson doesn't see." Cash defended me.

"I'd rather he gets back to work, not just laze around all winter."

"I'm not lazing around. It's only eight. I'm awake and here," I said. "When I see Lachlan, I'll go do any job he wants me to do, and I can help Cash."

"I told him to call Hawkins," Abi said softly, looking up at Cash.

"Any luck there yet?" Cash turned to me.

I shook my head, looking down at my boots.

"Ah, well, it'll happen. Until then,"—Cash took a step, reaching over me to the carafe, still full of coffee—"I have a job you can do."

"What's that?" I asked. "Time your clients?"

"Well, yes." He nodded, filling his own mug with coffee. "But after that, Quinn's arriving tonight. We need all the brawn to get her moved in."

Quinn?

Quinn Compton?

I still thought about Quinn Compton. I thought about all the ways her body moved with her horses as she rounded those barrels. I thought about the way her eyes would meet mine, the perfect shade of emerald to get lost in. And I thought about the way she called me off. *You're a playboy, you're childish, all you care about is who is keeping your bed warm and how soon you can announce at the NFR...*

"She hates me, you know that, right? She'd probably kick me out of her place if I showed up."

"Well, you did hit on her one too many times," Abi mumbled under her breath, yet still clear as day.

"Twice. I hit on her twice." If you'd call that hitting on her.

"And asked her out," Cash added.

"Which she promptly told me no," I reminded him.

"She's not overly fond of you, I'll admit that, but she didn't have much help packing her trailer, so I want to make sure she has help *unpacking* her trailer. Lachlan and Rhett are coming; it would go faster if you would, too." Cash walked back over to Abi, pulling her close to him again.

"Where is she staying?" I asked, not knowing of any place that was for rent around Alpine Ridge.

"The Richards had their condo open up; she paid for the year up front."

"Damn." I raised a brow. "The entire year?"

Cash nodded. "I think Jeff is going to ask her to buy it if she likes it, but she's getting in tonight, and we need the hands." Giving Abi a kiss, he plopped his hat on his head and slapped my shoulder. "She'll be here in a few hours. See ya there?"

Cash left through the back door, not even giving me a moment to answer him. I looked at my sister, who was studying me intently.

Out of everyone on the ranch, she knew.

She was the only one whom I trusted with everything. Maybe it was a twin thing, or maybe it was because I knew she would hit me with hard love and whip my ass back in gear. Whatever it was, she knew every single detail. There was nothing I would keep from

Abi. She knew why I wasn't getting jobs. She knew how I felt about Quinn, even after what she had said to me. She knew I was slowly falling apart and hiding it very well.

"You don't have to go help. I actually agree with you," she said, her tone mixed with a sigh. She walked up to me and wrapped her arms around my middle, her chin resting on my shoulder. I loved being her twin, but I loved how unique we were. "Quinn would absolutely hate having you there."

I let out a laugh. "I'll call Hawkins. Maybe he has some good news for me. And I'll find Lach. And help Cash until he heads to Quinn's." I wrapped my arm around her, squeezing her shoulder. "I'll stop 'lazing around.'"

Abi shook her head. "You know I didn't mean it like that."

"Sure you did, but it's okay."

She pulled away from me, giving me a soft smile. "Call Hawkins." Her smile vanished as she pointed at me, before turning and grabbing her book from the counter. "Now, if you'll excuse me, I have a chapter to finish before I tend to some horses."

"Enjoy." I raised my mug to her as she left the kitchen, leaving me in the silence.

Glancing out the window, I could see Cash greeting his client in front of the stables, a smile on his face as the girl jumped from her truck, the mud slushing onto her jeans and boots. Cash shook her hand and patted her shoulder, leading her into the stables. I looked down at my own jeans and boots—not a speck of dirt on them.

Quinn was right in everything she said to me that day. *Playboy, childish, more starch than man.* And it stung more than it should have.

THREE

Quinn

J UMPING FROM MY TRAILER, I slapped my hands on my thighs. Everything that I put in the trailer was finally in my own small condo, and the joy that radiated through my body was palpable. All the mixed emotions I was feeling while packing were gone, and contentment flowed through me. A stillness that I wasn't quite used to. Was this what life was supposed to feel like? Because if it was, I didn't want any part of it to change.

"That's everything." Lachlan, the only Hartwell I knew nothing about, came out of the condo, *my* condo. He flipped his hat forward again, giving me a quick nod. "Anything else?"

I shook my head. "No, thank you. I really appreciate the help."

"No problem." He walked past me, giving my shoulder a quick pat. "See you at the ranch."

"Bye, Lachlan," I called, waving even though he was already in his truck, before I jogged my way into *my* condo.

I was going to love calling it that.

Cash and Rhett were still inside, each grabbing a box and putting it in the correct room. The condo had an open concept, which I adored. The living room and kitchen blended into one space, the small kitchen island the only thing to mark which room was which. The stairs leading up to the two bedrooms were off to the right, and a small coat closet sat empty, waiting for my many hats and boots. There was also another small closet for a washer and dryer. A window let the natural light in, and I could just see all the possibilities I could do with it.

When I handed Jeff Richards, the owner of the condo, the check for the entire year's worth of rent, his jaw basically dropped. It was half my earnings from the year prior, but looking at the place…it was worth it. *My condo.*

"Do you have any pots and pans?" Rhett asked, opening a single box that was labeled *kitchen* to reveal two of everything. Two plates, two cups, two bowls, two sets of silverware, but no pans. He pulled out the plates and set them on the counter. "This is the only box that says kitchen."

"I have to go shopping. I need to get a few things." I smiled, excitement that I got to pick out my own things soon showing on my face. "Like a couch." I looked at the empty living room. "Or a futon."

"A couch. This isn't a bachelor pad," Cash said as he came up behind me. "Abi and Kyla could go shopping with you. I'm sure they'd have a blast."

"Is it weird I want to do it alone?" I pinched my brow and looked at my trainer.

He snorted. "Not at all. I take it you want to organize and unpack by yourself, too?" He looked around at my condo and the piles of boxes in front of me.

"Kinda." I shrugged my shoulders up to my ears.

"At least let us set up your bed." Rhett didn't even wait for an answer; he just bounded up the stairs two at a time. Cash gave me a smile before he followed, leaving me alone in the living room.

I pulled out my phone, bringing up the chat with my dad. I had updated my parents on the journey so far, but once I made it there, I got so caught up in the unpacking that I had forgotten to let them know I was already feeling settled.

Me

Made it and semi unpacked. Take a look.

I snapped a quick photo of my living room and kitchen and sent it off.

Dad

Looks good, pumpkin! Send a pic when it's all set up.

I smiled, huffing at his positivity when a text from my mother instantly followed. I opened her chat with a deep breath.

Mom

Why don't you have any furniture? You need
a coffee table, a couch, and a love seat. It
looks small. Can you even get a full couch in
there?

Inhaling, I typed out a response to her.

Me

I'm just getting settled. I have to go shopping.

Mom

Don't get too much. It's a tiny space, you're
used to our house, just make sure you stay
within your means, Quinn.

I locked my phone and shoved it in my pocket. The place isn't
too small. It's perfect. And it's mine.

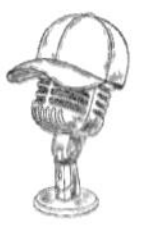

Two weeks later, I not only had a couch, but a coffee table, a small
dining room table, a bookshelf, and everything was unpacked and
where it should be. My photos lined the mantel of the small electric
fireplace, the orange glow of the fire filling the room as the sun set.
The small speaker played country music as I finished cleaning the

kitchen from dinner, and there was a small glass boot filled with some flowers sitting on the kitchen counter.

I was—to say the least—settled. Comfortable. *Home.*

With January coming to a close, I started to piece together my schedule. I knew this year would be packed with rodeo after rodeo, trying to earn as much cash as I could to make it to the NFR. I had to coordinate with Cash on the training, I had to make sure Hook and Charming were ready and up for journeys, and I had to sign up for the rodeos.

Last year, Cash handled all of that for me. Being his only client, he acted more like an agent than a trainer. He called the arenas, he got my name on the boards, he booked the hotels and stables, leaving me with no worries at all. This year it was all me. I had done it before, and I could do it again.

First things first...

I set up my laptop on the kitchen island, taking a seat on the stool. I pulled my water and phone near me.

Me

How many clients do you have now?

I typed out the quick message to Cash, setting my phone down to search for the local equestrian vet, only to pick it right back up again.

I flipped back to the message screen, opening a new tab and typing Abi's number.

The small dots began to dance right away, but instead of a text, a photo showed up of Hook and Charming in their stalls. Hook was reaching over, his lips curled up, and he tried to bump into Charming's in his pestering, big brother way. Charming's face was turned away from him, ignoring Hook's attention-seeking schemes. I loved those two. Each one offered something different, and the photo only showed it. Completely different, yet two peas in a pod. And I loved them more than anything.

Abi

Happy as can be.

Me

What vet do you use? I need to get them checked for the year. Any recommendations?

Abi

Most definitely, I'll shoot his info over to you.

Me

Thank you! I'll stop by later to say hi to them! I know I haven't been around.

Abi

No worries, it's my job, and we love having them here. Stetson and Wyatt have been helping—trust me, your boys are in good hands.

Wyatt Hartwell? Helping with horses?

I chuckled at the thought, not being able to picture him anywhere near the stables. How he and Abi were twins was beyond me. They were so different. I admired Abi in more ways than one. I saw how hard she worked at her stables and how much she cared for her family and the ranch. She turned Cash's life upside down—for the better—and managed to keep the ranch moving despite overcoming her own obstacles. Wyatt, on the other hand...he had everything handed to him.

I would have, too, if I had gone down the path my mom wanted me to. When I told my mother I was done with pageants, it put a rift in our relationship. Her exact words—and yes, I remember them, they ring through my head every now and then—were *"I won't be supporting this, you can do it, but you're doing it on your own."* So I did. I found that stable, I earned the money, and I bought my own damn horses. I worked my ass off to get to where I am, and there's nothing I would trade for it.

There was a small sliver of me that wondered if Wyatt was the same. Maybe he wanted more, too, but with the way he acted—the way he relished his life—told me that sliver was just a pipe dream.

That boy didn't work for anything.

Me? I could see exactly where my life would go, even after I was done competing.

There were a lot of things to consider, but ultimately I wanted to own and run a horse sanctuary. I wanted to take care of the retired racehorses, the retired show ponies, the horses that needed peace before they took their last breath. It was always something I thought of, something I would want to consider in the near future. Until then...

I'd compete.

And I'd save every penny I could to make that happen.

Wyatt didn't have any plans like that for his future. I was certain.

Pushing any and all thoughts of Wyatt out of my head, I dialed the number Abi sent my way, making an appointment for Hook and Charming, then scheduled my first event in four weeks, and then the next, and the next.

I was on a roll, and nothing could stop me.

Not my mother, not Wyatt Hartwell, not another injury—nothing.

That evening, after I had a few months of rodeos scheduled along with hotel room accommodations, I sped to the ranch. I hadn't seen my horses since I moved in, and my heart was feeling the heavy weight of horse mom guilt. The gravel crunched under my tires the second the paved roads ended and Hartwell Hills came into view. The Nova Luna Stable and Training Arena, freshly painted, looked like a completely different building from when I came here almost a year ago. Then it was brown and worn, the classic stables look that went on any ranch—but now the white paint with black trim, and the sign hanging above the entrance made it pop. It was, without a doubt, the most perfect building on Hartwell Hills.

I parked my truck in front and dashed inside, taking a moment to look at Cash's drawings that hung on the sides of the doors. It didn't matter how many times I saw them; they always put a smile on my face. More had been added in the year since he moved in, and they were just getting better and better.

I heard a whine and a huff, and Charming's bobbing head was the first thing I saw once I turned the corner.

"Ah, hey, baby boy." I reached my palm out, his nose nuzzling against it, no doubt looking for a treat. "Do you wanna ride tonight? We can go for a quick one."

He nodded his head, only proving my theory that horses understood the English language. I scratched behind his ears, cranking my neck to take a look at Hook. When I saw nothing but an empty stable, I turned back to Charming.

"Where's your brother?" I asked him.

"I have him."

I half expected Cash or Lachlan, but when I saw who the voice belonged to, I had to keep the irritation down. I was not in the mood to be hit on. I kept my expression vapid—a smile only lightly twitching when I saw Hook.

Wyatt Hartwell held onto my horse's lead, bringing him in from the pasture. Hook walked close to him, his stride quickening once he caught sight of me. Wyatt gave me his signature smile; his blue eyes sparkled the closer he got. He was wearing gloves on his hands, a gray, long-sleeve Henley, a backwards baseball cap, and jeans that were covered in...

I scrunched my nose.

"Is that mud?"

FOUR

Wyatt

I STOPPED.

What did she ask?

It had been months since I had last seen Quinn Compton, and I still found myself staring. Her brown hair was pulled into a tight ponytail, long enough to fall over her shoulder. She was dressed simply with no makeup, just a coat and jeans—but damn—I could still see every curve of her body. I was still taken by her; I could feel myself wanting to come alive with her. I still stood by what I thought when I first saw her. Quinn Compton was the most beautiful woman I had ever seen, even when she was looking at me like my very presence in the stable confused the hell out of her.

Pinching my brow, I looked down at myself. Mud caked the tips of my boots, and fresh mud splashed my jeans.

Okay. Seeing what transpired the last time we spoke, her confusion was valid.

I looked back up at Quinn.

"Yes?" I answered, raising a brow to her.

"I've never seen mud on you before." She took a step, reaching her hand out for Hook's reins. "What are you doing here, anyway?"

"Good to see you too, Quinn." I handed her the lead. "I work here." I gave Hook a pat on his neck, offering her a smile before moving on to my next task.

When Hawkins had come up with no committees to add my name to, I finally gave in and told Abi to put me on her payroll. The last two weeks, I had been spending my days with the many horses we boarded. I mucked the stalls, I bathed them, I would take them for rides—basically anything Abi wanted me to do, I did. Every now and then, Lachlan appeared asking for an extra set of hands, but more often than not, I went to bed smelling like a horse, no matter how many showers I took.

"You..." she paused. "Work here? With the horses?"

I chuckled. "Yeah, is that hard to believe?"

"Kinda," Quinn said flatly, folding her arms and cocking her hips. Hook nudged her with his nose, but her emerald eyes just bore into me.

My lips curled into a grin.

"Hey, Wyatt."

My attention went from Quinn to my sister, who was jogging in from the training arena. With a quick glance at my watch, I noticed that my shift was almost over, but knowing Abi, she would have one more thing for me to do. I'd say yes, not only because she was my sister, but because I found myself wanting to.

"I need you to—oh…" She stopped once she reached us. "Quinn!" Abi smiled, and not seeming to care that Quinn was holding on to a seventeen-hundred-pound horse, pulled her in for a hug. Quinn hugged her back, the confusion I was getting from her vanishing the moment she embraced Abi. "Cash didn't tell me you were coming by. You're not on his schedule tonight."

"No." Quinn pulled away, keeping her hands on Abi's forearms. "I just needed to see my boys."

"They're happy," I told her. "Hook and I have gotten quite close." I shoved my hands in my pockets and widened my stance, looking from her to the gelding next to her.

Truth was, he was a needy bastard. He required more attention than any horse I had met. I spent time with him before any other horse, and once I was done with his stall and went to another, he whined and huffed until I was back over with him. When he was in the pasture, he would follow me along the fence, changing his speed just to get me to play along. I would from time to time, and I always rewarded him with a peppermint. He didn't act that way with anyone else—just me. And damn, I quite enjoyed it.

"Excuse me?" Quinn's emerald eyes snapped towards me.

"He really likes Wyatt," Abi answered, a chuckle in her voice.

"He doesn't like anyone but me." Quinn turned to her horse, rubbing his nose. "He was hard to break."

"Well…" I took a step towards Hook, reaching my hand out. He nudged it, finding the peppermint I hid there. "We're buds. Did you need something, Abi?"

"Oh, no. Nope. Just wanted to see if you had gotten all the horses in from the pasture. It's supposed to freeze tonight."

"All twenty-seven in and accounted for. I'll get blankets ready."

"I'm thinking about taking Charming out for a ride. Is that ok?" Quinn asked, giving her horse another pat.

Frowning, I studied the girl in front of me. She was doing everything in her power to avoid my gaze, but I couldn't stop looking at her.

I cleared my throat. "Now? The sun is setting soon."

"Well then," Quinn scoffed, "I'd better get Charming saddled up."

With that, she gave Abi a grin, put Hook in his stall, and went to her other horse. I worked on the horses, getting them ready for the night, all the while she saddled up her white gelding. The stables were silent. Once she and Charming were out on the field, I went back to the black gelding.

"We're good, huh, bud?" I asked him, rubbing his nose. "I'll get your blanket."

I brushed him, loving the way his skin twitched under the bristles. He huffed once the blanket was over his body and gave my cheek a nudge as I tied up the front. I scratched behind his ear, digging in my pocket for another peppermint. Hook's nostrils flared, his tongue finding the candy instantly.

"Think you can do me a solid?" I asked him, knowing very well I wasn't going to get a response.

Quinn was here, and she'd be here for at least the year. There was the strong urge to turn on the charm, flash my wicked grin, tease her, and taunt her into giving me another chance, but again, after what happened the last time I tried any sort of move on her, that would be the worst thing I could do. There was something about her—there always had been—and I couldn't place the way she made my entire body react. It was different than anything. There was more to it. Lord knows I wanted to feel every inch of her, but I also wanted to hear her laugh. I wanted to see the smile I knew she had, even if I didn't deserve it. She still had zero interest. She wouldn't give me the time of day. And I didn't blame her.

Hook huffed, as if he was waiting for me to continue.

"Put in a good word for me? You know I'm a good guy, right? Think you could talk to your mom about me?" I asked him again, tempted to give him another peppermint to get on his good side even more than I already was. When I got no answer, I chuckled, stepping out of his stall and sliding the lock. "Sleep well, bud."

And just as I was walking out, I caught sight of the gorgeous girl riding her horse in the pasture, and my stomach flipped.

I was getting used to waking up with the sun. Did I like it? Not really, but I did it. At first, it was hard, and I hated everything that came with it. Especially the hours. I was constantly late, but my body started to get used to it. I woke up, dressed, made my way over to the main house for coffee and breakfast, and then I'd head to the stables with Cash while Abi got her son, Stetson, ready for school. The more time I spent working in the stables, the more I found myself enjoying it.

The routine was simple, but with almost thirty horses, it took most of our morning. Cash took the right; I took the left, which meant I had Hook to entertain. I'd hit his stall first, and when I finished, he would whine after me until I made it back to him. He had always made another mess, and my instinct was that he did it solely for the attention. But I cleaned his stall again. Filling the water he knocked over, putting the hay back into the feeder, and giving him more food, all while he bit at the hem of my coat, pulling me out of the way to get to his meal.

"Damn you." I pushed his nose away. "Good thing I'm done with your stall."

He huffed.

"How much does Abi charge to board a horse?" I called, knowing Cash would be able to hear me from the other side.

"Uhhh..." His voice carried. "Wish I could tell you. I want to say between five and six hundred a month."

I looked at Hook. "I think we should charge more for this one." I locked his stall, grabbing the bucket before moving to the next stall.

The shrill of my phone filled the space, getting a few reactions from horses around, and it only grew louder as I dug it from my pocket. Sam's—a fellow announcer whom I hadn't talked to in months—name flashed across my screen. I smiled.

"Hey Sammy!" I cheered, maybe a little too bright for how early it was.

"Damn, Hartwell." He chuckled in response. "Honestly thought I was going to get your voicemail."

"It's not that early." I raised my arm, forcing my sleeve down to glance at my watch. Okay, maybe it was still early. I thought it was later. Shit—I was really getting good at the stable hand gig. "Well, I guess it is. Why are you *calling* me so early?"

"It's late, depending on how you look at it."

I could hear his grin. Cocky bastard.

"Who'd you wake up next to?"

Sam was normally my wingman when we went out after rodeos. We'd find bars or hotels to go to after, doing a quick sweep for any buckle bunnies that had gotten left behind. It was easier that way. They wanted to have a good night, and I'd be more than happy to give it to them.

"Runner-up for Montana."

I raised a brow. It was once a rumor that I was going for all the rodeo queens. That I had a list and I was checking off each state. Sure, I'd had a fun time with a few...but Sam? Sam was the one checking them off his list. Every year, he tried to get the whole country. Every year, he came close to succeeding.

I pinched my brow, thinking of her name, only to come up short. "The runner-up, huh?"

"Just let her out of my room."

"And you decided to call me...why?"

"Where the fuck have you been?" He bit out, his tone changing almost instantly. "Last I knew, you were taking some time off, a few weeks tops if I remember correctly, and now here it is, almost two months later, and you're gone. I miss ya, man. Craig isn't as fun in the box."

"Get him drunk and he's a blast."

"Come on, man, your sabbatical is up."

Sam didn't know specifics. He wasn't there that night I made the biggest mistake. He was—if I remember correctly—already up with the rodeo queen for the night. That night, it was just me, Hawkins, some stupid cowboys, and the head of the Wyoming Rodeo Committee playing a game of pool. One too many beers in, one too many things said about a certain girl, and I snapped. A broken nose, a snapped cue stick, and a hospital visit later, I was asked to step away for a bit, promised the whole thing would blow over...only to be forgotten about weeks after. Hawkins blamed the alcohol; he said I wouldn't have done that under normal circumstances, but the truth was, I would have. I had heard them talking before we invited them over to play a game—I knew exactly what I was doing.

Even still, I don't regret hitting the guy; I don't regret causing him to miss a few rodeos thanks to his broken nose. I'd hit him again if I heard him say those things about Quinn any time soon.

The only thing I regret is losing my standings.

"This isn't a sabbatical." I heaved a sigh, shoving my phone between my shoulder and ear to try to work.

"I haven't seen your name come up for weeks. People are starting to ask about you."

"Yeah, well—no one is interested in my name anymore," I mumbled.

"That's horse shit."

I took a step into the stall and slid, looking down to see my boot covered in literal horse shit. *Nice timing, Sam.* I glared up at the horse in the stall, standing near the back. She wasn't one of ours, and her shyness told me she was new.

"This is your way of welcoming me, huh?" I whispered to her, dragging my boot against the wood.

"What?"

"I just stepped in horse shit, right as you said horse shit."

"You stepped in...where are you, Hartwell?"

"My ranch."

Technically, it wasn't mine. I owned five percent as of last year, two hundred and fifty acres of land that still needed to be plotted out. I had a request for when we finally did plot it, it had to be far enough away from everyone that I could have my own space, but close enough that I wasn't mistaken for the brooding, dark cowboy of Hartwell Hills. I still had no desire to do more than I was. Ranching wasn't what I was made to do. It was just a temporary spot until I could figure out my announcing career. *If* I ever figured out my announcing career. I was starting to really miss it.

"Idaho?" He clarified, his voice rising in question, a small squeak with the O.

"That's where my ranch is, isn't it?" I dropped the horse's breakfast and grabbed the pitchfork to scoop the hay. She made her way over to the black bowl of food, gave me a small nudge, and slowly began to eat.

"Well, perfect," he sighed, a grunt in his voice. "I'm heading to Boise. I'll come visit, pull you out of the stupor you've gotten yourself into."

"I'm not in stupor. I'm helping my sister while she's low on staff." Not technically a lie, but not the truth either. Abi didn't need staff to make the place run smooth.

Sam was silent for a beat, then said, "She asked about you, man."

"Who?" I asked, my interest piquing.

"Montana. You think I had the runner-up out of choice?"

"Kelly?" I raised a brow. "Why the hell is she asking about me?"

"Come on, man. She told me to remind you of that week." I could practically *hear* his wink.

"Okay, this conversation is done. I have stalls to muck."

"See you in a few days, and don't step in any more horse shit."

"Get some sleep." I slammed my thumb down on the red button, shoving my phone back in my pocket.

Kelly Fugal was the one girl last fall who almost—*almost*—made me forget about anyone else. Her year as a rodeo queen had officially started; she was on top of the world, and she took me right there with her for one week. If I didn't catch her making out with a bull rider after waking up in my bed that same morning, I swear there could have been something more with her. Why the hell was she reminding me of the time we had?

Then a voice sang through the stables, getting louder as she approached. Hook neighed, and Charming's head poked out of the stall. They knew her voice just as well as I did, and the thought of Miss Rodeo Montana, Kelly Fugal, vanished from my mind when Quinn Compton stepped into my view.

FIVE

Quinn

CHARMING'S FRONT HOOVES DANCED from side to side as he geared himself up, his heartbeat vibrating through him. Deep breath in, long breath out. I'd done it so many times you'd think I'd have it down by now, but even in the training arena, the tension still rose in my stomach. There was something different about being here—just me and my horse—versus being in a packed arena where the cheers motivated me. Here, all I had was Charming's body moving underneath mine. Our deep breaths in and out, our heartbeats beginning to match, his muscles tensing, wanting to go. And right now, he wanted to *move*.

I kicked him into a full gallop, the wind catching my hair and his mane as we bolted through the gate. I led him off to the right, to that first barrel, and he rounded it perfectly. The tip of my boot skimmed the edge of the lid, but it stayed up. *Phew*, I had to make those stay up, especially in training. Charming gained more momentum as he flew towards the second barrel, circling that one with just as much ease. We tilted off to the left, gaining a speed that could match a jet plane as we finally made it to the third barrel.

Piece of cake.

The barrel didn't stand a chance.

Charming zoomed back to the entrance of the arena, his body buzzing just as much as mine was. He halted and let out a loud huff as the smile formed across my face.

I loved it. Everything from the speed to the pulling back just in time to stop. Some people got their adrenaline rushes from jumping off bridges, extreme mountain biking down a rocky path, something that they considered dangerous, which could potentially kill them. But for me, this right here, on the back of a horse, was it. Nothing would ever compare to it.

I had the feeling nothing could stop me, even if it tried.

I leaned down and wrapped my arms around Charming's neck. "Good job, boy," I said, rubbing my hand along his coat. "Good job."

"Fourteen point nine!" I heard Cash shouting from the opposite end of the arena.

Pulling Charming back around, kicking him into a trot, I went right back to Cash, his dashing smile just as wide as mine must have been.

"Not bad. Best time of the night." He took a step on the dirt, a small limp to his step. "A few more runs? Get Hook." He nodded towards the stables.

I gave him a salute before dismounting Charming. Before every session, I saddled both of my boys, getting each ready for whatever

Cash may throw at us. Sometimes I'd switch in between, giving both of them the time they need in the arena. Other times, I'd be on one horse the entire ninety minutes. If that was the case, I took the one who didn't get to race on a long ride after. I was honestly hoping for a long ride with Hook, but it looks like we'd get to spend some time in the arena together racing barrels.

Hook was a stubborn boy; his affection only went towards certain people, mainly me. But the flash of Wyatt Hartwell handing him a peppermint and the way he talked to him sat in my mind, and it hit me in a way I wasn't sure how to take. Instinct was telling me to be annoyed, to remind the man that Hook was *my* horse, and he had his own, plus the other horses the Nova Luna Stable was boarding, he could bribe. But in reality, my stomach did a small flip when I saw the two of them together.

It was getting harder to pretend Wyatt wasn't around. He was always in the stables, and I mean always. He floated from stall to stall, giving each horse attention before moving on to the next. He would joke and laugh with Cash, take direction from Abi, and always acknowledge me there, even if I didn't pay any mind to him. Our eyes would meet for a brief second before the corners of his lips would tug. He'd nod and then break the contact, moving onto whatever he deemed worthy of his focus. But he'd always give me that same cocky smile, sometimes a wink.

And my damn stomach would do the same stupid flip.

I had to remind myself that it was how Wyatt Hartwell worked; it was how he flirted and got all the women he had been with. I wasn't an idiot. I heard stories about him from other barrel racers and rodeo queens, which only solidified my first impression of him. Playboy. Childish. Self-centered. Prideful.

Hear that, stomach? He's a playboy and only trying to get what he wants out of you.

So why—when I didn't see him at all—was I a little upset?

I traded out horses and took Hook back to the arena, whipping out a few runs with him in no time, impressed when the barrels only wobbled a little bit. Cash was impressed, too, ending the session with his normal pep talk of the horse is only as good as the rider and how far I've come, with a gleam of pride in his eyes. He'd pat my back, giving me his full support, and then I'd be left alone with my boys.

I removed Hook's saddle first, tossing it over his stall before giving him a brush down. Charming waited patiently in his own stall, his head poking over the wall, watching my every move. I looked up at him as I inspected Hook's shoes, pulling on some dirt that had lodged its way up in his hoof.

"You're next, don't worry."

He huffed.

Sweat started to seep from my brow. Once I was finished with Hook, I gave him an apple before heading in with Charming, taking the slobber on my hand as a sign of love. Moving from stable to stable, I glanced around, not admitting to myself that I was looking for a certain Hartwell. If he were here, would he have helped? He would have taken Hook, obviously, and I would be ready to head home. Would he give me that smile? Would he talk to me?

Would I let him?

I scoffed.

Talk? He'd try to hit on me again.

So no, I wouldn't let him.

Removing Charming's saddle, I flung it on the stall's wall just like the other one, and my phone began to vibrate in my pocket. My mind filtered through my contacts. I had friends from home, but they were the kind of friends we would go months without talking and still consider each other friends—they wouldn't be texting me. Cash was with another client... that only left my mom or my dad. My bet—mom.

Bingo.

Mom

> Haven't heard from you in a few days. How's Alpine Crest?

I furrowed my brow.

Me

> It's Alpine Ridge, and it's wonderful. You and Dad would actually like it.

Mom

> Oh, no wonder I couldn't find it on the map. Just checking in.

Me

> Doing great. Just finished a training session, heading out on the road in a few weeks.

Mom

> That's good.

And with that, the conversation was over.

Not that it surprised me.

I pocketed my phone and kept working with Charming, walking out of the stables twenty minutes later, my legs already starting to feel the pull from the day. I could go home and just sink into a nice warm bath and—

"Hey!"

A cheerful voice from behind me called, derailing my thoughts of a bath completely. Spinning, warmth spread across me once I saw Abi. She was the sunshine of Hartwell Hills, even after enduring everything she had, just being near her made anyone feel the joy she radiated. It still shocked me to learn how much she lost all those years ago. Her husband, her friend...holding everything in until Cash came back into her life. Even through all of that, her smile never faltered. She always made me feel welcome, like she wanted me there—not just because I was her fiancé's client, but because I was a friend.

"Hey, Abi." I returned her smile.

"How was training today?"

"Good. Really good. Your fiancé made me work both horses today." I rubbed my hand on my forehead, still feeling the slight sheen of sweat.

She scrunched her nose. "So you're pretty beat, huh?"

I sighed, slumping my shoulders. "I smell like a barn."

"I smell like a barn every day. I was actually wondering if you wanted to go out with Kyla and me tonight? It's her night out, baby free, and you've lived here for about...what? Four weeks now? Get out of the house and come out with us." Her eyebrows raised as she tilted her head, eagerly awaiting my answer.

The last time I went out was—hell—I couldn't remember.

The night Wyatt hit on me the first time, maybe?

Maybe after...but I'm pretty sure I left early.

Which meant it was about time.

My long soak could wait. This sounded much more appealing.

"Can I shower first?" I asked, pinching my brow and looking down at the state of my person. Horse shit on my boots, water-soaked jeans, dirt on my blouse...I could only imagine what my hair looked like. "Unless you want to hose me down?"

Abi chuckled. "Ha, you have plenty of time to shower. Kyla still needs to get Baby Poppy fed and down, but we'll pick you up, say...around eight? We're going to The Steel, so drinks are on us."

"Perfect." I gave her a nod. "This sounds great. Thanks for inviting me." I smiled, sensing the excitement growing in me.

"Of course, we thought of you. You're stuck with us—welcome to the fold!" Abi gave me a quick hug and a wave before she ran back into the stables, shouting, "See you at eight!" before she was completely out of earshot.

I rushed home, showered, and got ready so by the time Abi honked her horn at eight o'clock on the dot, I'd could run out of my front door. I gave my hair a little curl, chose a set of dangly earrings that matched my turquoise tank top, and threw a white lace shawl over it. I donned my least mud-covered boots with a pair of tight-fitting jeans and even applied a light coat of mascara. And when the horn honked, a slight buzz ran up my spine.

The side of me that was out more often than not was covered in hay, mud, and sweat from working all day, but I'll be the first to admit I loved being able to causally doll up. When I was in pageants, I hated it. I hated the flashiness that came with it. The teasing of my hair and the constant jewels that weighed me down—but this I liked. I could have my own simple style that made me feel gorgeous, even if I still smelled a little like a barn. Simple. Elegant.

Me.

"Okay." Kyla, Rhett's wife, twisted in her seat to look at me as I buckled up my seat belt. "You're adorable."

I blushed. "Thanks." I held back my smile and tucked a piece of hair behind my ear. "Normally I'm a little grungy, so I took the chance to dress up."

"Hey." Abi caught my gaze from the rearview mirror. "We have shit under our fingernails, and we live by it." Raising a hand, she wiggled her fingers.

I glanced at my nails and sure enough, there was a thin line of dirt. I scrunched my nose. "Remind me to scrub my hands when we get to The Steel."

"You're flawless," Kyla complimented again, turning back to face the front. "This is a girls' night, though, so I hope you're not expecting to pick up any guys."

"Oh no...no no." I waved my hand in the air. "Girls' night. One hundred percent. How's Baby Poppy."

Kyla let out a groan. "I love being a mom," she started, and I noticed Abi giving her a side eye. "But she's teething, and her sleep schedule is all messed up, and my boobs"—she reached up and grabbed her chest—"hurt so bad. I won't even let Rhett touch them."

"Welcome to motherhood." Abi chuckled. "Cash and I have started talking about adoption. He wants a baby, but we haven't been together that long—"

"He's adopting Stetson, right?" I asked, leaning forward in my seat, noticing the lights from The Steel coming into view.

Abi nodded, turning into the parking lot. "Yeah, after the wedding, we'll make it official, but we still want to build our family. Cash is dead set on a girl. Poppy has done a number on him."

Kyla leaned her head back on the seat. "Anytime he wants her, he can have her."

"You don't mean that." Abi popped the truck in park, gave herself one last glance in the visor mirror, and at the same time, we all undid our seat belts.

"No, I don't. But man...I love these nights." Kyla jumped from the car. "Come on, girls, first drinks, then pool." With a skip in her step, she bounded towards the entrance.

I followed Abi and Kyla, the loud country music hitting my ears the moment the doors flew open. The smell hit me next—stale beer and wings were a clear sign that I was at The Steel, the local hangout spot for anyone in Alpine Ridge. I had been a few times the previous year, mainly with Cash or Abi, but had yet to venture in since becoming a 'local.' My nights lately had been consisting of me lounging on my new couch, watching the same season of *Once Upon a Time* again, and eating the same salad for dinner. Tonight, it was going to be wings, and that stale beer, and I was thrilled.

The place was packed, laughter and pool balls breaking filling every inch of the space, even carrying over the music. My bet was that everyone in Alpine Ridge was here tonight. I saw a few of the ranch hands from Hartwell Hills, my next-door neighbor, with her boyfriend. And...

Wyatt sat at the bar with another man, both drinking from pint glasses, both laughing at the top of their lungs. He had his ball cap on backwards, his blond hair sticking out of the bottom under the lip in all directions, and even with the dim light of the bar, his bright blue eyes could be seen from any distance.

"Oh!" Abi touched my shoulder, giving me a squeeze. "Wyatt's here! Excuse me while I go torture him."

Abi left Kyla and me standing near the opposite end of the bar as she went and wrapped her arm around Wyatt's shoulder. He flinched, but his face lit up when he saw Abi, wrapping his arm around her waist.

"Yeah, that's torture." I chuckled, pulling my attention from the siblings to Jason, the bartender, trying to grab his attention.

"Hey Jason!" Kyla shouted, waving her arm in the air. Jason glanced our way, and he beamed as he gave us a quick nod.

"Rum and Dr Pepper coming right up!" He waved at us. "And for your friend?"

"You know me so well," Kyla cooed, leaning forward on the bar top. "And Quinn..." she looked over at me, narrowing her eyes. "I'm guessing a lager."

"Ooo, yes please." I wiggled in anticipation, winking over at Jason.

Jason wiggled his eyebrows. "I'll get Abi's up, too. Spiked Arnold Palmer, I'm assuming."

"That would be correct." Kyla did a little dance with her hips once her Dr Pepper was in front of her, taking a sip. "Perfection." She said hoarsely, raising her glass. "Cheers." We clinked our glasses together, each of us taking a long drink. Kyla turned back to Jason, and my gaze—completely disobeying what I wanted it to do—glanced down at the bar top to Wyatt.

"Hey," I began after taking a long swig from my drink. "Who's with Wyatt?"

Kyla's eyes went from me to him. "Sam, I think. He's one of Wyatt's rodeo friends. He got here last night. I guarantee he's trying to convince Wyatt to get back on the road."

I furrowed my brow. I knew Wyatt hadn't been to any rodeos recently, but a part of me figured it was from the season ending, taking a break just like I was before he ramped up his schedule, every weekend filled with rodeos.

"Why would he need convincing to get back on the road?" I asked, surprised to find I really wanted to know the answer.

"He's just—"

"Thank you, Jason!" Abi shouted as she came up in-between Kyla and me, interrupting Kyla and totally pulling us away from the conversation. "You guys up for a round of pool? Guys versus girls? Us against Wyatt and Sam."

"Two against three? That's hardly fair." I looked down the bar top at the two men, Sam talking into Wyatt's ear as he met my gaze. Wyatt twisted in his chair, and he hit me with the same cocky grin he would in the stables.

"Wyatt's actually really good at pool, and Kyla's the master, so it's a fair match, seeing as I suck at pool." Abi looked from me to Kyla. "It'll be fun."

Kyla glowed. "I'm down."

Glancing down at Wyatt again, I felt a small tingle in my stomach. I came out tonight to have some fun, to let loose a little. What better way to start than to beat Wyatt Hartwell's ass at pool?

"I'm game."

SIX

Wyatt

I REMEMBER WHEN MY brother first met his wife. He said the moment Kyla walked into The Steel, he saw her. Even though we were in the middle of a conversation, his attention went right to her. Rhett always went on about when he and Kyla met. He said that he can feel his entire body warm up when Kyla wraps her arms around him. Cash talked about when Abi walked into a room, all the noise drowned out, and she was all he could hear. My mom and dad had love radiating through them, no matter where they were in the house. Even when Lachlan's wife was alive, he talked about her like she was his entire world.

Me? I always looked around, saw my—for lack of a better word—target and then approached. I put on the swagger and the moves, found the perfect things to say to sweep them off their feet, and then, more often than not, I left with her. I had contacts, but nothing more than a one-night and one-night only.

I never fully understood any of it until I saw Quinn walk into The Steel.

The music and chatter from the crowd died down, and Sam—who was telling me a very interesting, not-so-interesting story—became a blur in front of me. All I saw was Quinn.

She was dressed up. Her jeans hugged her body perfectly. Even with the lace cover flowing down past her hips, I could see every curve. Every piece of her had a part of me growing a tad bit harder, but like always, it was her eyes and smile that drew me to her. I had never seen her like this, a faint layer of makeup that only added to her natural beauty—those emerald orbs standing out even in the dark. If only I could see them up close, drown myself in them, and maybe...just maybe...convince her to drown, too.

So, when Sam suggested a game of pool, how could I refuse?

Striking out with her numerous times didn't exactly set me up for success, but I had seen her watching me in the stables. Her gaze would follow my every move, and I swear there were times when she was going to say something to me, but ultimately, she never spoke. I would pretend I didn't notice her; I would keep working, but I could feel her eyes on me. There were a few times when I'd catch her staring, but I'd just smile at her and move on. But—she *was* watching.

That had to mean something.

Right?

After their first round of drinks, Kyla was the first to jump off her stool and head over to the pool table. Sam and I had already racked the balls, ready for a team game. Us, against all three girls. Abi wasn't an issue, but I had seen Kyla play. The former city girl had skill around the pool table—but Quinn was the wild card. Could she play? Would she tease me the same way Kyla did when she and Rhett played their first game?

I was suddenly very angry at myself for not wearing my cowboy hat.

"You guys ready to lose?" Kyla came up to the table, grabbing the chalk before reaching out for the cue.

Sam barked out a laugh. "Hardly."

"I don't know, Sam," I swung my cue over my shoulder, "Kyla's pretty good."

My gaze followed Quinn as she took the chalk from Kyla, rubbing it on the tip of her cue. Her eyes met mine, yet again for another second. She inhaled, and a smirk grew on those perfect pink lips.

"Who's going to break?" she asked, looking from Kyla to Sam.

They glanced over at each other, then Sam met my eyes. At the same time, we each shrugged a shoulder. Sam leaned on his cue and waved his arm in front of the table. "Ladies first."

Kyla raised her eyebrows and bent over the table, aiming at her shot before breaking the rack, the crack filling the entire bar. No balls sunk, which earned a laugh from Sam.

"I thought Wyatt said you were good, city girl?"

"City girl?" Kyla narrowed her eyes at him.

"Watch it." I hit his shoulder. "Rhett has a sixth sense when someone is flirting or giving his wife a hard time, and we don't want him showing up."

"Especially since he'll have to wake up my daughter to do so, and I will punch you for that," Kyla spat at Sam, pointing at him with her hip cocked.

He flinched, a huff of a laugh carrying over the table. "Not flirting, just loving the fact that I can claim solids now." Sam bent and aimed, sinking the green solid. "Your shot, Wyatt."

I studied the table, which was hard seeing as all I could focus on was the turquoise tank top on the other end of the felt. Licking my lips, I forced myself to ignore her and aimed, shot, and missed. It was because she wiggled her damn hips and leaned on the edge of the table. *Dammit.*

"Oof." Quinn caught my attention. "I could have made that shot."

I raised a brow and leaned on my cue. "Is that so?"

"It was easy."

"Well then." I stepped back and waved my hand over the table, offering her the turn. "It's your shot."

Quinn rolled her eyes, then her demeanor changed when she looked at the felt in front of her. She flipped her hair, and it fell to one side as she leaned, aimed...and sank three stipes.

"Shit," Sam muttered.

"Nice!" Kyla cried, giving Abi a high five. "I didn't see that shot."

Quinn smiled, a tilt to her head as she beamed with confidence. "My dad taught me."

"Are you going to let Kyla have a go or..." I trailed off, placing my cue on the edge of the table.

"Oh, no." Kyla handed her cue to Abi. "Technically, it's Abi's turn."

My sister, who hated this game almost as much as I hated riding a bucking horse, took the cue and missed her shot, not even trying to aim. She clenched her teeth. "Maybe I should sit this one out? I'll go grab the next round." Abi didn't even wait for drink orders; she just took off, and I watched as she spun, giving me a wink before making it to the bar.

I shook my head at her before giving Quinn my full attention once again. She was studying the stripes, her eyes narrowing as she stared. Sam copied her expressions and leaned in, aiming his cue. Once the ball bounced off the edge, he stood up and glowered. Kyla let out a small laugh and began to circle the table, her thumb at her lip as she concentrated. Like he had done with Quinn, Sam mimicked the way Kyla studied the balls, no doubt trying to see what she was seeing.

"You gonna keep mimicking me?" Kyla asked, not taking her eyes off the set.

Sam scoffed. "No, I see exactly how I'm going to win this game."

With a laugh, Quinn popped her hip. I made my way closer and closer to her, telling myself that I had to keep my hands to myself. What I wouldn't give to brush her hair off her shoulder and kiss under her ear.

"So, your dad taught you?" I asked Quinn, leaning in towards her.

She nodded. "He would play with me until I started beating him. How did you learn?"

"I grew up in a town where pool was the only source of entertainment."

"That"—Abi placed another beer in front of me—"is not true."

"It is," I remarked. I gave my sister a look, knowing full well she knew what we did when we were younger.

"You legit live on a ranch." Quinn gave me a small glare, which quickly morphed back into a smile before she said, "Pool couldn't have been your only source of entertainment."

"You made your own entertainment." That time, Abi jumped in. "When we were seven, he and Rhett jumped off the roof of the stables to try to land on the trampoline. Rhett landed safely. Wyatt broke his arm."

"My point has been made." Quinn held her palm out to Abi, but her eyes never left me.

"Okay, so I've done some pretty stupid stuff." I frowned. "But if I recall correctly, you were on the roof with us." I looked at my twin, raising my brow knowingly at her.

"Yeah, but I didn't jump. I climbed down the ladder to save you." She winked.

Quinn shook her head, laughing as she turned her attention to the table, aiming to take her shot, sinking two more balls. We were definitely going to lose the game. "What's another thing you stupidly did?"

"In the past or recently?" I took a step towards her, and her scent filled the air between us. Fruity—blackberries and coconut, and my mind went right to wondering if she tasted the way she smelled.

"Recently."

I raised a brow and went through the many stupid things I had done in the past two years, but for some reason, I landed on, "Not asking you out the right way." I responded, my voice heavy, leaning into her.

Quinn's eyes widened. "Well, sorry, I'm not a girl who likes a pick-up line."

A pick-up line? I had an arsenal of those, but she didn't want that, huh? So...why not cut to the chase? "Get a drink with me after the game." I locked my eyes on her, not faltering in the slightest.

"That's all you got?" Quinn pinched her brow. "Not even a 'let me buy you a drink,' just *get a drink with me.*" She took a step back. "Not even bothering with the pick-up lines now, are you?"

"You said you didn't like pick-up lines."

"Rhett legit asked me what I was drinking. His pick-up line was perfection." Kyla chuckled, leaning to take her shot since Quinn and I had seemingly forgotten about the game. "They aren't bad if they're cute."

"Yeah, but Wyatt's aren't cute," Quinn retorted. "You look like you belong on the dirt. How about we make it official?" With a roll in her eyes, Quinn looked over at me, giving me one quick smile—a tease?—before watching Kyla take her shot, with her head tilting just enough that her hair fell over her shoulders. I had the urge to brush it off to the side, tuck it behind her ear, and feel it between my fingers.

Damn, how could I get this girl to have one single drink with me?

"Ok then." I closed the gap she created. "What would it take for one drink?"

She shook her head, her lips parting as she let out a small breath. Her eyes searched my face before they fell. "Nothing, Hartwell," she said blandly.

"How about this," I said softly, standing so close to her that our breaths began to match up. "You beat me at this game, and I'll leave you alone. I'll walk out of this bar with my drunk friend—"

"Hey!" Sam interjected, but I ignored him.

"—and I'll stop trying to get your attention. No more pick-up lines. I win...you have that drink with me."

"A bet?" Quinn's lips formed a perfect smile, and damn, I wanted to kiss the corner of her mouth, taste that blackberry coconut flavor. "That's worse than *get a drink with me.*"

"Worried you'll lose?"

"No, I will most certainly beat your ass, so it doesn't matter anyway."

"Then what's the problem?"

Quinn licked her lips and turned to look at the table. I had lost track of whose shot it was. I wasn't paying attention. I think I took two turns...but hell...I couldn't care less about the game.

Finally, she blinked and turned to look at me. "Fine. It's a bet." Quinn reached out her hand, and I took it, giving it one firm shake to seal the bet. Her skin was soft as silk, and I held on a little longer than I should have.

"Kyla, whose turn is it?" she asked, not breaking contact with my gaze.

"Yours," Kyla answered.

Quinn raised her lips into a smirk and turned to the table, not hesitating as she bent and aimed...sinking the remaining stripes. She inhaled, studying the table for a second longer before walking to the other side.

"Eight ball, left corner pocket," she said right before she aimed, sunk the ball, and won the game.

Well...shit.

She straightened her back and did the same hair flip, handing her cue off to Abi.

"Hartwell," she said as she walked over to me, taking my own cue from my hands. "I guess it's time for you to take your drunk friend and leave."

Let me say that again.

Well...

Shit.

SEVEN

Quinn

WHEN WYATT BET ME he would leave me alone, I didn't actually think he would. But I saw him almost every day over the past week, and all I got was a nod and a smile if we just happened to cross paths. Was he intentionally making sure I knew he was following through with it? If that was the case, he was playing a different game. Besides, I should've been grateful he was leaving me alone.

He was giving me what I wanted, right? He wasn't hitting on me, he wasn't chasing me—he was simply...leaving me alone.

The least I could do was be grateful.

I unsaddled Charming after a training session, leaving Hook fully saddled for a ride. My legs were already achy, my muscles screaming for a hot bath, but my soul—and Hook's—needed the ride.

There was nothing that would ever compare to riding a horse. The only sounds were the thump of his hooves hitting the ground, his puffs of air as he breathed, and the surrounding nature around us. His body moving with each breath, his joints turning into liquid with each step. We had to work together, we had to trust each other in order for the ride to be worth it. And lucky for me, Hook had my complete trust.

Once outside of the stable, I mounted Hook and kicked him into a canter, heading right towards the lake. I had been at Hartwell Hills long enough to know the land better, and I would be the first to admit I had fallen in love with it. The rolling mountains were still snow-capped. Seeing as it was barely the middle of February, they would be that way for a while, but it only added to the scenery. The dark clouds had covered the sky, and a light snow was falling. The Hartwells owned five thousand acres, mainly all used for their many heads of cattle, but they had taken the time to build horse trails through the mountains, all leading to the gorgeous lake. The snow wouldn't stop me from getting there.

Once we reached the lake, I leaned forward and wrapped my arms around Hooks' neck, loving the way he groaned from the hug. The first time I ever saw the horse, I knew he was mine. I had worked so hard for years before I finally made the jump to buy my own horse, and the second my eyes found the nameless gelding, I just had that feeling. People talk about true love all the time—that's how it was when I saw him. The entire world clicked together, and everything made sense. I carefully approached him. The breeder actually warned me he was eccentric and harder to break, but that didn't change the feeling. My palm up, I giggled when he sniffed my hand, huffing when he found it empty. He gave me the most unenthused expression and blinked a few times before flicking his head away. The first thing that hit my head was my favorite TV show, *Once Upon a Time,* when Cora showed Hook a small jar, and he just looked at it, the same expression the horse had given me. *Sparkly dirt...*

"Hey, Hook," I mused at him. And then his eyes hit mine, and we connected. And from that moment, he was mine. I paid for him in full—with cash—and then loaded him into my trailer and took him home. I had already prepped the stables, knowing I was buying a horse, so I could make his transition as easy as possible.

My mother was shocked when I unloaded him and walked him around his new home. She watched from the house as I guided him through the small pasture and into the stable, giving him fresh hay, water, a blanket to call his own, and then I sat with him. All night long.

Once the morning hit, I brushed him, talked to him, and then went inside. And got the wrath of my mother. Because yes, I didn't tell her I was buying a horse.

I sat as she talked to me about responsibility, how she and my dad handled everything for me and the horses we already owned, and how she wasn't going to support me in the endeavor. I looked her dead in the eye, told her, *"I know, I got this,"* and proved to her I did. Three years later, I bought Charming. They never once took care of my horses. Now, Hook was seven and my pride and joy.

I dismounted, scratching him behind his ears, taking in the view of the lake. Small bits of ice still floated on the surface, and the snowflakes disappeared the moment they touched the water. Hook exhaled, his breath appearing at my side. He nudged my cheek, giving me all of two seconds of his time before he bent to pull at the grass that poked through the snow. I chuckled and patted his neck, stretching my own body and knowing the next day I was going to be sore, worse than I already was.

Thankfully, I didn't have training tomorrow.

Tomorrow was prep day.

I was leaving for my first leg—four rodeos over the week-end—first thing Thursday morning. I had to prep Hook and Charming, pack, confirm the hotel rooms, and make stable arrange-ments...tomorrow was going to be just as busy as today, minus the training.

I heaved a sigh, making a checklist in my mind of all the things I had to do before leaving. Hook raised his head, giving me another nudge.

"Ready to head back?"

I grabbed his reins and slid my boot in the stirrup, swinging myself up and into the saddle. I shifted my weight while Hook stood perfectly still—just like I trained him.

"Compton?"

I heard my last name as I nudged Hook back to the trail, and none other than Wyatt came into my view. Hook bobbed his head and let out a whine. Rusty, Wyatt's chestnut gelding, came to a full stop and let out a huff, his breath just as thick in the air as Hook's was. It was getting colder...if I was aware of it, so were the horses.

I heaved a sigh.

"What are you doing out here this far? It's getting dark."

"I could ask you the same." I raised a brow at him.

"I was working with Lach. He's not far behind." He gestured his head back. "It's supposed to start snowing harder. You heading back?"

He was so...mechanical as he spoke to me. No smile in his voice, no sparkle in his eye. And I...didn't like it.

"Obviously," I cleared my throat, "seeing as I'm on my horse."

He narrowed his eyes. "Alright, then, I'll ride back with you."

With that, he kicked Rusty into a trot, clicking his tongue. Hook whinnied, his muscles below me moving as we watched Wyatt get a little further ahead. I kicked Hook into a canter, catching up to him in no time. We slowed our pace, ending up walking the way back to the stables, letting the snow fall on us, and damn, he was right. The snow began to fall thicker, covering the rim of Wyatt's baseball cap and Hook's mane. It was a heavy, wet snow, soaking both of us. Wyatt was getting just as drenched, which meant Rusty and Hook would both need extra care before we headed our separate ways.

Once we got into the stable, we worked in silence. Rusty's stall wasn't far from Hook's, but far enough that we could work at our own pace. I focused on my gelding, removing each layer of snow-flaked fabric on top of him before reaching down to clean his shoes, finally ending with a good, deep brushing. Once his blanket was on and he was settled, I gave him a treat and made my way out of the stall.

"Are you headed home?" Wyatt asked, his voice coming out of complete silence. Deep and low, but solid. There was no light tease or flirt with his voice that I was used to. It was simply...him.

I would never tell him this, but I did love his voice. I could understand why he decided being a rodeo announcer was the route for him. He had a certain tone to him, one that could carry even if he didn't have a microphone. I should know—I've heard it. It was deep, and raw, raspy at times—probably after he talked for hours on end—but that didn't stop him. The man was born to talk. If he wasn't doing rodeos, I could envision him as an audiobook narrator—he had *that* voice.

So, the fact that he was keeping his conversation with me short and sweet, most likely just sticking to the bet he lost, rubbed me the wrong way. The man needed to talk.

I gave him a nod. "Yep. I have a lot to do tomorrow, so I need to get going to start that adventure."

He huffed a laugh, shoving his hands in his coat pocket and pulling out a peppermint. He took a step towards Hook and held out his palm. Hook snatched it up, nuzzling his nose against Wyatt's palm.

"Abi will kill me if she sees you get in that truck and drive off, knowing how bad the roads are."

"I can drive in winter weather." I protested. "I'm from Montana."

"True, but I also know you haven't eaten." He lowered his hand, shoving it back into his coat pocket. "The plows will be out before you know it. Come eat dinner, and then the roads will be safer."

I folded my arms, suddenly feeling the grumble in the pit of my stomach. I heaved a sigh, giving in. "I could eat."

He gave me a curt nod. "Perfect, I didn't really want to die today at the hands of my sister."

"Abi, commit murder?" I gave Hook one final pat, then made my way past Wyatt and out of the barn. "She's too sweet for that."

"You don't know my sister, then."

The main house of Hartwell Hills was where everyone gathered. Abi and Cash called it home, along with my favorite eight-year-old, Stetson, but more often than not, the entire family met here for dinner. Abi and Cash moved around the kitchen, Stetson was sitting at the table already playing on a video game, and Rhett and Kyla were taking turns dancing with their baby girl, Poppy. Once Lachlan arrived, it would be the entire family—and oddly enough, I felt welcome. My mom often complained that I never arrived for family dinner. Well, if it were like this, I would've been there every night.

"Hey, Quinn!" Abi called. "Glad you could join us. Cash, get her a plate."

I gave him a smile stuffed with sarcasm as he handed me the plate and silverware.

"I meant put it on the table for her," Abi scoffed.

"She's got it," Cash remarked, giving me a grin.

Abi gave her fiancé an eyeroll while Cash lightly kissed her on the cheek.

I waved the plate in the air. "I definitely got it." I chuckled, moving back to the table to claim my seat next to Stetson. "Hey, little dude," I said, running my hands through his unruly hair.

He didn't even move. All of his energy was poured into the gaming console in his hands.

"Stetson." Cash's voice dropped a few octaves. "Turn it off."

"Dad," Stetson grumbled, and shrugged his shoulders as his console dropped to the table. My heart swelled hearing him call Cash 'dad,' and I'm sure if mine did, Cash was ready to burst. I quickly turned to him to see if I could catch a hint of happiness. "Can I just beat this level?"

Cash widened his eyes. The joy and love for the kid were there, but he was in full-on dad mode right now. My dad was—well, used to be—the same.

"Save it." He grumbled, his jaw clenching. "You can play tomorrow."

Stetson sighed in protest, but shut off the video game, placing it screen down on the table. "Hi Quinn," he finally sighed, his voice was heavy.

"What were you playing?" I asked, hoping I could pique his interest back a little bit. Last year, he was excited to be on the back of a horse, helping me with barrels, and ready to be anywhere Cash was. "I didn't think you liked video games."

"Mario is really fun. That was Super Mario *Odyssey*, and I was really close to beating it." Stetson looked up at me.

"Ah, well, tomorrow then." I tried to give him some form of hope. "I've missed you at the arena," I admitted, nudging his shoulder. "I haven't had anyone to place the barrels for me."

"Once I'm on spring break, I can help."

Before I could answer, the back door slid open and Lachlan came bursting through, snow falling from his boots and hat.

"Fuck it's cold. I didn't think it was supposed to snow this hard." He removed his hat, placing it down on the small table next to the door, the drips of snow hitting the wood.

"Uncle Lachlan..." Stetson widened his eyes and tried to keep the smile from his face.

"Oh, sorry. I mean…Fudge, it's cold." Lachlan ruffled Stetson's hair a lot harder than I did, which earned him a laugh from Stetson as he attempted to fix it.

"It's supposed to snow through the night, which reminds me, Quinn,"—Cash caught my attention—"aren't you leaving tomorrow?"

I shook my head. "No, Thursday. Tomorrow is prep and packing."

"Ah…" Rhett sighed, his body in full rocking mode as he tried to comfort a fussy Poppy. "I miss those prep days. And the road. You should ask Wyatt for help. He was always making sur—ah, Poppy Girl." He stopped, jerking his head back as Poppy's arm flung out of her swaddle, her scream louder than before, barely missing her dad's head.

"Is she okay?" I asked, my gaze narrowing on the bundle in Rhett's arms.

"She has colic, and I can't walk her around like I do a horse, so"—Rhett looked down at his daughter and his motions became more extreme—"we bounce."

"And not sleep." Kyla pulled up a chair across from Stetson, folding her arms in front of her to lay her forehead down. "We're on night two."

"Here," Wyatt said, walking up to Rhett, his arms outstretched. "Let me take her." He did a 'gimme' gesture with his fingers.

"She'll scream. You think this is bad…once I hand her over, everyone here will lose their hearing." Rhett responded, looking at his brother as if he were crazy.

"Who was able to get Stetson to sleep when he was crying?" Wyatt raised a cocky brow.

"Sylas." Abi and Cash said in unison.

Wyatt gave them a glare. "Okay, when Sylas wasn't an option."

Abi tightened her lips. "He's right. Wyatt had a way with Baby Stetson."

Rhett took half a millisecond to decide to hand the fussy baby girl over to Wyatt. He took her gingerly, bringing her to his shoulder, his large hand resting on her tiny bottom. He began to sway, a small bounce to him, and then he began to hum.

The familiar country song filled the room, his hum—like his voice—was deep and soothing as he lightly moved around the room. The solid sound coming from him was most likely causing the perfect vibration for Poppy to feel, and soon she stopped fussing and curled herself into Wyatt's shoulder. But even when she was quiet, Wyatt kept humming.

And I couldn't stop watching.

The sun was out again, and all the heavy snow that had settled on the ground was already beginning to melt. It snowed through my entire prep day, making it hard for me to get back to the stables to get Hook and Charming ready. Thank God for Cash Callahan. Since the plows hadn't been out, I was home packing and confirming everything I could while Cash helped me at the stables, so when I pulled up Thursday morning, Hook and Charming were ready to go. I filled the tack with all the essentials and guided Charming in the trailer first, tying him up and rewarding him with a kiss.

When I came back for Hook, I stopped when I saw Wyatt already leading him out to me.

"Figured he was next," he said, handing me the reins. "When will you be back?"

"Monday," I answered, leading Hook into the trailer next to Charming.

"And you really are going to take both? You can leave Hook here. I'll make sure he's good."

"You're not stealing my horse, Hartwell."

"That wasn't what I was doing, Compton." He gave a slight laugh as he shoved his hands into his coat pocket.

"That's the second time you've called me Compton." I shook my head as I tied Hook up, making sure to talk loud enough for him to hear me. "Didn't think we were on a nickname basis."

"Compton isn't a nickname. I could give you one if you like, but then I'd be breaking the bet I lost."

I jumped from the trailer, landing right in front of him, the mud splooshing under my boots. "Glad you remembered the bet."

"Seriously, I can watch Hook."

"I always travel with both my boys. I rotate who I ride, and seeing as I have four rides this weekend, I need them both."

"Four rides? In three days? Isn't that a bit much?"

"Nope," I answered quickly. "Not for me."

Wyatt raised his brows and began to sway, his feet solid on the ground. He folded his arms as his body moved back and forth, back and forth, and damn...all I could see was him holding his niece, humming to her as she fell asleep in his arms. I wasn't one to fawn over men holding babies—hell, I didn't even know if I wanted children—but the sight of him being sweet...and gentle...and loving...was a side I hadn't seen. The inkling that there was more there hit again. Maybe he wasn't such a bad guy after all.

"I could come," he added hastily, snapping me out of watching him sway. "To the rodeos with you. It's been a while since I've been to one, and I'd like to get back to it. "

I pinched my brow, the vision of him holding Poppy vanishing. He hadn't been to a rodeo in *months*. He was missing *something*, and I had a good feeling what that 'something' was. The one remark reminded me he was exactly who I thought he was. "What, so you can keep marking off those Miss Rodeos off your list?" I bit, folding my arms.

He flinched, taken aback. "Um...no. To help you."

"Wyatt," I sighed, dropping my arms, closing the trailer door. "I don't need help. I put my schedule together and confirmed everything. I don't need to babysit you while I'm at it."

"Babysit? Quinn, I don't need to be babysat—"

"I'll be back on Monday," I interrupted him. "I'm sure you can keep bribing my horse with peppermints when I get back." I locked the trailer and gave Wyatt one last look.

Turning on my rig, I watched Wyatt in the sideview mirror, his arms still folded as he turned to go back into the stables. The image of the sweet and gentle Wyatt became clouded by his chasing girls—chasing me—helping me be grateful that he had been sticking to the terms of the bet.

EIGHT

Wyatt

"THE LAST TIME YOU asked me to babysit, Stetson flat out refused and ended up going with you, remember?" I placed my palms on the kitchen island, mimicking my sister's stance. It barely crossed my mind that someone said I was the one who *needed* babysitting, not three days ago, and now I was the one being asked *to* babysit.

Abi bit her bottom lip, her eyebrows furrowing with an expression that screamed worry. *Please, Wyatt,* she begged silently, *watch my kid.* Being the asshole brother I was, I'd let her stew for a little bit. Except my sister didn't know the meaning of the words 'little' and 'bit.'

"That was almost a year ago, and now you'll have Stetson and Poppy. Stet will be thrilled to help entertain her for a day." Her hands moved from the counter to her sides, her expression still pleading.

"A day?" I repeated, louder than I intended. "You and Rhett want to trust me"—I pointed to my chest—"with your kids for an entire day."

"Well, afternoon into the evening. We'll be home shortly after bedtime, but..." Abi raised a shoulder. "Stet can stay awake until Cash and I get home."

"Where are you guys going? The four of you? The ultimate double date?" I pushed myself off the counter, swinging my arms until they landed on my hips.

Abi's face fell as her hands slid across the marble counter, her fingers coming together as she fiddled with the engagement ring on her left hand. She was being quiet...unusually quiet. Whereas before she couldn't stew...it seemed to be all she wanted to do now.

"Abi," I drew out her name.

"Cash and Rhett were able to sign up for a rodeo in Boise. A few cowboys had to back out, and they had some room, so they were able to jump on."

"Boise? Tonight?"

As much as I hated to admit it, my stomach dropped the moment I knew they were going to the Round-Up, a rodeo I had announced at a time or two. It wasn't a huge event by any means, but still, it was *my* rodeo. Cash and Rhett would probably bring home a couple of hundred bucks each, but seeing as they both just did rodeo for their own enjoyment and not for their careers, they most likely got a call and signed up last minute. And yet—I didn't get any kind of call from the committee. The look on Abi's face was all the proof I needed to know she was even hesitant to tell me where they were going. That stung a little harder than it should have.

I missed being behind that microphone. Every time I thought about what I was missing out on—the rustle of papers as we followed the line up, the judges in our ears calling out scores, the view being the best one in the entire house, the excitement that just came with being there—whenever those memories even remotely passed through my brain waves, I could feel a piece of me shatter. Working on the ranch was one thing, helping me figure out that rodeos weren't everything I had to look forward to, but it didn't completely kill the void that only being back in that booth could fill.

I licked my lips and heaved a sigh, pulling myself back together to look at my sister.

She let out a long breath through her rounded lips. "Sorry, I know it sucks to know we are all going to a rodeo while asking you to stay behind with the kids—but—"

"Abi." I stopped her, raising my hand. "I'm the one who fucked up, remember? Just because I can't participate doesn't mean that Cash and Rhett shouldn't." I swallowed, putting on my best face. "You don't think Stet will want to go?"

She huffed. "Oh, he will, but we want to go to dinner after, as yes"—she lifted her hands air quoting—"the ultimate double date. Which includes a restaurant and drinks, and no kids allowed. You're great with the kids. Stet and Poppy love you."

"I know they do," I said with a cocky grin, waggling my eyebrows. "I'm the best damn uncle any kid could have."

But damn, I'd rather be at that rodeo.

"I'll pay you," Abi added quickly.

"No, you won't." I gave her a pointed glare. "You know damn well I'll watch them. I've finally seen *Bluey* and kinda want to watch more."

"Not too much screen time, please. That kid has become addicted to his Nintendo."

"Well, why did you let your *fiancé* get it for him for his birthday?"

"He was turning eight. It was a big deal," she defended. "We didn't think he'd get attached to Mario."

I chuckled, rolling my sleeves up. "I'll hide it. When are you guys leaving?"

"Around one, enough time to get some chores done, and Cash has a few clients this morning. Oh." She lifted a finger in the air. "Kyla needs you to stop by her house so she can fit the baby carrier on you."

I pinched my brow. "Why?"

"You can't do night check and feed the horses while carrying a baby, can you?"

"Hell no, but...looks like Stetson is learning night check tonight because I am not wearing a baby carrier." I shook my head, firm on my decision.

But I made a liar out of myself when I did indeed go to Kyla's, where she showed me how to put on Poppy's chest carrier. She hooked me up and slipped Poppy inside, her little blue eyes facing me, a smile on her small lips. Kid was cute, I'd give her that. She had the Hartwell eyes with her mama's hair, and she knew she had her Uncle Wyatt wrapped around her little finger. Kyla went over all the things I needed to know in detail, and I took mental notes. I'd watched Stet a few times, but never when he was as young as Poppy. I may have been good with him, but I traveled a lot, plus I didn't think Abi and Sylas were trusting enough to leave me alone with him. I could get the kid asleep, I could rock him and put him in his crib, no issues. I could hum until he calmed and began to hum along with me, but Abi or Sylas was always with me.

"Dumb question…" I asked, looking down at my niece as she cooed. "Well, a few. Can she sit up yet? Can she hold her head up? Can she…walk?"

"Don't be an idiot, Wyatt." Kyla rolled her eyes. "She's four months, what do you think?"

I pinched my brow. "The last bit was a sarcastic joke, but—"

"Yes, she can hold her head up, but not for long. We haven't mastered sitting yet, and if I come home and she's walking, I will murder you."

"Harsh."

"I'm not ready to chase a toddler. And Wyatt." Kyla spun, her gaze hitting mine like a million swords. "No horses. Not yet."

I gave her a salute and then began to pull Poppy from her carrier.

A few hours later, Stetson, Poppy, and I stood on the front porch of the main house, watching the two couples roll away, the dirt trailing behind them. Poppy breathed a few sounds, her legs going crazy as I held her back against my chest, her little bum fitting perfectly in my palm, and Stetson stood with his arms folded, his brow furrowed as he watched the car vanish from sight. We stood in silence for a few moments, as if what I was about to say was going to cause them to turn the truck around and never allow me to babysit again, but finally, I looked at Stetson and said:

"Wanna ride a horse?"

Poppy took in her tummy time on the stable floor, her wobbly head following us as Stetson readied his horse for a ride, and I slipped the bridle onto Rusty, the baby carrier slung over my shoulder. Marshmallow bobbed his head, leaning down to Poppy on her blanket, even licking her hair and making it stick up in all angles. Rusty kept giving me looks, no doubt wondering why a horse as trained and perfect as him was going to be walking next to a younger gelding like Marsh. I swear I even saw him roll his eyes.

I looked down at Poppy as I pulled the baby carrier off my shoulder.

"Damn," I muttered. "Now I have to give her a bath."

"You'll have to anyway," Stetson grunted, hoisting the saddle up and over Marsh, "If you don't want Aunt Kyla to know she was on a horse. Is she riding with me!?" He perked up, his eyes wide.

"She's not gonna be on a horse." I tightened Rusty's lead. "Your aunt said no walking and no horses, and I don't want Kyla to hate me. I'll have her in the carrier while I walk Rusty. She's a Hartwell, girls gotta get used to horses." I looked back down at Poppy, holding herself up on her elbows, Marshmallow's nose sniffing her head. Her little face was trained on the big white beast in front of her, mouth open, eyes wide with fascination. Marsh huffed, Poppy flinched, and I noticed snot on her forehead. "I will be giving her a bath."

Moments later, Stetson was mounted on Marsh, and I had baby Poppy settled against my chest in her carrier as I guided Rusty around the outdoor arena. Rusty huffed, wanting to move as fast as Marsh was, but he kept by me, his nose finding Poppy and giving her little nudges. Stetson led Marsh in a canter around the arena, passing us a few times while I took Rusty soft and slow, letting Poppy get used to the animal next to her. I hummed the same Shania Twain song that Mom would hum for us, the same one that calmed her the other night, as Rusty's hooves hit the ground with a thump. Poppy never fussed as we walked, her eyes wide with wonder, completely enchanted by either my humming or Rusty. My bet was on the latter.

"Pretty damn sure she's gonna love horses. Look at the way she's looking at Rusty." I shouted across the arena to Stetson.

"Just you wait. She was born to ride!" Stetson called, slowing Marsh down to my other side, sandwiching Poppy and me between the two horses.

"What do you think she'll do? Breakaway roping? Trick riding? Dressage and show jumping at the Olympics?" I tickled her back through the carrier and felt her legs kick.

"Barrel racing, like Quinn!" Stetson replied. "I can teach her! Quinn taught me! I'm an expert."

I had been doing really well, not thinking about Quinn while she was gone for the weekend. And now, thanks to my nephew, she was officially back on my mind. I lasted almost two days. It was harder not to think about her while she was here, seeing as she was in the stables more than in her own home, and fuck...I hated making that stupid bet.

In the back of my head, I had her. I was good at pool; I'd win and then sweep her off her feet during a drink. Hell, I just wanted to get to talk to her. But then, after, once Sam and I left The Steel, all my mojo left, and the next time I saw Quinn, I couldn't think of a single thing to say to her. At first, I wasn't going to hold up my end of the bet. My plan was to approach her, lean against the stall, and ask her out again and again until she finally said yes, but then when I froze...even I was confused.

No girl had ever made me freeze up like she did. No girl had ever caused me to shut down.

I was good with women. I could talk to them, flirt, and tease like it was in my job description. No strings, no commitments—just a good time.

Maybe Quinn wasn't supposed to be just a good time? Maybe Quinn was supposed to be more?

But I couldn't get to her. She was impossible to break through.

When I offered to go to rodeos with her, my hope was to spend time with her, to let her see the kind of guy I could be, and it would be a lie to say I was shocked when she said no. I wanted to talk to her. I wanted to hear her laugh. Get to know her. I wanted to help her thrive. But she didn't see that. All she saw was me chasing the rodeo royalty.

When in reality—I hadn't wanted to chase anyone since I had set my eyes on her again.

Poppy let out a long, loud coo, bringing my full attention back to her. It didn't even occur to me that I had stopped walking. I tugged on Rusty's lead and took a step, inhaling as I looked at my niece.

"Barrel racer, huh?" I gave her bottom a pat. "I can see it. She's gonna love speed." I let go of Rusty's lead and let out a 'hiya'—his signal to gallop—and he took off. Stetson laughed and kicked Marsh into a run, chasing after Rusty. I could see Poppy on the back of a horse, her smile wide as she rounded every single barrel. Just like...

Stetson's 'yee-haws' and shouts pulled me back into the moment, only slightly forgetting that Quinn Compton could teach Poppy how to ride the way she does.

Stetson and I closed up the stables, getting the night check done in record time, even with a baby strapped to my chest, and then made our way to Rhett's place. After Poppy was bathed and dressed in a pair a footie pajamas that I was jealous of, I gave her a bottle and we watched a few episodes of *Bluey*. Those stupid dogs were more entertaining than half the crap I'd seen on television lately, and when it was time to turn it off and get Poppy in bed, I found myself saying, "One more episode." I rocked Poppy until she was calm, her fingers wrapped around my thumb, and placed her into her crib right before she drifted off, the same moment I heard the front door open.

"Aunt Kyla," Stetson whisper shouted. "Poppy *loves* horses!"

I chuckled, pushing Poppy's dark hair back, leaving her room with the light click of the bedroom door, only to find myself facing Kyla, who looked like she couldn't tell if she wanted to kill me or hug me. Her mouth dropped to say something, but I stopped her.

"Don't worry." I raised my hands. "I had her safely on my chest while I walked Rusty around. But she was completely taken by him."

"No shit. She's a Hartwell." Rhett smiled, his hand running along Kyla's shoulders.

Kyla's face softened. "You didn't have her *on* the horse?"

"No, Kyla, I didn't have her on the horse. And...she's not walking."

Kyla scrunched her nose. "Sorry to be a buzzkill."

"Not at all, just being a good mama." I gave her a quick side hug before turning to my brother. "What score did you get?" I asked him, watching Kyla sneak into her daughter's room.

Rhett grinned, waggling his eyebrows with pride. "Seven point two."

"You were supposed to let the other guys win." I smiled at my brother. "And Cash?"

"Scored a ninety-three."

"Damn." I raised a brow.

"Wyatt," Kyla whisper-yelled as she came back into the living room. "She's dead asleep. How!? She won't fall asleep for me...only Rhett."

I gave my brother a look and shrugged my shoulders like it was no big deal. "I'm the Poppy whisperer." I gave her a wink. "Hey, Stet." I reached out for my nephew, grabbing onto his shoulder. "Let's get you back home. It's late."

Kyla pulled me in for a hug, thanking me for babysitting one last time. I let her know Marsh attempted to eat her, but she was, all in all, a good baby, didn't even fuss once. Kyla made a comment on how I was now the designated babysitter, and I gave her a quick grin and thumbs up, pushing Stetson out the door.

Stetson recounted the entire night on the walk back. Once we got to the main house, I had to hear the story for a third time as he told Cash and Abi, only stopping when Cash pushed him up the stairs to get him into his own bed, giving me a quick thanks before he disappeared upstairs, grumbling, "Okay, okay. You have school tomorrow."

"Thank you," Abi sighed, following me to the front door. "I saw Trevor there."

Trevor was the head of a rodeo committee in Idaho, close friends with the guy I punched. I bit the inside of my lip and kept any thoughts of that night away.

"Oh yeah...how did that go?" I asked, my hand on the doorknob, my other reaching up to rub the back of my neck.

"Good, I guess." She shrugged her shoulder. "Told me to tell you to call him."

I gave her a nod, pulling her in for a side hug. "I will, I will," I assured her, knowing damn well I wouldn't. "Enjoy your night, sis."

"Night, Wyatt. Thank you again."

She shut the door behind me, and I heard it lock. I stuck my hands in my coat pocket and started towards the bunkhouse, stopping only when I saw a familiar truck pull up. The ground crunched as Quinn pulled to a stop, jumping from the cab the moment the engine was cut. She slammed her door and stomped—literally stomped—to the trailer.

Narrowing my eyes, I slowly approached. I thought she would be back tomorrow, not close to ten on a Sunday night.

"You're back early," I said once I knew I was close enough, keeping my pace slow.

Quinn shot her gaze towards me, her ponytail whipping around her shoulders. "Don't."

I raised a brow in question. "Don't what?"

"Don't say anything tonight. I'm getting my horses in their stalls, and then I'm going home, and I don't want to hear it from you tonight."

"I wasn't going to say anything. Need help?"

She dropped her arms, a loud groan escaping her as she looked up to the sky. "No, Wyatt. No. I don't need help. I can take care of my own horses. Please just..." She sighed and looked back at me. "Just leave me alone."

The anger that radiated from her was palpable. Just looking at her, I knew her weekend didn't go the way she wanted it to—but—I wasn't going to press. I dropped my chin and looked at my boots, kicking the dirt before I twisted towards my bunkhouse.

"Alright," I sighed. "Well...if you need me"—I pointed to the bunkhouse—"you know where to find me."

She didn't respond. She just stood and kept her eyes on me, holding my gaze until my back was turned and I couldn't see her anymore, still gorgeous even through the frustration of whatever was plaguing her.

NINE

Quinn

I ALWAYS THOUGHT IT was a cliché when I heard someone say the shower would wash away every bad thing from the day—or in my case, the weekend—but there I was, in my shower, standing under the hot stream of water, trying to let it do exactly that.

The weekend was a disaster to say the least. The stables I had booked for Hook and Charming the first night only booked me to have one horse, and since they didn't have an extra stall, I had to beg for them to let my boys share. Then the hotel was expecting me the following night, so I ended up sleeping in my truck—which is not set up for camping—and I came in last on my first ride. During Saturday's adventure, Charming and I pulled a seventeen point nine, bringing home a small check, but then I had a no score, knocking down all three barrels, on the third run. And who just happened to be there at that ride...

My mother.

With her current Miss Rodeo Montana, Kelly Fugal.

Of course, she was there the time I landed a no score.

She came up to me with a large smile on her face, wrapping me in her arms as gingerly as she could so as not to mess up her hair, congratulating me on a 'good try.' She asked about Alpine Crest—as she still called it—and how she just wished I could come home once in a while. And then she placed her hand on her queen's shoulder and walked away from me. I stood, forcing the tears not to well in my eyes, as I held onto Hook's reins as tight as I've ever held them.

I loaded both horses in the trailer, got them settled in the stables—each having their own stall this time—and went to my hotel. I canceled my Sunday ride, canceled the boarding and hotel reservations. Then I popped in my headphones and watched my favorite episode of *Once Upon a Time* as I burrowed myself in the sheets, happy with myself in that the tears I kept in never fell. I slept in, went and ate brunch at a local café, and then drove—only to hit traffic on the way home.

Pulling into Hartwell Hills, of course, the first person I saw after a monstrous weekend was Wyatt. I just wanted to get my horses in the stable and climb into my own bed. Not get confronted. So—I did just that.

And now the shower would wash it all away.

I knew I could do this; I did it last year, so why was this time a complete disaster? How did I manage to set myself up for failure? I messed up booking two stalls, I messed up the hotel confirmation, I knocked down a total of three barrels—in one ride—and managed to barely keep myself together after seeing my mom. How. The. *Hell*, did I manage all of that in a span of three days?

And why wasn't the shower working?

Turning off the boiling hot water, I dressed and made myself a cup of tea. Curling up on the couch, I instantly turned on a comfort show. Shockingly—*Once Upon a Time.* Nothing would ever create the same calm that Captain Hook did, telling Emma he loved her for the millionth time. I wasn't even a crazy romantic, but there was something about their relationship that had me glued to the screen the minute they came together. The moment the title hit, my mind slowed down. Same with the night before at the hotel—if it wasn't for this show and becoming one with my bed, I most likely would have broken down.

A large part of me was saying I needed to double-check all my bookings for the next leg to make sure I didn't make the same mistakes again. Five rodeos in seven days, I have two 'rest' or travel days—which now that I think of it might help. It wasn't going to be travel, rodeo, travel, rodeo the entire seven days. I had seen other racers and cowboys compete twice in one day, and I figured with two horses, it was a no-brainer—I could, too. I knew I could do it—but right now...in the exact moment in time...I needed to *not* do it and just...relax. If only...

The heavy vibration of my phone, still shoved into my bag by the front door, made it hard to relax. With a groan, I retrieved it, not bothering to unlock it before I plopped back on the couch. A text from Cash.

Cash

You're home?

Me

> Saw me drive up, huh?

Cash

> No. Wyatt texted me. Said you looked frustrated. All ok?

I dropped my phone in my lap, my head falling back on the couch cushions. I inhaled through my nose and exhaled through my lips, then raised the phone.

Me

> I'm fine. Just a bad few runs.

Cash

> I say this with love, but I don't want to see you at the stable tomorrow. We got your horses. Rest and take the day. Restock your fridge and don't think about rodeos. Recharge.

I was tempted to give him the saluting emoji, my go-to emoji when he gave me a task, even if that task was to not do anything at all. Instead, I simply replied.

Me

> I'm fine. Talk later, ok. Thanks, Cash.

Saluting Emoji Sleep well, Quinn.

I gave the screen a soft smile. Even if Cash couldn't see it, I hoped he knew it was there. Locking it, I tossed it to the other side of the couch, curling back up with my tea. The phone vibrated again a few minutes later, lighting up. I looked at it and heaved a sigh when I saw whose calling. *Mom.*

I let it go to voicemail.

Despite what Cash ordered, I headed to the stables the following afternoon. I had slept semi-decently—albeit on the couch—but woke with the determination to shove the bad weekend behind me. The only way to do that was to move forward. But before I dug into the logistics of it all, I went to where my heart would be happy, where—following Cash's orders—I could recharge. And that was with my boys.

The stables were quiet when I arrived, with only a few ranch hands and Cash prepping the arena for a client. With him distracted, I went straight to Hook and Charming. Charming was pulling fresh hay from the bag, and Hook was standing with his head down, his tail flicking back and forth. Opening the tack, I grabbed a few finishing brushes, planning to make both my boys shine, starting with Hook.

"Hey, mister," I cooed, stepping inside his stall, only to come in contact with a pair of legs. I tripped forward, surprisingly catching my balance before I ran headfirst into my horse's stomach, losing my grip on the brushes. I placed my hand on Hook's coat and looked at the source of my fall. "What the hell are you doing?"

"Hiding," Wyatt answered. He was sitting on the floor of Hook's stall, his back up against the wood wall, his legs outstretched in front of him, ankles crossed. His baseball hat was backwards, and a large mud stain was splashed across his chest.

"Hiding?" I parroted. "In my horse's stall?"

"I just finished cleaning it." He gestured to the pitchfork leaning up against him. "I figured I'd take a quick break before moving on to the next."

I bent, grabbing the brushes I had dropped, before shooting him another glare.

"And the best place for a break is *my* horse's stall? To hide?"

"It's quiet in here," was his response.

I huffed. He was soaking up the exact thing I wanted. I blinked at him before turning back to Hook, raising the brush to his coat. He raised his head and nudged me with his nose, a sweet hello.

"Are you just going to sit there while I brush him?" I asked, my back to Wyatt.

He inhaled. "Can I?"

I spun, meeting his gaze, his baby blue eyes fixed on me. He didn't even blink; he just stared at me, holding me down with his sincere question.

"You just want to sit there?"

He gave me a crooked smile. "Yeah."

I took a deep breath, still holding eye contact, deciding it wasn't worth the fight or annoyance. "I guess that's ok."

"Thanks," he said, twisting his hat forward to lean his head on the wall with a thump. "How was it this weekend? Hook looked ragged; you must have really worked him. How did you do?"

I paused, not sure how I wanted to answer. I still had so many things to go over to figure out what I did wrong, so many logistics to comb through. I could ask Cash. Even though he had stopped coming with me, he booked and planned all the things last year. I simply showed up. Maybe that was my first mistake—thinking I could actually do it.

Nope. I told myself. *You can do this.*

"Couldn't have been better." I finally answered, settling on the vague answer.

I walked to Hook's shoulder, catching Wyatt nodding from the corner of my eye.

"You seemed upset last night." His voice slowed, almost as if he were choosing his words wisely.

I heaved a sigh. "It was just a hard weekend. Next week will be better."

"I'm sure it will."

"It will," I agreed with him. "I made a few mistakes, but I won't be making them again." I looked over at him, noticing the way his eyebrows pinched.

"Made a few mistakes? You mean, you knocked over a few barrels?"

"Oh, what?" I tilted my head and let my hair fall. "Did you watch it on the *Cowboy Channel*?"

He gave a soft laugh. "No, I didn't. Just guessing by the way you came home last night."

"I was tired. It was a long drive."

"What happened?" His voice was soft, calming almost. The same chill flowed through my body with the way he spoke that did when fictional characters declared their love for each other. It was uneasy, yet completely comforting.

I pursed my lips and dropped my arms to my side, then began. "I messed up the reservation at the stables, and they almost wouldn't let my horses share a stall. I thought I booked a hotel, but I got the days mixed up and ended up sleeping in my truck. I came in last, knocked over barrels, saw my mom—you know…" I took another deep breath, not believing I just mentioned my mom in front of Wyatt. I tensed and forced myself to continue. "All the normal things."

"You messed up reservations? Stable and hotel? How?"

My shoulders relaxed, and the fact that that was what he chose to ask me about changed my entire demeanor. I wasn't exactly sure what I would do if he asked about my mom.

"I just mixed up the days while I was booking, an honest mistake. And I swear I booked two stalls, but…I guess I didn't. It was just the one place, though." I ducked under Hook's neck, giving him a soft caress. "They let them stay in the one stall, but they upped my price and made me sign a waiver in case anything happened that they wouldn't be responsible."

"Make sense. But—did you just overbook yourself, so…it slipped your mind?"

I shrugged my shoulder. "Cash did this for me last year. He finalized everything. I guess I was overconfident." I sighed, looking over at him. He opened his mouth to speak, but I pointed at him. "Don't say anything. Mistakes happen. I just can't let them take over."

"Mistakes do happen, but you don't have to do this alone, you know. I'm sure Cash would still help you book things, at least until you get the hang of it. Hell, I can help." He stood, dusting off his jeans and his palms. "But I gotta ask, why travel with both horses. You did last year, too, right? I know seasoned riders travel with two or more, but this is only your second year—why take both?"

"It's..." I looked at the gelding in front of me. Hook was fast, he was energetic, and he was a spitfire who got the best scores. Then I turned to Charming in his own stall. He was calm, he was precise, he was everything Hook wasn't all wrapped into one package. I had to have both of them. "It's important to me. I can read the arena and get a good feel as to who will perform better. The louder the crowd, the more Hook gets pumped. He runs faster, he performs. The smaller the rodeo, Charming's my man. They are my heart and soul, and it's really important to me they both come. I need them." Looking back to Hook, I scratched behind his ears, and he let out a soft groan.

"Who were you riding when you knocked over the barrels?" Wyatt asked.

Twisting my lips, I responded, "Hook. I made the wrong call."

"No, I wouldn't say that. I haven't really seen you 'make a wrong call' since you got here." He air-quoted right before shoving his hands in his pockets. "Well, except not going out with me, but that's beside the point."

"Really, Wyatt?" I raised a brow and shot him a glare.

"Come on." He cocked a devilish grin. "Just trying to make you smile."

I shook my head, actually feeling a smile tug at my lips. I tightened them, keeping that particular emotion down.

Wyatt cleared his throat. "What's your next step? You have more events this weekend, right?"

I nodded. "I'll be gone for seven days, five rodeos."

"And everything is booked?"

"I hope. I'm going to double-check as soon as I'm done here." I answered, my hand gliding down Hook's back. I'm not sure why I felt compelled to talk, why I felt comfortable with Wyatt, but I swallowed and said, "What if I can't do it? What if I am overconfident? What if I make the wrong call again and again and ruin my shot? You have no idea how much this means to me. I can't mess up again."

Wyatt's eyes grew hooded, his chin dipping as he looked at me, his contact not once faltering. He inhaled, a deep, slow breath. "You won't but—"

"But?" I stopped him.

"No, it's not a bad but." He chuckled. "There's no harm in having someone there to root for you and hype you up and take care of things when you can't."

"And who's that? My mom? My dad?" I laughed at the thought. "Cash?"

"I can come. I can help. Truly Quinn, this isn't about me chasing bunnies like you seem to think I do. I want to help. No more mess-ups. No more fallen barrels. I know you can do this; I've seen the determination. Not many women can say no to me, but you've managed to shoot me down several times, and that takes more determination than barrel racing—"

"Wyatt," I sighed, raising my head in exasperation.

"I'm kidding," he laughed. "Well, about you shooting me down, but not about coming with you. I can help. I can take care of the horses, I can cheer from the stands, I can make sure your horses get two stalls and you're sleeping in a bed and not your truck." He met my gaze, taking a step back from me, not forward. "Think about it at least. If you want help looking over your schedule tonight, I can help there, too. I've helped Rhett plenty of times."

"You're serious?" He couldn't be serious.

He twisted his lips in a smile, his blue eyes beaming. "Think about it and let me know. I'll let you have time with your boys."

With that, he left the stall.

My mind was buzzing. *Would it really be bad to have him with me?*

TEN

Wyatt

I F I WEREN'T IN the kitchen, I wouldn't have heard the knock. It was so light, but it was there. Two steps and my hand was on the doorknob, swinging it open—a rush flying through my chest when I saw who was standing there. Quinn held her laptop to her body, and she took a few deep breaths. Her eyes trailed down slowly, but then popped back up, blinking rapidly as she looked away.

"Quinn?" My voice rose at least an octave in surprise. Trying to shrug that off and play it cool, I flashed her a smirk and leaned against the open door.

A light blush spread across her cheeks when she looked away, her gaze anywhere but on me.

Pinching my brow, I looked down at myself, my frown vanishing with the realization of the reason for her blush. I stood shirtless, my gray sweatpants sitting low on my hips, I was barefoot, and my hair was still wet from my shower. I raised a single eyebrow, folding my arms across my bare chest, using my shoulder to prop me up on the door. I would be lying if I said that the fact that her blush was because of me didn't send confidence roaring through my veins. Now, if only she'd act like that when I was clothed.

She cleared her throat and swallowed so hard I could see her throat bob.

"I was thinking," she finally croaked. "Maybe it wouldn't be a bad idea to have you come along with me. I was looking at my schedule, and I seem to have…" She trailed off, her jaw clenching.

"Come on in." I held up a hand and stepped back from the entry, giving her plenty of space to cross the threshold into my small apartment. She passed me, her scent wafting through the air between us. This girl was around horses nonstop, yet she still smelled of coconut. I grinned, inhaling it in. "Let me just go get a shirt on," I said, closing the door behind her.

"Please," she said hastily. She placed her laptop on the small kitchen peninsula, and as I walked to my dresser, I caught her licking her lips, the blush on her cheeks still visible.

Tugging a simple black hoodie over my head, I approached the peninsula where Quinn was opening her laptop. I pulled the stool out and took a seat, watching as her fingers ran against the mouse pad.

"Okay, what did you seem to do?"

"First," she started, "I'm not sure how I managed to do this, so you're not going to ask any questions about how I screwed up so bad—"

"You didn't screw up," I mumbled, and she kept talking as if she didn't even hear me.

"But I was looking at my schedule," Quinn continued, her eyes moving all over her computer screen. "I have five rides coming up. One in Idaho, New Mexico, and Colorado, and two in Arizona. I have this planned over seven days, and in confirming everything when I got home,"—she paused and turned her laptop to me—"I noticed that a rodeo hadn't confirmed me as a rider, and a few boarding stables only had me booked for one stall."

"Okay, easy fixes." I slid the laptop closer to me, now seeing the multiple screens she had opened. A rodeo website, stable confirmations, and a document with her schedule and travel plans. First, I went to the rodeo website, already having an idea as to what was going on. There had been times when Rhett was too eager to get to the next step that he didn't—

"Second," she said, catching me off guard from my thought. I looked up at her, my brow raised. "This is strictly business. If you do anything outside of helping me here and on the road, I will punch you."

I chuckled. "Noted. I'll be good." I gave her a smirk, which quickly vanished as soon as I saw her vacant expression. I cleared my throat. "So, I'm looking at the rodeo. Looks like Flagstaff?" Right to business.

"Yes, which happens to be the first rodeo this weekend. Phoenix, Albuquerque, Grand Junction, and Boise all confirmed." She looked down and picked at her nails.

I hummed. "You scheduled them in a circle." I motioned with my finger in the air, thinking of the map in my mind. "Good plan."

"It made sense, and the dates worked. I just missed Flagstaff."

"Okay, first thing, let's get that confirmed. Did you pay your fee?" I asked, and when her answer was a shrug, I inhaled and gave her a knowing nod. "We'll do that. Then the stables." I opened the browser tab and pulled up her registration form. "How many rodeos did you book at a time?"

"A few months in advance. I have my life planned up through May."

"Mainly weekends, right?"

"A few weekdays."

I nodded and scrolled through her forms, tilting my head in confirmation. "Well, this is easy—you didn't submit the registration."

"What?"

I spun the computer to her. "You never submitted the form for the Flagstaff Rodeo."

Quinn pinched her brow. "I didn't?"

I shrugged. "It happens. I can't tell you how many times Rhett didn't finish his registration."

"How many times? And you handled it for him?" She furrowed her brow, the expression of disbelief not hard to miss.

"You'd be surprised how many times. And yeah, I'd help the best I could. When our schedules aligned, he packed, and I took care of this. I made sure to book everything. Rodeos, hotels, camp sites, stables. All of it. He traveled with his mare, Buckle, but I was easy. No horse required." I quickly scanned through her form, adding any details I could.

"So, committees hired you because of Rhett?"

I scoffed. "Hell no. I may not ride any events, but I made a name for myself." I kept my concentration on the submission, not closing the browser until I got the *Welcome to the Rodeo* banner. I quickly moved to the stable website, searching in her email for confirmations.

Quinn just...watched. She was studying me as I worked, leaving me in silence for a bit. This was something I actually liked to do, the organization of it all. The planning, the prepping, making sure it all ran smoothly for Rhett. Then I'd relax as we traveled, knowing everything was booked and taken care of.

"Why don't you ride in any events?" Quinn asked, breaking her silence, placing her hands on the counter.

I met her gaze and raised a brow in question, giving her a dubious look.

"I mean," she continued, "I've seen you do tie down. You were terrible, but I can see you doing this now, and you're like...a completely different person."

I pinched my brow.

"I mean..." she started, pausing as if trying to find the words that weren't going to be a direct insult to me. "I just didn't think you would be the one people went to for"—she waved her hand in front of me—"all of this."

The corner of my lips tugged. "All of this?"

"You don't seem interested in this."

"I'm going to need you to define *this*." I mimicked her hand gesture from earlier.

She slumped her shoulders. "I didn't envision you being so organized when it came to rodeos. I just saw you as the one who tagged along and let everyone else take care of everything."

I gave her a grin. "Rodeos take work, a lot of planning. It's a lot for one person to handle and, Quinn..." I heaved a sigh. "This is my career, too. Not just a hobby."

I could visibly see her chewing on her bottom lip. Her jaw tensed.

Studying her, I finally answered her question from before. "I don't do livestock events because I grew up mutton busting and hated it. That's the start. Now it's because I don't want to hurt myself."

"You jumped off a roof," Quinn said, her tone void, like she couldn't believe my reasoning. "But you won't ride livestock events?"

"I've done more than jump off a roof, but yeah, that *is* a huge reason. I've seen Rhett tear muscles and Lachlan break bones. My dad has a bad back, and a few bull riders have retired early due to injury. Hell, I saw my brother-in-law die. I love to ride horses, but...when I have control of them." I broke eye contact and went to the browser for the boarding stables. "I grew up a Hartwell. We live and breathe rodeo. And I just found my own way to love and enjoy it."

"Announcing."

"I like to talk." I shrugged a shoulder, giving her a quick grin before turning back to the computer screen. "Can you pull up all the boarding confirmations?" I turned the computer to her and waited.

After a few moments of silence, watching her tap away at the keys, she slid the laptop back to me with several browsers open.

"Okay, this is just as easy; just pray they have stalls."

"Praying."

After sending a few emails to the stables and myself her schedule, I closed Quinn's laptop. "What about you?"

"Huh?"

"How did you start barrel racing?"

She inhaled, letting out a long breath through her nose. "My mom was a rodeo queen. As much as she tried to get me into that part of the rodeo world, I wanted to do my own thing—a little like you, I guess."

"You were a rodeo queen?"

"Up until I was about thirteen, then I stopped to work at a stable. I bought Hook and started training and just...knew it was the right thing for me." She slid her laptop close to her, her hands running along the closed lid. "I wasn't the rodeo queen type."

Looking at her, I could absolutely see her as the rodeo queen type. Quinn was beauty personified. I could picture it, clear as day. A crown on her hat with her hair teased and curled to perfection, her smile bright and radiant. Her hands on her hips, with her chest jutted out, displaying her brand-new sash. Her lips red, her shadowed eyes with long lashes, her blouse perfectly pressed, and her jeans free of any dirt. Custom chaps that caught your eye as she rode and waved to the crowd that just saw her be queened...

And even though I could see it, she was right. It wasn't her.

Her hair was natural, cascading down her shoulders in waves, not a forced curl in sight. Her skin was flawless, a slight blush to her cheeks—most likely residual from earlier—but it still created the perfect glow to her. She wore a light coat of mascara, but no other makeup adorned her skin. She didn't need it—she was stunning without it. Her lips were perfectly pink and kissable, even without lip gloss or lipstick to make them pop. Just looking at her sent heat through my body, a bolt of lightning shocking my entire being. Months ago, I had come to the conclusion she was the most beautiful woman I had ever seen, and looking at her now, seeing her in the most casual clothing, horsehair still lingering on the cotton—I stood by it. There was an urge to pull her to me, to feel her soft skin, her hair weaving through my fingers. I wanted so much more with her than I had ever dreamed. This feeling...just from looking at her.

Quinn was perfect. In every sense of the word.

"I need you to stop looking at me like that," Quinn said softly, filling the silence that began to hang in the air.

"Like what?" I asked, my voice husky, furrowing my brow.

"Like you want to kiss me."

I took a breath, not realizing I was looking at her that intently. But...

"I do want to kiss you," I smirked, knowing that lying wouldn't do me any good. "There's no other way to look at you."

She rolled her eyes slightly and looked away from me, her gaze falling on the window. "Wyatt, what was the second point I made when I first got here?"

I pushed myself up from the stool, heaving a sigh. "Strictly business." I held up three fingers. "Scout's honor."

"Then stop looking at me like that." She met my gaze, and the gleam from her emerald eyes told me I was still looking at her like I wanted to cradle her face, take her mouth with mine, and taste her. I broke eye contact before I made that a reality.

I inhaled, holding my breath for a beat before exhaling heavily, my hands finding the pockets of my sweats. "According to your schedule, we leave on Wednesday for a full day of travel." I took a step closer to her, only tempting myself more to kiss her. I balled my hands into fists in my pockets. "I'll tell Abi I won't be around, and I'll get the horses prepped for the drive."

"I can prep the horses—"

"Quinn," I stopped her, "Let me *help*. You focus on packing for five rides, and I'll prep the horses."

Her eyes narrowed for a millisecond, then she nodded. "Okay, fine. You prep the horses. I'll pack, and we leave for Flagstaff on Wednesday." She grabbed her laptop and once again held it to her chest. "Thank you, Wyatt," she said, her voice sweet. "For everything...except the awkward moment for a second there."

I raised a brow. "Nothing was awkward. Happy to help."

"See you tomorrow?" She opened the door and slipped through before I even had time to respond. Then, she was gone.

"Tomorrow," I repeated to an empty apartment.

ELEVEN

Quinn

THE DRIVE TO FLAGSTAFF was twelve hours without stopping every few hours to make sure the horses had hay and water, and suddenly, I was very thankful I had a co-pilot with me. Four hours into the drive and Wyatt insisted we stop at the next gas station. The second I shifted my truck into park, he hopped out of the cab, flopping his baseball cap on his head.

The truck was packed to the brim with all of our luggage—mainly mine. Wyatt assured me he was a light packer. Me? I had several hat boxes, outfits in garment bags, my own suitcase with toiletries and hair accessories, and several pairs of boots. On top of everything I needed, I had all of Hook and Charming's things in the tack. Wyatt had a single duffel bag, one pair of boots, and one baseball cap. When he opened the back seat of the cab, his eyes widened, and the exact words that came out of his mouth were, "You pack like Rhett," before he shoved his bag in on top of the massive pile of my things.

I filled the tank, went into the building to use the facilities and grabbed a few snacks, and came back to Wyatt still in the trailer with the horses. I checked on my boys, seeing them happy as can be in Wyatt's care, and then returned behind the wheel. Wyatt offered to drive but reluctantly gave in when I told him I was more comfortable behind the wheel. We played music—country mainly, with the random Panic! At the Disco and AC/DC song thrown in, and Wyatt surprised me even more when he began to sing along to Shania Twain.

The conversation was light, sometimes not at all, as the world passed us. When we did talk, it was "I can't believe you listen to Panic!" from Wyatt, and "I can't believe you knew every word to every Shania Twain song that played" from me. Talking to Wyatt became easy when I wasn't worried about him pulling the moves on me. Our conversation began to flow, as if we were the type of friends who didn't text each other good morning; we just picked back up where we left off. And then when the silence took over, it wasn't awkward; it was comfortable. Even if his comment from the other night still sang in my head.

I do want to kiss you.

The way he said it made me think he wasn't saying it to flirt, and the way he was looking at me made me think it was more than just a fling. More than how he would look at the other girls. I would have to remind myself of all the stupid things he had said to me in the past. I had to ignore that small little flutter in my core.

At the next stop, I let Wyatt take over the wheel, but the tunes stayed the same. I pulled a book out to read, and Wyatt still sang along to the music. When he finally asked me what I was reading, I showed him the cover—the latest Matt Haig.

"I'll have to send that to Abi. Is it good?" he asked, returning his attention to the road.

"It's wonderful. Cash mentioned that Abi likes to read. He said they are on bookshelf number two." I chuckle, returning to the book.

"Mainly fantasy...romance...books." Wyatt furrowed his brow.

"Does one have a dragon on it?" I groaned. I was up for a good fantasy novel, mainly fairytale retellings, but I wasn't jumping on the dragon rider train quite yet. I'd wait for the buzz to die down.

He twisted his lips. "Not that I know of? But I don't pay much attention."

"Well," I shifted in my seat, my eyes going right back to the words on the page, "maybe someday."

"You guys should start a book club when we get back. Abi would be thrilled."

We grew silent again, Wyatt lowering the music as I read, and at the next stop, he pulled both horses from the trailer to let them rest their legs. They walked and stretched, each staying close to Wyatt as they moved. Hook tugged on the lip of his baseball hat while Charming pulled at the leaves on the few trees that were around, but when their time was up, they both went back into the trailer without complaint, and then Wyatt drove the rest of the way to Flagstaff.

We arrived at the stables ahead of schedule, and we both took the horses to their stalls for the night, giving them the prince treatment for putting up with the long drive. Once they were settled, we took the short journey to the hotel. After checking in, Wyatt grabbed his bag, and I started to open the garment bags to find the right outfit for tomorrow, the right hat, the right boots, stopping only when Wyatt appeared from behind me. He grabbed a luggage cart and began stacking all my things—and I mean *all* my things, leaving the back seat of my truck completely empty before he rolled it to the elevator for me. I followed, not exactly sure what to say to him, catering to me. So...once we were in the elevator, I settled for the simplest thing.

"Thanks." I leaned against the elevator wall as the door closed. Wyatt gave me a smile.

"You really only brought the one duffel?" I asked, raising my head, looking at all my bags in the cart on top of his single bag.

"Three jeans, seven t-shirts, seven button-downs, socks, underwear, toothbrush, and all that jazz, one pair of boots—"

"Hat?" I raised a brow.

"When have you seen me in a cowboy hat?"

"When you announce."

"Well, yeah, it's part of the uniform, but even working in the stables, I'm wearing this." He pointed to his baseball cap. It had the Hartwell logo on it, and the sides were distressed, but in a way that you could tell he's worn it for years, not purchased that way. "I'm not big on cowboy hats."

"Why not? They look good on basically anyone."

"True. I wear them when I have to, but since I'm here to help you—baseball cap."

I shook my head at him. "We'll fix that."

The elevator door opened, and Wyatt waited until I was in the hall before he pushed the cart through. Our rooms were a few doors down from each other, but he helped me unload the cart—forcing me to stay inside while he returned the cart to the lobby. I didn't protest as he pushed the cart out of the room. It had been a long time since I had been taken care of like this; not even Cash was this generous when he traveled with me last year. I watched him disappear back into the elevator before shutting the door and locking all the locks, then looked at every garment bag, every hat and boot box, and my suitcases, a smile spreading across my lips—all brought on by Wyatt Hartwell.

I knocked on Wyatt's hotel room door shortly after eleven the next morning. We had time before we had to go to the arena for registration, and the man needed a hat. He opened the door with a smile. Dressed comfortably in a gray tee and jeans, his hair wet and messy, most likely from a shower, he looked refreshed even after the long day of travel we had just had.

"Here to ask me out to lunch, Compton?" His smile turned into a smirk as he leaned against the door frame, his arm stretching over his head.

I raised an eyebrow and crossed my arms over my chest.

"Nope...right. Sorry." He shifted and raised a finger as he chastised himself for flirting. "Habit. Hi, Quinn."

"Get your shoes on, Hartwell." I lowered my arms and spun on my heel. "We're going to get you a hat." I waved my hand in the air in a *follow me* gesture as I began to walk down the hall.

"I have a hat," he called after me.

"Not the right kind of hat. Come on."

I heard the door close, then open a few moments later. I made it to the elevator and pressed the button down to the lobby, seeing Wyatt jog down the hall from the corner of my eye. He had grabbed his baseball cap and put his boots on in a hurry, his jeans tucked and sticking out in all the wrong places. He situated himself once the elevator was closed and didn't question me as we walked to the truck and climbed in. But once the doors were closed, he shifted in his seat.

"We're going to get me a cowboy hat? I have plenty of those at home." He protested.

"At home, not here. You're going to rodeos, Wyatt. You gotta look the part. You'll stick out like a sore thumb wearing that old thing." I tapped the bill of his hat, forcing it down. "I don't care that you're not announcing. You need a damn hat."

Wyatt took off his hat, ran his fingers through his damp hair, and placed the cap on backwards. "I can have Rhett overnight me one—"

"Nah. I'd rather get you a new one for this adventure."

He chuckled, shaking his head as I left the hotel parking lot, going to the closest store I could find already programmed on my phone's GPS.

"And here I was hoping for lunch, I get a new hat instead."

"We can get lunch after," I assured him. "Hat now, then food. We don't have time for a custom hat, so I hope a Boot Barn will suffice."

Wyatt let out a long, exasperated, over-exaggerated sigh. "If you really think I need a hat—"

"You're wearing a hat that looks like you got it when you were five. Boot Barn will be like a crown after wearing that."

"Don't. Diss. My. Hat." Wyatt snapped each word, the sarcastic tone floating through the air.

I couldn't help my smile from slipping out, but didn't remark. The comfortable silence went on until I pulled into the parking lot of Boot Barn. The country music blared through the speakers, but Wyatt went directly to the back wall, where the hats lined the shelves. I jogged in front of him, my ponytail bouncing behind me as I made it to the hats first. I had to stop him from picking a plain brown one with no flair or attitude. Wyatt needed a hat that fit him.

"What's your hat size?" I asked, grabbing a black hat with a silver bull skull on the band. "Seven?" I flipped the hat upside down before twisting to Wyatt. Catching his gaze, I plopped it on his head.

He looked handsome, I would admit that, but black didn't fit him. He wasn't broody enough. No one would look at him and say, 'You *must* be the grumpy cowboy that all the girls pine after.' That wasn't him. I plucked it from his head and put it back on the shelf.

"What was wrong with that one?" he asked, watching my every move. "It was nice, and it fit."

"You're not a black cowboy hat kind of guy. White?" I picked up another hat, white with a black rim, and Wyatt just stood still as I again plopped the hat on his head.

Finding a mirror, he caught a glance of himself, raising an eyebrow. "Cash would choose this hat." He traced the rim with his thumb and forefinger.

Rolling my eyes, I caught sight of a hat I knew would fit him, even if it were an eyesore. Black alligator leather with a turquoise pattern on the brim. Completely hideous, yet...perfect. I turned, facing Wyatt with enthusiasm, just in time to see him place the white one back on the shelf.

His jaw dropped as soon as he saw the hat I was holding. "Oh, fuck no," he grumbled.

"Just try it on."

"No." He bit, his eyes wide as he took the hat from me, waving me off. "Go over there. I can pick my own damn hat."

I raised my hands in surrender. "Fine, fine." I backed away from him, using my thumb to point behind my shoulder. "I'll go over there," I mimicked him.

I began to wander through the women's clothing section, getting completely distracted by the earrings, all the while trying to keep my eye on Wyatt. He tried on a few more black ones, some deep brown with jewels around the headband, another white one—but each one he picked up, he studied and put back down. None seemed to capture his vibe. Either that, or he was being honest when he said he didn't care for cowboy hats. It wasn't until he picked up a light brown Stetson with a turquoise emblem on the headband that he stopped and looked at himself from all angles in the mirror.

I could feel my lips twisting into a smirk as I watched him trace the brim, adjust it on his head, and raise and drop his chin, taking himself in. Eventually, he hooked his thumbs in his jeans pockets, cocked his hips, and posed. Not wanting to miss this, I raised my phone and snapped a picture of him. I could see his face in the mirror, the smirk he was giving himself, his blue eyes shining through. It was *his* hat. If I could see it in a photo, he could see it in the mirror.

"What do you think?"

The sound of his voice made me flinch. Quickly locking my phone, I looked up at him. He was still wearing the hat, and up close it was even more perfect.

"That's it." I smiled up at him. "You found your hat."

His smirk grew, his eyes shining even brighter now that he was in front of me. He removed it and replaced it with his baseball cap. "You almost had it with the alligator one."

"That was a joke," I admitted, "but glad you tried all your options. See?" I reached up and patted his shoulder, realizing for the first time how much taller he was than me. "Cowboy hats aren't all that bad. Now you'll fit in. You even have dirt on your jeans."

Wyatt's grin turned into a full ear-to-ear smile, complete with a laugh as we made our way to the register. He even bought my earrings.

TWELVE

Wyatt

THE TEXT FROM HAWKINS pulled me away from the chat with my sister. It had been weeks since I had heard from him. Weeks of silence and then 'not so good, good news?' What did that even mean? Hawkins had been radio silent for weeks, only solidifying that I was most likely never going to announce again. Keeping busy at the stables and being with Quinn was a nice distraction from the fact that I was still off committee lists, but now—Hawkins had my full attention.

Not even bothering to text him back, I hit his number to call.

"Hey, Wyatt," he answered quickly, a slight shake to his normal, solid tone.

"Hey, Hawk."

"I take it you saw my text."

"Yeah, care to elaborate?" I took my new hat from my head and tossed it on my bed, glancing at the clock on the nightstand. 2:30 p.m.—I had to meet Quinn soon. "Quickly," I added.

"In a rush?" he asked.

"Yes and no. What did you mean by not so good, good news?"

"I saw your name on a committee for Reno."

My entire body flinched, and at the same time, a knot began to form in my stomach. I couldn't have heard him right. The Reno Rodeo was huge, one that I had yet to announce at. It was just as big as Days of '47 in Utah, or Cheyenne Frontier Days in Wyoming...if my name was on the list for announcers, maybe my fuck-up wasn't as bad as I really thought.

"Hawk, that's great news, not just *good* news," I said, my voice ragged as I soaked this in. My mind ran through past events. I screwed up in October of last year, I bummed around until the NFR, then came home. Bummed around some more...then finally started to work. I never fully felt like myself. I missed the piece of me that I found behind the microphone. This...this was hope in the form of a phone call.

I counted on my fingers. Three months until Reno. "For the entire week?" I asked, my hopes rising slightly even though I knew in the back of my mind there was a 'not so good' portion of this news.

"Well, that's the thing."

My shoulders slumped. Dude didn't miss a beat. "I saw your name in the running, but they haven't decided yet. Lucas is head of the committee this year, and he and Archie are pretty good friends..." He trailed off, not even needing to finish his sentence.

I rolled my neck back, closing my eyes. Of course, Lucas Tuck was friends with Archie Rollins, AKA the man I punched and caused to black out after breaking his nose.

"That's the catch," I grumbled. "So, my name may be there, but it's not gonna happen, is what you're telling me."

The knock on my hotel door forced my attention. I heard Quinn's faint call of my name, and I stood, grabbing my hat from the bed and giving myself one last look in the mirror. I didn't dress up like I would if I were working, but I still wanted to look presentable. Hell, people know my name, and if what Hawkins was telling me was true, people were starting to see me again. My focus tonight would be on Quinn and her horses—that's why I was there. But I wouldn't complain if someone came up and talked to me.

"That's what I'm tellin' you," Hawkins sighed. "I'll keep hyping you up, man, but—"

"Wyatt, are you ready?" Quinn called from the hall.

"Listen, I have to go. Thanks for calling me and letting me know. If something comes of it, great...if something doesn't,"—I opened the door and came face to face with Quinn—"great." That last *great* came out differently than the first, and I gathered it had everything to do with the stunning woman standing in front of me. "Thanks, Hawk." I lowered my phone and took Quinn in.

I had seen this girl dressed up and playful in a bar, beating my ass at a game of pool. I had seen her in a T-shirt with jeans and worker boots, her hair pulled into a tight ponytail as she cared for her horses. I had seen her in lounge pants and a tank top, reading a book as the world passed her by. And now, I was seeing rodeo Quinn. She was dressed in full uniform, a turquoise button-up that had her sponsor patches sewn in, with a belt buckle from a win last year shining on her waist. Her hair was lightly curled under her hat, and her eyes...*fuck* her eyes. Emerald green and beaming with confidence. I could get lost in those eyes...

And apparently, I was staring.

"Ready?" She chuckled, her body swaying to break me from my stupor.

I cleared my throat and gave her a nod, grabbing my coat before shutting the door behind me. In one swift motion, I put on my hat and slipped my phone in my pocket, doing my best to shove the call away.

"Who was that?" she asked, gesturing to my phone, more or less my ass.

I gave her a smirk. "Hawkins."

"And Hawkins is...?" She drew out the s.

"An announcer buddy. He's been keeping me up to date on all the committees, trying to get me back in the game."

"Are you not already 'in the game?'" She air quoted.

"It didn't occur to you that I haven't been working lately?"

I pressed the elevator button, my gaze drifting to the numbers rising as the elevator came up. I listened to the mechanics of it, jabbing the button again with my finger, willing it to come a little faster. I most definitely didn't want to be talking about my employment status with Quinn—or anybody for that matter—and I was taking it out on the elevator button.

"You haven't been working?" she answered, offering me a frown with a hint of confusion spreading across her features. "I figured you were taking the winter season off."

The doors opened. I let Quinn step in first, then followed, once again jabbing the L button to the lobby.

"Did something happen?"

I twisted my lips and frowned. My inner monologue screaming, *Well, she's gonna find out somehow*. But...I really didn't want to go into specifics. That 'somehow' was not in the elevator.

"Remember how we came to the conclusion I've done some pretty stupid things?" I gave her a side eye.

"Yeah?" She huffed.

"Let's just say my most recent stupid thing topped every other stupid thing and..." I heaved a sigh. "I'm not announcing."

"You didn't lose your card, did you?"

I shook my head. "Nah, not that drastic. But stupid enough to cause a rift in my career."

An astronomical rift.

At least I had some semblance of hope now. My name was on a committee. The Richest Rodeo in Americas committee. This whole thing could blow over soon...*ish*. I wasn't expecting to get Reno; that was a long shot. Almost as delusional as getting the NFR this year—but my name was back on a committee list. And that was something.

Leaving it at that, we worked our way through the lobby and to the stables, where her boys were waiting patiently. Hook bobbed his head, whining as we got closer. I dug in my pocket for the peppermint I put there just for him and held out my palm. Quinn laughed as Hook and I shared a moment, her eyes all for Charming. She hooked up his bridle and lead, guiding him to her trailer.

"Looks like you get the night off, bud." I rubbed Hook's nose. "See you in a few hours."

He huffed, making sure to be the loudest horse in the stables as we left.

"Stop spoiling him." Quinn smiled at me as soon as I made it back to the trailer, just in time to see her hook up Charming and shut him in before she jumped off the back.

"Never."

The arena was already packed with cowboys and cowgirls by the time we arrived, and Quinn was buzzing with anticipation. As soon as she parked the truck, I jumped into action, grabbing my hat and practically jogging to the trailer to tend to Charming.

"I can do this." Quinn's voice was clipped as she came up to the trailer.

I had it unlocked already, the door open, and my body halfway in to get her horse when I stopped in my tracks and pointed at her. "I'm here to help you, remember? Get checked in. I'll get him saddled, and then you can warm up."

Quinn held my gaze for a moment too long, biting her lower lip before she finally gave in, dipping her chin so the brim of her hat covered her eyes. She lingered a second longer before her feet jerked into action.

"Okay, I'll be right back." She flashed me a smile, then, without another word, she dashed off.

I guided Charming out, hooking him to the side of the trailer before I opened up the tack shed. Clean shoes and hooves, check. Brushed coat, check. Saddle blanket and reins, check. I strapped Charming up to the nines, picking the breast collar and bridle that matched Quinn's blouse, and once he was done, he got a peppermint.

"He looks good, ready to ride." Quinn came up behind me, forcing me to look over my shoulder as she reached out for Charming's nose. "Hey, handsome man," she cooed as Charming searched her palm for a treat. "You gave him a candy, didn't you?"

"Maybe." I sang, giving Charming one final scratch before dropping the brushes back in the tack. "I have to earn their love somehow."

"Oddly enough, I don't think that's a problem. Hook is practically your horse now."

"Oh, right—it's your love I have to earn."

"Wyatt!"

The call of my name made me stop, not even getting to hear the comeback that I knew was right on Quinn's lips. The smirk my stupid ass comment rewarded me faded as she glanced behind my shoulder. A cowgirl, her bright pink blouse covered in sponsor patches, came dashing up to us, her face beaming as she got closer and closer.

"Wyatt!" She called again, practically jumping into my arms. "I haven't seen you in so long. What has it been? Two years?"

"Hey...April," I chuckled as she buried her head into the crook of my neck. "Yeah, about that I think."

April pulled away from me, and before I could even react, her mouth was pressed against mine in an all-consuming kiss. Her hands slid down my chest until she gripped my waist, and a soft moan left her lungs as she broke the kiss.

"Two years too long," she whispered, a moan lingering as she fluttered her eyes open.

Me? I was too stunned to say anything back.

Thankfully, Quinn wasn't.

"April Grant, right?" She took a step forward as she cleared her throat, breaking whatever spell April was under.

Ha...I knew the spell. I had only been trying to cast it on the girl to my right since meeting her.

April released me and took a step back. "Oh yes, hi. I'm so sorry. I just...haven't seen him in a long time and got"—her eyes shifted over to me—"carried away."

Quinn shrugged. "I don't mind. I'm Quinn, by the way." She held out her hand. "Quinn Compton. We'll be racing against each other this evening."

"Right!" April stepped to my side, taking Quinn's hand and shaking. "You're Lance and Helen's daughter. Great to meet you." Once she let go of Quinn, her attention turned right back to me. "I didn't know you were announcing tonight."

"I'm not." I reached out for Charming's reins. "I'm Quinn's assistant for lack of a better word."

"He's agreed to help me with my horses this trip," Quinn added, tilting her head to me, giving me a cheeky smirk. "So yeah, assistant sounds about right."

"You're traveling together?"

"Yup." Quinn popped the P.

"Oh, I had no idea." April furrowed her brow for a millisecond before offering me a knowing grin. "I miss hearing your voice. I was hoping since you were here—"

"Nah." I interrupted her. "Still technically on sabbatical." That's what Sam called it? Right? "But it was good to see you. You're right—it's been way too long." I reached up, moving a flyaway hair from her shoulder, making sure it was perfectly blended in with the rest of her golden locks. I could literally see her swoon with one gesture. Now if only that would work on some *other* barrel racer.

"We're all going out tonight after the rodeo. Join us," she cooed, taking a step closer to me, her hands landing on my chest.

Normally, I'd jump at the chance, but tonight, I couldn't think of anything better than hanging out with Quinn. I didn't even know if that was in the cards, but looking at Quinn right now, I didn't want to be anywhere else.

"Ah." I turned on my disappointed sigh. "You know I'd love to, but I'm here with Quinn. I gotta help her with Charming and make sure everything is okay. Plus, we leave early tomorrow morning for Phoenix—"

She frowned, pleading almost as she slumped her shoulders. "Okay, then. If you're sure. But..." She raised on her tiptoes and gave me a chaste, fleeting kiss, one that would have sent me into a spiral wanting so much more before. "My number is the same if you change your mind."

I hummed, the knot in my stomach unraveling as she walked away. Blinking, I turned back to Charming, noticing the pinched, smug expression on Quinn's face right away. It was a mixture between amusement and...was that...jealously?

It can't be. Quinn? Jealous? Over me?

I was reading too much into it.

She most likely just wanted to tease the hell out of me for what just happened.

"Don't say anything," I said sternly.

She pursed her lips, waving a hand in the air. "Wasn't gonna."

"You look like you were gonna."

"Oh, but Wyatt." She placed her hand to her chest, doing her best impression of April, adding a bit more Valley girl flair. It was fucking adorable. "It's been too long. Two years too long."

I raised an eyebrow. "She's a very talented girl." I motioned back to where April had come from. "She just got overly excited."

Quinn let out a soft chuckle. "Go chase if you want. Don't stop on my account."

"Chase?" I repeated the word, a coy grin spreading across my lips. "Come on, Quinn, there's only one girl I want to chase right now." I handed her Charming's reins, holding her eye contact for longer than necessary. There I go...getting lost in the sea of emerald.

I blinked, forcing myself back to dry land. "Come on, let's get you in that field for a minute before the race." I bounced my eyebrows, turned to shut the tack shed, and walked off—grateful when I heard Charming's hooves his the concrete from behind me.

Thirteen

Quinn

I beat April.

By three seconds.

Not that I was counting.

After my win, Wyatt bounded up to me, a skip in his step as he wrapped his arms around my waist, lifting me off the ground. I squealed as he laughed into the crook of my neck, sending a warm, fuzzy feeling through my spine that I couldn't quite explain. He set me down and shook my shoulders, congratulating me on the run, teasing slightly that he'll have a girl kiss him before every ride, as it seemed to spark just the right motivation in me. I gave him the longest eye roll I could, which in turn got me the widest smirk he could muster right before I playfully shoved him away.

I silently loved the fact that he was there to cheer me on and be by my side. Cash was fantastic to have, but he would start listing ways I could go faster and harder the next go around. With Wyatt, it was just...fun. He was excited to see me win and had just as much energy as I did after. The adrenaline that pumped through both of us was strong enough that it could be boxed and saved for another night.

"Quinn," Wyatt began, opening the tack and placing the saddle on the pole, grabbing a brush to toss at me. "You just won the Flagstaff Rodeo. What are you going to do now!?" He put on his best announcer's voice, I swear, even adding a southern twang to it.

I raised an eyebrow. "Shower. Watch my comfort show. Sleep." I ticked off my after-ride routine in my mind.

That was one thing I didn't factor in—how would Wyatt fit into my routine. I guess, in the back of my mind, he would do his thing, and I would do mine. There wouldn't be anything to question or plan. We'd go our separate ways. Nothing to overthink.

"You're supposed to say something different. Like you want to go to Disneyland or buy a new pair of boots. Didn't you ever see those commercials after the Super Bowl?" He ran his hand down Charming's bare back, giving me a wink which I promptly returned with an annoyed glare.

"You're channeling a commercial from the nineties, before I was born, you realize. I've never been one for Disneyland, and I have too many boots, plus I like to shop for hats."

"Last chance, Wyatt!" April's voice came up to my side, singing as she got closer to us. If she drew out his name any longer, she'd run out of air. "Come out with us?"

I looked over at her mid brush, my hand stopping on Charming's coat. She slowed her pace, her eyes heavy on Wyatt. Wyatt met my gaze over Charming's back, raising both of his eyebrows.

"Quinn can come, too. I'm sure we'll all have a great time." She placed her hands on her hips, a tilt to her stance. "For old times' sake?" she begged, her bottom lip popping out in a pout.

Wyatt gave her a small chuckle. "Thanks for the offer, but I have a horse to take care of. You're going to be in Phoenix, yeah? Maybe then."

April met my gaze, then turned her eyes back to Wyatt, "Okay, okay. Tomorrow night then, in Phoenix." She begrudgingly accepted defeat. "Great ride today, Quinn."

I gave her a tight smile, definitely not thinking about how I beat her in the back of my head. "You too."

She scrunched her nose and rose to her tiptoes, kissing Wyatt on his cheek before leaving us alone. I saw the faintest tint of pink spread across his face after her small kiss, and he inhaled long and slow, holding his breath for a few seconds before exhaling through his lips.

Was he wanting to say something else to her? If he wanted to go, he could. I wasn't going to stop him. My plans after a ride were always the same. I relaxed in my own way. I'm pretty sure Wyatt's plans always consisted of a different bar, a different girl, a few hours of sleep, and then back on the road while his brother drove. I told him this was strictly business between him and me, and there were no stipulations as to what he did after the rodeos. As much as I was beginning to enjoy the time we spent together, I had zero control over what he did...or...*who* he did.

That thought settled uneasy in my stomach, a knot forming. Yet another feeling I wasn't sure how to explain.

"You can go, you know," I finally said to him, my arm moving for the first time since April had arrived. Wyatt was basically done brushing his side of Charming, while I had only touched a small spot.

"Nah." Wyatt tossed his brush back into the tack bag, taking mine from me to brush out Charming a lot faster than I was. "I'm beat. Plus, we have a busy day tomorrow and have to leave early for Phoenix. I'll go out tomorrow night if I feel up to it."

"Just don't stop on my account." I took a step back, my hand gliding on Charming's coat as I walked around him to unhook him from the trailer.

The corner of his lips lightly tugged. "You're not stopping me from doing anything. Except for wearing my hat."

I grinned, catching sight of him before stepping into the trailer with Charming. He never once took off his cowboy hat, well, that I was aware of, and I still stood by what I said that morning. That hat suited him. He looked damn sexy in it.

Wait...*nope.*

I did not just have the thought that Wyatt was sexy.

I inhaled, and like Wyatt did a moment ago, I held in my breath for a few beats before exhaling. I hooked in Charming and left the trailer, making sure to walk on the opposite side of the truck from Wyatt. He was barely climbing into the passenger seat as I started up the engine, twisting his torso to buckle up. I blinked and returned to the conversation we were having *before* my thoughts went some-where they weren't supposed to.

"We should just toss the other one." I popped the truck in gear and left the arena, catching the "Oh, hell no" that Wyatt mumbled under his breath.

Dad

Hey, Pumpkin, how was Flagstaff?

Me

Sixteen point nine – won the night.

Dad

That's my girl. Your mom said she saw you last weekend.

Me

Yeah, in Wyoming. Did she also tell you I lost that night?

Dad

She may have mentioned it.

But you won tonight.

Me

I'll win tomorrow too. Charming was a bit wide around the barrel, but I'll tighten up in training and ride Hook tomorrow. Team roping was great tonight.

Dad

When is team roping not?

Me

Well, it's been missing its best heeler for years.

Dad

Good thing there's still a Compton on the dirt. Proud of you.

The loud knock at my door sent a shock through me, my phone falling out of my hands. My dad would text a few times a week, and we would always end the conversation the same way. My mom may not be proud of the rodeo path I'd taken, but my dad always made sure I knew he was, even if he didn't show it in person. His last few words would always cling to me—*proud of you.*

I heaved a shaky sigh as I picked my phone up, sending a quick goodnight text before making my way to the door. By how late it was, it could only be one person. I opened the door, slowly at first to peek through, opening it wider once Wyatt came into full view.

"It's late, Hartwell," I sighed, leaning my forehead against the door.

He shrugged a shoulder. "Couldn't sleep, thought I'd check on you."

"I'm good." I lifted my head to look at him, those blue eyes sending a shock through me I'd force myself to forget. "If you can't sleep, why not head out? I'm sure everyo—"

"Nah." Wyatt slid through the door, making his way into my room. "I'm tired; I just can't sleep."

Watching him take in the room, I shut the door and locked it behind me. "And...what do you expect me to do about you not being able to sleep?"

He cocked an eyebrow. "There are lots of things you can do, Compton."

"Get out." I pointed towards the door, not having the brain capacity for this, but also feeling a hint of relief when he just crossed his arms over his chest and smirked.

"Whoa, jumping the gun there?" His smirk grew to the right. "My mind was actually on that TV show you mentioned."

"TV show?" I mimicked his stance, popping my hip out to the side. I was in my pajamas already—shorts and a sleep tank—and my wet hair was braided and lying on my shoulder. I noticed him eyeing me up and down, taking a deep breath in before he took a step. He dropped his arms and reached for my laptop.

"I didn't bring my computer, so I thought maybe—"

"You want to watch a TV show?" It was my turn to raise an eyebrow at him.

"Yeah, why not?" He held out my laptop. I eyed it, and then him, seeing the truth across his face.

The man looked tired. His eyes were heavy with dark circles I had never noticed before, sunken into his skin. Even his cocky smile was weaker than normal. Maybe a comfort show was what we both needed.

I took my laptop from him. "Fine, but I'm picking the episode."

"Fine by me. I think I just need the noise."

"Your room has a TV, you know." I settled on the bed, pulling the comforter over my lap and pulling open the streaming app.

"You don't think I scrolled through it?" Wyatt asked, lying next to me on the bed, over the covers. He looked comfortable once he settled his body, wearing those same gray sweatpants he was wearing when we planned the entire thing, and a plain black tee. He lay on his back, propping the pillows behind his head, laying his hands on his chest. "Other than news and a few porno films, there was nothing."

"Excuse me?" I blinked, looking over at him.

"Don't worry, I didn't buy any."

"But you looked."

"The titles were displayed." His voice rose as he gestured to the TV that hung on the opposite wall. "With a huge *mature audience only* right next to them. That's when I decided your laptop must have something better than *Barbarian Nights.*" There was a chuckle in his tone, a tiny snark of embarrassment hidden there.

I clicked on *Once Upon a Time* and found my favorite episode. "That was not the title." I gave him a small chuckle and set the laptop between us, twisting to lie on my side facing him.

Was this weird? Having Wyatt in my bed next to me while we watched a show? It wasn't too cozy, was it? It wasn't too intimate? Wyatt seemed as chill as could be, his eyes already focused on Killian

Jones giving his crew orders, his breathing steady and relaxed, not a care in the world that he was in bed with me.

"It was. There were others, too." Wyatt sighed, his gaze drifting over to me. "I could list them off for you." He raised his hand, one finger pointing as if he were ready to tick them off one by one.

"Please." I pushed his hand back down. "Don't. Just..." I pulled my hand away and shoved it back under my pillow. "Watch the show."

We watched in silence for a few moments, Wyatt never once moving except for the soft rise and fall of his chest, all the while me still relatively freaking out that a man was lying next to me in my bed. I was far from a virgin, but the two men I had been with never shared a bed with me after. This was a new feeling, having a warm body next to me, even above the covers, just simply being. And that warm body was one of the most promiscuous men I had ever met. How many hotel beds had he left in the middle of the night? How many people did he cozy up to after sleeping with them? Did he lie with them like he was lying with me—or was this completely new for him, too?

It was on the tip of my tongue to ask him, but I bit it down. Keeping my random thoughts that once again I shouldn't be having to myself. Inside thoughts only...

This was nothing. Just two people, watching a show together.

The show where the two characters kiss at the end...

Dear Lord, what was I thinking of picking *this* episode?

"Who's that?" Wyatt asked, his finger jabbing towards the computer screen.

"Mary Margaret and David," I answered. "Snow White and Prince Charming."

"And who's that?" he asked as Regina came onto the screen.

"Regina," I said. "She's the Evil Queen."

"And—"

"Emma, and Hook." I interrupted him.

"Who are they?"

"Emma is just Emma, and Hook is..." I trailed off, even I was confusing myself, "Hook."

"Charming and Hook. You totally named your horses after this show."

"Yes. Now shhh. They have to find the map."

"Why?"

I laughed softly, shifting on my bed. "So, they can get off Neverland."

"Wait." He plopped his hand down. "They're in Neverland? What are they doing in Neverland?"

"Trying to find Emma's son."

"Why?"

"Because Peter Pan kidnapped him."

"So, Peter Pan is the bad guy? Wait..." He hesitated as the scene changed to the past. "Who's that?"

"Wyatt," I dropped my head, lifting my chin to the ceiling. "Just please watch the show."

"It's a little confusing."

"This is season three. How about when we get back, we can watch it from the beginning, okay?" I mumbled, feeling the vibration of my phone coming from somewhere on the bed. Sitting up,

I reached for it, finding it faster than I thought. *Mom* flashed across the screen. I pursed my lips, inhaled deeply, and ignored the call, setting the phone face down on the nightstand.

I shifted back into the bed. Pulling the covers up to my chin, I looked at the man lying beside me, his focus now one hundred percent on me.

"You could answer that you know," he said. "It's your mom."

I shook my head. "No, I don't really have the brain power for that right now."

"But you have the brain power to follow this show?" He raised his brow and turned back to the screen.

I followed the show, no problem. This was my go-to episode. I didn't need any brain power for it. Talking to my mom, on the other hand...

I swallowed. "I don't need to think about this. I've seen it a million times. No brain power needed. Now shhh." I raised my finger to my lips. "This is the best episode."

Wyatt followed my cue and returned to the episode, not asking another question the entire time. Hook saved David, they talked to Henry, and Emma kissed Hook—all the amazing things from the episode still hit the same in my chest like the first time I saw it. A smile grew on my face, watching Emma kiss the man who had just helped save her father, knowing he was falling in love with her right then and there. I snuck a quick glance at Wyatt, not quite knowing what to expect from him, only to see him fast asleep next to me.

His head tilted towards me, his dirty blond hair ruffled from the pillow, his lashes long, and as they kissed his cheeks, hiding his gorgeous blue eyes. He had a light scruff to his face, the right amount in my opinion, and his lips—lightly parted, perfectly pink. My eyes wandered to his chest, rising and falling just as softly with each breath he took with his fingers splayed out on his stomach. One knee was bent up, the other stretched out, comfort personified. He looked...

Beautiful.

Pinching my lips together, I sat up softly, closing the laptop and placing it on my nightstand. I flicked off the light and returned to face him. He didn't stir as I moved; he just...rested. Not wanting to wake him, I gave him a soft smile he would never see, and I drifted off—sleeping like the dead next to Wyatt Hartwell.

FOURTEEN

Wyatt

WHEN I WOKE UP next to Quinn, my body a little cold from sleeping on top of the covers, I was tempted to scoot closer to her. Pull her to me and warm both of us up. I'd bury my face in her hair and breathe her in. I'd kiss her neck and wake her up, muttering *good morning* in her ear while she stirred under my touch, and she'd—

Kick me out.

So, before I could give in to any of *that,* I climbed out of the bed and snuck out.

Then I cheered when she won in Phoenix. And declined going out again, because the idea of watching another confusing show with Quinn was more appealing than spending time drinking with others. Sure, they were bummed, but once I saw the smile on Quinn's face when I turned them down, that was worth more than a drink.

This time, I made sure not to fall asleep on her bed.

It was getting harder to keep things strictly business like she had asked, and I had to bite my tongue from time to time to keep all the things I wanted to say to her at bay. The reason it was getting harder? That small tint of blush on her cheeks I would notice with every stupid comment. It appeared right before the eyeroll, right before she would point at me and remind me this was all business. But that small shade of pink told me otherwise. She was having just as much fun as I was.

Albuquerque was similar—Quinn won for the third time in a row, but that night, she welcomed my hug once she jumped from the saddle, that same amazing laugh filling my senses. And when I knocked on her door for the nightly episode, she had it cued up and ready to go—actually starting on episode one that time.

"I thought we were going to wait until we got back to the ranch?" I asked, propping myself up on the pillows as she snuggled into the blankets.

"Why wait when we can start now?" She hit play, and I watched the world of her favorite show unfold as it began to make a little more sense.

I made sure not to fall asleep on her bed that night, though it was harder this time. I could smell her coconut lotion even through the blankets, I could hear her steady breathing, I could feel her warmth spread through the bed—even warming me. And every time she would let out a small laugh, I couldn't help but smile.

Once we reached Grand Junction, it was almost as if she and I had been doing this for years. My focus was the horses—and not doing anything stupid, like kissing her—and hers was checking in and making sure she was ready to go. Not having the stress of saddling her horse being on her definitely helped her ride, and I expected the same results tonight as she had given the past three rides—a win.

She didn't even hesitate once we parked, jumping out of the truck to go check in as I made my way back to Hook. She had been rotating them, giving them each their moments to shine, but I was glad to see Hook excited for tonight. I saddled him up, picking the flashiest breast collar I could find in the tack shed. The diamonds that lined the leather stood out against his black coat, and damn, the gelding looked like he was ready to win a show. I scratched behind his ears, praising him once again, before unhooking him from the trailer.

I started to lead him to the back field, knowing Quinn would warm up there before the event started, when my eyes caught her at the registration table talking to Sam. She beamed a smile as he laughed about something, making me quickly change my trajectory, throwing Hook for a little loop.

"Sam!" I shouted cheerfully, trying to hide the jealously that was settling in the pit of my stomach. "I didn't know you were announcing tonight!"

"Damn right. Boise, too. Good to see you back in the arena!" He slapped my shoulder as I came up. "All it took was this beauty pulling you out of your funk, huh?" He grinned, motioning towards Quinn.

"Quinn." I looked over to her, clearing my throat. "You remember my drunk friend from that night at The Steel, don't you?"

Quinn gave me a single nod. "Sure do, he was just reminding me of the bet you made, and I was telling him how you've obviously failing at it."

"I am *winning* that bet." I gave her a wink.

"Yeah…" Sam chuckled. "Failing. Big time." Sam's attention went from me to Hook, reaching his hand out to let Hook study him. "And who's this?"

"He's mine, Hook. Just wait till you see him ride." Quinn smiled, taking the reins from me. "Thanks for saddling him up, Wyatt."

"Ready for your warmup?"

"Yep." She gave me a slight smile. "See you after?"

I gave her a small nod, shoving my hands in my pants pockets.

"See you too, Sam. Oh, Wyatt." She tapped the brim of my hat. "Nice hat." Then she clicked her tongue, and she and Hook walked away towards the back field.

Once she was out of earshot, Sam's arm flung around my shoulder. "I think it's safe to say you won her over."

I looked at him, raising a brow. "She still can't stand me. She agreed to let me come along to help with her horses since she had a hard time the first weekend."

"Uh-huh, yeah…" Sam reached up and tapped the brim of my hat, mimicking Quinn's actions from seconds earlier. "Nice hat." He let me go, taking a step back to the registration table. "You should come hang out with us tonight in the booth. It's Jeff and me."

Just the idea of being back in the booth sent a chill up my spine. It had been months since I last watched a rodeo from that perspective. Watching Quinn from the stands was one thing, but seeing her from the ground, seeing every single detail...

"I wouldn't be in the way or anything?"

"Fuck, no. Jeff will be thrilled. You can help us throw the clown under the bus."

"Who's the clown tonight?"

"Hector Fields."

"Damn, he's good."

One thing I loved about my job was keeping up with the clown and his antics. Clowns—being trained bull fighters—were more than jokes, but their job was to keep the crowd entertained between events and give the announcers shit. Hector was one of the best, and he and I had been known to put on a hell of a show. He would go into the crowd and pick fans to hype up, or he would hide and have me find him just from the shot on the big screen, and he would always be willing to go out for a beer after. We never talked about what he would do at the next show—I just had to learn how to keep up.

"He'll be thrilled to see you, too. It's been way too long, man."

"Don't get too used to it. I'm not *back* back." I admitted.

I wasn't even getting used to it. I still hadn't heard back from Hawkins about Reno, and as the month got closer to ending, the prospect of announcing there was getting smaller and smaller.

"You haven't heard anything about Reno, have you? Has the committee chosen its broadcasters?" I asked out of pure curiosity.

Sam shook his head, "No, I'll be in Alberta that weekend, so I'm out. I was contacted, though, and had to turn it down."

"You're choosing Alberta over Reno?" I raised a brow.

"Gotta represent my home rodeo, man—just like you'll always choose Alpine Ridge on the Fourth, I'll always choose Alberta."

"Nothing compares to the Hartwell Rodeo."

"I beg to differ." He slapped my shoulder again. "Come on, let's head to the box."

A few hours later, I sat between Sam and Jeff as they replayed every ride, hyped the crowd up, and gave Hector a run for his money. And I just took it all in, loving every second of it. I missed this.

When I was six, I rode my first sheep across the dirt at the Hartwell Hills Fourth of July Rodeo. Dad had tried to convince me to go again at a few more local rodeos, even at home, but I politely declined. At least, I thought I politely declined. Ask my mom and she'll say it was more tantrums and screaming no at her. When I was seven, I gave in and did it again, and I cried after, demanding that I would never *ever* get on a sheep again. When I was nine, I sat with my mom in the stands, watching Rhett at thirteen being the youngest tie down roper that year, Lachlan riding in bareback, and my Uncle Levi riding around on horse with a microphone. The next year, they built the announcer box, and I begged Uncle Levi to let me up there with him.

And then I was hooked.

Every Hartwell had their thing with the sport. Rhett was tie down, Lachlan was bareback, Abi would barrel race for her own enjoyment—but when the opportunity was given to me to pick my event, nothing caught my eye. I hated riding sheep. What made my family think I'd want to ride a bucking horse? Rhett tried to get me to do team roping with him one year, but I held the rope like it was a foreign object. Nothing fit me—until I was behind that microphone.

The box with Uncle Levi was my place. At ten years old, I knew that was where I was supposed to be. And I was good at it. We worked together for years, learning each other's quips and how to taunt the clown. He always said I was a natural. When Uncle Levi retired when I was twenty, he handed me the mic; that box became mine.

Now, twenty years after that first time with Uncle Levi, I couldn't do what I loved to do—even when it was in my reach. The microphones were right there on the tables. The screens were showing us every angle, and the clown was throwing all the jokes tonight. And all I could do was sit...and listen...and pretend to be okay with it.

While Hector and Jeff were bantering back and forth, I dug through my pocket, pulling out my phone and hitting Hawkins's name.

Me

Any word on Reno?

Those damn dots took way too long to dance.

Hawkins

Not yet, don't worry, man, I'll keep you updated. When I know something, you'll know something.

"And tonight we have eight fine ladies to show those barrels whose boss—" Sam began his voice echoing through the speakers.

I perked up, not wanting to miss Quinn. I stood, leaning my palms on the table, watching the first racer round the barrels, knocking over the second barrel. I clenched my fist in victory, and the grunt of 'yes' came out of my lips before I could stop it. Not me wanting the other racers to fail. Loosening my hand, I shoved it in my pocket, clearing my throat before pushing myself off the table.

My gaze caught Sam's, and his eyebrow rose higher as he followed me.

"I saw that," he whispered, covering the mic with his hand.

I just shrugged my shoulder and turned my attention back to the arena.

"And Quinn Compton," Jeff began, "on her second year, one of the youngest barrel racers this season, on a winning streak right now, and tonight should be no different. And there she is out of the gate riding her gelding, Hook—"

If he thought he was hyping Quinn, he could use a little more guidance. I blocked him out and focused on Quinn. Sam hit my arm with the back of his hand, trying to get my attention as I followed her every move. Barrel one, barrel two, barrel three—and Hook shot out towards the gate. Quinn's smile was brighter than the diamonds on Hook's breast collar.

She was...quite the show.

"A fifteen point six for Compton tonight, keeping on with her streak and—"

"Tell me you like the girl, without telling me you like the girl." Sam chuckled, pulling on my belt loop, forcing me back in my seat. "I caught on at The Steel, but you, sir, are long gone."

I inhaled, not even bothering to answer him. I was long gone.

After the barrel racers, I left the box, wanting my victory hug from Quinn more than I wanted to stay and see the bull riders. I jogged down the metal stairs, jumping off the last three, my boots hitting with a thud, and I took off, knowing exactly where she would go. Hoping she would want to see me as much as I wanted to see her, I felt my feet fly on the ground, weaving in and out of the people who had to get their last cup of beer before the bulls took center stage.

I rounded the corner, the smile bursting from me as I saw her come into view.

The only thing that stopped me was the woman she was talking to, and the fact that the smile that I'd seen on the last few rides wasn't there as the woman talked. I slowed and approached Quinn, completely out of breath.

"Quinn," I said, my voice ragged. "Quinn!"

She turned, a slight smile forming once her eyes caught mine, but she stilled. I stopped next to her, forcing my arms to stay at my sides. I could see the stress that lined her eyes, her knuckles white as she gripped onto Hook's reins. The heavy breath she let out shook my entire core. She should be celebrating another win, but she was...heavy.

"Wyatt, this is my mom, Helen Compton. Mom—Wyatt Hartwell."

The woman, Quinn's mother—whose phone calls I couldn't help but notice when they had been ignored this entire weekend—gave me the fakest smile I had ever seen. She held out her hand and said in an exaggerated, joyous tone, "Oh, a Hartwell. Wonderful to meet you!"

FIFTEEN

Quinn

WHEN I RACED OFF the dirt, Hook shaking with the thrill of the ride, the last person I expected to see was my mother. I was hoping for Wyatt, even though I knew he was in the box, I had a feeling he would rush to find me—it had become our thing after all—but my mother derailed that the second she came into my view.

The word *congratulations* didn't even pass her lips. The first thing she said was, "Your father told me you were going to be here today; I was hoping to see you *before* you got on the back of a horse."

I pursed my lips together, thinking to myself that was the last time I told my dad my schedule.

"You could have found me before my event," I said in response. "I didn't know you were going to be here." I looked around. "Where's your queen?"

She folded her arms over her chest. "She's carrying the flag."

I nodded. "That's great, Mom."

"Why didn't you tell me you'd be here? I had to go searching for you. I found your trailer before you." My mom lectured, her voice stern as she looked down at me, even though we were the same height. I couldn't figure out what was hidden in her eyes. Disapproval, hatred, despair? Anger. How many emotions could two eyes hold, and why did she have to be so good at hiding them?

"Mom," I sighed, tightening my grip on Hook's reins. "You know I'm doing this, you know I'm traveling this year to make it to the NFR, and you know I've signed up for major PRCA Rodeos—which this happens to be—"

"I think you should at least share your schedule with me. That way, I know where you're going to be. Your father knows. I shouldn't have to hear it second-hand from him. We used to do this together, Quinn."

"No, Mom, we did—"

"Quinn!" I heard Wyatt's voice boom overhead, saving me from whatever I was about to say to my mother. "Quinn!"

And just like that, my mother turned into the most perfect person on the planet.

And I guarantee it had everything to do with the man at my side.

Wyatt shook her hand as he gave her his award-winning smile, no doubt taken by her. "Yes, Ma'am, Wyatt Hartwell."

"Your name has quite the reputation in the sport; there's been talk about why a Hartwell hasn't been seen this season yet."

"Yeah, well, my brother is taking some time off to be with his wife and newborn, and I...well—" Dropping his chin, his smile faded. He let out a sigh before looking back up at my mom. "I'm here for Quinn. I'm sure you caught your daughter's ride, though. Fan-fucking-tastic if you ask me."

My eyes shot at my mom the same time she blinked back at Wyatt's language, but her smile grew, and her eyes turned back to me. "Yes, of course," she said, her voice rising by at least two notches. Fake as can be. "I'm always so thrilled to see her in action."

Thrilled? To see me in action? Ha...no, there were more things she was interested in than watching me ride. She was there for her queen and, at that moment, Wyatt.

"What was my time, Mom?" I asked, my voice completely toneless.

"Oh, Quinn. You know it's not about the time." She reached her hand out to me, gently placing her palm on my arm.

"Actually, Mom, it's all about the time," I grumbled, tempted to jerk my arm away.

"Fifteen point six," Wyatt answered for her. "Last night was a seventeen point nine, and the night before that was sixteen flat. She's been coming in first all weekend and damn." His eyes turned to me, catching my gaze for a split second. "She's amazing to watch."

My mom sighed, turning her attention back to Wyatt. "I would love to see your brother back. Do you know if he's riding at all this year?"

Wyatt blinked. "I'm not traveling with him this year, couldn't tell you what his plans are."

My mom hummed. "Shame. But you—" She leaned in slightly, her attention now completely focused on Wyatt. "I'm sure you'll be back in the announcer box soon, right? Rodeo is missing your voice."

Wyatt flashed her another sideways smile, taking one step forward to grab Hook's reins. "Maybe someday, but...not anytime soon."

"I know Kelly would love to see you again. She speaks highly of you."

I blinked and felt my entire body freeze. Kelly...and Wyatt?

Wyatt inhaled sharply, and a grin I hadn't seen before lightly spread across his lips. "Kelly Fugal?"

My mother gave him a prideful gleam. "Miss Rodeo Montana."

"Miss Rodeo Montana," he repeated matter-of-factly, like he didn't need to be reminded who she was.

I inhaled. Neither did I. Kelly Fugal already had my mother's attention; she didn't need Wyatt's as well. But then my mother said—

"She said you used to date?"

My head flipped to Wyatt, probably a lot faster than it should have. His gaze caught mine, a single eyebrow raising to his forehead. He cleared his throat.

"We went on a few dates," Wyatt answered, rolling his shoulders as his body shifted back towards me. "It wasn't meant to be, obviously. She's sweet, though. Will you tell her I say hi?"

"Of course." My mom smiled.

Wyatt gave her a nod. "Quinn, I'll get Charming unsaddled and in the trailer for you." Wyatt pulled the reins from me, and I reluctantly let him, his eyes meeting mine for the briefest moment.

If I could've screamed at him to stay, I would've, but all I did was close off, my arms folding across my chest as he took a few steps away from me.

"Pleasure to meet you, Mrs. Compton." His attention turned to me. "See you at the trailer."

I nodded back to him, not saying a word.

"Pleasure to meet you, Mr. Hartwell," Mom called after Wyatt, who simply turned and gave her another smile.

Once he was out of earshot, she took a step closer to me. "A Hartwell," she whispered. "Quinn, you didn't tell me you were traveling with a Hartwell. I knew they lived in Alpine Crest—"

"Ridge, Mom. Alpine Ridge." I corrected her. She didn't even take notice.

"But I had no idea you were close with them. This could help you. And are you dating him? Honey, that's—"

"The farthest thing from the truth." I took a step back from her. "Wyatt is just..." I paused. What was Wyatt exactly? My horse's assistant? A rodeo hand? I rolled my shoulders and picked the easiest answer. "He's a friend."

"Oh, honey." She stood up straight. "The way he was eyeing you, you two are more than friends. Even mentioning Kelly didn't turn his eyes away from you. That's a good thing; he could help you—"

"Help me what, Mom?" I snapped, knowing exactly what she was going to say.

He's a Hartwell. He's well known in rodeo. Was he that well known to be able to have sway with the judges? Changing times wasn't common, but it did happen. She saw him only as a way to help me climb the ranks, just by being his girlfriend.

"I don't need help. In any way. He came to take care of the horses so I could focus on riding," I bit out. "I'm doing this on my own."

Her lips pursed as she stepped away, the almost joyful expression on her face turning back into that unreadable emotion—that time mixed with dissatisfaction. I won tonight. Scored the best I had all weekend, and the only thing she cared about was my social standing. Who I was dating. How I was getting to the top of the leaderboards. It didn't even phase her that I did all of that, that I got myself there. I trained. I worked. I pushed. I did whatever it took. And she didn't care in the slightest.

I bit the inside of my lip to stop myself from saying anything more.

"Apparently," she finally began, breaking the silence, "you can't. He's here to help you, right? I'm assuming because you're still healing from that injury last year? You can't do everything because you're slower? He's unsaddling your horse, getting him in the trailer, and he's probably going to go collect your check. Can't you see that you aren't doing this on your own? You're keeping him from his career just because you are too stubborn to admit defeat and stop while you're ahead."

I flinched. I? Was keeping...*him*...from his career?

"Mom, I..." I choked. "I have to go."

"Oh, come now, Quinn..." She dropped her arms to her side, her bracelets jingling against her jeans.

But I didn't stay. I blocked out her voice and walked away. She shouted my name a few times, but I held my shoulders as high as I could and made my way through the crowd to my trailer. I wanted out of there. I wanted to crawl under the covers again and forget this entire encounter had happened. I won tonight. That's all I needed to focus on.

But the only thing running through my head as I stepped closer and closer to my truck was the fact that she was more interested in the man by my side than my own accomplishments. The only way I would get anywhere was if Wyatt helped...no...not just Wyatt—a Hartwell.

Nothing I did was good enough, was it?

Not for her, at least...

I climbed into the driver's seat of my truck and turned the engine over. I could feel Wyatt's eyes on me from the passenger seat, the concern that flooded him basically palpable. I swallowed and met his gaze.

And as much as I hated to admit it, I saw Miss Rodeo Montana. Did he want to be with her right now?

"Tonight would be a good night to go out, huh? I bet you're wishing April...or even Kelly...were here." I said softly, holding back the tears that wanted to come out.

He heaved a sigh, lifting his hand to my hair, lightly tucking it behind my ear.

"I'm not going anywhere tonight, Quinn. Didn't you hear? I'm here for you."

Sixteen

Wyatt

QUINN WAS SILENT AS we settled Hook in the boarding stall. She was quiet when we drove back to the hotel. She was quiet when she swiped her key card. And when I knocked on her door for our nightly episode of *Once Upon a Time*, she said, "Not tonight," before shutting the door in my face. I stood there, staring at the number plaque, wanting to barge in and pull her close to yank her out of whatever had taken her cheer away. I'd only seen her like this once before, right when she got home from her first weekend. And then she had done the same thing. Closed off.

This wasn't her. The urge to break down the door was getting stronger and stronger. But the more I stood there, the more I realized I knew absolutely nothing about what was wrong other than the fact that it had to do with her mother. Therefore, I knew nothing about how to comfort her.

When my sister's husband, Sylas, died almost six years ago, I knew exactly what to do. Abi and I worked and thought on the same plane. Her grief was mine, and simply being there for each other, just letting her cry on my shoulder until she fell asleep, listening to her break and beg for him to come back, that was what she needed. I was enough for her in her darkest times. But this was Quinn, and even though we had spent basically every second together the past five days, I had no idea who she really was and how to make her feel the joy that was taken from her. I didn't know if I was going to be enough for her.

So...I gave in to her desire to be alone and went to my own room and lay awake all night long, wishing tonight was the night I fell asleep over the covers. When the sun rose, I went to meet her in her room. She was packed and ready to go, but I could tell her eyes were heavy. I had seen that with Abi multiple times when she would cry herself to sleep. Did Quinn do that last night? My chest ached at the thought.

I grabbed her bags and piled them on the cart, making sure to work quick so she wouldn't have to lift a finger. Then I loaded the truck and forced her into the passenger seat. She didn't protest. She just buckled up and raised her knees to her chest, plopping her head on the headrest.

"Sleep well?" I asked, not entirely knowing what to say to her.

"Not really. Thank you for driving," she responded, her head rolling to look over at me. She gave me a slight smile before turning back to the window.

"I drive, you relax." I popped the truck into gear and stepped on the gas.

I drove the entire way to Boise, keeping conversation light as the landscapes passed us. She read. She slept. She relaxed. Focused on anything but the road in front of her. And in the silence, the silence that never felt awkward between us, questions began gathering in my mind.

What was her favorite color? *Turquoise probably.*

What was her favorite food? *That one I didn't know the answer to.*

What was her favorite movie? *If I had to guess, a fairy tale.*

What was her favorite book? *Peter Pan? With how much she loved Hook...had to be it.*

What did she like to do in her spare time? Where did she grow up? What was her first rodeo experience like? *I want to know all of these answers.*

If she could be doing anything but barrel racing, what would it be? *Another answer I couldn't wait to find out.*

When I first saw her, I knew there was something about her. Even now, seeing her like this, I still wanted to know what it was and how I could find out. I wanted to really, truly, get to know the woman who was next to me. To find out what exactly makes her smile and tick, even to find out what makes her cry. There had to be a way I could get all of those questions answered. There had to be a way to break down whatever stood between us to make *this* not so impossible after all. This weekend only proved that.

And as we sat there—the silence growing as she turned the page of her book—I started to form another type of emotion. Fear. I was actually getting scared of the knot forming in my chest.

I had never ever felt this way about someone before. I never saw myself settling down with anyone, not giving myself the option to grow close enough to want that with someone. I saw my family, my sister, and brother each finding love and growing their lives, but the fact that I had no plans in that area didn't bother me. I knew what I wanted to do with my life, and a family just didn't fit into it.

But Quinn...

I wanted her to fit.

When I first saw her, I knew there was more to her than the beautiful woman who caught my eye.

When I first saw her, I knew no one would ever compare to her.

Even when nothing I tried worked to get her attention, I still couldn't stop thinking about her. She didn't want to be chased, yet I didn't want to chase anyone else. I didn't want to *be* with anyone else.

Even in silence, she was all I wanted.

And that scared the shit out of me.

When we made it to Boise, we settled the horses and checked into the hotel, and once again, she asked to be alone. I made some stupid comment about how I needed to find out what happened to the Huntsman, and when she rolled her eyes and gave me a slight smile—giving me hope she was still there—she promised we would pick it up again, and that she wouldn't leave me hanging like that. I opened my arms for a hug, and relief flooded me when she stepped in, her cheek resting against my chest. Her warmth spread over me, her chest shaking with each breath. I hated seeing her this way, and once again, I just stood there, wishing I knew exactly what was going on through her mind. We said goodnight, and I didn't move until I heard her door click shut.

She came in fifth the next night.

And more silence crowded the truck as we drove home.

I pulled into the ranch late, the lights of the Nova Luna Stables still illuminated above the door as if Abi was expecting us. I parked the truck far up, the back of the trailer near the door for easy access. Quinn jumped from the cab and made her way to the back. I jogged to beat her, grabbing hold of the lock.

"Go inside and stretch your legs. I got the horses." I nodded towards the house. "Cash will want to see you anyway."

"Wyatt—" She shrugged. "I can do this."

"I know you can, but I'm here for *you,* and you've had an extremely long few days. Go inside and then head home. I'll take care of your boys. Okay?"

If I couldn't find the way to talk to her, I could at least do this.

She kept my gaze for several moments before she exhaled as her shoulders dropped.

"Okay," she sighed. "Thank you."

I watched as she disappeared into the main house, and I stepped into the trailer, unhooking Hook and Charming before leading them into the stables and to their stalls. I brushed them, gave them fresh hay and water, treated them both to a peppermint, and went through the motions of night check. The entire time, Quinn was on my mind.

The stable grew quiet, nothing but the light huffs and puffs of a few horses, and by the time I was done, her truck and trailer were gone—and my single bag, with my new hat sitting on top of it, was sitting outside the stable.

Locking up, I bent and picked up my bag, plopping my hat on my head on top of my baseball cap, and solemnly made my way to the bunk house.

It was cold and dark, and missing something. *Someone.*

"Jesus Christ, man," I mumbled to myself, tossing my bag off to the side. "It's been seven days."

But in reality, it had been a lot longer than that.

And I wasn't about to spend one more night without her.

An hour later, I knocked on her front door with the toe of my boot. Quinn opened the door to her condo, her hair wet and braided, already comfortable in her pajamas. I gave her a cheeky grin and held up the pizza box from June's Pizzeria in town and a bottle of Moscato wine. Quinn leaned against the door and placed her hand on her hip.

"What are you doing, Hartwell?"

Even though I could see how tired she was, the small smile she gave when she caught sight of me made me weak in the knees. I mimicked her grin.

"You left me hanging. I gotta find out what happens to the Huntsman."

"Spoiler alert...," she began. "He di—"

"Nope. La la la," I sang loudly, using the fist that gripped the wine bottle to cover up one of my ears. "You can't spoil it."

"Do you know what time it is?" she asked, the sweet smile I loved so much growing on her lips.

I looked at my watch. "Just past midnight."

"And you brought pizza and wine?"

"Hey..." I took a step, basically forcing her to the side to let me in. "We ate nothing but gas station snacks all day yesterday and only ate breakfast this morning. Plus, I'm not sure if you ever had pizza from June's." I stepped into the living room.

I had gotten her address from Cash, and already I was impressed with what she had done with the place. It had that homey feel that any place but mine had to it. An open concept blended the living room and kitchen, the separation marked by a gray sofa with throws and pillows facing a small TV next to the fireplace. Photos of her horses hung on the walls, and scattered with them were photos of landscapes or paintings, none of her family or her. The dim light made it look cozy, a place where I could picture her relaxing, and the scent of coconut wafted through the air. The smell of Quinn.

I set the pizza box down on the coffee table and followed Quinn as she moved to the kitchen, grabbing two plates and two glasses.

"I only have two of everything, so you're washing your own plate," she noted, plopping on the couch and looking up at me.

I chuckled and opened the bottle of wine, thankful I went for a screw top instead of a cork. "Har har, noted."

Quinn pulled her legs to her chest, grabbing a throw that was hanging on the back of the sofa.

"Did you really come here to watch *Once Upon a Time*?" Her soft voice filled the space, and I met her gaze.

I swallowed. "Well, yes and no." I picked up the glass and poured some wine for her, gingerly handing her the cup. Her fingers brushed mine for a second too long as she took it from me.

"What's the no part?"

I met her gaze. "I didn't like that you were upset. I didn't want you to be alone."

She pursed her lips and inhaled, her chest rising as she found the words. "I don't want to talk about it," she finally whispered.

"I'm not expecting that. I'm expecting to eat pizza, drink some sugary wine, and find out what happens to the damn Huntsman." I pointed at the TV, taking a seat next to her. "Can we do that?"

She held my gaze, her eyes darting back and forth as she stared into me. Then a full smile formed, and she nodded.

"Yeah. We can do that."

She leaned forward, grabbed the remote, and flipped open the box of pizza. "Oh yes," she hummed. "Pineapple on pizza. Looks like you and I have something in common, Hartwell."

*Pineapple on pizza...*favorite food? Check.

I leaned back into the couch, the theme of *Once Upon a Time* hitting like an old friend, when I noticed Quinn's gaze on me. Her lips moved as she studied me, her eyes never faltering.

"What?" I finally asked, admittingly loving the way she was looking at me, but always desperately wanting to know what was floating through her mind.

"You know, about a year ago...I thought you were too full of yourself, too cocky..."

I narrowed my gaze. "Ouch."

"I'm beginning to think I was wrong about you." She sighed, lifting her slice of pizza. "You're not so bad, Hartwell."

"You're not too bad yourself, Compton. Now shh." I raised my finger to my lips, "I'm watching."

She giggled and settled onto the couch, her legs stretching out in front of her, her toes coming awfully close to being shoved under my thigh. She was comfortable, she was smiling...she felt like mine.

SEVENTEEN

Quinn

"**Y**OU'RE TOO TIGHT!" CASH called, his voice barely audible over Charming's hooves hitting the dirt. "Loosen it up!"

He had placed five barrels in a straight line for me to weave in and out, back and forth, front to back, over and over again. Charming was loose one ride last week; if he were tighter, we could maybe cut back time a little. And the man wanted me to *loosen* up.

"I'm trying to be tight!" I yelled back at him.

I yanked on Charming's lead, and he turned, his snout so far left I could see his entire profile. I felt the edge of the barrel against my boot. *Shit, shit, shit.* Don't. Fall. I looked over my shoulder, a breath of air leaving my lips as the barrel wobbled but stayed upright.

"Remember when I said loosen up!?" I heard Cash's voice.

I slowed Charming down, his hooves digging into the dirt as he halted to a stop.

"I'm trying to be tighter. We were loose in Albuquerque. If I tighten up—"

"You'll knock barrels over. If I remember correctly, you won Albuquerque." He folded his arms over his chest. I opened my mouth to talk back to him, but he spoke first. "None of this 'yeah, but I could have won by a few milliseconds' crap."

I narrowed my eyes at him, hoping the glare stung. The way he raised his brow told me it didn't.

"Do it again, but loosen up." He turned his back, completely missing the smile I flashed him before I turned Charming and did it again...loosening up just like he said.

Some people went to the gym—which, sure, I loved a good run—but for me, nothing beat training. Riding always got me out of whatever funk I was in. Especially if a certain parental figure caused that funk. And today was no different. We'd been home for two days, and my mother's words still lingered in the back of my head. Every time I closed my eyes, I saw her face as she told me I couldn't do this, that I was wrong, and she was right. That I was slower because of an injury I thought I'd recovered from. I didn't even have a twinge of pain in my leg anymore, which proved she was wrong, but that moment replayed like a broken protector screen, showing the same twenty seconds over and over. The only thing keeping it out was the fact that I was going to train, that I was going to ride. So, when I finally climbed back into the saddle, I could feel the moment slightly lift, and my energy went right back to where it was supposed to go.

I kicked Charming into full speed, and we weaved in and out of the barrels, his concentration just as focused as mine. This time, no part of me or my gelding touched a barrel. I rounded him a few times, up and down, until even I was out of breath, and we halted right in front of Cash.

He clapped those nice, slow claps you see in movies when the protagonist gets a victory.

"See what happens when you loosen up?" he teased, raising a single brow.

I rolled my eyes and smiled, tilting my head down at him. "I still say I could go tighter."

Cash shook his head and messed with his rolled-up sleeves, taking a step into the arena. "You're off tomorrow, and back in the arena Friday. When's your next trip?"

"Next weekend."

Which reminded me, I wanted to ask Wyatt to look over the confirmations again. I could probably travel alone this time; I didn't book myself like I did that first weekend, but a quick check of things would be nice. I made a mental note as I dismounted Charming to ask him that night.

Since he had shown up at my doorstep with pizza, he made it a habit to come over every night since. He brought a different kind of takeout each time, all from his favorite local places, and a new wine or beer. We'd watch an episode, maybe two, and then he'd leave. He never asked me about what happened at Grand Junction. Instead, he'd ask mundane questions as the show played in the background. *What's your favorite color?* Turquoise—haven't you guessed that yet? *Yeah, I guess that's obvious. How did you find this TV show?* A commercial, Snow White is one of my favorite fairy tales, and they sold this show well. *Snow White? Not Peter Pan? With how much you love Hook, I'd assumed Peter Pan.* Have you even seen the cartoon of

Peter Pan?! When his answer was no, I gasped—instantly going to the old Disney cartoon. He hated it and halfway through begged me to go back to *Once Upon a Time*.

I let him ask his silly questions, and I would answer them with no issue...but when I thought about questions to ask him, I froze. Mainly because I wasn't sure if I wanted to know the answers. *Did you really date Kelly? Did you really keep a running tally of the rodeo royalty queen to sleep with? You wouldn't have any sway with the judges...right?*

I honestly found myself really enjoying the few hours with him every night. I didn't want to bog it down with stupid questions that wouldn't change anything. Wyatt wasn't anything more to me than a friend, and learning the answers may change that. The answers may prove that what I thought of him to begin with was right, or that my mother was right.

Now that I thought about it, when Wyatt was around, I wasn't thinking about my mother.

That hadn't even crossed my mind until now. She had tried to warp him, too, and here I was, almost letting her. But here he was, showing up with pizza, beer, and nothing more than a smile as we settled in and watched a stupid cartoon from the fifties. He didn't seem to have any interest in what his name could do for me...so...why should I?

"How many rides this time?" Cash asked, stepping towards me.

I gripped Charming's lead. "Three. Friday, Saturday, Sunday. I don't even have to travel far."

He nodded. "Good, you need some easy weekends like that before summer hits."

"Summer..." I sighed. "It's going to be epic. Need help with the barrels?" I motioned behind my shoulder.

He shook his head, "Nah, got another barrel racer coming and she's too loose."

"Too tight, too loose—you can't win, can you?" I chuckle, leaving him alone in the arena to put Charming away.

Glancing at the clock, a small smile spread across my lips when I saw I had enough time for a quick ride on Hook. All I had to do was unsaddle Charming, and then Hook and I could be on our way.

"You needy bastard. I don't have any more treats for you." I heard the mumble as I walked closer to Charming's stall, the grin growing wider as I witnessed Hook pulling on Wyatt's cap. "I'm out of peppermints because of you."

"Maybe you should stop feeding him peppermints. Then he would leave you alone." I clipped, opening Charming's stall, letting him walk in.

"Your horse," Wyatt grumbled as he pushed Hook's nose away, "is a menace."

"You love him."

Wyatt scoffed, scratching behind his ears. Then there's me, ignoring the small flutters in my entire body.

Wyatt smiled. "I do."

"I was going to take him on a ride..." I began, not really knowing where I was going with this. I pulled on Charming's saddle, stopping before I could unhook him. "Wanna come?" I finished, shocked at even myself. His jaw opened slightly, a small grin appearing as his whole eyes widened with the same shock.

"Wyatt!" A call echoed through the stable before Wyatt had a chance to answer me, but when I looked behind him to see who was demanding his attention, I couldn't help but grin.

"Abi and Kyla." I nodded behind him, watching as his sister and sister-in-law got closer. Finally, I met his gaze, and he blinked, turning to look over his shoulder, only to be handed a baby.

Poppy giggled once she looked at her uncle, the cute toothless smile beaming as she reached up and grabbed his hat.

"Designated babysitter." Kyla folded her arms, smiling at her brother-in-law.

I chuckled and reached a finger out to Poppy. She grasped it, her other hand gripping onto Wyatt's shirt with dear life as she looked at me like I was stranger danger to the extreme.

"I don't remember being asked to babysit." Wyatt raised a brow, looking at Kyla.

"Can you?" Abi asked, coming up to my side, resting her elbow on my shoulder. "I need to steal Quinn and Kyla, and Rhett is out for the night."

"Steal..." I turned to Abi. "Me?" I pointed at my chest. "You know, you could ask me like a normal person if I have plans, not kidnap me last minute."

"Well," Kyla said, "in her defense, this is last-minute for everyone. Dress shopping."

Wyatt looked over at me. "Dress shopping? Wedding dresses?"

"Yup, and I need Quinn. So...please babysit the little?"

"Why do you need me? I'm not in the wedding." I asked, looking from Abi to Wyatt to Kyla. She gave me a sweet smile and looked at Abi.

Abi parted her lips to speak, but instead of words, a shriek escaped her when Cash's arm pulled her away from me.

He turned and kissed her temple. "Did I hear dress shopping?"

"Yes, and you're busy. But..." Abi turned to her fiancé. "Can you get Stet from school?"

Cash kissed her nose. They were adorably disgusting. I loved them.

"Of course. I demand photos."

"That's illegal if I remember correctly." Wyatt quipped, shifting Poppy so she sat in his arms, her back to his chest. She began kicking her legs and flaying her arms, seemingly giving him a hard time as he struggled to keep her still, but I could tell—he loved it.

"I'm not sure about illegal." Abi turned to look at her brother. "But now you have two jobs: keep this man busy and watch Poppy."

"I take my jobs very seriously." He tickled Poppy's tummy, and she let out a small giggle. Then his eyes met mine. "Rain check on the ride?"

I nodded. "Sure, because I guess I'm going dress shopping."

I sat on the small white sofa next to Kyla, a sparkling water in hand, waiting for Abi to come out of the dressing room. Abi asked us all kinds of questions when she picked the styles, and ultimately she grabbed three dresses, one picked by each of us. Each style was different, yet stunning, and surprisingly, no massive princess dresses were picked. We each chose a dress that suited Abi. Simple. Elegant. Timeless. I even pulled experience from my inner rodeo queen from when I was thirteen, picking a dress that I would wear versus what my mom would make me wear.

The first dress she wore was Kyla's pick, a short skirt with long lace sleeves that flowed down her arms. Her brown cowboy boots went with it nicely, and when she spun in front of the mirror, holding her hair up in a messy bun, I could picture it.

"Cash would love this one." I smiled, watching as she studied herself in the mirror.

"Cash is going to love anything you pick," Kyla responded, raising her glass to her lips. "That is one thing I regret about my wedding. I wore jeans."

Abi chuckled and turned to us, taking a step off the podium to reach for her own glass of sparkling water. "Well, when you get married weeks after meeting the guy." Abi gave her a knowing smile.

"Wait, what?" I looked at Kyla, my hair falling over my shoulder in curly waves, wanting in on the story. "You didn't have a wedding ceremony?"

She shook her head. "Nope. Rhett and I got married after two weeks, and it was supposed to be temporary."

"I still take full credit for that." Abi raised her glass at Kyla before taking another drink.

"Two. Weeks?" I widened my eyes. "How did you even meet?" I raised a brow in question.

"He was a one-night stand that failed." Kyla gave a small smile into her glass, her cheeks blushing. "My ex came to the ranch, and Abi told him I was married. Rhett showed up at the right time, and

I asked him to pretend to be my husband, and well...he took the part very seriously. We got married in the courthouse. It's a fun story if you think about it. But we didn't get to do any of this. No dress. No wedding party. No ceremony. I wish we could."

Abi spun again. "Vow renewal. Have an actual wedding this time." Twisting her torso, she looked at Kyla. "I'll accept nothing less than matron of honor."

"Sorry, Abs. That title goes to Grace."

Abi narrowed her eyes. "Fair. Bridesmaid then."

"Grace?" I questioned, looking over to Kyla.

Taking a sip of her drink, Kyla nodded. "My best friend. She lives in Arizona."

"And hasn't visited since you first moved here," Abi remarked, glancing over her shoulder at Kyla.

"She came out when Poppy was born." Kyla defended, her voice raising louder, almost echoing. As if she knew how loud she actually was, she bit her lip.

Abi gave a silent chuckle. "For two days. You know I think she's great, I just wish she'd come back. I'd like to think we'd be friends."

"She won't. Something happened and she won't tell me what."

"How do you know something happened then?" I raised a brow, leaning back into the couch.

"Best friend intuition." Kyla answered.

"She'll be back," Abi said certainly, "Especially if you renew your vows. I bet Rhett would be all over marrying you again."

"We've talked about it. Maybe on an anniversary."

"What's your wedding going to be like, Abi?" I asked, shifting back to the bride. "Big ceremony, courthouse elopement?"

"Ceremony. In the stables. It's only fitting." She ran her hands down her stomach. "I love this, but...sorry, Kyla. It's not the dress."

"Agreed, next!" Kyla raised her glass in the air, and Abi disappeared behind the curtain. "Congrats on your rides this past weekend," Kyla said to me, leaning in and bumping me with her elbow.

"Thanks, it was a great weekend." I smiled, thinking back on all but the last ride. "One step closer to the NFR."

"You should be proud. We all are—everyone watched. Wyatt made sure we knew exactly where to catch each ride."

"Wyatt?" I gave a small laugh. "He was more into it than anyone, I think. Once he got the hat."

"He needed that. He needed out of the bunkhouse, out of the stables. He needed to be reminded why he loves the rodeo."

"Amen!" Abi called from behind the curtain. "Don't get me wrong, I love my brother, and the help he's doing around the stables has been fantastic, but he's been"—Abi tossed one of the dresses over the curtain—"happier since you guys got back. Kyla's right, he needed that. He's been"—she scoffed—"not himself after what happened with Archie. I'm honestly starting to get nervous he's never going to get back in the booth."

"What happened with Archie?" I asked, furrowing my brow at the curtain.

"He just...messed up." I heard Abi's faint voice. "He needed to get back to rodeos. I think even being near his old friends and people who recognize him has been helping."

"We ran into my mom in Colorado. She sure knew who he was." I flinched, not exactly sure why I decided it was a good idea to bring her up. I raised my glass to my lips and widened my eyes. Maybe they didn't hear me.

"Your mom was Miss Rodeo America, right?" Kyla asked, raising her own glass.

"Yeah, she's the coach for Miss Rodeo Montana, and she let it slip that Wyatt and Kelly used to date. So yeah, Abi, he's definitely around his old friends."

"I wouldn't call Kelly a friend, and I wouldn't classify the week they were together as dating," Abi answered. "An old flame, maybe, but my brother has plenty of those."

"Like the entire rodeo royalty?" I asked, clamping my lips shut the second the words left my mouth. I glared at my glass of sparkling water, wondering if there was any trace of alcohol in this thing. Why the hell was I bringing up the questions I didn't want to know the answers to? I couldn't ask him, but I could gossip to his sister? *My age is showing.* I bit my lip and looked at Kyla.

"I know for a fact that it was Sam going after the royalty, not Wyatt." Abi gave a slight grunt. "Wyatt wanted to have fun, sure, but he wasn't about checking names off a list. I bet you he's slept with fewer people than you think."

"But he was with Kelly?" I mumbled, looking down at my drink again. "My mom seemed to think that mentioning her name to him would have him spinning."

"There could have been more with her, but it didn't last long. I think he caught her with a—hey—Kyla—can I get your help with this."

Kyla shot up, handing me her drink before she peeked into the curtain. Seconds later, she stepped back out and gave me a sweet smile. "Zipper got stuck."

"He wasn't about checking names off a list?" I asked softly once Kyla got back to me, taking her drink back.

I heard Abi bark a laugh. "No, my brother may be a playboy, but he's not *that* promiscuous. He wants to have fun, fewer responsibilities when it comes to certain things, and to feel free in a way. But it's not a different girl every single night. In fact...now that I think about it, he hasn't been out or brought anyone home in a while. I think the last hook-up I saw was Melanie, and before her...I honestly can't remember. He's too busy looking at someone else."

I opened my jaw to say something, but once Abi stepped out of the dressing room, I was stunned into silence, not even registering anything she said about Wyatt. She stepped out into the light of the shop and up on the small pedestal, still facing us. She was absolutely radiant.

She was wearing my pick. A cream satin gown with spaghetti straps, a V-neck, with the fabric cascading down her body, flowing down her legs over her boots. There were no pearls or beads. There was no lace. There were no designs to draw you away from the woman wearing the dress. Just her beauty, her elegance. Her blue eyes moved back and forth between us.

"What? Is it that bad?" Abi asked, her hands running down her hips.

"No Abs..." Kyla set her glass down on the table in front of us and stood, closing the gap between her and Abi. "This is..." She lightly touched Abi's shoulders and spun her to the mirror, and the entire room glowed once Abi saw herself. "Oh my God."

Abi studied herself in the mirror, her hand moving down her body, her breath completely gone. Just like us, she was stunned to silence.

She lifted the skirt, popping her toe up to show her boot, giggling a little once she saw that yes, they still worked perfectly with the dress. She bent slightly at the waist, her cheeks turning full on pink once she turned to us.

"I'm not trying my pick on." Her voice cracked. "This...this..."

"Is perfect," Kyla whispered. "I know there are probably a million other words I could use to describe it, but perfect fits. Quinn"—she turned to me—"isn't it?"

I smiled at Abi. "It is," I whispered back.

"I'm never taking it off." Abi declared, wrapping her arms around her torso.

"Well." I stood. "Eventually you have to."

"Cash will take it off for you." Kyla joked.

Abi cut her a look but then blushed. She let out a breath and held back her emotions, turning back to us. "Okay, okay. Enough about me—"

"But you're the bride?" I narrowed my brow. "This is literally about you."

"It's your guys' turn." Abi spun, the skirt flowing over her boots. "I'm thinking purple with brown hats?"

Our turn.

"Abi, I don't need—" I started, waving a hand in front of me, wiping away what she was just implying.

"Quinn." Abi turned, her hands finding my shoulders at the same time her blue eyes found mine. I never noticed they were exactly the same as Wyatt's. And suddenly, she had my full attention. "Do you know how important you are to Cash?"

I gave a small nod. He was important to me, too, so of course I hoped I was important to him.

"So, you know how important you are to me. I know we haven't known each other very long, but I'd love for you to be next to Cash and me on our wedding day. I'd love for you to be a part of the wedding party."

The love in her voice carried through to me, and I felt my heart begin to swell. How was I supposed to react to this? Obviously, my answer was yes. Abi had entered my life a little over a year ago, and even though most of that year was spent with me on the road or training, Abi had managed to become someone I could look up to. She had a way of making you feel loved, making you feel wanted—part of her family—and now, her hands on my shoulders, I couldn't help but feel exactly that. Loved. Wanted. A part of *her* family.

I took a deep breath and let my body move on its own. I wrapped my arms around Abi's neck and buried my face in her hair. She gave a small laugh, her arms squeezing me tight.

"I take it that's a yes?" Her voice rose with her laughter.

"Of course. I'd be honored." I pulled away and held her at arm's length, locking onto her blue eyes. "But purple?" I raised a brow.

She dropped her chin, her shoulders shaking in a silent laugh. "Okay, I'll admit, I have no clue how to pick colors for a wedding.

All I knew was my dress had to be white." She looked down at her body. "And it's not even that."

Kyla and I shared a quick glance, and a new affection filtered between us. We mirrored a smile, and at the same time, grabbed Abi's hands to pull her towards the rows of colorful dresses that Kyla and I could try. We tried pink, purple, navy, black, brown...but ultimately settled on a brown hat, brown boots, and a turquoise light flowy dress.

"The men won't know what hit them." Kyla spun, the skirt flowing around her knees. "Imagine Poppy in this color. She is the flower girl, right?"

Abi chuckled, now sitting on the same couch Kyla and I were, back in her jeans and sweater. "Stetson will carry her and the rings. It's going to be perfect. Maybe we'll all be on horses!"

"In your dress?" I looked at Abi in the mirror. "My mother would have a heart attack."

"I'm getting on a damn horse in my wedding dress." She pointed at me, her cheeks blushing as the smile grew across her face, nothing but pure joy radiating from her. I had no doubt I'd see both her and Cash on a horse that day.

EIGHTEEN

Wyatt

I KNOCKED ON QUINN'S door at 8 p.m. on the dot, just like I had the past few nights. Tonight, I carried a six-pack of Alpine Ridge's finest beer—it was Corona—and sushi. I wasn't sure if she was a sushi person. So far on these nightly episode escapades, I had discovered she loved pineapple on pizza, was big on teriyaki chicken and fried rice, and picked the onions and pickles off her burgers. Sushi wasn't my favorite, but if Quinn liked it, I'd eat it.

She opened the door wearing a tank and yoga pants, her hair in a braid that hung over her shoulder, looking just as sexy as she had the past couple of nights. I wanted to greet her by pulling her into me, but as always, she leaned on the door frame, folded her arms, and raised a single eyebrow. I raised the six-pack and plastic bag.

"I was told the next episode we meet Belle." I smiled, tilting my head.

"We do," Quinn replied. "Any guesses on who's her Beast?" She stepped to the side, letting me cross the threshold. She shut and locked the door behind me, meeting me in the living room where she already had glasses ready for us. I had brought wine two nights and beer on the others. This girl was prepared…and expecting me.

"Have we met him?" I set everything down on the coffee table, smiling at the wine glasses sitting there.

"We have." She nodded, reaching for the plastic bag. "What are you feeding me tonight?" She let out a gasp. "Sushi!" Her waist snapped back up, her eyes wide as she looked at me.

I pinched my brow. "Is that a yes? Or a no to the sushi? Because I can order June's."

"I love sushi."

"Is there any food you don't love?" I asked, twisting open a Corona. Quinn met my gaze, her brow raised in question. "You know, just in case I bring the wrong thing, and you are forced to eat whatever food you have here."

She breathed out a laugh, grabbed a beer and a container of sushi, and plopped on her couch, one leg tucked under her body. "I'm not fond of Thai or Indian food. The spices and tastes are just off to me, and if you ever give me a mushroom, I will hurl it at your face."

"No mushrooms. Got it. But sushi is fine."

She used the chopsticks to pick up a roll, waving it in the air before stuffing it in her mouth, doing a small little dance on the couch as she chewed. I watched with a smile, taking control of the remote to cue up the episode.

"Oh, you'll never guess what happened today at the dress shop." Quinn grabbed my attention right as I clicked on *Once Upon a Time,* Snow White's face filling the screen.

"What happened?" I glanced at her quickly before hitting play.

"Abi asked me to be in her wedding."

"Cash asked me that today, too," I admitted.

He began the conversation with, *"Just know you're second choice, but you mean a lot to Abi...and well, you've grown on me."* I laughed and said I only tolerated him, but that I'd be proud to stand by him and my cousin. Lachlan was going to be his best man, and I his only groomsman. When I asked about Rhett, seeing as in the years since Sylas had passed, Cash and Rhett were closer, Cash replied with he'd rather it be me up there...then quickly added that someone had to watch the baby.

I was still finding it hard to grasp that a year ago, I was still holding a grudge against the man.

"I thought you two hated each other?" Quinn asked, basically reading my mind.

"We had a rough patch there, but Abi basically forced us together."

"Abi has a way of doing that, doesn't she?" Quinn picked up another roll. "Apparently she's the reason Kyla and Rhett are married."

I barked a laughed, "Yeah, she is."

"You two have the same eyes, did you know that?"

I raised a brow. "Well, yeah. She's my twin."

"Who's older?"

"Me. Only by a few minutes."

"Who got better grades in school?"

"Abi. Hands down."

"Who's more reliable?"

"I think that depends on who's relying on us." I locked onto her gaze.

"Do you guys have that twin telepathy?"

I shrugged my shoulder. "Maybe? I guess? I tend to feed off her emotions when we're in the same room—one look at her and I know what's going through her head, even when she's putting on a smile for everyone. And we always seem to text each other at the same time."

"Who's the better rider?"

"Me."

She raised a brow and twisted her lips.

"What?"

"I've seen you on a horse a total of one time, maybe twice."

"I taught Stetson how to ride."

"You can't be the better rider." Her voice drew out, disbelief flooding the air between us.

"You haven't seen me *really* ride." I leaned forward a tiny bit, giving her a small wink. "You owe me a rain check, remember?"

She hummed. "Well, Abi did mention horses at the wedding, so maybe then."

"The wedding's in June. Hopefully before then." I raised my eyebrows and turned back to the television. The screen had already dimmed from lack of movement.

"June? Reno's in June. I signed up for that one, and a few others that month. It's gonna be a busy summer." She wiggled her hips into the cushion, settling into her seat more.

"It's before Reno, that's for sure, and let me take a look at your schedule. I'll make sure nothing overlaps."

Her lips tilted to a soft smile, her eyes catching mine for a second before darting back down to her food.

"You wouldn't mind checking over this next adventure, would you? I can do this journey on my own, but having you look it over would put my mind at ease."

I took in a sharp breath. "Sure, I can. After we meet Belle?" I pointed at the screen.

Quinn let out a laugh. "Sure, after the episode." She flopped her head on the back of the couch cushion, her gaze still trained on me.

I had to hide the fact that I skipped over the small tidbit that she said she could do the next adventure on her own. I was hoping it would become a thing—us every weekend going from rodeo to rodeo. Even if she wanted me there just for company, I'd lean back on the trailer and let her do everything, and I'd be content just watching her. I knew she could do it, I just wanted to watch her.

I looked at her longer than I should have, taking in her pink cheeks, her emerald eyes, and different tints of brown in her hair, weaving through the braid. I noticed the small freckles on her cheeks that I hadn't seen before and the way her lips curved into a soft cupid's bow. There was nothing fake about the woman in front of me, and I had a feeling that no matter how many times I looked at her, I'd never catch all the details.

I let a breath out through my nostrils and turned back to the television, finally pressing play on the episode. We sat in silence for a few moments, watching Belle's story unfold. I even muttered "I should have known" when I saw who her Beast was, earning me a "it was kinda obvious" from Quinn.

Once the episode was over and the credits rolled, Quinn shifted, unfolding her legs and pulling them close to her chest. "Are you—" She stopped, inhaling a deep breath. "Are you going to be Cash's best man?"

I shook my head. "No. That's Lachlan. Just a groomsman."

"Kyla's her matron of honor?"

I nodded. "I'm assuming so." I looked over at her, seeing the dots connect in her mind, connecting in mine, too.

Cash told me they weren't going to have a big wedding, but Abi wanted to keep to some traditions. She'd walk down the aisle after the wedding party. Meaning—

"Looks like I get to walk you down the aisle, Compton."

"What the fuck did you get into?" I groaned as I scraped the brush through Rusty's coat. Spring was officially in full swing at Hartwell Hills, and mud was everywhere. My normally chestnut colored horse was now a dark, deep brown, and his coat was hard and crusted. I scraped at the dry mud, his tail whipping back to hit me. "Don't." I looked at my horse, tempted to tug his mane.

He huffed and shook his head.

"I swear the fields are nothing but mud," Abi called from the other stall, her voice carrying through the air between us. "Marshmallow is as black as Onyx."

"Oh joy," I grumbled, pulling a dry patch from Rusty, which earned me another loud whine. "Can't wait to get to that stall."

"Stetson will do his own damn horse. We have others to tend to. And I swear, these horses aren't going back into the field until after it dries."

"Abi," I dropped the brush to my side and walked to the barrier, draping my arms to get a good look at her. "It's spring on the ranch...it's going to be wet for months."

She was squatting next to the horse's hind legs, putting just as much pressure on the comb as I was. She let out a long groan and stood. "How long do you think it will take the two of us to de-mud and bathe all of these horses?"

I inhaled, looking at my sister. The Nova Luna Stables housed thirty horses, and currently, we were at full capacity. The horses stayed for a few weeks to a few months; others had become permanent residents.

"If we both take fifteen..." I let out a puff of air through my lips. "We'll be done by fall."

Slumping her shoulders, she lifted her chin to the ceiling. "You'll never get any announcing jobs if I keep you here brushing horses."

I huffed a laugh, pushing myself back into Rusty's stall. "Hawkins told me he saw my name in Reno, but they're cutting it close."

"Reno?" Abi parroted. "That would be a cool one to get your comeback. I'd come to that one."

"Quinn's on the board."

Abi's head popped over the wall separating the two stalls. "Really?"

"Yeah, I was looking at her schedule last night. She's booked herself up until the Fourth of July."

It was Abi's turn to rest her arms on the wall, the brush dangling between her fingers as she looked at me. "And are you going to travel with her?"

I raised a brow and looked at my twin. "Worried I won't be around to help here?" I joked.

Abi shook her head. "You know I'd rather you do what you love than working here, but I *am* curious now." She dragged her voice a little as she spoke the last few words. Knowing her, she's been wanting to talk about this. When it came to talking to me, it wasn't like Abi to hold anything back, so my interest was definitely piqued.

"Curious about..." I stopped brushing Rusty and walked to the wall, coming up to her side.

"What's happening between you two?" she asked, and before I could say anything in response, she kept going. "Last I knew, Quinn hated you—"

"She doesn't hate me...anymore," I emphasized *anymore*, knowing full well that months ago she wanted nothing to do with me. But the feeling of sitting next to her on her hotel bed, and in her car, on her couch watching that stupid show—her arms around me after a win—all of those moments were too strong to say she still hated me. I was growing on her—even she would admit that.

"Okay, she's not overly fond of you, but having you there helped, I can tell." She met my gaze. "That first weekend, she would text Cash and complain, but we hardly heard from her this time around. We heard from you more about making sure we followed, so…I'm just curious as to what is going on inside your head." Raising her arm, she used the end of the brush handle to tap on my forehead. "This is Quinn we're talking about, and last year…"

"She shot me down."

"Multiple times." She deadpanned. "And called you childish, and didn't she say you were more starch than man?"

"I haven't starched my Wranglers in months."

"She was…" She swayed her head and shrugged her shoulders. "Wondering about you the other day. It just made me wonder what your intentions are with her."

"You know, same as always. Flirt, tease, chase, eventually get her to see how amazing I am." I flashed her a grin, which faded the moment I looked at my sister.

Abi dropped her arms and let her groan echo through the stable. "I'm being serious, Wyatt. I just want to know what your plans are when it comes to her. Quinn is becoming a friend; I like having her around. Quinn is—" She paused, taking a breath. "She's funny, she's smart, she doesn't take anyone's shit. I've never seen a girl that young as determined as her. I don't want you to—"

"What?" I snapped before she could even finish the sentence. "Screw it up for her?"

Abi pursed her lips together.

"Alright, Abi." I tossed the brush to the ground. "I get it. I'm a fuck up. The playboy. I have made some pretty stupid mistakes when it comes to women, but I can assure you, I have absolutely no intention of screwing things up for Quinn. Do I still have feelings for her?" *Fuck yes, more than I did before.* "Eh...a little, but right now, I'm happy just being her friend. She makes me smile. She makes me laugh. And she's been putting up with my shit. If she wants me to go with her, I will jump at the chance to see her shine again, but she told me she wants to go alone. So, she'll go alone. I respect that of her. You said yourself she's determined, and I see it. I guarantee you, I won't screw anything up for her. Her goal is to get to the NFR. One of my mine is to help her get there."

"Wyatt," she sighed, "I didn't mean—"

"I know what you meant," I interrupted her. "But Abi...I just need you to trust that I won't mess things up for her. I didn't last weekend. I flirted, sure, but she's hard not to flirt with."

"You're losing that bet, aren't you?"

"Oh, terribly." I nodded vigorously, placing my hands on my hips. "But proudly so."

Abi held my gaze for a long time. "You have more than 'a little' feelings for her, don't you?"

I met her gaze once more, the brim of my ball cap shadowing my eyes. "Yeah. I'm fucking falling for her. And you're making me walk down the aisle with her."

Abi smiled. "That wasn't intentional." She pointed at me.

I clenched my teeth and shook my head. "You just like playing matchmaker."

"No, I wouldn't call it that. But...I *am* on your side. I'll always be on your side. I want to see you happy, and if Quinn makes you happy..." She trailed off, raising one shoulder to her ear.

"She makes me very happy," I said, almost a whisper.

Abi smiled at me. "I'm rooting for you. So, don't screw it up so I can keep rooting for you."

I was tempted to give her a salute. Instead, I turned my back and waved a hand in the air. *Don't screw it up so I can keep rooting for you.* Trust me, sis—I won't. I'm falling way too fast and way too hard.

Nineteen

Quinn

MY ENTIRE DRESSER VIBRATED as my phone buzzed loudly on the wood. I craned my neck to look at the screen from where I stood, practically buried in my closet, only to see the word *Mom* accompanied by her photo. I ignored it, returning to the closet where I was carefully placing shirts in garment bags for my upcoming weekend. I was leaving the next day for three rides, and my entire room was a mess with hats and shirts tossed everywhere, and my living room was lined with every pair of boots I owned and belts hanging off the couch. It was only three days; technically, I needed three shirts, three hats, three pairs of jeans, and boots—but this is how I worked. I wanted to see everything and pick what felt right for the ride. The last thing I needed was my mother calling me.

The last time I *spoke* to her was at the Grand Junction Rodeo two weeks ago. She had given me a few text messages here and there, each one earning her a simple *K* or *Yes* response from me, but nothing other than that. I really didn't want to talk with her. Not after the 'apparently, you can't' comment she made.

What I hated even more was that it was sticking with me.

Was the fact that I had someone with me the only reason why I had a good weekend? Would I have made more hiccups and mistakes if I had gone alone? What if she really was right—what if I couldn't do this? What if...

The past two weeks at home had been full of training, training, and more training to prove to myself I could. When Cash was with other clients, I'd take one of my boys out and circle barrels in the fields or run around the cow pastures. And when I wasn't in the saddle, I'd go to the gym and work on my core and leg muscles. Abi and Kyla cheered me on from the fences, acting as my own personal hype team, but other than the girls' day when we went dress shopping, I hadn't had much interaction with any humans besides Cash.

But then there was Wyatt.

Wyatt...

Every night without fail, Wyatt came to my place with food and drinks. He saw me at the gym one afternoon, and after that, the options he brought became healthier and protein-filled. As much as I was loving the burgers and pizza...a baked chicken with a side salad was probably the more feasible choice for staying in shape and building muscle. He commented on how hard I was working and that someone had to make sure my diet followed the plan. I would roll my eyes, and he would just stand there and smirk as he popped a cherry tomato in his mouth. Then he'd get settled, and we'd watch the show together.

But what really sent my mind for a loop was the fact that I looked forward to him coming every night. I looked forward to sitting with him and listening to his stupid comments about the show. I looked forward to inching my toes closer and closer to him, knowing if I were to sneak them under his thigh, he wouldn't protest. And I really looked forward to getting a hug from him each night—him always drawing it out longer than really necessary. But I would sit in it, breathe him in, and just...enjoy the feel of his arms around me. He was warm and welcoming, solid and safe, a friend I needed in the moment. And as much as I hated to admit it, that's exactly what he was becoming—my friend. And something else that sent my mind for a loop? Something else I would never admit? Every time he was near, butterflies flew like crazy in my stomach.

My phone buzzed again, that time louder, as if it were taunting me.

Mom.

I sighed, tossing the garment bag on the bed and placing my hands on my hips, staring at the mess until the phone stopped. Bending to grab a hat box, a low groan left my lungs when, yet again, my phone started to buzz.

That time, a text.

I tapped my screen.

Dad

> Answer your mother, please. She just wants to know if your schedules overlap.

I typed out a quick one-thumb message.

Me

I'm packing. Tell her I'll call her from the road.

I wouldn't...but maybe it would hold her over until then.

Dad

Come on, Pumpkin, one quick call.

Me

I will when I'm done packing. Promise.

Dad

We both know you won't.

Then, another name dropped down on my phone.

Mom

You'll text your father, but won't answer my calls. Quinn Compton...

I gave in before I finished the sentence and tapped her name, the ringing through the speaker causing that same knot to appear in my stomach.

"About time, Quinn," Mom answered.

"Hi, Mom."

"Where are you this weekend?"

"Northern Idaho."

"Kelly and I will be in Colorado, Chelsea and Jada, too."

I racked my brain to think about who those girls were. I knew Kelly—Mom never stopped talking about her—but Chelsea and Jada? Second and third attendant, maybe? I blinked and pushed the useless information from my head.

"That's great, Mom. I'm sure Kelly is thrilled."

"What the hell happened in here?" Wyatt's voice came booming up the stairs, and even though my mother was already talking in my ear, a small smile spread across my face. A few nights ago, I had stopped locking my door, knowing he would just come in, *wanting* him to come in.

"I gotta go, Mom. Wyatt just got here—"

"Oh!" Her tone automatically changed. "Wyatt Hartwell. You are seeing him, then?"

"No, Mom. I'm not. He's just a friend."

"Quinn!" Wyatt called. "Boots have taken over your living room, did you know this?"

I laughed. "Mom, I have to go. Have a good time in Colorado."

I hung up before she could say anything back, shoved my phone in my pocket, and made my way downstairs. Wyatt stood in the middle of the living room, a box of pizza balancing on one hand, a bottle of ginger ale in the other. Our eyes met, and he beamed, small crinkles forming in the corner of his eyes. Those wrinkles only made me smile; the pure amusement that radiated off of him as he stood in the midst of all my boots was contagious.

"You have more boots than any normal person would have in their lifetime, and why are they all in the living room. Better question? Where were they before they were in your living room?"

I chuckled and tossed the hatbox I was still carrying on the chair. "There are twenty-one pairs of boots here, Wyatt, and they were in my closet. I'm packing." I took the pizza box from him. "Pizza? I thought I had to eat healthy."

"Cauliflower crust and veggies. It's basically a salad." Wyatt spun in a circle, looking at all the boots. "Twenty-one pairs...how long are you gone for? A month?"

"Three days."

"My question still stands about the boots."

I headed into the kitchen, hearing him follow.

"I like to see my options," I said, placing the pizza box and my phone on the kitchen island.

My phone buzzed...again...with the same parent calling. I turned the phone screen down and caught Wyatt's look. No one really knew about my relationship with my mother. Cash knew snippets—enough to know I didn't really have her in my corner—but other than him, I never talked about her. And even though I could see the question filtering through Wyatt's face, I cleared my throat and moved on.

"Cauliflower crust, huh?" I sighed, opening the pizza box. "Never tried it."

He inhaled. "It's disgusting, so I apologize in advance."

"You know." I gave him a sideways glance before pulling a slice from the box. "I go to the gym and work out so I don't have to watch my weight. I eat what I want, when I want." I took a bite and chewed and...oh...yes...Wyatt was so wrong. It was delicious. I hummed as I chewed. "I learned my lesson as a kid. I will never, ever count calories."

"Who the fuck made you count calories as a kid?" He furrowed his brow and leaned on the counter.

For a quick moment, I debated lying, but for some reason, I didn't want to lie to him. Even if the truth hurt a little. "My mom. For pageants. But when I stopped those, I stopped counting. I love food, and I'm grateful I never developed a bad relationship with it." I took another bite. "But you're very wrong." I chewed, closing my eyes and savoring the taste. "This is delicious."

"Glad you like it." Wyatt smiled, his eyes on me, a slanted grin on his lips as he accepted the change of subject.

My phone, however, didn't. It began to buzz once again, and I swear, the vibration just kept getting louder. Was that a thing? Did phones know you were avoiding calls and purposely become more violent when you didn't answer? I glared at it.

Wyatt pointed at it. "You can answer that, you know. Don't let me stop you."

"It's not important." I spun, reaching for two glasses, a little disappointed I had forgotten to pull them out.

"Who is it?"

Shaking my head, I turned the phone over, Mom's photo blaring between us. I watched until it stopped, then flipped it over again, sliding it further away. Ignoring it, I grabbed the ginger ale, the cap making the perfect *pfft* sound as it released with the twist. Wyatt was silent, his eyes following my every move. I filled both cups and handed one to him before he finally spoke.

"She's uh—" He began, a crack in his voice. "—not very supportive? Is she?"

I heaved a long sigh, met his gaze, and then shook my head. "No," I said simply.

He was quiet, his eyes darting as he tried to find something to focus on, but like always, he settled on my eyes. The bright blue orbs filled with concern as he took a deep breath, in and out, focusing on me. My body just froze, feeling the chill my mother always brought with her. She could take anything that I found joy in and ruin it. Even a night with Wyatt.

To think…months ago I would have never imaged him sitting here with me. I would have never thought I would consider him a friend. And once again…I found myself not wanting to keep this from him. My simple 'no' wasn't enough. He made me feel different. Like I wanted to open up, and I almost wanted to tell him everything. He made me feel warm and safe just sitting across the island from me. That frozen feeling that was creeping up after his one simple question began to fade as I looked at him.

"I don't really talk about it," I said softly, breaking eye contact to look at my fingers.

"We don't have to."

"No, it's not that." I sighed. "It's that no one really ever asked me."

"No one?" His brow pinched.

"I mean, my friends all saw the way she was when we were growing up." Twisting my lips, I shook my head. "Maybe it's the norm where I grew up. There are a lot of pageant moms, and some get into it more than others. That was my mom. She supported me when I did pageants. She was only proud of me when I did pageants."

"That can't be true."

"Oh, but it is." Widening my eyes, I took a long gulp of my drink, wishing it were something stronger. "I asked her, and she responded with silence. I quit pageants when I was thirteen. I hated everything about it. Well…that's a lie. I loved the horsemanship—"

"Obviously." Wyatt opened his palms with his comment, a grin flashing across his lips.

I couldn't help but smile back, my stomach doing a little flip.

"Obviously," I repeated, mimicking his gesture. "I went to work at a stable. I worked my ass off. I saved every penny I made and bought Hook on my own when I was seventeen. I started racing with him and bought Charming three years later. She wasn't proud of my work at the stables; she wasn't impressed that I bought my own horse. She couldn't care less when I signed up for my first rodeo. She has never gone to my rides on purpose, and she doesn't call with congrats or send inspiring text messages. She appears with the rodeo queen she coaches, and even then, it's by accident that we run into each other. The only way my mother would have supported my life choices is if I went down the exact path she did.

"But obviously…" I raised my brow at him, loving the smirk he gave me. "I didn't, so therefore, I'm her biggest disappointment. And if I'm being honest, that's not even the tip of the iceberg when it comes to her."

"You're the furthest thing from a disappointment," he replied softly. "If she can't see that—"

"Are you going to say she's not worth it? Didn't your parents support you no matter what?" I cocked my head and glared at him. His eyebrows rose as he blinked a few times. I straightened my posture. "Sorry, that came out meaner than I meant it."

"No, it's okay. They were supportive in their own way." He shrugged a shoulder. "I mean, they didn't support me when I decided to streak down Main Street."

"There's a story there."

"There is, but..." He shifted. "For another day." He stood and walked around the counter. "My parents were proud of me even if I made decisions they didn't care for, so I can't imagine how you feel when it comes to your mom, but I hope you know you have support now. Cash, Abi, Kyla...me." He faced me, his palm resting on the counter as he lowered his chin to look at me, those blue eyes boring into me again. His voice lowered. "Maybe someday she'll see how phenomenal you are, until then"—he reached up, his fingers lighting brushing my hair from my shoulder, the touch from his knuckles grazing across my skin, creating a sizzle that was hard to ignore—"you have me to remind you."

Did he know what he was doing to me at this moment? My breath hitched, and my heart rate began to pound as I stared into his eyes. I could still feel the path his fingers took against my bare shoulder when he moved my hair. I could hear his breath; I could practically feel his heartbeat against my chest even though we were still inches apart.

"I'll always remind you how perfect I think you are."

Oh God...

Months ago, if Wyatt had said that to me, I would have thrown a comeback or something his way. Knock him off his high horse and tell him to get some mud on his boots. But now...after spending countless hours with him, laughing, talking, feeling him against me with every hug he offered...learning who he truly was...

My knees went a little weak.

And with the way he was looking at me, I could tell he wanted to kiss me. His eyes trailed from mine, to my lips, to my neck, to my hair...before they settled back on my lips. Desire flooded through him and into me, and I could feel the heat, so palpable I could almost taste it.

"Absolutely perfect." He sighed, his voice breathy as he locked eyes with me again.

He leaned ever so slightly to me—a breath away from me...when a ping came from his pocket, then another and another.

The moment gone, I quickly stepped back, picking up my glass of ginger ale and gulping it down as fast as I could. Thank God—or whoever was watching—that someone had demanded Wyatt's attention because as much as my knees were shaking...I could not have just almost kissed Wyatt.

After my glass was empty, I looked back at him, still frozen in the same spot, his concentration on his phone.

"What is it?" I asked, my voice raspy from chugging an entire twelve ounces of ginger ale in one gulp.

Wyatt bit the inside of his lip. "Nothing." His phone made the locking sound before he set it on the counter and slid it down by mine. It hit my phone with a thump before they both sat still on the counter. He heaved a sigh. "Ready to watch an episode?"

His smile was gone. The glint in his eye that was there just seconds before had faded.

I nodded. "Yeah. I think you meet a very pivotal character tonight."

His smile returned, but it wasn't the smile I had grown to know. There was something behind it.

"I sure hope it starts with an H and ends with an ook." He pushed himself off the counter and made his way to the living room.

"You're an idiot, you know that?"

"Yeah, but..." He groaned as he sat down on the couch. "You enjoy having me around. Just admit it. I'm a joy."

I licked my lips and sat down next to him, close enough that my knees rested against his thighs. He could pull me into his side at this point in time, and I wouldn't care. I would welcome his touch, his warmth, his scent. I did enjoy having him around. I wanted him around. I wanted all of—

Nope...not that far yet.

I opened up the app and cued up the episode, quickly glancing around at all my boots, still spread around the living room floor. Tomorrow I'd pack up the pairs I picked in my truck. I'd pack my backseat full of garment bags, hat boxes, and suitcases full of God knows what in them...leaving the small space for Wyatt's one duffel bag.

"Come with me," I said suddenly, not even second-guessing it.

Wyatt raised a brow and looked over at me.

"This weekend, come with me to the rodeos. I'm sure your favorite horse...you know the one that starts with an H and ends in an ook, would be thrilled to know you're there to take care of him."

The smile I wanted came back. Even the sparkle in his eyes returned.

"I thought you'd never ask."

TWENTY

Wyatt

MY ENTIRE BODY JERKED as I pumped my fist and cheered, watching as Quinn disappeared behind the gates after her fourteen-second ride. I'd decided to sit in the stands for these rodeos, and I could still see her smile from here. She took first, and Kurt—the announcer on duty tonight—just called that she was now the time to beat. Kurt was good; he got the crowd roaring, and damn, they cheered for Quinn. She had this in the bag. Just like last night and the night before, Quinn was topping the charts. And she was riding the high.

I waited a few seconds before side-stepping past everyone, taking the stairs two at a time until I was back behind the stands. My heart was racing; I couldn't get to her fast enough. She couldn't go far. If she won, the reporter would want to talk to her. I could imagine her still on Hook, letting him turn in circles as they waited. With how fast he was going, I'm sure his sassy ass still had some pent-up energy, so she'd be taking her time to calm him down. Yet, I still ran as fast as I could to the back of the arena, jumping onto the lowest metal bar once I reached the gate.

"Quinn!" I bellowed once I caught sight of her.

Just like I guessed, she was still on Hook, his head bobbing up and down as he tried to settle. Hook turned before she did, his hooves bouncing as they made their way over to me.

"Did you see that!" Quinn exclaimed. "Fourteen seconds flat! Fourteen! Pretty sure that beat your mom's time."

My grin spread as I remembered that day at the ranch. The entire Hartwell family was sitting in the tiny indoor arena. Quinn rounded some barrels, she taught Stetson how to race, Rhett beat my ass at tie down, and my mom showed Quinn how it was done. The other thing that stood out in my mind was that it was the first time I had actually tried to hit on Quinn—and her exact words: "*If you would get your ass off the gate and saddle a horse, I'd be more inclined to talk to you.*" If only she knew that months later, she'd be the one inviting me to her rodeos.

"I got it all on film," I assured her, reaching out to pat Hook on the nose. "I'll make sure to send it to her—but knowing them, they already saw it." My parents were still traveling after their retirement, but they always made sure to follow the rodeo. They basically had *the Cowboy Channel* on as background noise.

She wiggled her hips in the saddle, a breath of relief leaving her lungs. Quinn's cheeks were flushed, her hair was disheveled, and her shirt slightly askew on her shoulders—yet I had never seen her this ecstatic. I wasn't sure if it was the fact that she knew everyone was supporting her—watching her—even from Alpine Ridge or across the world, or if it was simply because she was doing what she was meant to do.

"Compton," a rodeo hand called. Quinn turned to the voice. "You won! They wanna see you on the dirt."

"Coming!" She slid from the saddle and handed me the reins, not even a second thought as to who she was handing off one of her boys to. She just gave me a wide smile and took off towards the gates.

I climbed over the gate, landing on my feet in front of Hook. He moved and nudged me with his nose to get my attention, but I turned just in time to see Quinn adjust her hair, straighten her shirt, and step out onto the arena dirt.

"What a ride, Quinn! You must feel like you're on top of the world." The reporter's voice rang through the speakers, almost drowning out the crowd.

"I am. It's been three nights of amazing rides. But it wasn't just me; it was Hook also. I always try to gauge who to ride, but these past few nights it's been him, and he's really performed." I could hear Quinn's smile through the speakers. The excitement she carried traveled through the microphone and into the crowd, and I suddenly wished I were right next to her. I wanted to see her there, not just hear her. "We trained and worked really hard to get here, and it's one step closer to the NFR."

"If you keep up with rides like this, you'll definitely make it there. Congratulations on tonight, and we can't wait to see where you go."

Quinn was beaming when she collected her check, and she had a bounce in her step as we unsaddled Hook. She hummed as she guided him to the trailer and locked it. Flipping her hair as she got into the driver's seat of her truck—the joy basically radiated off of her at this point. I had never seen her like this, and I couldn't stop staring as this new side of her came out. The Quinn I knew was scheduled, she was structured, she was calm. Tonight, she was acting as if she were a Coke bottle that had been shaken and was ready to burst. I loved every minute of it.

Her gaze met mine in the silence, and her eyes widened, the expression never leaving her.

"What?" She removed her hat and plopped it on the dash, her fingers quickly moving to run through her hair.

"Nothing, you're just cute like this." I smiled at her.

"What?" She repeated, her smile widening as she scrunched her shoulders. "I'm excited. I won. Three nights in a row. Nothing to stop me or pull me from this mood, so you'd better relish it while you can."

"Oh, I am." I chuckled. "I love seeing every new side of you, but you're too energized. I'm kind of wondering what you've done with my Quinn."

"Your Quinn?" She raised a brow, but the smile didn't fade.

"Yeah, *my* Quinn."

"Well, *your* Quinn is on a high, and no amount of bad news or anything else could bring me down from this." She put her hands on the wheel and ran her palms against the leather before kicking the engine on.

I tightened my lips, my smile all but fading for a split second.

Bad news? I could give her some bad news.

Reno passed on me.

I had gotten the text from Hawkins right after she told me about her relationship with her mom, and in the grand scheme of things, it didn't seem as important. In that moment, I wanted to focus on Quinn, hating that a stupid text saying, *Sorry, man, maybe next year* was enough to pull me down into the depths with her. When I locked my phone and slid it across the counter, we both accepted it and ignored the dread that the devices held. Then she was sitting next to me, closer than she ever had before. And then she asked me to come with her this weekend, and the fact that I was still unemployed in the rodeo world didn't matter at all.

I let out a breath through my nostrils. "There's gotta be another way to get this energy out of you, then. I bet the hotel has a gym. You could go for a fifty-mile run."

"That sounds terrible." Quinn kicked the truck into gear.

"*Once Upon a Time*? Pretty sure something big is going to happen. We can run in place or do push-ups until you pass out from the adrenaline rush."

Quinn let out a soft chuckle. "You do not want to watch that show every night. It's been fun, and I'm loving the rewatch, but push-ups sound just as bad as the run. I can't believe I'm going to suggest this, but..." She gave me a glance, her smile spreading. "I think we need to go out."

Shock spread across my face. Going out was my thing. My thing to get the night really going, not Quinn's thing. Quinn was the shower, bed, and early to rise kind of person. Abi even told me about a night when she traveled with her—telling me Quinn didn't even finish her drink, and that she was stressing that they had to leave early the next morning. I wasn't sure if I heard her correctly.

"Go out? I'll ask again...who are you, and what have you done with *my* Quinn?" I deadpanned, emphasizing the *my*.

"Oh, come on, Hartwell." She leaned over and tapped the brim of my hat. "You can even wear your ball cap. No cowboy hat required. We'll go back to the hotel, get changed, and then find the best honky-tonk northern Idaho has to offer."

"A honky-tonk?" I parroted. "You taking me line dancing, Compton?"

"We could." She raised a brow. "I'm pretty good at line dancing. Do you know how?"

"There are a lot of things you don't know about me." I leaned towards her, lowering my voice.

Her eyes widened as she spun to look at me. "Google it, right now. Find the best place we can go line dancing." She pointed at my lap, most likely gesturing to my phone.

I chuckled and leaned over, digging my phone from my pocket to follow her instructions, Googling *best western bar in northern Idaho*.

Forty-five minutes later, I knocked on Quinn's hotel door. I had replaced my cowboy hat with my Hartwell ball cap, not even giving myself a second look in the mirror before making my way to her room, and the moment Quinn opened the door, I regretted not changing my clothes.

Quinn was...well...*fuck*...

She managed to dress up a simple denim top, pairing it with a white lace skirt and white boots, with a turquoise necklace hanging from her neck. Her hair had been brushed but was still wild, and a new light brown hat perched on her head. Her eyes were bright, her cheeks had a pink tint, her lips were shiny and perfectly kissable, and the glow that surrounded her was impossibly bright. I almost had to squint. But there I was, staring into the light. I had seen Quinn dress up before, but this...this was...

Rendering me speechless.

And I was the one who loved to talk. I was the one who had words for everything.

But not this. Not for her.

There were no words to describe how beautiful she looked.

All I could do was stand there and take her in.

"Ready?" she asked, moving quick as she stepped out into the hall, shutting the door behind her, her haste not even pulling me from my stupor.

She made sure her door was locked, then, in another quick movement, she spun, her white skirt billowing around her. I had to remind my legs how to move. *One foot in front of the other, Hartwell. You know how to walk.*

"What's the place called?" she asked, spinning again to face me, her hair flying in all directions.

I coughed, "It's uh—" I stumbled. Damnit...if I didn't watch myself, I'd trip over my own boots. "The Westerner."

"Seriously?" She chuckled. "And they have line dancing and pool tables?"

"I can't promise dancing, but I can tell you right now we're not playing pool." I blinked, my ability to walk finally being returned to my legs. Quinn was already down the hall, so I had to jog a few steps to catch up with her. "You beat my ass that one time, and I can't make another bet."

"We can think of something, can't we?"

"No pool." I pointed at her.

She rolled her eyes. "Fine, no pool."

Together, we walked out onto the street, the night air still chilly even though we were well into spring. I was still in my jeans, T-shirt, and flannel...I could only imagine how cold Quinn must be feeling. I glanced at her legs, noticing the small goosebumps that prickled her skin. My gaze trailed up to her arms, and the same goosebumps spread over her shoulders. The urge to run my knuckle down her bare shoulder was extremely potent, as was the temptation to shed off my flannel and drape it over her shoulders, but with the way she was moving, she probably didn't even notice the cold. So...instead of giving in to my impulsive thought of touching her, I shoved my hands in my pockets.

"Here we are!" Quinn skipped the final three steps to the door and reached for the handle. I beat her to it and pulled it open, the thick music reaching all the way to the street. "Oh my God, the *vibes*. Good pick, Hartwell. Drink first, then dancing." She grabbed my sleeve and pulled me to the bar. She didn't have to drag me—I would willingly follow her anywhere she'd want to go at this point.

Pushing through a small crowd, we sat at the bar top and ordered two lagers, and the second the bartender laid eyes on Quinn, he knew exactly who she was. He leaned in, his voice a little shaky as he made sure she was, in fact, Quinn Compton. When she nodded and leaned forward, he was so completely lost, I was shocked he remembered to serve us our drinks. Apparently, the local rodeos were bigger than college football in The Westerner, and the bartender—Brad—was a huge fan of barrel racing. Meeting Quinn was the highlight of his night. And, once they started talking, I was invisible. Her smile grew as Brad recapped her rides the last few nights, even commenting on her ride tonight. Quinn blushed and giggled as the conversation started to flow through them. And that wonderful pit of jealously grew in my stomach. I heaved a sigh and spread my legs a little wider, making sure my knee was touching her. I grabbed my drink and took a long gulp, my eyes flying between Quinn and Brad.

Reminding myself that Quinn was not mine to be jealous over, I pulled my phone from my pocket. A good doom scroll would hopefully distract me.

Heading directly to the PRCA website, I checked Quinn's standing, not even shocked when I saw her sitting in third place. I clicked on her profile and scrolled. It had all her past times and events listed for the year so far, including tonight's win. I had been the one to constantly check her stats—and she was going up and up. There was no doubt in my mind that she would be number one soon.

My phone pinged, and a text banner dropped.

Abi

> Quinn was amazing tonight! She must be over the moon.

Me

> She is. Just checked her standing. Third in the nation.

Abi

> Damn—does she know?

Not sure, but she will.

Make sure she celebrates. I know she's big on her schedules, but…get her out.

"Hey, Compton," I said, a little spark in my chest when she turned around from Brad. I raised my phone and aimed it at her. "Smile," I said, looking at her from over the top of my phone.

Quinn raised her chin and smiled at the camera, her beauty almost just as mesmerizing on the screen as it was in real life. I lowered my phone and looked at her on the screen, making sure to mark it as a favorite before I sent it off to Abi.

"Who's that for?" she asked, leaning away from Brad and close to me. Her hat lightly touched my forehead as my screen lit up in between us.

Oh my lord, she's at a bar! Good job, bro.

It was her idea.

I think you're rubbing off on her.

Oh—I saw the announcement. I'm sorry, Wyatt, it wasn't meant to be. They're missing out.

"Who's missing out?" Quinn said, pulling my attention back to her.

I locked my phone and shoved it back in my pocket. "No one. Just had to show Abi proof of you in a bar."

"Wyatt." Quinn's voice dropped. "No deflecting. Who's missing out?"

I licked my lips. "No one," I repeated.

"Is it her?" Raising her glass, she lifted her pointer finger and gestured behind me. "Is she missing out on Wyatt Hartwell?"

Twisting my torso, I saw the group of girls she was pointing at. A brunette stood in the middle of the group, raising a cocktail to her lips, and when her eyes met mine, her grin turned downright sexy. If Hawkins or Sam were next to me, hell, even Lachlan or Rhett, I'd stand up and make my way over to her, make sure she wasn't 'missing out' on anything. But I had a photo in my phone to prove that I was already sitting next to the most gorgeous woman in the bar, and there was nowhere else I'd rather be.

I turned back to her, a single eyebrow raised. "You playing my wingman?"

She shrugged her shoulder. "Why not? There are a lot of girls here who could be your type." She looked around the room. "I kinda wanna see you in action."

I leaned in. "I told you, Quinn, you're the only one I'm chasing."

"Oh yeah?"

"Yes."

"Then tell me who's missing out?" She arched her back and raised a brow.

My lips curved as I sat back up, reaching for my lager. I took a sip and let it loose. "Reno. They took my name off the broadcaster bill. I was hoping to announce."

She narrowed her eyes, her back straightening. "I didn't know you put your name in for the committee."

"I didn't, but it ended up there anyway. You know I'm not taking time off by choice."

She leaned in, the gleam in her eye telling me she wanted more of the story. "Okay, I know you said you did something stupid..."

"I did."

"But let's be real here, *how* stupid a thing did you do to end up with your name taken out of committees?"

I heaved a sigh and took another pull from my drink. "Started a fight that ended with me and the other guy going to the ER. He just happened to be a head of a committee that has some strong connections, and now I'm having a hard time finding any jobs. Hawkins has been trying to help, but has had no luck. I was hoping Reno would be a shoo-in."

"Why did you get in a fight? No wait—" She held up a palm to stop me before I could even begin. "You slept with his wife?"

I jerked my head back, my eyes widening and brow pinching. "Why the fuck is that the first thing that popped in your head?"

She shrugged, "I don't know. I figured it had to be dramatic in order for you to really get pissed. I've known you for three months now—"

"Four...almost five." I corrected her, doing quick math in my head. Five. Five months, we have been in each other's lives.

"—and I've never really seen you upset." She kept talking as if she didn't even hear me. "I mean, I've seen your smile fade, but it's not like you to start a fight."

"Well, yeah...I did start it, but it wasn't because I slept with the man's wife. I wouldn't be the guy someone cheats on their husband with, and before you start,"—I noticed her jaw open and close, her lips tightening—"it's almost happened. Found out she was married and put a stop to it."

"So what caused it then. What made you so mad that you had to send someone to the hospital?"

They were talking about you, how you were cheating your way to the top because there was no way you could climb that high after an accident like you had. How you were sleeping with the judges to change your times. How you were riding on your dad's coattails, and that you had no idea what was really waiting for you. And how if you were already cheating...maybe they could get something else out of you in order to get you higher...

But I couldn't tell her that, now could I?

"Honestly, it was so long ago I don't remember," I lied.

She narrowed her eyes and raised her glass to her lips, but before the glass touched her lipstick, "Boot Scootin' Boogie" began to play over the speakers, louder than the rest of the music. The entire bar erupted in cheers, and people began to gather in the center of the room. Quinn let out a sharp gasp and placed her beer on the table, grabbing my sleeve once again, pulling me through the crowd, the topic at hand all but forgotten.

"Show me your moves." She smiled, stopping us once we reached the middle of the dance floor, forcing me to stand next to her as the entire place started dancing in sync. I knew all the steps by heart—you don't grow up in Alpine Ridge and not learn this dance, so as my feet moved on their own, I watched Quinn the entire time, and fell a little harder.

We danced, we drank, we talked and laughed, we played a game of darts—which I let her win—then right before last call, Quinn linked her arm in mine, and we made our way back to the hotel. The topics of Reno, my fight, or her mom not coming up a single time, making the statement Quinn had said hours prior that no bad news could kill this high a fact. And this time, on the walk back, I draped my flannel across her shoulders. I walked her to her door, not even worrying that she had my shirt, and stood in the hall as she stepped inside. We said a soft goodnight, the air heavy between us, and I turned—my room just down the hall, yet too far away.

"Hey, Wyatt."

I turned, seeing her head poking from her door. I raised my brow in question.

"I really am sorry about Reno, but...you'll still come with me, right? I'm there for six of the ten days, and I'd really love you to—"

"I wouldn't miss it for the world."

Her eyes smiled. "Night, Hartwell."

"Sleep well, Compton."

TWENTY-ONE

Quinn

Dad

Have you seen your standings?

Me

Not done yet, Dad, keep watching.

Dad

Third! And it's only May.

Mom

Where will you be this weekend?

Me

Home.

WHEN MY DAD CREATED a group chat—in his words, a way to keep my mom involved—I begrudgingly complied. Dad was his normal upbeat self, always trying to steer the conversation towards me. Mom never acknowledged it. And I just ignored it.

The idea that she could be at any of the rodeos last weekend hung in the back of my mind, but then I won. And Wyatt was there. And then I took first again. And Wyatt was there. And on the third night—when she was nowhere to be seen, and the first person I wanted to see was Wyatt—the idea that she could have been there didn't even cross my mind.

Rodeos always sent a thrill through my body, but nothing like this past weekend. I was on a high, and when I said nothing could stop it, I meant it. Even now, days later, simply sitting on Kyla's front porch, a beer in my hand as we watched the sunset, I could still feel the buzz. The texts from my mother didn't even bother me. I wasn't entirely sure if it was because of my wins and standings, or if it was that I hadn't seen the one person who always managed to jet set this feeling into oblivion—but whatever the reason, I was going to soak it up and ride it.

Baby Poppy sat in her mom's lap, Kyla bouncing her as her giggle echoed off the porch ceiling. Kyla sang a 'bababa' as Poppy's smile widened, watching her mother with those vibrant blue eyes.

"Does Rhett have blue eyes?" I asked, glancing up at Kyla to see her deep brown eyes.

"He does," Kyla cooed, her voice high as she smiled at her daughter. "She got her daddy's eyes and her mama's hair." She tickled Poppy's brown hair that had been growing in.

Rhett's eyes…Wyatt's eyes.

"She'll be known for her eyes." I leaned over and tickled her tummy, which warranted me the cutest chuckle I had ever heard. "All the Hartwells are. I can spot Wyatt's in a crowd now."

"Oh, really?" Abi piped up, her head rising from the back of the chair.

"They're hard to miss." I shrugged my shoulder.

They were also the first things I looked for after a ride. His eyes were always full of excitement, pride…Dare I say… a certain four-letter word? No. I really didn't dare. He always gave me that look, one that sent shivers down my spine and butterflies in my stomach. It was no wonder why girls would fall for him easily; anyone could get lost in those baby blues. Even me.

Wyatt's friendship was becoming more than I thought it would. I found it easier to talk to him, wanting to let him in even more. He took my crazy family dynamic and rolled with it, making sure I knew he was there to support me when my family wasn't. He made me forget every word my mom had or hadn't said to me throughout the years. He made it easy. He made me laugh; he made me *want* to laugh. Even though he was willing to settle for watching a show and nothing else, he made me feel comfortable enough to try something new. With Wyatt, I wanted more than the routine we settled into. And then when we got there...I wasn't quite sure how to act. I could tell just by looking at him that he wasn't one hundred percent sure either.

Every single moment from the other night came flooding back. Did he think going to that bar was a date? When I took my time getting ready to go out, my stomach was certainly flipping. I had to give myself a physical pep talk in the mirror, reminding myself that it was Wyatt Hartwell, that I was not getting dressed up for him. He was a playboy, a womanizer, a flirt. Yet, when I opened that door, my breath stopped, and the pep talk went out the window. I saw the way his lips parted, I saw the way his back stiffened, and the way his eyes sparked as he took me in. I would be lying if I said I didn't like the way that felt. When the cold air hit my skin, I pretended it was a cold shower—washing away any feelings that could be mustering their way through. Two friends. Hanging out. Having a few drinks. It was no different than sitting and watching a show. Except it was extremely different. I went from reminding myself he wasn't the kind of guy I wanted to reminding myself to stop looking at him.

When the bartender began to flirt, I leaned in and smiled, soaking up the attention of someone else. Telling myself I wasn't secretly wishing it was Wyatt. And then what did I have to do? Mention the girls who couldn't take their eyes off him. Maybe, my mind told me, if I saw him interact with another girl, I would remember why he was just—and only could be—a friend.

You're the only one I'm chasing, Quinn.

He couldn't still be chasing me...could he? Sure, he flirted, but that was Wyatt. He flirted. He used those baby blues to his advantage. He knew exactly what they did.

"I was so happy when Poppy's eyes turned. I was hoping she'd get her daddy's eyes." Kyla leaned forward and rubbed Poppy's nose with hers, her words bringing me back to the here and now. "When are Leo and Lottie coming home?"

Poppy began to babble, shoving her fists in her mouth.

"They'll be home before the wedding. They wouldn't miss it. But then I think it's off to France?" Abi narrowed her eyes, questioning herself.

I laughed. "You don't know where your parents are going?"

"After they retired, I couldn't keep up with them. They came home for Poppy, Thanksgiving, and Christmas, but they've been enjoying being stress-free." Abi waved her hands in front of her.

"Stress-free?" Kyla repeated. "I wonder what that is like."

"We'll find out when we retire." Abi sighed.

"Your life is a lot less stressful these days, my friend." Kyla chuckled. "I'm dying for my next book recommendation."

"*Discovery of Witches*, for sure. It was fantastic, but Cash brought home a fantasy book for me, and I'm devouring it." She widened her eyes. "It's been nonstop since the first page. I made Cash go get the next two in the series, and he said he's going to read it when I'm done."

"The dragon one?" I asked, looking over at Abi.

Abi tightened her lips, the grin breaking through. "The dragon one." She raised her bottle to her mouth.

I rolled my eyes, "That book is everywhere. Is it good?"

"Is. It. Good?!" Abi leaned forward, her voice getting louder with each word. "You both need to read it."

I scrunched my nose. "I'll wait, thank you, but this does remind me"—I looked from Kyla and Abi—"Wyatt suggested we start a book club."

"There's a book club we can join." Kyla popped up. "It's called the Smutty Grannies, and they meet once a month at the bookstore in town."

"The...Smutty...Grannies?" I repeated.

"Spicy books." Abi wiggled her eyebrows.

"Gathered that." I chuckled. "I'm sure bringing a sexy book on the road is just what I need."

"When are you leaving again, Quinn?" Abi asked, changing the conversation, shifting in her chair to face me.

"Not for two weeks, even then it's just Utah and Nevada. I'm trying to stay in the circuit."

"Rhett said Wyatt's been helping set your schedule. I used to think Rhett did all of that, but I guess it was Wyatt." Kyla situated Poppy on her lap. "He's been helping, right?"

I nodded and took a swig of my beer. "Yes, ma'am. I'm honestly not sure what I would do without him at this point. He's confirmed all my schedules, takes care of the horses and drives, and lets me read or just relax. Seriously—he's been a Godsend."

The girls grew quiet, and I looked from side to side at them. Abi's eyes met Kyla's as she let out a sigh.

"Okay." I pushed down the air in front of me. "I get I wasn't the nicest to him when we first met, but...you guys know Wyatt. I had no idea he did all that stuff. Maybe"—I shrank—"I judged him too harshly when I met him."

"He's a good guy," Kyla added. "A bit immature, but he's growing up."

"He better. He's thirty." Abi scoffed.

"Twenty-nine." I corrected.

Abi shook her head. "We celebrated our birthday three weeks ago."

My head snapped in her direction. "I missed your birthday? Three weeks ago? No one told me." I added sheepishly.

"It's just a day. Normally, we're so busy even we forget. But, if I remember correctly, he headed over to your place with a pizza and ginger ale." Abi settled in her seat. "He skipped out on family dinner to watch that show with you, and we've always spent our birthdays together."

A knot formed in my stomach. "He didn't say anything."

"Well, neither did I. Really, Quinn," she met my eyes, "It's ok. Cash and I celebrated. But with Wyatt, he may love the attention, but when he has his eye on something, that's all he can see. Therefore, you were the forefront of his mind, not our birthday."

I closed my eyes tight. "We're just friends," I mumbled before opening my eyes again. Kyla and Abi were giving each other another stare-down. "Really. We're just friends."

My phone pinged on the side table, thankfully distracting me from the conversation. I glanced down at the screen until I saw the name.

Wyatt

Tell Abi to let you go. It's show time.

I grinned, a slight heat rushing to my cheeks. Picking up the phone, I thumbed my reply.

Me

Hell no. I'm having fun. The show will be there tomorrow.

Wyatt

Fine. I'll watch without you. I have that app too, you know. *tongue sticking out emoji*

"What time are we meeting for dresses tomorrow?" I asked, setting my phone down. But Kyla and Abi answered with silence, both of them boring down on me. The only sound was Poppy's coos. I looked back and forth at both of them until I finally gave in. "What!"

"You like my brother," Abi stated blankly.

"We're friends." I reiterated, drawing out the word as long as I could.

My phone pinged again, and both Abi and I looked down at the screen.

Wyatt

Oh, I have your schedule confirmed—all settled there. And I forgot—what episode are we on?

I didn't pick up the phone to answer; I just let the banner go black with the rest of the screen before I made eye contact with Abi. Her eyebrows raised.

"We're friends," I said again.

"You've said that four times now." Kyla gave me a side glance as she moved Poppy to her shoulder.

"I'm trying to get it through your head."

"Just being frank here." Abi leaned back in her chair. "You're not fooling me."

"Me either," Kyla added, her voice raised to appease Poppy, who buried her face in her mom's shoulder, her fist working to get to her eyes.

I sat back and watched as Rhett came out to take his daughter, giving Kyla a kiss on the temple before humming into his daughter's ear. Shortly after Rhett disappeared into the house, Kyla said goodnight to us and followed him. Abi offered to walk back with me to the main house and stables, and on the way, her phone rang, and by the blush on her cheeks, a dead giveaway that it was Cash on the other side. I could see the light in both of their eyes, and even though I kept telling myself that Wyatt was just a friend, I was having a hard time fooling myself, too.

Wyatt opened the bunkhouse door, actually wearing a shirt this time, and his smile spread across his face. I made it to my truck, took one look at the bunkhouse, and without even thinking twice, I bypassed my truck and the next thing I knew I was knocking on the door. He had shown up to my house every night for the last few months, always with food and drink, and here I was... empty-hand-ed. I raised my palms in the air.

"Pretend I'm holding a pineapple pizza and a six pack." I took a step into the threshold. "We're on season two, episode thirteen, by the way."

"Ah, right." Wyatt shut the door, following me into the living room.

I had been in his place above the bunkhouse once, and even then, I mainly stayed in the kitchen, but I took in my surroundings. It was probably no more than five hundred square feet, the living room and kitchen sharing a space, the queen-sized bed just a few steps to my left. It was nothing special, nothing to fawn over. No part of it screamed Wyatt Hartwell. I twisted my lips and plopped on the couch in front of a small flatscreen.

"This is where you bring girls?" I asked, instantly regretting it.

"I haven't brought a girl here—or been to a girls' place"—he plopped down next to me—"in months." He tossed me the remote. "Season two, episode thirteen. How was girls' night?"

"Good," I replied, cueing up the episode. "I mentioned the book club."

"Yeah?" He raised his brows. "What did they say?"

"That we should join one that meets at the local bookstore. Abi said they read mainly spicy books." I gave him a sideways glance.

His eyebrows raised even higher. "Oh...really? If you have Tik-Tok, you can get some great recommendations from there."

"No. No TikTok. And I won't be joining the Smutty Grannies."

"The Smutty Grannies? Oh, that's fantastic, and I really think you should join."

"I won't be doing that."

"Come on, you can't just live off of rodeos and *Once Upon a Time* your entire life. Join the book club."

"There's more in my future than a TV show and rodeos, you know. I'll have to retire sometime."

"Tell me."

I met his gaze. "Tell you...what?"

"Your future. What does your future hold after you're retired, after we're done watching this TV show?" He shifted himself on the couch so one leg rested between us, his knee close to mine, his arm draped on the back of the couch.

My future. I could count on one hand those who asked me what I wanted to do with my future. My dad, my first boyfriend Orion, Cash, and now Wyatt. I licked my lips...did I want to tell him? Telling him about my mom was easier than this. This dream was mine and mine alone, but the look on his face, the eagerness he was showing to hear everything...I trusted him to hold it close, too.

"A horse sanctuary," I answered, my voice soft.

His eyes twitched, his lips curving up into a smile.

"I want to have a place where retired racehorses can go to live their last years. I want to take care of sick or older horses that were going to be sent to slaughter. I want to find companions for blind horses, and I want horses to feel safe and comfortable, taken care of. I doubt it will ever happen, but" —I pulled my legs up to my chest—"that's my future."

Wyatt's smile stayed soft, his eyes flitting from my own, dancing as he searched my face. "What would you call it?" He finally asked.

"I..." I stumbled. "I don't know. I never really thought about it, to be honest. I have no idea where I'd put it. I'd need a lot of land and a building and a barn and...well...it's going to be a long time until I can make that happen. I'm only twenty-two, almost twenty-three—" I stopped, my jaw dropping as I remembered the small tidbit that Abi shared earlier. "You had a birthday, and you didn't tell me?"

Wyatt shrugged, pushing himself off the back of the couch with his elbow. "It wasn't a big deal."

"Not a big deal...you turned thirty. That's a big one."

"Well then, good thing I spent it exactly how I wanted to, huh?" He smiled at me. "This sanctuary, let's call it 'Once Upon a Rescue'—"

"Yeah, no. That's not what I'm calling it."

"It'll happen."

I tilted my head, my hair flopping down over my shoulder. I noticed his gaze trail down my shoulders, lingering there a little longer before his eyes snapped back up to me.

"Until then,"—he shifted again—"you went up the standings. You're second."

"Second? Last I saw, I was third!"

"Rising up. And it's only May," he whispered, his voice husky as he leaned forward.

My entire body screamed to jump into his arms, pull him close to me, and tell him that I wouldn't be second if it weren't for the support that he gave me. All the double-checking my schedules, all the times he saddled and fed my horses as I checked in. Maybe my mom was right, that I couldn't do this on my own, but he made me feel like I could—and damn, I wouldn't be here if it wasn't for him.

But instead of tackling him, I bit my lip and sighed, saying instead, "I should probably tell my dad. He'll be excited."

Shifting on my side, I pulled my phone from my pocket, pulling up the group chat.

Me

Hey! Check out the standings. Second.

The message turned to read, but a few moments passed before the dots appeared, followed by a screenshot of my smiling face in the number two slot on the PRCA Website.

The excitement from the news drained as it hit that mom didn't even take the time to message me back herself. I read the message a few times and then showed the phone to Wyatt. He read the texts and met my gaze, his smile never faltering.

"I guess now's not the best time to tell you I can't go with you in a few weeks?"

"Really?" I scrunched my nose, lowering my phone down to the couch, my shoulders slumping. "The only reason I'll accept is if you're announcing at a rodeo."

He drew in a sharp breath with his teeth, "No. If only. I need to help Cash with wedding stuff."

I relaxed. "Oh, okay. I'll accept that, too. I'll hate not having you there, believe it or not...I really enjoy you there."

"I figured, but hey,"—he sat back—"I made sure your mom won't be at any of the rodeos. Well...I made sure Miss Rodeo Montana wasn't going to be there. I figured if she was there, your mom was there. I can't have her killing your high."

That time, I did tackle him, wrapping my arms around his neck as we both fell backwards on the couch.

TWENTY-TWO

Wyatt

Please tell me you saw that!

You're going to hate me more than you already do…

YOU MISSED IT.

I didn't mean to.

Hartwell…

Me

sends mirror selfie

Quinn

Okay, fine. I accept for wedding things. But Wyatt! 13.8!

Me

Fuck yeah, Compton.

"WHO ARE YOU SMILING at?" Cash's reflection came up behind me, stretching his neck to look at my phone.

Lachlan, Cash, and I came to the small men's shop, the same one that fitted my dad for his wedding, and Lachlan for his. Henry Collerwood still ran the shop. Though it was updated to fit the times, he still ran things the same way. Currently, I stood on a pedestal, three mirrors surrounding me, allowing me to see all my best views. I had on gray slacks, a black belt, and a white button-down layered with a gray vest hanging open to reveal the deep, vibrant purple tie. Cash was donning the same ensemble, but topped with a white hat, the black rim around the crown replaced with the same color purple. When Lachlan stepped out of his dressing room, his sleeves were slightly rolled up, showing off his tattoos, and tie undone. You could see it in his face that he was not thrilled with the color selection.

"How come we have purple, and the girls have turquoise?" He grumbled, shoving his hands in his slack pockets.

Not dropping my phone, I snapped a photo of Lachlan and sent it right off to Quinn.

Quinn

Damn, he's looking good. Remind me, is he single?

Me

And too damn old for you.

"Quinn picked the turquoise from what I hear, and it worked on both her and Kyla." Cash turned to the mirror and began fiddling with his tie.

"Quinn looks amazing in anything," I replied absent-mindedly, watching those little dots dance on my screen.

"So it's Quinn that got you all smiley over there?" Cash nodded his head in my direction. At the same time, a text came through.

Quinn

I'm all for an age gap romance. Give him my number.

Me

Fuck. No.

"We're texting. Is that a bad thing?" I shrugged, stepping off the platform at the same time Lachlan stepped up.

"Seeing as the woman has shot you down more times than you care to admit, it's a bit strange. What changed?" Lachlan worked on his sleeves once more, rolling them up to his elbows before moving to his tie.

What had changed? If I were to rewind the clock to when my fist hit Archie's nose...the world seemed to slow down. Even though I was trying to act like nothing was different, life moved in slow motion. It wasn't until I accepted it that I finally broke, not entirely sure what was going on with my life, until she raced back in it in January. These past months with her were as if everything was being pieced back together. Rodeos, pizza, sushi, TV shows—she was bringing me back to life without even knowing it.

Everything made sense with Quinn. Natural even. I couldn't help but flirt; I couldn't help but stare and push down that urge to kiss her, but she had become so much more than a girl I wanted. She had become what I would consider a close friend, and by the way she was texting me—by the way she hugged me that night—I'd say I was a close friend to her, too.

Everything changed, but at the same time, everything stayed the same.

"Nothing changed," I settled on admitting, locking my phone before I had a chance to read her reply.

"You're not playing her along, are you?" Cash asked, furrowing his brow at me in the mirror.

"God, not you, too. Abi and I already talked about this." I slumped my shoulders.

"Well." Lachlan turned. "How many women have you been with in the past two years?"

I squinted and tried to pull up a number. It wasn't massive by any means, but the number was up there. "Am I counting repeats as one?"

Cash and Lachlan froze, both staring at me with an eyebrow raised.

"I'm kidding—"

"Are you?" Lachlan stepped off the platform.

"You can't blame us for worrying about her. She's young and doesn't need to be—"

"I'm not playing her." I held out my hands, stopping Cash from saying anything else. "The last girl I had over was Melanie...and if I remember correctly, Cash, you had no issues with her being over. This is Quinn. This is different. I haven't been with anyone since she came back into town, and I don't plan on seeing anyone else. I need to talk to her, tell her how I really feel, and see what happens."

Cash narrowed his eyes. "Hold up. How you really feel?"

"Don't act like Abi hasn't told you." I folded my arms and looked at my soon-to-be brother-in-law.

"She hasn't. I don't pry. She tells me things if she needs to. When it comes to you, she's pretty private—she was even shocked when I told her I wanted you by my side at the wedding. She's pretty sure we still hate each other."

"Yeah, well, right now, I do," I clipped.

"Can we circle back to this how you really feel thing, because that's new." Lachlan spun his finger in a circle in front of him, rewinding the last ten seconds. "I thought you were just hitting on her like you've always done."

"I mean...it may have started that way, but now—" I heaved a sigh. "I really...really...*really* like her. I don't want to say the other word quite yet, even though I know damn sure that's where it's headed. I don't know if she feels the same or if she really sees me as a friend, but…" I dropped my arms and looked at them. Cash done up to the nines, looking exactly as he will in a few weeks. Lachlan a scruffy 'nice' mess with his tie half done, his sleeves rolled up, and a glare on his face. They both eagerly waited for me to finish. "I want to tell her how I feel soon, and we'll see what happens. If she'll have me, I'm hers. If she wants me as a friend, I'll be that, too."

The thought of telling Quinn how I felt came as easy as deciding to announce at a rodeo. Every time I was with her, I was warm. Whenever she smiled, I felt a buzz fly through my body. That spark of electricity happened whenever she touched my skin, even if it was a light brush, it was there. When her arms wrapped around my neck, I inhaled her coconut scent and fell a little harder each time. I waited for her texts to come and counted down the minutes until I was next to her again. I wanted all of her, and I hoped she wanted all of me.

I just had to tell her.

TWENTY-THREE

Quinn

IN THE PAST FIVE months, I'd gotten dressed up twice. Dressing up made me feel fun and free, and I didn't get to do it enough. But this time, standing next to Kyla in the same turquoise flowy dress, my hair with a curl and makeup bringing out my best features, I felt like a princess from my show. And having Wyatt keep sneaking grins at me while Abi and Cash exchanged their vows didn't help the feeling.

Each groomsman, including Stetson, wore the outfit Wyatt sent me a photo of, but paired with a gray cowboy hat, the same purple band around the crown. Even Rhett—sitting in the audience with Poppy in her turquoise dress—matched the men. Abi was stunning in her cream gown, her blonde hair curled around her shoulders—and the looks that Cash kept giving her were everything. Love etched into his eyes, not once faltering from her. I hated that I couldn't see her reaction, knowing what these two went through to get here.

Abi's father, Leo, stood in front of Abi and Cash, and when he announced them, Mr. and Mrs. Cash Callahan, Cash took a step towards his bride and wrapped his arm around Abi's waist, dipping her as he kissed her. Everyone in the crowd cheered for them. And my eyes hit Wyatt's.

He flashed me a cocky grin that turned into a wide, gorgeous smile, and my stomach flipped.

My weekend without him was fine. I came in the top three on each ride, and I even visited a few bars on my own—but I missed him. I missed watching the show with him until I fell asleep, I missed his cheers that, somehow, I always managed to hear during a ride, and I missed his arms around me when I made it back to the trailer. We texted every day, and he would call right before I would climb into bed, but it didn't amount to him being there.

When he waggled his eyebrows at me, I gave him a slight eye roll, and then Abi, Cash, and Stetson walked back down the small aisle, followed by Lachlan and Kyla, and finally Wyatt and me. He held out his arm to me, and I lightly held onto his elbow as we passed the six rows of guests. The wedding party, including Rhett, was whisked away by the husband-and-wife photography duo to the field behind the stables, where six horses waited for us.

"She's really making us get on a horse?" I leaned in and whispered to Wyatt.

The photographers started shouting who belonged to which horse, which honestly made me laugh because—duh. I couldn't imagine Abi getting on Hook in her wedding gown.

"You doubted it?" he whispered back.

"Who saddled them?" I asked, reaching up to Hook, loving the way he was decked out in a turquoise ribbon hanging from his neck. I glanced over at Rusty, Wyatt's horse, noticing the same ribbon around his neck.

"Lach and I did, while you girls were getting all dolled up." His arm moved, and his fingers gracefully intertwined with mine. It was a natural feeling to link our fingers together; I didn't even flinch. "You look gorgeous, by the way. The most stunning woman here tonight."

I felt the heat rush to my cheeks, but I forced it down, pulling my hand away from his. The spark lingered. "You're supposed to say that to Abi. No one is prettier than the bride."

"No," he sighed, reaching out for Rusty's lead. "Cash is supposed to say that Abi, Rhett is supposed to say it to Kyla, but I"—he took a step towards me, our gazes locked—"I want to say it to you."

Our eyes stayed locked, and my lips parted as a small gasp left my lungs. He *wanted* to say it to *me*. The air stilled as we breathed the same breath. My brain was filtering, trying to find the perfect comeback to get us out of the tension, but I didn't have time to say or think of anything before the photographers began to circle everyone, the woman holding the camera obviously a little intimidated by the horses.

"Alright, men, can you help the ladies onto their horses? We just have a few shots with the wedding party, and then you're free to go mingle with the guests until we get the couple shots done." The woman shouted for all of us to hear, and the six of us moved.

Wyatt placed his hand on the small of my back, gracefully taking the small bouquet of lilies I was holding. I slipped my boot in the stirrup, commenting to Abi about how grateful I was for the boots as I hoisted myself onto Hook. Wyatt helped me smooth out my skirt, then handed me my flowers. I watched how, in one swift motion, he swung his leg over Rusty and settled himself in the saddle. He gave me one last wink and then smiled for the camera.

Wyatt dancing with a baby on his hip was hard not to watch. Poppy was all giggles as he swung his hips back and forth, flipping her in circles and dipping her down as he sang every single word to "Any Man of Mine." He didn't even notice me staring; he was just having fun with his niece. Kyla had a close eye on him, her and Rhett dancing alongside him, but I could tell she was having just as much fun watching Poppy as I was. I just hoped the photographer caught it in motion. Resting my chin in my palm, my free fingers rubbing the fabric of my skirt together, I took in the entire Hartwell family dancing and laughing together, even Lachlan looked like he was having a decent time.

Abi spun, almost falling into Cash's arms, before she let out a laugh and pulled him close to whisper something to him. He nodded, kissed her, and then she lifted her skirt and made her way to where I sat alone at the table, a little skip to her step.

"Okay." The bride plopped down in the chair next to me, her cheeks flushed and hair slightly tousled, yet still gorgeous. "My feet hurt."

"You're wearing boots." I gestured to her feet. "The same style boots you wear every day. How do they hurt?" I chuckled at her.

"I don't normally dance in them, or walk a ton, or leave them on...all...day. Plus..." Abi lifted her leg. "These are new. See how not covered in mud they are?"

"They're perfect, Abi." I smiled at her. "But really, shouldn't you be out there?" I nodded towards the crowd, where Cash danced next to Stetson, looking like a complete idiot as George Straight played over the speaker. "Maybe get your husband off the dance floor before he embarrasses himself?"

Abi turned and blushed as she watched her new husband. "Let's be real, when does he not embarrass himself?"

"He's a pretty solid guy...this is the strangest I've seen him. But seriously,"—I leaned my elbow on the table and bore into her—"get out there with him and then make him rub your feet later."

"Well, what kind of host would I be if I saw one of my bridesmaids sitting here alone and I didn't pay attention to her?" Abi leaned forward to mirror my posture, giving me a wry smile.

"I'm people watching," I said, straightening my back, noticing Abi do the same. "Also, I'm wondering why in the world you didn't invite Oakes Ashford?"

"The bull rider who rents the arena? Why would I invite him?" Abi chuckled.

"Cash tells me he's here at least three times a year, and they get along." I shrugged and raised a palm. "Plus..." I shrunk. "He's nice to look at."

Abi let out a loud laugh, which gained the attention of Wyatt and Cash, that is, until "Boot Scootin' Boogie" started to play and the dancing crowd cheered. I raised an eyebrow over at Abi.

"'Boot Scootin Boogie'?"

"Wyatt told me to play it." She waggled her eyebrows at me, biting her bottom lip.

"Of course he did." I held back my chuckle, shaking my head, looking over at Wyatt, who simply stuck his tongue out between his teeth at me as he and Cash started the moves, Poppy still giggling in his arms. I couldn't stop watching the entire time...that stupid grin on my face that I couldn't seem to get rid of.

"People watching, huh?" Abi asked, her tone flattening as her grin spread. "Are you sure you're not Wyatt watching?"

I jerked my head to her, "I told you—"

"Yeah, yeah." She waved me off. "Just friends. Listen." She leaned forward again. "I normally don't go airing my brothers' secrets around, we're each other's safe space, you know, but...Quinn..." Her voice lowered. "I've never seen him like this. He's been different these past six months, almost as if something or"—she nudged my knee—"someone got his ass to grow up a little bit. He likes you...really likes you. So if he decides to say something to you tonight...just...hear him out."

Hear him out.

My heart lurched into my throat. I had to swallow it down.

"Mrs. Callahan!" Cash shouted from the dance floor. "I will make them replay this song!"

"Oh God. He already Mrs. Callahaned me." She flipped her hair but turned back to me, the grin wild on her face. "Just...hear him out."

I nodded once, not able to do much more than that.

"Miss Quinn!"

Before I could black out from what Abi had just told me, Stetson appeared, his hands latching onto mine before I could react.

"Uncle Wyatt says you *have* to dance to this one."

I inhaled and blinked, pulling myself from the stupor. "Oh, did he?" I smiled.

"Yes, come on! I need a partner!"

I laughed as Stetson dragged me out with him, placing me in the front of the line, sandwiched between him and Wyatt. I let the music and the steps drown out everything Abi had said. *He likes you, really likes you...just hear him out.*

Hear him out? What if I didn't want to hear what he was going to say? What if I already had an idea as to what he was going to say? He's told me over and over again that I was the only girl he was chasing. That I was the one he wanted to kiss. Hell, he spent his birthday with me without even telling me it was his birthday, and then he said it was exactly where he wanted to be.

I knew to him it was more than friendship. I knew he wanted something more...

I just...

Didn't want to ruin what we were.

It didn't matter what my heart was yelling at me—that maybe he was worth trying, that maybe, *just* maybe, he wasn't who I thought him to be at all. He was chaos, but maybe my structure needed the chaos? Maybe his chaos needed my structure? With him, I had done things that I hadn't thought about in a long time. A game of pool, late nights watching a show, singing along with Shania Twain during the long road trips, heading to a bar to celebrate wins, and opening up about a hard part of my life that I'd rather forget.

But I did all those things because he was becoming a friend.

And I couldn't—*wouldn't*—ruin that.

Hear him out.

"Alright, Stet," Wyatt said, his voice husky and deep. "My turn to dance with Miss Quinn. Can you take Poppy back to her mom?" He leaned over, handing Stetson his cousin.

Stetson rolled his eyes. "Okay, fine. But you can't fall in love with her."

Wyatt and I furrowed our brows and looked at Stetson at the same time.

"Excuse me?" Wyatt asked.

"Uncle Rhett fell in love with Aunt Kyla. I like Miss Quinn. Don't. Fall. In. Love." Stetson glared at his uncle and then turned to walk back into the crowd.

"Well, that was terrifying." I looked at my *friend.*

"Apparently, Stetson is into older women." Wyatt reached out, his palms up. "Dance with me?" he asked, the smile steady on his lips.

Line dancing ended and was replaced by a slow and smooth country song. I knew the deep voice that drew the couples together, and I couldn't help but reach out and take Wyatt's hand. He pulled me close, his scent enveloping me. There was a hint of hay to his scent, and I knew it had attached to him since he began working in the stables. It worked for him. No heavy cologne like I had smelled before, no Axe body spray to cover up anything he may not want there. It was just him. Just Wyatt. Hay and strawberries...and the sunset.

I wrapped my arms around his neck and let my body lie flush against his, and he gently began to sway us.

"Have I told you that you look breathtaking tonight?" he said softly into my ear.

"I believe you used the term gorgeous, but yes, you have. Think of another pick-up line." I arched my back to look up at him. His eyes were hooded as he was studying me, sending my stomach into flips already.

Flips I promptly ignored because we were just friends.

I've ignored them before...I can ignore them again.

"That wasn't a pickup line, simply stating a fact."

"Well." I swallowed. "Thank you. You don't look half bad yourself."

"It's the hat, isn't it?" He grinned. "Cash wouldn't let me wear my ball cap."

"Good. I would have protested and burned the ball cap if you had worn it. Even Stetson is wearing a cowboy hat. You had to match them," I joked, happy that the serious tone that was there less than five seconds ago had already seemed to lift.

"You wouldn't burn my hat."

"Oh, yes, I would."

"I'd make you buy me a new one."

"A new cowboy hat, you mean."

He raised a single eyebrow, his smile spreading from ear to ear.

I cleared my throat. "You do look handsome tonight, Wyatt."

"Thank you," he said softly, his hands sliding from the small of my back up my spine.

He stopped swaying.

I stopped swaying.

His eyes darted as he looked at me, his lips parting slightly, his breath becoming uneven.

My breath became just as uneven, just as ragged as I inhaled sharply, filling my lungs with the courage to...stop.

"I..." I stumbled. "I need you to stop looking at me like that."

"Like what?" he asked, his voice just as unsteady as mine.

"Like you want to kiss me."

We've had this conversation before. I knew we had. And by the low grin on his face, he remembered it too.

"I've already told you I do. You know you're the only one I want to kiss."

I slid my hands down to his chest, feeling the way his lean muscles sculpted even under his layers of clothing, and I shivered. If I gave in to this right now and let him kiss me—I could feel him. I could take him in and relish in the idea that he wanted me...

But that would risk...

Him.

I pushed myself away and, for the millionth time, swallowed the pit that was settled in my throat.

"Wyatt...I..." I met his gaze. "We're friends. I..."

"Quinn," he sighed. "Please, just hear me out."

Hear him out.

I turned, my feet moving on their own volition as I barreled my way through the crowd, the song we had been dancing to ending suddenly. Were we really dancing for that long? Did our silly banter about his hat choice and staring at each other really last more than three minutes? If so...why did it feel like seconds?

"Quinn, wait," Wyatt called after me, his footsteps not far from mine. Soon, he was in front of me, stopping dead in his tracks, forcing me to do the same. "Don't—"

"I can't hear you out," I said suddenly.

Wyatt froze, his arms drooping to his sides.

"Wyatt." I took a single step towards him. "I don't think you know how much you mean to me. You've become so much more than a friend. You're..." I fought for the words, coming up short when the only one hit my mind. What did Abi call it? "A safe space for me. Someone I can trust, and seriously, I never thought I'd say that about you. I love having you around. I love talking with you and watching our show, and eating random foods. I love everything about you—but as my closest friend."

Wyatt rubbed his lips together. "Friends?"

I nodded, biting the inside of my cheek. "I can't let anything screw it up. Please..." I whispered, begging him. "We can't screw this up."

His gaze never once left mine. We were quiet for a moment, longer than the song we had just danced to, it seemed, but finally Wyatt took the steps that lay between us. He leaned in, kissed my cheek, and whispered.

"We won't screw anything up. I promise. Friends."

Then he walked past me, leaving me staring into the open field as the sun set slowly over Hartwell Hills.

TWENTY-FOUR

Wyatt

F RIENDS.

We were friends.

And I couldn't screw that up.

I didn't want to screw that up.

I wanted to spend every waking moment with her. I wanted to watch her fall asleep, and I wanted to see her wake up. I wanted her to shove her freezing cold toes under my thighs as we watched the show, and I wanted to find another show to watch after this one was over. I wanted to keep guessing what foods she liked, find out which ones made her hum as she took that first bite. There were so many things I wanted with her.

And if the only way to get those things was to be her friend...

Then I'd take it.

She came back into the wedding reception a few moments after I did, and I shifted, removing myself from the self-pity of being shoved into the friend zone. I pulled her close for a side hug, tempted to kiss her temple, but stopped myself.

I wanted so badly to tell her how I felt, drop that other L word that I had never said to someone who didn't have the last name Hartwell. Her words, *"I can't hear you out, you've become so much more than a friend. You're a safe space,"* rang in my ear on repeat, and there was no way I was going to get them out anytime soon.

Letting her go and losing all the warmth that came with her, I went straight to my brother and held out my hands.

"Give me the baby," I demanded.

Rhett held his daughter a little tighter. "Excuse me?"

"I need a distraction, and it's her bedtime. You know I'm the Poppy Whisperer, so hand her over. You and your wife stay out a little longer." I waggled my fingers in a 'gimme' motion.

Poppy smiled and let out a small giggle, but her tiny arms reached out for me just the same.

"You sure?" Rhett asked, adjusting his hat once Poppy was free from his arms.

"Yup." I popped the P, giving Poppy my cheesiest grin. "Maybe we can watch *Bluey.*"

Poppy babbled, her hands reaching up and yanking the hat from my head. I could feel my hair standing on end—the gel I had used to try to tame it before the ceremony did absolutely nothing to help.

"I'll have Poppy asleep before you guys get home." I gestured towards Kyla, who stood next to Abi and Quinn, leaning in and listening to whatever Quinn was telling them.

Most likely, that she had to shoot me down—again.

"You okay?" Rhett tilted his head, coming into my vision, blocking Quinn out.

I nodded, smiled, and looked at my niece. "I'm perfect. Come on, Poppy Girl, let's get you to bed."

Poppy responded by shoving her entire fist in her mouth.

"She's teething. You can give her some Motrin, the bottle is in the fridge." Rhett's voice faded as I began to walk away, waving my hand in the air.

I gave the woman of my dreams one last look, happy to see the smile had returned to her face. Tickling Poppy, I made my way over to Quinn, noticing how her smile only slightly faded when I approached them. Kyla reached out for her daughter, but I turned my hip.

"Nope, I got her. I offered to put her to bed, just"—I turned to Quinn—"wanted to say good night. Thanks for the dance." I gave her a wink and a grin, then turned my back.

"Wyatt, wait." I felt her hand on my elbow, and I spun around, staring into her emerald eyes. "Please tell me we're okay."

"Quinn," I sighed, stepping close to her so only she could hear me. "We're more than okay. I promise. We have Reno to plan. Yeah?" I asked, raising my brow.

I could see her shoulders relax. She nodded. "Yeah, it's in a week."

"I'll come by tomorrow to double-check everything. Sound good?"

Her smile grew, but only by a smidge. The fear that we weren't okay still lingered in her gaze. She inhaled, her shoulders rising as she took a breath.

"I promise, Quinn." I leaned in and kissed her cheek once more, feeling the zing that traveled through my lips the second they touched her skin. "We're good. We'll meet up tomorrow."

Her cheeks tinted a slight shade of pink as she rolled her lips. "Okay." She smiled and turned to Poppy. "Good night, sweet girl. Be nice to your uncle."

"She will be. I'm the Poppy Whisperer," I sang, trying and failing to make my voice sound like a psychic.

But Quinn laughed, so it must have worked.

A bottle, a dose of Motrin, and forty-five minutes later, Poppy was asleep in my arms as I swayed back and forth in front of her crib. My vest was hanging over her crib, and her tiny fingers had wrapped their way around my purple tie with a slight smile on her lips. Such a peace to her—not even realizing what was bursting through my chest. I lay her down gently, brushing the hair from her forehead, stood and loosened my tie, still watching my niece take soft breaths.

"Ah, to be a baby," I whispered, leaning my elbows on the edge of her crib. "You got it made, you know. Just—when you get older, don't fall for a guy who doesn't love you back. It makes life harder to love someone so much, knowing they don't want you the same way you want them. Maybe it's for the better? Maybe I'm just *friend* material? But with her—fuck Poppy Girl, I love her. She's worth it. She really is. You'll find someone like your mom and dad, Cash and Abi...you, Poppy, will be loved always. Just don't screw up like I did and fall for the wrong girl."

Rubbing my knuckle against her cheek, I pushed myself off the crib and left her room, my heart a little heavier than normal. I kept loosening my tie, hoping that if I relieved the tension there, it would relieve it in other places. I even went as far as to start unbuttoning my shirt, pulling it away from my neck.

I wasn't sure if I liked this feeling or hated it.

I wasn't used to it.

Kyla was leaning against the hallway arch once I made it a few steps out of Poppy's room, a soft smile upon her lips, and before I could react to the possibility of me saying fuck in front of her sleeping daughter—she held out her arms and pulled me into her.

"You didn't screw up," she whispered, and I heaved a sigh and held my sister-in-law a little tighter.

Friends. I could do friends.

Checking her Reno schedule was something we had planned, and it would be weird if I came without food and beer—right? So, I ordered her favorite pineapple pizza with cauliflower crust from June's, grabbed the beer I watched her drink three of that first night, and opened her door.

The day I came over and she yelled, "It's open!" gave me a new hope for our relationship, and ever since then, her front door had been open for me. And tonight, I walked in to not only boots everywhere, but hats and blouses and Wranglers strewn about all over the living room.

"Where are we supposed to sit?" I chuckled, tilting my torso to set the beer and pizza down on the coffee table.

Quinn rounded the corner from the kitchen. My *friend* basically hopped in, her laptop outstretched in front of her.

"I'm packing. You check, I pack."

I bent back up, taking her laptop from her, meeting her emerald eyes.

Fuck, she's gorgeous. Confidence radiated off her, and the smile she carried as she backed up and did a little jig made the room brighter. Even now—wearing a tank and pajama shorts, no makeup, her hair in a messy bun—I could practically see how soft her skin was, and my mind wondered if it felt how it looked. The curves of her body that had been visible even in winter clothing were now more prominent. I was basically being held together by a thread. If only she had let me talk, I could be pulling her close to me. I could be kissing her in the midst of all her things, feeling her against me as we moved together, humming in tandem as we explored.

Shit...it was going to be a lot harder than I thought.

Being her friend was going to be the death of me.

"We leave in four days, and you're packing?" I moved a blouse on top of another, finding a place to sit on the couch.

"I have a system." She came around the edge of the couch, grabbing two of the beers, popping them open, and handing one to me. "It's six days in Reno. Five rides—six if I make the qualifier—"

"You will," I interrupted, looking up at her through my lashes.

She narrowed her eyes and gave me a tilted grin. If only I could kiss that grin.

"I may not, but that's okay if I don't." She held her palms out in front of her. "I'm pretty sure I booked everything correctly, too. Two hotel rooms, two horse stalls, and I made sure I was registered for all the events. You would be proud."

"Damn," I chuckled, typing in her password—because yes, I knew her password to her phone and laptop. *Was that a perk of being a friend, or did that mean there was more here?* "Why am I even here?"

"Shut it. I need you to double-check me." She lifted her bottle to her lips. "Just to be safe. Eventually, I'll get this done by myself."

"Ah, then you won't need me anymore." I gave her a cocky smirk. I prayed she would always need—or want—me around.

"Impossible." She pointed at the laptop. "Check. I'm going to go get my garment bags." She spun on her heel and dashed up the stairs.

I checked, and checked, and checked, and...she had everything handled. Two hotel rooms. Two stalls. Five rodeo registrations. There was one more thing. I pulled open a tab to the Reno rodeo, clicking on the royalty tab, and skimmed. We'd miss the Miss Reno Rodeo pageant, but that wasn't what I was looking for. I found the list of royalty who would be attending. No, Miss Rodeo Montana. My grin turned into a full-fledged smile. Without this distraction, I had no doubt that she'd make it to the championship night.

Seconds later, a few garment bags were tossed down the stairs, landing with a thump at the front door.

"Need help?" I called.

"Nope!" Her voice echoed through the stairwell. I just laughed and returned to the task at hand.

If it isn't Wyatt Hartwell, I see across the lobby.

I read the text, furrowing my brow, looking up, and scanning the room for my friend. I hadn't seen Hawkins in months—not since that night I ruined my career—and he was honestly the last person I'd thought I would see here. I caught onto his waving arms instantly, and I shook my head, shoving my phone in my pocket.

Quinn and I had arrived in Reno only a few hours before, and after we settled the boys, we came straight to The Grand Sierra Hotel. The next day was going to be busy, especially for Quinn—and I knew she would want to go right to bed. I even doubted we'd watch *Once Upon a Time* tonight.

I spun, placing my hand on her shoulder, giving her the heads up I'd be right back as she checked us in, then sprinted across the lobby to my friend.

"Hey Hawk!" I grabbed his hand, pulling him to my shoulder to wrap my free arm around him. "Been a long time. I didn't think you'd be here."

He pulled away and shrugged. Hawkins was built, his black hair always sticking up at odd angles, even under his hat.

"Didn't think you'd come. Sorry, man, they chose my name over yours." He spoke quietly, dipping his chin.

I grinned. "You announcing the next couple of nights?" I asked, raising a brow.

Hawkins met my gaze and nodded. "Yeah. Up until the championship. I'll sneak you into the box. Sam's here too—not working though, just hanging around."

"I'd love to get in the box, but"—I turned to look at Quinn over my shoulder. She bobbed her head and took the key from the receptionist—"I'm here helping Quinn."

"Compton?" He raised a brow. "The same girl—"

"Yeah." I chuckled, stopping him before he could go any further. "One in the same. She's riding, heading to the NFR. And traveling with a high maintenance—"

"Who's high maintenance?" Quinn came up to my side, slapping my hotel room key on my chest. "Not me."

I barked out a laugh. "No. Your asshole of a horse."

"Oh, Hook?" Quinn smiled, and damn if my knees didn't turn to Jello. "The one you love more than your horse back home? That one?" She teased, then turned to Hawkins. "Hi, I'm Quinn." She held out her hand.

Hawkins smiled and grasped her hand, shaking it lightly. "Hawkins Warren, nice to meet you finally. I've seen you ride, and Wyatt here certainly loves to follow your career. I've heard a lot about you from this guy."

Quinn raised her brow and looked over at me, "Is that so, Hartwell?"

I sucked in air between my teeth. "I would lie but..."

"Wouldn't do you any good," Quinn quipped. "I'll let you two catch up, I'm beat so"—she jerked her thumb over her shoulder—"would you hate me if I skipped the show tonight?"

"Not at all. Get some rest. I won't be far behind."

She bobbed her eyebrows once, gave Hawkins another nod, then left me there with her coconut scent still lingering.

"About time you settled down." Hawkins drew out.

I snapped my neck to him. "Settled down?"

"You've been pinning after her for how long now?" He put his hands on his hips, "I mean, she's the reason why you're not getting any jobs, isn't she?"

"She's not *the* reason why I'm not getting any jobs, and no...I haven't settled down. We're just friends," I grumbled, hating the way it slid off my tongue.

"Sure, with the way she was just looking at you before that elevator opened, the way she didn't take your shit...you two are not just friends. I'm happy for you. Glad it finally happened."

I bent and grabbed my duffel bag, tossing it over my shoulder. "Nothing happened, Hawk. I can assure you, she made it very clear we are just friends."

"Ah, great." He slapped my shoulder. "Then come on out tonight. There's a lot of local places we can hit up, a lot of bunnies just waiting—"

"Nah." I shook my head. "I'm actually tired. We had a long day in the car and then settling her asshole of a horse. Sorry, man. Maybe another night? With Sam?"

Hawkins raised a brow, giving me the same expression Lachlan would when I would tell him I was going straight home and then ended up in the bed of someone else. No doubt Hawkins was thinking I was headed right up to Quinn's room.

"I'm serious," I groaned. "She doesn't even know the reason why I'm not getting picked by committees. Just that I did something stupid and fucked up, and now no one will hire me. I'm not planning on telling her either—at least not here. She doesn't need to know some asshole was talking shit on her when she's worked so hard to get here."

"Sooo, you're just...friends?"

I nodded. "Just friends. Plain as that. Now..." I situated my duffel bag on my shoulder again. "When does Sam get in?"

TWENTY-FIVE

Quinn

WYATT TOLD ME HE checked, double checked, and *triple* checked, even that Miss Rodeo Montana wouldn't be anywhere near the Reno Rodeo today. So, someone please explain to me why I was staring at my mother from across the parking lot?

It looked like she just got here, three other girls climbing from her truck that read *Miss Rodeo Montana Kelly Fugal* in big, bold, red letters. None of them was dolled up. Kelly at least had her sash on, but other than that, they looked exhausted from what I presumed was their drive.

I came in second. I just had a fantastic time, and I was on my way to find Wyatt when I saw her. I took a step back, hiding myself behind my gigantic black horse, and slowly walked past their truck and to my trailer. Wyatt was there, bouncing on his heels just as I expected him to be, and when I latched Hook onto the side of the trailer, he scooped me up and spun me in a circle.

I held on tight and buried my face in the crook of his neck, not even caring that my white hat fell to the ground. I inhaled his scent and forced my brain to let go of the image of my mother and focus on the thought of him. It was hard for him to be here, too. He told me last night that the committee chose his friend Hawkins to announce instead of him, and he admitted that it stung slightly. When I told him he could go home, he quickly made sure that I knew he was here for me, and the fact that he wasn't in the booth didn't matter.

If he could be present for me, knowing that there was something better for him, then I could at least try to be present for him when the knowledge that my mother was here was shoved in the back of my brain.

"Fifteen point seven, Compton!" He put me down, and I instantly missed his scent. "You just gotta make the top ten to be in the championship. Well on the way!"

Looking off to the side, I dipped my chin to see if I could catch any glimpse of my mother. "Well, since I didn't compete in the first couple of rounds, we'll see."

"Nah." He used his thumb and forefinger to lift my chin to him. It was then that I noticed he had my hat in his other hand. When did he bend down to get it? He plopped it back on my head. "You got this in the bag. You know that?"

My shoulders slumped, and I gave him a soft nod. "Let's get Hook settled and then head back to the hotel, I'm tired..."

He pinched his brow slightly, his smile fading before he blinked away his expression, giving me his bright smile once again. "As you wish."

"Ah...*The Princess Bride* has officially entered our friendship." I unclipped Hook's breast collar, giving Wyatt a smirk, grateful that I could think about something else for a moment. "One of my favorite movies."

He took a sharp inhale through his teeth. "So, if I tell you I've never seen it—"

"No," I cut him off, pointing a deep yet sarcastic glare his way. "That's a deal breaker. It's a classic."

"I was doing other things as a kid; I didn't really watch movies." He tilted his head, giving Hook his attention as he spoke. "I mean, I watched *Die Hard*."

"Of course you did." I chuckled. "I'm fixing this. *The Princess Bride* was what sparked my love for fairy tales. You can't be my friend and not know that movie. How did you know to say 'as you wish' then?"

He laughed, and I couldn't help but smile. I loved his laugh. It filled my stomach with butterflies every time and always managed to drown out all the noise of any surrounding area.

"Just because I haven't seen it doesn't mean I don't know girls go feral for that line." He scoffed, his expression turning cocky as he pulled the leather on Hook's saddle loose.

I tightened my lips. *Oh.*

I pushed that little comment aside, blinking a few times to really erase it. "Well, I'm still fixing this. We're watching it tonight."

"Hell, no. Hook just agreed to take them to Neverland. We're watching our show."

Our show.

"Fine, but when we finish this series, you're watching it." I pointed at him.

"As you wish," he sighed, his voice low and smooth. So smooth, so low, I had to shove the flutters down.

He was so close to me then, all I had to do was...

I cleared my throat and stepped back from him.

An hour later, my horse was happy, my hair was washed and braided, and Wyatt stepped through my hotel room with two to-go salads. I plopped on the bed and grabbed my laptop, opening it up to cue up the show just as Wyatt sat down next to me, sliding a salad and a fork my way.

I dwelled on the idea of my mother being here during my ten-minute shower, telling myself that's all I would give myself to think on it. It wasn't her fault I let it get to me; she was simply doing her job as Kelly's coach—right? I shouldn't let her doing her job affect mine.

But it did.

Every. Single. Time.

I went down the same rabbit hole.

And I could already feel myself falling like Alice.

That's why I only gave myself ten minutes. So, I couldn't fall.

Wyatt fluffed up the pillows on the headboard, getting comfortable as he waited for me to find the right episode. He stabbed his salad with his fork, shoved what seemed to be the entire head of lettuce in his mouth, and then waved his fork in front of my laptop. I took his gesture like a little wand, his fork magically starting up the show, so to make him smile—even with a mouthful—I pressed play and settled myself next to him.

We were quiet, no words needed as we ate and enjoyed the crew landing in Neverland. Wyatt's comments began to reminisce on the first time we ever watched this show together, ranging from him saying, "Well, now that all makes sense" to "I honestly should have seen that coming." When he shouted at the TV that Henry was about to trust the wrong person, it sent my soft laughter through the room, and without realizing it, I scooted closer to him. Once the episode was over, I managed to burrow myself under the covers, the laptop seated closer to our feet.

"So..." Wyatt began, his voice a little heavier than normal.

I hummed. "So."

"I saw—"

"My mom?" I finished his sentence.

He met my gaze and nodded once. "Miss Rodeo Montana wasn't on the list, but apparently—according to Hawkins—there was a royalty change, and she was available."

I shrugged as best I could under the covers. "It happens."

Wyatt shifted his body towards me, one single eyebrow raised as he folded his arms across his chest.

"I have four—maybe five more runs. I don't know how long she's going to be here, or if she even knows I'm here, but I know I won't get the support from her. I won't get the congratulations on the rides or the good lucks beforehand. I'm just worried that I'll knock over the barrels, or fall off and hurt myself again, or not make it to the championship event, or—"

"Stop." Wyatt cut me off, and I did as he asked, biting on my bottom lip. "Can I ask..." He swallowed. "Why do you need her support or congratulations?"

A shaky breath left my lungs. "She's my mom. I may not want to see her, but it still would be nice to get that praise. Did you know..." I rolled my eyes at myself. "No, you don't, because I haven't told you how far this goes. When I signed up for my first rodeo, I told her I entered the pageant. She and Dad came and sat in the stands, and she looked so thrilled. But then, after, when I went up to her after winning the event, she had her arms folded across her chest, her glare heavier than I'd ever seen it. Dad gave me all the praise, saying he was so proud of me and that he couldn't believe I did that all on my own. My mother said, 'This isn't what I wanted for you,' and then turned and walked away. She has never supported me since."

"And your dad?"

"He loves my mom; he does what she says. He's come to a few events, but never on his own. It's always the ones where mom is with her queen. He says he watches my races when he can, and he'll send me texts, but"—I scooted closer to him—"I just want her to be proud, you know? And I want the fact she isn't and never will be to not get to me and ruin my chances at doing what I love."

He studied me, his blue eyes searching my face. Reaching up, he tucked a piece of hair behind my ear and then wrapped his arm around my shoulder, pulling me against him. My head rested perfectly against his body, and I fit, despite the blankets that separated us. I molded into him, turning to face him as I wrapped my arm around his waist.

"I know this isn't the thing to say right now, and I'm no therapist, and yes...my upbringing was very different, but—" he took a deep breath. I felt his chest rise and fall, his heartbeat picking up. "Kyla's talked openly about her relationship with her mother to

Rhett, and when I met her mom, I saw the distance between them. They're working on it. But Kyla...she knows she fits here with us, with Rhett. Sometimes, family chooses you, and those people are the ones you need to focus on. I can promise you—" He shifted slightly, and I raised my chin to look at him. "You fit with us. You are more loved with my family—with me—than you'll ever be with anyone else."

I gave him a soft smile and settled myself back down on his chest. "I know," I whispered.

"One more episode?" Wyatt sighed, his fingers tapping on my shoulder.

I left his warmth, grabbed my laptop, and pressed play, settling myself right back to where I was next to him, and before I knew it, I was sound asleep right there, using Wyatt Hartwell as a pillow.

TWENTY-SIX

Wyatt

I SADDLED CHARMING, PICKING the perfect breast collar and bridle to match Quinn's turquoise blouse. She had to add a few sponsor patches to her shirts, but the color still popped. She had everyone's attention. She definitely had mine.

She slept next to me all night, her warmth calming my body in every way. It was a new experience for me, just *sleeping* next to someone, not wanting to disturb them in the slightest. Once the episode was over, I closed her laptop with my foot and, using my legs, managed to get the small blanket at the end of the bed over my body, all without waking her. I kissed the top of her head, pretending she was mine even if it was only for a minute, and then fell asleep. We woke up at the same time, in the same position, and I quickly left for my room. We acted normal during breakfast, the banter the same as always, with a little flirting thrown in, but nothing unusual—except the fact that she had used me as a pillow in the back of my mind.

My pocket vibrated once I finished with Charming, thankfully pulling me out of the Quinn spiral I was finding myself in. *Just friends. Remember that, Hartwell. Just friends.*

Hawkins

Yeah…we'll meet you at the trailers?

Me

Perfect.

I shoved my phone back into my pocket. Plans. With just the guys. For the first time in—well…six…maybe seven months. I was going to get rusty if I kept saying no to friends.

Quinn came back to the trailer with her number and two water bottles. She handed the number and water to me and spun on her heels so I could pin it to her shirt.

"There's a crowd tonight," she muttered softly, twisting open her bottle.

I moved the wavy hair her braids created off her back and shoved the water bottle under my arm, working on the first pin on her right.

"There's a kids' fair tonight—more families, fewer drunken dates." I looked at the back of her head as I pinned the final pin. Holding her shoulders, I shifted her torso slightly, and she met my gaze over her shoulder. "You nervous?"

I felt her body rise with a deep breath. "No."

"You sound a little nervous." I gave her a tilted smirk.

"Maybe a little," she admitted. "This is a big crowd—bigger than I'm used to."

"One step closer to the NFR, Compton."

"For you, too, Hartwell. I fully expect you to make your way over to that announcer box tonight." She gave me a sexy grin, one I assumed she wasn't trying to make sexy, but failed because my heart fluttered.

If only she knew how much I wanted to kiss her.

She did—I'd told her plenty of times.

If only she'd let me.

"I will. Hawkins will welcome me with open arms."

"I thought that was you." The voice of the woman neither of us wanted to see carried over the crowd, and we broke our eye contact to look into Helen Compton's direct stare.

"Your father didn't tell me you were going to be here." Helen crossed her arms. "You didn't say anything in our family chat either."

I held on tighter to Quinn's shoulders.

"I'm here, Mom," she said solemnly.

Helen let out a hum, and her chin tilted to me. "Wyatt, nice to see you again."

I gave her a nod. "Just here for Quinn."

Another hum. I pinched my brow watching her eyes dart from me to Quinn. "Yes, well, she needs the help. I just wanted to say hello since you didn't yesterday, but now I need to get back to the girls. They're carrying the flags—Kelly is holding the American Flag, so make sure you congratulate her."

I felt Quinn's entire body stiffen, and once Helen was out of earshot, I spun her to face me. Her eyes were already sunken, her lips tight as she was no doubt replaying her mother's words over and over.

"Hey." I leaned down to meet her at eye level. "We aren't going to spiral here."

"We?" she parroted, a shake to her voice.

"Remember who is really proud of you. The ones *you* find most important. Those are the people you want in your corner. I'm here not to *help* you, but to watch you. And Quinn—I love what I see. Do *not* let her get in your head. Do *not* let her take this. You deserve this more than anyone. The only thing that matters right now is you and this ride."

Her breath shook. "You love what you see?"

"You kicking ass and heading to the NFR? Yeah, Quinn...I fucking *love* what I see."

Her body relaxed, and a soft, closed-lip smile formed, her cheeks turning pink as her eyes stayed steady on me.

"You need to get back there," I reminded her, moving her hair from her shoulders. "I'll be waiting for you—okay?"

She nodded, letting out a shaky breath before reaching for Charming's reins, giving me one last hopeful look before she made her way to the back of the arena.

I watched her stride go from hesitant to firm and confident, her hand reaching up to stroke Charming's nose. And when she turned the corner, she gave me one last look, one last gorgeous smile, before she vanished.

TWENTY-SEVEN

Quinn

I LOVE WHAT *I see.*

Wyatt was right. Wyatt was absolutely, one hundred percent, right. The only thing that mattered in the moment was the ride—and getting back to him afterwards. And in order to do that, I had to beat my time from last night.

I mounted Charming and spun him in circles, his speed ramping up.

I fucking love what I see.

"Amber coming in with a seventeen point nine, a seventeen point nine. But now we're heading to Montana, native, barrel racing's princess, I've heard her be called—"

Huh...that's a new one...

"—Quinn Compton riding her gelding Charming. Now, last night, she pulled in a fifteen point seven, and the time to beat for tonight is a fourteen point four. I really think—just watching her these last couple of rides and even seeing what she's done in the past—she can beat it."

I blocked out the announcer's voice—I was certain it was Hawkins—and tightened my legs around Charming, feeling his body move as he gained the speed. When I rode, nothing passed through my mind. All I could hear was Charming's hooves hitting the dirt, all I could feel was the pounding of his heart and mine syncing up, and all I could see were those damn barrels. But tonight...tonight I saw the prize. I saw Wyatt ready for me. I felt his arms wrapping around my waist, lifting me off the ground. I heard his laugh in my ear and his joy ringing through my body. I could see his lips against mine.

I rounded Charming over the first barrel. We went right and saw the dirt fly around his hooves. He huffed and picked his speed back up, rounding the second barrel. I let out a laugh as we booked it to the third, rounding it, and then we flew down the arena and into the gate.

"And she's beat the top time tonight and set the time to beat for the Reno Rodeo—Quinn Compton pulling in a thirteen point eight! Did you see that ride? Thirteen point eight! That's going to be a tough time to beat for the entire Reno Rodeo, sending her straight to the championship—"

With one thing—one person—on my mind, I slowed Charming to a trot and circled the back, not seeing him anywhere. My heart rate picked up, but then logic set in, and I made my way straight to the trailer. If he weren't by the gates, he would be there. As

Charming got closer, my blood pumped through my entire body. He was so close...

Dismounting Charming, the buzz still flying through my veins, I stopped in front of my trailer. Seeing no one there, I huffed a breath.

"Wyatt?" I whispered.

"Compton!"

I spun, seeing him running through the few people who were behind the arena to get to me. My heart pumped, and I bolted, taking off running towards him. I jumped into his arms and wrapped my legs around his waist. I could feel him stumble a few steps back before he caught his balance, and his arms tightened around me.

It felt so good to be in his arms, it felt so...perfect...so right.

Don't think about what could go wrong, Quinn—don't let that stop you.

He was the prize waiting for me. He was my biggest supporter. He was my best friend. The man I was falling for, even though I was trying so hard not to. And here, in his arms—I could stay here forever.

"Please tell me you saw that?" I asked, my body still shaking.

"Saw it? Quinn, you didn't hear me?" He arched his back slightly, raising one eyebrow as that stupid cocky smirk took over his face.

Hear him? Wait...

"What?" I giggled, putting the pieces together before he had to say anything.

"Hawkins let me announce your ride." He tilted his head, biting his lower lip.

"Barrel racing's princess?" I smacked his shoulder.

"I knew that would get you." The cocky smile that appeared sent my pulse racing. This...man...

I grabbed hold of his neck, his arms steady on me, creating a small seat, and with one hand, I slapped his shoulder. He laughed, tossing his head back.

"You announced my ride, and the best thing you could say was that I'm your barrel racing princess."

"As much as I want you to be my princess—you're everyone's princess, Quinn."

If there were any time to kiss him, it would be this moment, right here. I could make it real. I could fall in love with him. I could—

"Come on." He chuckled, setting me down on my feet. "Let's get Charming settled and then watch the bulls. Yeah?"

I took a breath, a small ping of disappointment calming the emotions that just kept building. "Yeah."

I reached for Charming's reins, and the routine of taking off his saddle and getting him comfortable turned natural. We worked in tandem, stealing little glances at each other. I thought about what I could say to him, tell him that maybe I was wrong—maybe there was something more here, and I was just too afraid to admit it. Maybe, just maybe, we could be more. Maybe I could hear him out. The one thing that didn't pass my mind was my mother and the way she lingered near the trailer. I could feel her there, sensing her eyes on me, but it didn't matter. What really mattered was my smile when I talked to the reporter about my time, how even she was impressed, and how the world would be watching me. My cheeks flushed when I saw Wyatt's reaction to that statement, and then when his hand slipped in mine as he pulled me to the stands where we watched the bulls, *he* was the only thing that mattered.

"Dear God." I leaned up against the trailer after the rodeo was over. We never really stayed this long after; we normally went to settle my horse after my event, but tonight we stayed. My legs were killing me, my eyes were heavy, and I still wanted to kiss Wyatt. "I have never been this tired after a rodeo." I took my hat off, closed my eyes, and hit my head against the metal of the trailer, the thunk echoing. "Ow…" I grumbled.

"Never? Not even after that one weekend where you booked two rides in a row?"

"We won't talk about that night." I opened my eyes and looked at him. He had his hands shoved in his pockets, his stance wide, his stupid ball cap back on his head, and his blond hair sticking out in all directions. "But yes—even this night takes the cake. I can't wait to get back to the hotel and watch a show and just…pass out."

After talking to you, of course.

"You'll be back in the hotel in no time."

"Hartwell! You coming?" Hawkins came running up to Wyatt's side, knocking his ball cap off his head. "Need a ride?"

Wyatt laughed, twisting his torso to watch as his friend bounced on his heels, obviously still pumped with the same energy he used to announce the bull riders.

"Yeah, sure. Let me just make sure Quinn's good. Whose truck?" Wyatt asked, bending to pick up his hat.

"Mine—the red Ford parked in E lot."

Wyatt waved at him before turning back to me, taking a deep breath.

"You're..." I stammered. "Going out tonight?"

"Yeah, Sam's in town for the night." He smiled, not even phased by the fact that I just turned into stone.

"But..." I swallowed, stopping myself before I could become *that* person already. "Just..." I paused again, looking into his eyes. They were telling me something. There was definitely a message there. A silent request for permission, making sure I was alright before he took off? It wasn't like he *had* to watch a show with me. He wasn't required to sleep next to me and listen to anything I wanted to say. We were friends. Friends didn't make friends hang out with them.

I inhaled and gave him the best smile I could muster. "Don't make any bets with any girls, okay?"

Dropping his chin, he shook his head, his laugh rumbling through his entire body. He took a step towards me and kissed my cheek. "That's an easy promise. I may not be chasing anymore, but..." He heaved a sigh. "No bets. I'll see you in the morning? We're just going to Pure Country Canteen, you know, the authentic honky tonk." He waggled his head, and I just smiled at him. "I won't be out long."

I nodded, biting the inside of my bottom lip before I begged him to stay. He took a step back, banged on the back of the trailer, then left.

I went to settle in Charming, making sure to give Hook some attention before finding the nearest drive-thru with the worst food I could possibly eat, then promptly went back to the hotel. I walked into my dark room, tossed the bag of food on the bed, and stripped down to my underwear. I didn't need a ten-minute shower tonight, knowing that Wyatt wasn't going to be coming into my room—hell, I could take a bath. So, after I ate the disgusting taco, that's exactly what I did.

And the silence was getting to me.

I slunk down into the tub, the tips of my hair dipping under the water, and closed my eyes. I could just see myself from an outsider's point of view. All I needed was bubbles and a glass of wine, and I was the girl who had just been dumped by her boyfriend. Except that was the furthest thing from the truth. I was the girl who chickened out a few weeks ago, pushing the man she was falling for to arm's length. I told myself it was because he had become too close a friend to screw things up with. I wanted to get closer to him, not find myself hurt later down the line because he was *that* guy. The guy who had more numbers for booty calls than friends to talk to on his phone. I didn't want someone who had slept with a lot of women. Wyatt was friend material—the fact that I wanted to kiss him today was just a lapse of judgment. Just a lapse of judgement...

I'd eventually find a guy who was everything that I wanted. Someone who would put me first. Who would show me they cared for and loved me without even trying. I wanted someone who made my knees weak when they smiled, and whose eyes I could get lost in. I wanted someone I could trust, someone I could talk to without any fear of what they would think. I wanted to be chased. I wanted to be teased. I wanted to be told I was gorgeous. I wanted...

Wyatt.

I wanted to hear him out.

I desperately wanted him.

And I wanted to tell him all these realizations.

I *needed* to tell him all these realizations.

Standing from the bathtub, I dried myself, did a fast braid to hide the wet ends of my hair, and dressed in the cutest outfit I could find in less than five minutes. I grabbed my hat, slipped on my boots, and rushed out of the hotel.

The bar was loud, crowded, and smelled like stale beer, and I spotted him the second I walked through the door. Abi and Kyla always had this look on them when they saw their husbands. Their eyes would glaze over; their cheeks would blush, and that stupid smile that proved that they were in love would spread across their faces. Me—right now—in this exact moment...I'd bet one million dollars that's exactly how I looked because every person in the bar faded as Wyatt was the only one who came into my view.

My feet moved on their own, going directly to the pool table where he watched as Hawkins took his shot. Hawkins missed, and Wyatt began to study the table, and right before he bent, I stepped in between him and the table. His smile grew, and his eyes widened with surprise.

"Quinn—" he whispered.

I swallowed and quickly cupped his face in my palms, the pads of my thumbs rubbing his jaw lightly.

"Wyatt," I whispered back. "I..." I stumbled, taking a shaky breath before looking into his eyes, and suddenly every word I had conjured up on the drive over was gone. All I could think to say was, "I want you to chase me."

Then, I pulled his mouth to mine and finally...*finally*...kissed Wyatt Hartwell.

TWENTY-EIGHT

Wyatt

QUINN TASTED LIKE HONEY. And smelled like coconut.

I dropped the pool cue, hearing it hit with a smack on the bar's concrete floors, and threaded my fingers through her hair, most likely pulling her braid looser than it already was. She hummed, and I tried to take the moment deeper; the shock of Quinn kissing me was gone, and the urge to lift her over my shoulder and take her away was growing. But I slowed and let her control the pace.

She broke the kiss and locked my gaze, letting out a soft gasp, and blinked. Then—I wasn't sure if it was shock or regret that flashed through her eyes—but she quickly covered her face with her palms and buried her face in my chest.

Hawkins and Sam stared at me; the same stunned look splashed across their faces, with their eyes wide as their goofy smiles grew wider. I wrapped my arms around Quinn's shoulders, holding her gently as her breathing picked up. I shook my head at Hawkins, dropping my jaw and raising my brow—hoping to convey that I had no idea this was in the cards for tonight—but also that he and Sam were no longer a part of my plans. They both waved a hand in a 'shoo shoo' gesture, having my back as the best wingmen in the world.

I cleared my throat and trailed my hands down Quinn's back. "Quinn," I rasped, "Do you want to—"

"Dance?" Her head flew up. "Yes. Please."

"I was gonna suggest we—"

Quinn grabbed my hand, grasping it tight, yanking—literally *yanking*—me to the small dance floor where, of course, the band stopped their fun country song and replaced it with a slow romantic ballad. Without looking at me, Quinn spun, her arms flying over my head to rest on my shoulders. I gently put my hands on her waist, but didn't move. We didn't dance.

"Hey, uh..." I whispered, my cheek resting against her temple. "I think we're supposed to be moving. Swaying at least?"

She trembled. "I had thought of so many things that I wanted to tell you." She swayed her body lightly. "But the moment I saw you, every thought was gone."

"Do you want to tell me now?"

Her breath shook her entire body, and I pulled her closer, feeling her start to calm. "I don't remember, but—I can try to." Her hands ran down my chest, the pulse of her palms vibrating through me.

"Honestly?" I moved my legs, starting to turn the sway into a dance as the band sang a love song that I needed to get the title of. "The kiss kinda said everything."

"Do you know how badly I wanted to kiss you after my ride?" She arched her back slightly, her eyebrows pinched.

"Probably as much as I wanted to kiss you," I admitted, taking the moment to bend and give her a light, chaste kiss on her lips. "Kisses always say everything."

She let out that sweet hum and then rolled her lips together. "Well, not everything. I just...thought it was the best thing to get my point across in the moment."

I raised a brow. "What happened to not wanting to screw this up?" I lightly ran my knuckle up her neck until my fingers wove into her hair.

She bit her bottom lip, "I think...you're worth the risk. But if we figure out that this isn't going to work—"

"Who said it's not?" I questioned, but she flew over my words.

"—we can agree to remain friends because, Wyatt...I've never had a friend like you, and you're too important to lose, but..." she paused her fingers tickling the back of my head as they worked through my hair. She raised on her tiptoes and pulled me down to her for another kiss. Her mouth met mine, and my body exploded. Our tongues danced with one another, seemingly in rhythm to the song, better than our bodies were. And her moans, her light hums of approval as I took it deeper, were only fueling the fire. Pressing my body to hers in every way imaginable, her fingers continued to tickle and play with my hair, all while we kissed and kissed. Both of us breaking for air, she took a deep breath. "That..." she gasped, her eyes fluttering open, "is worth everything."

"Whoo!" A cheer traveled across the dance floor, breaking my concentration on Quinn as I turned back to my friends at the pool table. They gave each other a fist bump and me a thumbs up.

Quinn let loose a small chuckle and proceeded to bury herself in my chest.

"We have options." I kissed the top of her head. "We can get out of here or..." I pulled away to take her in. Her cheeks flushed, her lips puffy and perfectly kissable, her emerald eyes drowning me even though her hat was creating the perfect shadow. My train of thought vanished. "Fuck, you're gorgeous."

Leaning down for another kiss, Quinn pulled away. "We can get out of here or...?" she trailed.

I slumped my shoulder and nodded towards Hawkins and Sam. "We can go beat their asses at pool."

Quinn chuckled. "I'm down for a game of pool, as long as you kiss me after each shot I make."

I cocked a brow, the corner of my lips tilting up. "You said I couldn't make any bets tonight."

She lightly kissed me. "This is the exception."

Later—well, after last call was shouted—we said goodnight to Hawkins and Sam, and we found ourselves up against Quinn's hotel room door. I just couldn't get enough of her. In the past, I'd already have my hand up the woman's shirt, and soon after, I'd have us in the bedroom with our clothes probably strewn on the floor. Then, we'd be in the sheets, and I most likely had already forgotten her name.

Not here. Not with Quinn.

Never with Quinn.

I kissed her slowly, my hands tangling in her hair, her fists gripping my shirt, soft hums and moans coming from both of us. I traced her jaw, lightly opening her more, allowing me to devour her, taste her. Her hands loosened and slid up my chest, finding their way under my button-down and into my collar, her fingertips making my skin blaze with heat as they touched their way to my neck.

It took everything in me not to touch her in the ways I've dreamed about since the first time I saw her, the desire growing stronger with each swipe of my tongue against hers—but I had to savor this, savor *her*. I could still feel the way her body ached and twitched under her thin tank top. I could still feel her need with the way her leg lifted and wrapped around my own, keeping me in place. Her hips moved as my hands ran down her sides to her ass, lifting her off the floor gently. I pinned her there against the door with my hips, and she let out a moan, dropping her head back with a thump—giving me perfect access to her neck.

I kissed, I licked, I sucked...I did everything I thought about doing...except taking it one step further and opening that hotel room door.

"Wyatt," she said breathlessly, her fingers pulling on my hair once again as she gripped me. "What do we do from here? What does Wyatt Hartwell do?"

I lifted my head and kissed her chin. "In general...or..." I trailed, pressing my lips to the spot under her ear that drove me—and apparently her with the sound she made—wild.

"Well, I'm pretty sure you're supposed to be in my hotel room right now. Pretty sure we're wearing too much clothing. Pretty sure you haven't kissed me enough." She inhaled and found my lips, that same damn moan filling me.

Fuck, I could listen to her sounds all night long. I'd be the reason for these moans. I'd discover exactly how to touch her, how to kiss her, how to tease her in order to get these moans. I'd take them and bottle them up, listen to them on repeat if I could.

"I could," I muttered against her lips. "But—"

"But?" She groaned. "No buts."

"So many buts here." I grinned, squeezing her ass and loving the way she wriggled in my arms. "I promised you I wouldn't screw this up."

"That was before I did," she murmured, her lips following my chin as I lowered her back to the ground.

"You didn't screw anything up. If anything, you made it better. You're too perfect to rush this," I whispered, brushing her hair from her shoulder, lightly kissing her skin there.

"We can totally rush this."

"Oh, hell no. I'm taking my time with you. There's no way I'm fucking this up. You, Quinn,"—I kissed her—"are the woman I've thought about for months. I'm an absolute fool for you, and I'm treating you exactly how you need to be treated. Adored, savored, cherished, appreciated, admired…" I swallowed. "Loved." I kissed that same spot again below her ear, and she let out a soft giggle.

"It's like you opened a Google tab for words to say."

"I can open another one if you'd like. Words to describe Quinn Compton. Sexy." I kissed her neck. "Determined." I kissed her chin. "Carefree." I bit her bottom lip. "Stunning." I kissed her lips. "Fucking perfect."

"Sexy and stunning are the same thing." She laughed.

"Two different things in my book, and you are most definitely both."

"You already have me, Wyatt. You can stop it with the pickup lines." Her smile told me otherwise. She liked the stupid little pickup lines, which made me wonder if she liked them from the start. I convinced myself, right then and there, she did.

"But you said you wanted me to chase you." My eyes focused on her mouth, stopping myself from kissing her again.

"I do." She leaned forward, her hands cupping my face. "In my hotel room, preferably naked."

My eyebrows shot up, and I physically felt my heart begin to thump, thump, thump faster and faster in my chest. I took a long, slow breath through my mouth.

As amazing as that sounded...

"Not tonight," I whispered, kissing her again. "It's well past two in the morning, you have a ride tomorrow, and I know you—you want to get to sleep so you can be focused on that."

"No, I want to focus on you," she begged breathlessly.

"We have more than tonight, Quinn," I whispered to her.

"Promise?"

I sealed the promise with another kiss, breathing her in before stepping back, already missing her coconut scent.

"I never break a promise, just FYI. I'll see you in the morning. Get some rest." I gave her a wink, and then did the hardest thing I've ever had to do. I walked away from her, only to give her one last glance before opening the door to my own cold, dark hotel room.

TWENTY-NINE

Quinn

WYATT GREETED ME WITH a kiss at breakfast the next morning. He greeted me with a kiss after my ride. He greeted me with a kiss when I got behind the wheel of my car. Basically, whenever Wyatt could greet me, he did so with a kiss. And each time I fell a little harder for him. But even with the shift in us—nothing changed. We went through our normal ready routines, he cheered for me at every ride, and he was there lifting me off the ground, even if I didn't land a top spot. He was still my best friend. The only difference was that we couldn't keep our hands off each other. We were always touching in some way. Holding hands, his arm draped over my shoulders, mine on his biceps, his lips on mine.

But he still wouldn't come into my room—not even to watch *Once Upon a Time*. I practically begged him, telling him he could sleep above the covers again—all I wanted was to be curled up with him and maybe a make-out session where I just happened to lose my top. But he channeled his inner gentleman, telling me we had time, and he didn't want to rush anything.

I got where he was coming from, but damn, it was hard. With each kiss, each touch, each glance, he wiggled his way into my heart deeper than he already was. So, yes, maybe he was right—we had time. I wasn't going anywhere, that was for sure. And by the way he was acting, I didn't think he was either. Wyatt Hartwell currently had all of me, whether he knew he did or not. I was so gone for him.

I made it to the Reno Rodeo Championships, still having the fastest time in the entire event, and they were predicting me to win. Both Wyatt and I agreed I should ride Charming—he had brought in the fastest ride, and if I had any hope of beating that, he was my best bet. I wasn't expecting to beat it by any means, but if I could think about the prize at the end again, I could get damn close.

The only thing managing to weasel its way into my brain space was that my mother was still around. Kelly had carried the flag each night, and her attendants kept close by her like they belonged in a small high school clique. I'm sure they were all amazing, friendly girls—I just wanted absolutely nothing to do with them.

Nerves began buzzing through my body as Wyatt and I saddled Charming, his hand trailing against my shoulders each time he was behind me, and we walked to the back dirt together. As soon as I was mounted in the saddle, he kicked my boot from the stirrup and used it to lift himself into the air, kissing me deeply before he fell back to the ground.

"See you on the other side." He grinned, waggling his eyebrows at me.

"Compton!" I heard the attendant call my name, and I kicked Charming to move after blowing Wyatt a kiss.

Charming began to walk to the side, his head bobbing as we waited for our moment, and when that moment finally came, I kicked him into full speed, and we flew. The roars from the crowd faded and turned into a blur of colors as my focus rounded on that first barrel. We went left, and Charming rounded it perfectly. I squeezed his body, feeling him gain speed as we raced to the right barrel. My toe flared out, touching the barrel every so lightly—but I could feel it moving. The barrel was going to fall.

Shit, shit, shit...

Letting go of the reins, I leaned over, touching the top of the barrel, feeling it steady beneath my hand right before Charming ramped up again to aim his nose at the third barrel. I looked behind me for a second, and the barrel was still standing.

Yes!

We rounded the third, and the breath I had been harboring ever since my foot touched that barrel let loose—and I laughed.

The colors came back into the crowd, the cheers reverberated through my ears, and the announcer's voice hit as soon as I saw that time on the clock. Twelve point seven.

I beat it by one fucking millisecond.

"With a time like that," Hawkins's voice roared through the speaker above my head. "That's going to be hard to beat. I can guarantee you, barrel racing's princess took it home with that time! Quinn Compton just flew through the dirt, breaking the arena record twice this summer—unbelievable!"

Charming slowed as we moved through the gates. The one person I wanted to see right there, sitting on the gate with his feet locked behind the metal, his cowboy hat skewed on his head, and the cocky grin I loved brighter than the lighting in the arena. While Charming was still in motion, I swung my leg over and jumped, landing with a bounce right in front of Wyatt. Before I could climb the gate like I planned, he jumped, and his hands were cradling my face, his mouth covering mine.

"I am so..." he said against my lips. "In awe of you. I can't believe I saw that, I can't believe—"

"Believe." I cut him off, kissing him again, draping my arms over his shoulders.

"I'll take Charming, and you know they are going to want to talk to you. I hear you beat an arena record tonight." He leaned back, and his smile grew, his lips lush from our kisses.

Mine widened as I looked into his baby blues. An arena record. I beat the arena record.

"Barrel racing's princess, Quinn?" I froze at that shrill voice.

I met Wyatt's gaze, biting my bottom lip. I felt his fingers drum against my waist, and his quick nod gave me the courage to turn around and come face to face with my mom.

"Mom," I said flatly.

"What's with the new title?" she asked, folding her arms over her chest. Her hair was winged, perfectly stiff, and her jewelry that hung from her ears, neck, and wrist glittered even in the low lighting of the black dirt. She was royalty, not someone who would be here around the livestock animals, but here she was, her eyebrow perched up a little too high and her lips twisted—not even a hint of praise for her only daughter.

"Wyatt gave it to me," I replied.

"I think it's a bit childish, don't you?"

"Mom—"

"And now the entire Reno Rodeo is going to be blasting it on social media, the Cowboy Channel will pick it up—"

"I hope they do," I heard Wyatt mutter as he stepped closer to me.

"What will everyone think that you gave yourself this title, one you most likely didn't earn? I've followed your times. I know what you've done this year. Your father has been keeping me up on it since you won't, and Quinn—this is just the last straw I can take." Her voice rose, and her arms dropped to her side. I could see the moment that anger seeped into her eyes, and something happened to me at the same time.

I found myself not giving a shit.

"This is all *you* can take?" I pointed at her, making sure my feet were solid in front of Wyatt. "I'm sorry, but what exactly have you been taking? I moved out of your house. I found my own place. I hired my own trainer. I bought my own horses. I got myself here with no support from you, Mom," I shouted, gesturing towards the arena. "I just broke the fucking record! Or did you miss that because the only thing you got was the nickname my boyfriend gave me? You said you've been following my times? Did you happen to miss the one I just ran? Twelve point seven, Mom. Twelve. Point. Seven. I'd like to see your precious Kelly get that score. I have worked so hard.

I have done everything and have gotten nothing from you in return but disappointment. So if anyone has taken anything, it's me."

"Now, Quinn—"

"No...Mom, you don't get to interrupt me. I have been dying for your praise. I have been praying for you to say something the least bit supportive...but all I get is that the nickname is childish? Mom..." I dropped my arms to my side, my shoulders slumping as the fire left my body. "Do you even care?"

She blinked, heaved a sigh, and folded her arms.

"I expected better from you, Quinn."

I shook my head. "No." I raised and dropped my shoulders all in one breath. "You don't." I looked at my mother, trying to find a tiny bit of love there—but felt nothing. The only thing that was there...was void and empty. "I can't worry about this anymore. I can't see you and let it ruin my entire career. If you see me, please don't talk to me. I'll do the same if I see you."

I turned back to Wyatt and touched his chest gently for some feeling of warmth before I reached to grab Charming's reins. I held my breath and waited. I listened to her exasperated sigh, and the footsteps that took her, the slight jingle of her jewelry fading as she got further away.

"Hey, wait," Wyatt said softly, laying his hand on mine that was resting on his chest. "You just broke the record—and won the championship—so..." He nodded towards the arena. "You need to get back out there."

And just like that, with the look in his eyes, the confidence and excitement came flooding back into me. I raised myself on my toes to give him a fast kiss, because I could never kiss him enough, before I bolted and ran to the arena entrance, where, yes—they were waiting for me. And as soon as that mic was handed over to me, as soon as the crowd cheered, the last five minutes ceased to exist.

Steam wafted from the bathroom the second I opened the door, already dressed in my shorts and tank with my fingers working to braid my hair in record time. This shower seemed to do the trick; the other one months ago didn't. It washed everything away, including the giant weight that was pressing on me. Everything that had been building and building the past six months didn't seem as heavy, and where I knew the shower and telling off my mom wasn't the answer, for now, it worked. For now...I felt different.

My phone had been going nonstop since we got back to the hotel. First, my dad called to congratulate me. Thankfully, he didn't mention my mother, which meant she hadn't talked to him about it yet, or he simply stayed away from the topic. He was followed by Abi and Cash, Stetson raving about how he was so excited to see me in the Hartwell Rodeo next month. Kyla and Rhett sent me messages as well, and others followed from sponsors, to fellow riders, to older friends from Montana, and my heart was so full. I didn't think it could get any fuller, but then I saw him. The one person who I never thought would make me feel like my heart was buzzing, already relaxing.

Wyatt was on the bed with his hair wet from his own shower, his legs crossed and head resting on his arm, scrolling on his phone as he patiently waited. Earlier this week, when he scrolled through that Google tab to find the words that described Quinn Compton, he called me fucking perfect—but now, that was him.

I climbed over him, gaining his attention as he raised his arm for me to slide on top of him, resting my head on his chest. I heard his heartbeat, steady and calm—the exact rhythm I needed to fully relax to.

"Hey," he said softly, kissing the top of my head.

I hummed. "Hey."

"You broke a record today." Even with his voice soft, I could hear the euphoria that settled there.

I rested my chin on his chest. "I did."

"And you won the Reno Rodeo Finals." He beamed with pride.

"I did." A broken whisper filled the air, a soft laugh I tried to contain.

"You brought home your biggest check yet, and"—he turned his phone to me—"you're number one in the standings."

"Wait, what?" I pushed myself up and off of Wyatt, grabbing his phone from his hands. There was my photo, my cheesy photo that's required when you enter the PRCA, larger than the others below me, with my home and hometown right above my earnings. "Oh...whoa."

"That's not the reaction I was expecting." Wyatt leaned up on his elbow, his fingers running up and down my arm.

"No, that's a proper reaction. I never got this high last year."

"I think breaking a rodeo arena record twice in five days would do that." He kissed my shoulder, and the small zing it created radiated down my arm. "How do you feel about it?"

"Is this real?" I asked him, meeting his gaze, those baby blues piercing into me. "This isn't real, is it?"

"It is. You won. You stood your ground and proved to the entire world that you really are—"

"Don't say it." I smiled, giving him a side eye.

"Barrel racing's princess."

I rolled my eyes. "I hate that nickname."

"You love it."

"I think I preferred it when you called me 'Compton.'"

"I can still call you Compton, but I'll take full credit for your official nickname."

"It better not stick."

He kissed my shoulder again. "I hope it does."

"Wyatt." I tossed his phone onto his chest.

He chuckled, moving his phone to the floor before he turned and wrapped his arms around my waist, pulling me down to the bed and to him. I giggled, scooting closer to him, feeling his arms settle against me, his nose rubbing against mine. He began to study me, his gaze moving from my shoulders as he moved my braid to my back, his fingers making lazy circles once my skin was bare, to my eyes, and finally to my lips. He inhaled, held his breath for a beat, then exhaled, slow and steady.

"Please tell me you're going to kiss me now." I wiggled against him, sliding my hand under the hem of his shirt.

He shivered under my touch but didn't hesitate. Kissing me, slow and sensual, he acted as if he had unlimited time. Every inch of me that he touched began to tingle. When his fingers moved, I could still feel the heat they caused, like his fingerprints were etching themselves into my skin, staying there for as long as I'd allow them to. The slow heat began at my toes and climbed all the way to my stomach, lingering there until my core couldn't take it. It fluttered up into my chest, spreading the warmth carried through every piece of me. All with his kiss, my body hummed. My chest swelled, ultimately making me stop to catch my breath. I gripped onto his shirt and rested my forehead on his chest.

"Quinn," he said just as breathlessly as I felt. "I've never..." He paused, running his hand up to my shoulder, tracing my jaw line as he lifted my face back up. "I've never felt this way before." He swallowed hard, his Adam's apple bobbing. "Tell me I'm not making this all up. Tell me this means more to you. Tell me this isn't going to end when we get home tomorrow."

"I'm pretty sure I called you my boyfriend in front of my mother." I let out a soft chuckle, this time using my fingers to trace his jaw. I gripped his chin with my thumb and forefinger, pulling his lips back to mine. "You literally just took my breath away with the way you made me feel. This is so much more than I think either of us knows. This isn't going to end. Like you said...we have more than tonight."

I rolled, gently pushing him onto his back, crawling to lie on top of him once again. His heartbeat was quicker this time, and his eyes were filled with something other than patience. Heat flooded him, and I was there to feel it.

I kissed him, taking his hands in mine and guiding them to my waist, once again feeling the shivers as his palms found my skin. He took over, trailing his hands up my stomach, stopping only for a brief moment before he cupped my breast. I moaned into his mouth, pressing myself into his touch.

He dropped his head and heaved a sigh. "Quinn, I don't want to rush you…"

"We don't have to rush. I just want this Wyatt, nothing more. I want that breathless feeling again, and I want you to be the one to give it to me." I kissed his chin, the words like a featherlight touch across my skin. "Will you please give me that?"

"As you wish." Then he kissed me deeper, harder. His hands began to explore my body as he turned me on my back, his lips and fingers finding every sensitive area that even I didn't know existed, giving me exactly what I asked for.

THIRTY

Wyatt

QUINN'S LAUGH ECHOED OFF the stable ceiling, and still after two weeks, I wasn't used to that laugh belonging to me. I was, however, used to that laugh being *because* of me.

"Oh, hell." Quinn's laughter carried. "You're going to need a shower."

"Or a haircut," I grumbled, stepping away from Hook in his stall. He shook his head in pride, giving me a *ha-ha, I did that* teenager vibe. I had just finished cleaning his stall, giving him a pristine place to call home, and the way he decided to thank me was with a kiss...a very slobbery kiss that formed my hair into an alfalfa on top of my head. "He only managed this because he took my hat off." I bent, yanking my Hartwell ballcap off the ground, shaking all the hay off.

Quinn rested her arms over the stall. "You know what would have stopped that?"

I lifted my gaze to her, knowing exactly what she was going to say.

"A cowboy hat," we said in unison.

I raised a brow. Quinn tightened her lips into a line, and her expression gleamed.

"He wouldn't take off the cowboy hat. He wouldn't know where to grab." She touched all around the brim of her hat, adjusting it on her head. Once every inch of the brim had been touched, she dropped her hands on her thighs. "Plus," she continued as she opened Hook's stall, "I love the way you look in that hat."

I raised my chin. "Oh, really?" I reached for a towel, rubbing the top of my head to remove at least most of the horse slobber before shoving my ballcap back on, backwards of course.

"Mmhmm." She dug in her pocket. "I even..." she mumbled as she unlocked her phone and started thumbing through the few pictures she had in her gallery. "Snuck this."

Showing me her screen, I saw myself looking in the mirror at Boot Barn, the hat I had chosen that day perched on my head. For being a photo taken from a distance, in the middle of a store, it was a good shot. And it made me smile, knowing she snuck it even when she claimed she hated me.

"That's cute," I replied, keeping the heat from my cheeks. "Because I have this." I unlocked my phone, not even needing to go to my gallery, just flashed her the lock screen. It was Quinn, on Hook, flying through the arena during a ride in Reno. The background was blurry, but her, and the excitement on her face was clear as day.

"I'm your lock screen." She pinched her brow, watching me through her lashes as her lips formed a tight smile. Her eyes were wide and wet.

"Who else would be my lock screen?" I curved my lips, shoving my phone back into my pocket as I leaned in to kiss her. She still tasted like honey. Still smelled like coconut. The two things I was finding myself completely addicted to.

Hook let out a loud huff behind me, his head bobbing just right to knock off Quinn's hat.

"You little—" she grumbled, bending at the hip.

I reached up and scratched Hook's ear, his entire head turning towards me, basically cuddling into me.

"No hat is safe." I chuckled.

"He's just jealous." Quinn plopped her hat back on her head.

"Of me kissing you, or you kissing me?"

"Would you be surprised if it were both?" She tilted her head and squinted. "He took the moment away. I'm your lock screen, and he took the moment away."

Laughing, I wrapped my arm around her waist, pulling her to me. "Good thing we can just pick up right where we left off."

At dinner that night, Quinn sat next to me, our legs basically glued together. With only a few days until the Hartwell Rodeo, everyone was moving and talking about things that still had to get done in preparation for it. Lachlan had moved the bulls and calves over a few days prior, and I had already been in the announcer box, making sure I had everything I needed to give the crowd a good show. There were more kids signed up for mutton bustin' this year, and Stetson was quite annoyed he was now out of the age range, trying to convince my sister that he could—in fact—ride saddle bronc. Cash was the first saddle bronc rider of the night, and Rhett was leading tie down; we even had bigger names—like Oakes Ashford and Ty Grant—signed up for bull riding. The only thing that would make this even bigger is if Lachlan was riding bareback—but still, this was shaping up to be the Hartwells' biggest rodeo yet.

"We need to check the stands, make sure the food trucks are booked, confirm the volunteers for tickets and clean up, and oil the chutes," Abi said, listing off everything with her fingers. "Oh." She raised one finger. "And fireworks."

"They're being delivered tonight," Lachlan said, not even looking up from his plate.

"Maybe we should think about doing a drone show next year," Kyla suggested, handing Poppy her sippy cup. "Those are becoming big at other rodeos."

"I say stick to fireworks," I retorted, taking a bite of my chicken. "What would Lachlan do if you took the fireworks away?"

Lachlan shook his head. "I'll look into drones, Kyla."

"We can head over tonight." Abi stood. "Lachlan can handle the fireworks being delivered, Rhett, Cash, and I can oil the chutes and check the stands. Kyla—you can drag the dirt."

Kyla acknowledged Abi by lifting Poppy's small plastic spoon in the air.

"That leaves me." I looked at my sister, who gave me her cheesy smile. "Designated babysitter."

A harumph came from Stetson as he glowered at his mother. Where he was at the age where he could be of some use in the arena, it was also the age where he would get in the way once he got bored. He was a Hartwell—he loved the rodeo as much as all of us, but he firmly believed he belonged on the horse, not prepping for it.

"Ah, come on, Stet." I leaned over, my elbows resting on the table as I stared down my nephew. "It will just be the four of us."

"Four!? Quinn, too?" He asked, his head twisting to Quinn.

She nodded rapidly. "Me too."

"We can teach Poppy how to barrel race," I said, half mumbling, raising my glass to my lips.

From the corner of my eye, I saw Kyla twist her torso, glancing at me before returning to her daughter. Stetson's eyes widened as his jaw dropped, then he bolted out of his seat, cleaned up the table, and rushed out to the stables.

Quinn chuckled, giving my freshly washed hair a quick kiss. "I'll follow him and saddle up Charming. He's calm. Kyla—are you ok with that?"

Kyla stood, reaching for her daughter. "She loves horses, and she's ridden with her dad a few times, graduating outside of her carrier. I'm sure she will be just as excited to hop on with Uncle Wyatt."

Poppy reached her arms out as soon as Kyla turned, her fingers gripping the air. She had begun to babble more these days, forming simple words like *mama* and *dada*, and I lived for them. They were adorable in their own way, and now with her fingers reaching out to me, her eyes wide as I held her close, I swear I heard—

"Is she saying my name?" I looked over to Kyla.

Kyla scoffed, "Ha, no. It's a sound, *wah-wah* maybe. She's been forming new sounds—"

"Wah-wah sounds like Uncle Wyatt to me." I smiled back at my niece, rubbing my nose against her. I was rewarded with a giggle.

Kyla raised her brow. "It's a sound, Wyatt. Trust me, when she finally says your name for real—"

"Oh, Kyla." Abi chuckled, coming up behind her. "Let him have Wah-wah."

"Yeah." I furrowed my brow, twisting my face to try to get another giggle out of Poppy. I turned to her. "Uncle Wyatt," I said, nice and slow, catching every syllable.

Quinn's chin rested on my shoulder, her hands on my waist. "Uncle Wyatt." She parroted.

I looked at my sister-in-law, who just glowered at Quinn and me as we said my name over and over again, all the while Poppy babbling *wah-wah*.

"Fine," Kyla succumbed. "I'll give it to you."

Looking back at Poppy's blue eyes, her cute little smile on her face, Quinn's chin on my shoulder...I felt on top of the world.

Poppy kicked her feet and waved her arms, making holding her against my chest harder than it should have been, but her little squeals made it worth it. Quinn and Stetson set up barrels and took turns rounding them, but once Stetson ultimately got bored, he led Marshmallow out of the pen and bet Quinn he could race her to the lake. Quinn hollered, "You're on!" and then they both took off.

Poppy laughed, a squeal really, and I kicked Rusty into a walk. I held on to her tightly as I watched Quinn and Stetson get smaller and smaller as they made their way to the lake. And Poppy and I just enjoyed the view.

She began to babble: *baba, mama, wah-wah, dada,* and I would respond: *Really, tell me all about it, that's the coolest thing I ever heard Poppy Girl,* and by the time we made it to the lake, she and I had a whole conversation. She said *wah-wah* more than any other babble, and each time it pulled at my heartstrings. I knew it wasn't for me, that she hadn't made that association just yet, but I could pretend and still soak it in. I never thought about having kids, but Poppy was making it quite hard not to imagine it later down the line. Especially if it was with the woman who was standing next to my nephew, her hands on her cocked hips, her hair wind-blown, and the sexiest smirk on her lips, watching me slowly walk up on Rusty.

"I thought you said you were a fantastic rider?" she mocked.

"I'm holding precious cargo." I tickled Poppy's stomach, and she gave me another giggle.

"Here, I got her." Quinn held out her arms, taking Poppy from me as I dismounted so I could lead Rusty over to the other horses. "You know," Quinn said the moment I got to her side. "I've lived in Alpine Ridge for seven months now. I've ridden all over the ranch, and I'm still taken with how beautiful it is. It's gorgeous in the winter, it's perfect in the spring. Summer is to die for...I can't wait to see the fall."

"It turns orange." Stetson reached out, taking Poppy from Quinn. "Every tree." He kept talking as he took Poppy to the edge of the water.

"Hey, be careful. Riding is one thing, but let's stay away from the water, okay?" I told him.

Quinn slid her hands on my arm, tugging me close to her. "You really do have a beautiful home, Wyatt. I don't think you know how lucky you are."

I kissed her temple, keeping a close eye on Stetson and Poppy. "I am now that I have you. Before it was just okay."

She slapped my chest. "I'm serious. This is all yours."

"Well, five percent of it."

"Five percent?"

I nodded. "Yep. Lachlan has fifty, since his dad owned half. He got it when his dad died. Rhett has forty. Abi and I both have five."

"That's an odd way to split it up."

"I don't want more than that. I would have taken less if my dad hadn't mentioned building a house at some point." I shrugged the arm Quinn was holding, forcing her to let go. She didn't step away, most likely knowing what I was planning on doing next. Ever since we first kissed, she could predict my moves, so when she leaned into me, letting me slip my arm around her shoulders. It felt more natural than anything. "Eventually, the two hundred and fifty acres that have my name on them will have something attached to them.

Even if it's a small house, so I don't have to live in the bunkhouse anymore."

"But you love the bunkhouse," she teased.

"Sure, all two hundred square feet of it," I replied, sarcasm dripping from my voice.

"Oh, it's bigger than that."

I laughed. "I've never counted."

"Two hundred and fifty acres, huh?" She rested her head against my arm. "I could think of a lot to do with two hundred and fifty acres."

It was dark by the time we arrived back at the stables. Poppy was already asleep on my shoulder as I led Rusty into his stall. Quinn gently took the sleeping baby from me to let me dismount, handing her right back the second my feet touched the ground. Poppy whimpered and curled her fists around my shirt.

"She still hasn't had a bottle," I whispered to Quinn.

Quinn rubbed Poppy's back and then reached up to give me a chaste kiss. "I got Stetson if you want to take her to Kyla's. We'll do a night check."

"Meet me in the bunkhouse?" I asked, leaning closer to her.

She nodded, awarding me with one last kiss.

"Uncle Wyatt." We stopped and both looked to the front of the stall where Stetson stood with his arms across his chest. "I told you not to fall in love with her."

Quinn barked out a laugh, but then stopped the moment Poppy stirred, slapping her hand over her mouth. "Ope." She bit her bottom lip and widened her eyes. "I got him, you go put the baby to sleep."

I shook my head at Stetson, sticking my tongue out as I passed him.

Poppy woke up the moment I walked into the cabin, getting fussy as I changed her and found pajamas. I gave her a bottle, and she settled, falling right back asleep in my arms. I swayed as she got comfortable, the same Shania Twain song filling the dark space around us, then slowly set her down in the crib. Last time I was here, I used Poppy as a sounding board, heartbroken after being turned down by Quinn. Now, I was here, and my heart was so full it could burst, knowing she was waiting for me and that she was mine.

"Hey, Poppy Girl," I whispered. "I was wrong...fall in love, okay? Find that person and do not give up on them."

And I would never—ever—give up on Quinn.

Rhett and Kyla arrived soon after, Kyla hugging me before going to check on her daughter, but I went right to my brother. Once an idea popped into my head, it was hard to get rid of it. And swaying with Poppy, seeing Stetson and Poppy by the lake, having Quinn there for my stable chores with her laughter filling my senses, an idea formed. And I just needed to talk to Rhett.

"Hey," I leaned my palms on the kitchen island and looked at my brother. I knew later I'd need Lachlan and Abi, but for now...forty percent would do. "Can we talk?"

THIRTY-ONE

Quinn

"WITH JUST FIFTEEN MINUTES to go until the show really gets going, how about we start with some mutton bustin'?" Wyatt's voice blared through the speakers, still calm and collected even though he was riding on Rusty. When he told me he was going to switch it up, ride *and* announce at the same time, to—and I quote—*'Show you just how amazing of a rider I am,'* I couldn't help but roll my eyes at him.

I knew he was a good rider. I've seen him ride in the arena—granted, it was the worst tie down I had ever seen— and I've seen him riding on the field working. I've seen him riding with a fancy wedding suit on and with a baby being held to his chest. But apparently, according to him, I hadn't seen a good show until he had a microphone in his hand. And I wouldn't admit it to him, but he was right.

He was dressed to fit the part. His Wranglers fit him just right, the blue button-down stretched against his biceps, and his blond hair stuck out from under his Boot Barn hat. He had his script in one hand, along with the reins, and the microphone in the other. His baby blues could be seen even under the shadow of his hat, and his smile gleamed. I had heard his voice several times over the speakers—I had heard the way he could rile up a crowd—but I never *watched* him. He was in his element, and anyone could see the exuberance flying from him. I couldn't take my eyes off him.

"And we're starting with six-year-old Tersea Kuster—"

The chute opened, and the sheep busted through, the little girl holding on for dear life until she fell off, landing face-first in the dirt. The crowd gave a collective groan, but Wyatt moved on, announcing her score and hyping up her ride before introducing the next rider.

After all the kids had their moment, Wyatt led Rusty off the arena, and the high school riders went in with the flags. I began to weave through the crowd, wanting to get as close to Wyatt as I could. I may have plenty of time to prepare for my event, but I was missing something.

And according to Abi, that was an important something.

"And bringing us our National Anthem"—he came into view, and I felt that spark in my stomach. That one I was trying to ignore for so long, and now that he had been mine for almost a month...I was trying to figure out how I ever ignored it—"Kendell York from Alpine Ridge High. Please stand and face the flag—"

"Wyatt!" I whisper hissed, coming up to the side of Rusty.

Wyatt turned, welcoming me with his perfect smile. He had an earpiece in his right ear, the wire trailing down his back to the battery pack that was hooked to Rusty's saddle. Twisting his neck at an angle, he took it out with the hand that was holding the microphone and lowered them both to the horn. I watched as the red light on the mic turned black.

"Get out there and respect the anthem," he whispered back, leaning down close to me, his tease sending chills down my spine.

"Abi says Cash gets a kiss for luck. I'm pretty sure he's out there kissing your sister right now—"

"He'd better not be late. He's up first." He cocked a grin.

"—and Rhett always kisses Kyla after, right? So...when are we going to kiss?"

He raised a brow. "Well, seeing as we are both busy at the moment, you know, I got this microphone and a sponsor list, and you have to go get Hook ready, I don't think we'll be able to carry Rhett's tradition...or Cash's. But we could start our own." He cocked a grin and motioned to his stirrup, sliding his boot from it, giving me the leg up I needed.

Repeating the move he did to me just weeks ago, I used the stirrup to hoist myself up, my lips meeting his instantly. I reached for the horn of the saddle, using it to keep me upright as we slowly kissed. His fingers weren't in my hair, his hands weren't roaming my body. I wasn't humming or moaning into him. I was holding on to the saddle, praying I didn't slip—but this kiss was *the* kiss. That same spark flew from my stomach, reaching every inch of me. My body heated just from his lips, his taste...just *him*. I wouldn't have guessed seven months ago that this man—who I once said was more starch than man—would be sending this thrill through me. It had only been a few weeks, but it felt like so much longer. I would never have guessed that Wyatt Hartwell held my heart. My whole heart.

"Wyatt," I whispered against him. It was on the tip of my tongue...*I lo*—

"The anthem is over..." he whispered back. "I'll see you on the dirt."

I gave him one last chaste kiss before lowering myself down, removing my boot from his stirrup. Taking a few steps back, I could feel the pull tugging me to him.

"Meet me after? For the fireworks?" he asked, moving Rusty's nose to the gates.

I nodded, watching Rusty jerk his nose back, the microphone dropping into the saddle. I held back a chuckle and resisted the urge to flash him finger guns. "Sure, if you don't fall off. Maybe stick to announcing in the box?"

Wyatt gasped, dropping his jaw. "Prepare to be amazed at my skill." He curved his lips, shoving his earpiece back in his ear, and flicking the mic back on, all with the same hand, his other never loosening on Rusty's lead.

Rolling my eyes, I slunk away from him, keeping my eyes on him until he gave me a wink.

Cash scored an eighty-seven, then joined Abi and Stetson in the stands. Rhett clocked one of his best times with a seven-point-one, kissed Kyla over the gate like always, then took Poppy in his arms and wove in and out of the cowboys and cowgirls. And Wyatt let out the loudest cheer when I finished my ride, disappearing from the arena. Even if he didn't have a microphone in his hand, anyone would have been able to hear him scream, "That's *my* girl." And I guarantee that even though the sun had set and the sky was ready for the fireworks, anyone would have been able to see the heat in my cheeks.

I watched the rest of the event with the other barrel racers, but while my peers were watching the bull riders, my eyes were trained on Wyatt. He was still on Rusty, and even though they were behind the gate, they stood close enough that Wyatt could see the action and tell off all the scores as the judges sent them his way. His face had a light sheen of sweat, the sleeves on his button-down had been rolled up several times to expose his toned forearms, and his hair on the nape of his neck was damp—but even through the miserable heat—Wyatt looked happier than I had ever seen him before.

He didn't drop a beat the entire night, not missing a single outcome or score. He said the Cowboy Prayer with love and announced every single sponsor like they were a dear friend. Wyatt certainly knew how to gain the attention of the entire crowd and keep everyone on their toes.

And it was my turn to be captivated by him.

He had told me plenty of times that he was amazed watching me, that he was—in his words—in awe. The things he had said to me over the last few months stuck with me more than anything, so much so that they began to play on repeat in my head before a ride. But now...it was finally my turn to see Wyatt the way he saw me.

Wyatt was so much more than I ever imagined. More than I gave him credit for. Wyatt was...

Perfect.

"It's been a wonderful night here at the Hartwell Arena, we've seen amazing rides from America and Canada's greatest cowboys and cowgirls. This little rodeo of ours has grown so much, and we can't wait to keep building it up. It was such an honor being your broadcaster tonight, back in the saddle—doing the one thing I love almost as much as the woman who has claimed me as hers. I'm Wyatt Hartwell, and Alpine Ridge, if you turn your eyes to the south sky...you'll see the best firework show this side of Boise."

The first firework shot up in the sky, the screeching causing everyone to turn their heads, gasps and cheers following, and then the lights dimmed in the arena. Fireworks shot through the air, one after another, the pops and booms echoing—and while those held everyone's attention, I ran to him.

When I rounded the corner, he was already standing at Rusty's side, taking his hat off to rub his forehead with his arm. He inhaled and raised his chin to the sky, the look of pure happiness radiating off him. He was tired, he was most likely sore—but he was *back*.

"Hartwell!" I shouted, gaining his attention instantly.

I jumped and landed right where I was supposed to be. I wrapped my legs around his waist, my hands on the nape of his neck, feeling his hands finally on my waist, holding me steady.

"Damn, Compton." He chuckled. "You almost just took me out."

I kissed him, loving the way he had to catch his balance again as he shifted to hold me tighter against him, his mouth moving in perfect sync with mine.

"You're spectacular, did you know that?" I arched my back away from him softly.

"Spectacular?" He parroted. "I don't think I've heard that one before."

"You always say I'm the amazing one—"

"Well, you are."

"But you—" I kissed him again, soft and sweet, a chaste kiss that only left me wanting more. "I wish I had seen it sooner. We could have been *this* sooner."

He cocked a grin. "I tried. You're the one who hated everything I tossed your way."

"I take it all back. You're the opposite of everything I said."

"I don't remember half of it—"

"I do." I shifted to trace his jaw, feeling the stubble that had grown since he last shaved. "None of it is true. I just wanted to believe it was. I was such an idiot for not seeing you."

"Hey." He narrowed his eyes. "Don't call my girl an idiot. I promise you, Quinn,"—he met my gaze—"*this* is going to last a long time. I told you, I'm a fool for you. I'm a goner. I'm in—" He paused. "I'm in too deep."

Me too. My stomach did a jumping jack, small flutters filtering all the way to my fingers. "I don't want to say it yet—" I whispered.

"You can say anything."

I blinked a few times, feeling my heart beating in my chest. I wanted to. I could scream it from the rooftops—let the entire world know that I was in love with Wyatt Hartwell. But all I managed to say was—

"I feel so much more with you, and I want it all."

Maybe that is exactly what I was supposed to say. Maybe those words were stronger than those three tiny ones that everyone wants to hear at some point in their life, because the moment the words left my lips—the moment they hung in the air—Wyatt's blue eyes got heavy, his breath picked up, and with a soft *fuuuck,* his mouth was on mine.

Not breaking the kiss, he moved, taking us away from the crowd that was still engulfed in the fireworks that were booming overhead. A few grunts and *moos* from the livestock came from nearby, but I was too focused on Wyatt's breathing and moans to pay any attention to where we were going. All that mattered was that I could keep kissing him. I honestly didn't care who saw—that way, everyone would know he was mine.

My back gently hit a wall, my hat flopping to the ground, all while Wyatt drank me in. He shifted, one hand still firm on my ass, the other slinking up my waist, finally cupping my chin. His lips broke free from mine, and I gasped for air as he kissed my neck and down to my shoulder. This man knew exactly where to kiss to ignite my senses, and we hadn't even had sex yet.

In the few times we had touched and teased, he asked me what I liked, how I wanted to be touched—and tonight—fully clothed up against a building behind the Hartwell Arena, he was putting all those questions to practice. My body shivered as his hand trailed my collarbone, cupped my breast, his fingers grazing my side—it wasn't enough, yet it was almost too much.

"Please tell me you're coming over tonight?" I begged, my hands grasping at his collar.

"Why wait," he whispered in my ear, "when we can play now?"

"Now?" I gasped, locking my gaze with his.

"Just a tease." His smile was so wide, I could feel it against my skin. He nibbled on my ear. "Tell me I can, Quinn. Please tell me I can touch you."

"Yes," I breathed. "Please."

He kissed me again, his tongue not wasting any time dancing with mine. His free hand worked on my belt buckle, and he pulled on the button and slid it to the most sensitive part of me. I gasped the moment his warm fingers found my center, my head falling back on the wall. His fingers began to move in slow, lazy circles as his lips found and kissed my favorite spot right below my ear, driving me more insane than his fingers. I withered against him wanting so. Much. More.

"The only reason why I'm spectacular, Quinn," his voice was hauntingly low against my skin, giving my earlobe a little nip, "is because I'm wanted and loved by you."

Fireworks built inside me as the real ones boomed outside, the grand finale happening in me mere seconds before it was lit into the sky.

THIRTY-TWO

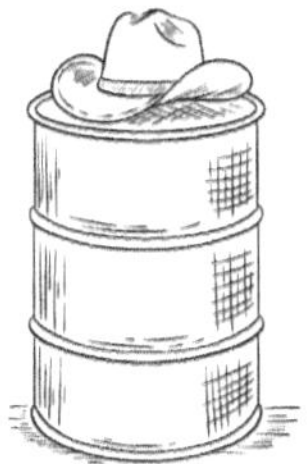

Wyatt

"Okay...I can't handle this anymore." I placed my hands on my hips and glowered.

"Can't handle what exactly?" Quinn questioned, her voice trailing while her eyebrows raised as high as her hairline.

I met her gaze, my own lips curling when I caught the way she bit her bottom lip.

"All the damn boots." I opened my arms and swung my torso. Yet again, I found myself surrounded by her many pairs of boots. One time, I had counted, but I swore, looking at them now, scattered everywhere, more had joined the fold, including a green suede pair with fringe galore. "I can't believe you do this every single time you travel. You pull them all out and then put them all back, only to do it again in a week. I can't take it anymore." I tried my hardest to pull disappointment in my voice, show the smallest amount of annoyance, but Quinn's growing smile and the blush on her cheeks made that physically impossible.

"I have to see all my options." She grinned.

"You've told me that, but why every single time?"

"We're going to be gone for a while this time. Days of '47, Frontier Days, Denver—we're in for an adventure before it settles for the fall, so I have to make sure I have everything I need. Don't worry," she added as she flipped her hair over her shoulder, twisting on her heel to put her back to me. "There will be plenty of room for your one duffel bag. That's all you need, right?"

Circling my lips in an *O*, I let out a breath. "That's a low blow, Compton. I may have to up it and decide to pack every hat I own just to spite you."

"You mean your one hat?" She glanced at me over her shoulder, her eyes bringing on the tease.

Narrowing my eyes, I stepped over three pairs of boots. "I have more than one hat. I'll pack every single one of them in a huge hat box so your boots won't hurt them and bend the rims."

"You're gonna to need to stack them because my boot boxes will be taking up the entire back seat, so there will be no room for your three hats." She spun again, leaning against the kitchen island, that same teasing gleam in her eyes.

"Or," I sing-songed. "You can bring three pairs of boots like a normal person." I kicked over a pair of boots, and the gasp that Quinn let out was utterly adorable. Her jaw dropped, and her cheeks flushed.

The playful banter over boots quickly left my brain space, and all that was left there was her. My breath stopped as I stared at her. Her lips moved as she forced the smile to stay down; keeping the annoyance on her face must have been harder than even she anticipated, and the sparkle in her emerald eyes only gave away that she wanted to play.

I had gotten to know her more in the past month since we started...dating? Is that what we were doing? Our nights of *Once Upon a Time* had turned into multiple episodes, kisses on the couch, and her leading me up to her bedroom every single night. I hadn't slept in my bunk house in weeks. I had yet to make any sort of lasting move on her, always stopping before things got too far, but that didn't mean I wouldn't tease. I touched, I licked, I *savored* every inch of her. I loved finding different ways to hear her moan, make her come—and yet I still had yet to be inside her.

It was absolute torture. Yet, she was worth the wait in every way.

I didn't want to rush her. Rush us.

I needed her to know she was more than that to me—more than what I was known for.

Every night before she fell asleep in my arms, I would remind her. *We have more than tonight.* She would repeat it, snuggle into me, and drift off. I would fall asleep shortly after, and more often than not, we woke up in the same position even before our alarm clocks rang. I had never slept so deeply.

Quinn scrunched her nose at me; the attempt to stay mad completely failed. I strode over to her, clearing the distance between us in no time. With ease, I lifted her onto the island, her knees quickly parting for me to step in and bring her chest flush with mine. Her arms rested on my shoulders, and our noses brushed together.

"We're fighting over boots." She giggled.

"Light bantering. I wouldn't call it fighting. I just love seeing you get riled up."

She hummed, tilting her head back, her hair falling down her back. "There are more ways to get me riled up, you know."

"Oh, I know." I kissed the bottom of her chin. "I can think of plenty." I softly nipped her neck, giving her a light kiss where I bit.

"I love it when you do that," she whispered. "There's so much I want you to do."

"Compton..." I said huskily.

"I know, Hartwell. We have more than tonight." She cocked her head and mimicked my voice, hitting the deep tone perfectly, might I add. "That's your catchphrase."

"It's a good one."

"It is."

Before I could answer, she kissed me, deep and raw. Her hands slid into the hair at the nape of my neck as she pulled me closer.

Fuck this, I thought. We did have more time, but that didn't mean we had to wait...and wait...and wait.

There was no screwing this up anymore. I was in this, and I knew Quinn was, too. What was the point of waiting? She knew she was more to me...

"Quinn," I whispered into her. "How about—"

The loud, shrill sound from Quinn's phone made me stop and offer up a truly annoyed eye roll. Lowering my head to her shoulder, I tried to ignore the ring so once it was done, I could scoop her up and run upstairs...finally make her...

"It's a FaceTime," she said, her hands sliding down my back. "My dad."

I gave her a soft kiss and stepped back. "I'll pick your boots." I used my thumb to point behind me at the mess, just as Quinn jumped off the counter to reach for her phone.

"Don't you dare." She glared at me, pointing at me with her index finger. "Hey, Dad." Her tone changed the moment the *vroop* signaled the start of the call.

"Hey, pumpkin," her dad's voice was a lot deeper than I imagined, but unlike her mom, I could hear the smile he was giving her.

At least one parent cares.

"Hey, Dad," she repeated, her tone more melancholy than it was two seconds ago. "What's up?"

"Just wanted to check in on you. You have a big week coming up, don't you?"

Quinn walked into the kitchen, setting her phone down on her little stand as she reached for a glass. I went back into the living room, right in the middle of all the boots, and studied them, trying to keep my focus on the boots and not the conversation with her father. I didn't know the man, heard her talk about him rarely—was he going to crush her like her mother did?

"I have the app ready to go. I can't wait to watch. You going for the gold?"

"Of course, what else would I go for?"

"Any plans afterwards? We'd love to have you up here for your birthday."

I pinched my brow. Birthday? How did it just now occur to me that I didn't know her birthday? I knew this woman's favorite foods. Favorite colors. Favorite books and shows. I knew how to make her laugh and ways to make her mad. I knew almost everything there was to know about her—except her damn birthday.

"No, I have so many events after...I need to be here to train and make sure I'm ready. I only have a few more rodeos to count towards the NFR. August and September are going to be really busy. In October, I should slow down a bit. You know how it is."

I glanced at her in the kitchen as she filled her glass with water from the tap before she grabbed her phone again.

"I'm packing now, see?" She flipped her phone so the camera faced me. I saw an older man, gray hair neatly styled, with emerald eyes and a full beard. Lance Compton waved at me through the screen, his smile just as wide and as bright as Quinn's.

"Wyatt's helping me pack."

"More like helping you narrow down which boots you can donate," I shouted.

"None of them!" Quinn shot back.

"You must be the boyfriend Helen told me about. I hate to tell you, but she picked up that trick from her mom."

Quinn dropped her arm, the phone going with it as she shook her head, letting out a long sigh before raising her phone again. "Thanks for that, Dad. But yes—Wyatt—"

"The boyfriend. I like that better." I pointed at her, keeping my eyes on a pair of boots I hadn't seen her wear before.

"—My boyfriend is here to help. We leave in a few days for Utah. But I really should help him before he starts to throw out my boots."

"Alright. I'll watch you in Utah and text you then. Consider coming up for your birthday, okay? We miss ya."

Quinn tightened her lips and nodded. "Maybe. I'll talk to you later, ok?"

"Love ya, pumpkin."

"Love you, too."

The *vroop* sounded again, and Quinn tossed her phone on the couch, plopping down after it. I stepped over a pair of boots, taking my seat next to her. Picking up her hand, I turned it so I held her palm. I ran my fingers over her lifelines, noticing the way her fingers twitched. She smiled and cuddled into me.

"We can leave the boots out and just order pizza and watch *Once Upon a Time*...right?"

"We can clean up the boots while we wait for the pizza, but yes. I like that pair, by the way." I pointed to the black pair with blue and turquoise embroidered flowers that sat in the corner. "I've never seen you wear them."

"Those are one of my favorite pairs. I have a matching hat."

"Take them? To wear on Gold Medal night?"

She sighed and turned her hand, grasping onto mine to bring it to her lips. She kissed my fingers. "Okay."

"So..." I started. "Am I allowed to know your birthday?"

She puffed. "August second."

"And we're not celebrating...why?"

"Nothing really to celebrate. Twenty-three is no big deal."

"Every birthday of yours is a big deal."

"You turned thirty without telling me." She rested her chin on my shoulder, glaring at me.

"Ha...okay, I'll give you that."

"I don't want or need to celebrate it. All I want is to be with you on my birthday. Okay? Can we do that? With burgers, and sushi, and ice cream, and pizza—"

"Pretty much the entire town's takeout menu?" I looked down at her.

"And you."

"And you." I kissed her nose. "Okay. Deal. No celebration. Just me, you, a shit ton of food, and *Once Upon a Time*."

"Deal."

Then we sealed it with a kiss.

THIRTY-THREE

Quinn

I JUMPED FROM THE back of the trailer, lifting my arms above my head, stretching my back, and letting out a long groan. Why we thought driving from Cheyenne all the way back to Alpine Ridge was a good idea, I'd never know. Even with switching halfway and stopping to let the horses out, the already long drive turned into fourteen hours, and my body was sore from the weeks of rodeos we had just endured.

Okay, endured is the wrong word.

I loved every second of it.

Utah's Day of '47, a weeklong rodeo event, was straight out of my dreams. I won almost every round, and when I held that gold buckle, I couldn't even explain the joy that radiated from me. Even if I didn't make it to the NFR, that moment in Utah made everything worth it. In Cheyenne, I may not have won the top slot, but I made enough to keep my standings. I was still first in the nation—still on my way to accomplishing my goal.

And Wyatt was there. Cheering me on, jumping with excitement as I dismounted my horse, kissing me every time. He would tell me how amazed he was, how lucky he was, and how much he loved watching me. I could feel it in his voice that he meant every word. Every time he whispered in my ear, I melted a little more. Every time his lips met mine, the warmth in my chest spread a little further.

Wyatt climbed out of the truck, shutting the door and jogging around the front to meet me, his arms slipping around my waist. I dropped my arms on his shoulders and snuggled my head under his chin. His woodsy and strawberry scent hit me, and I breathed him in.

"Never again," I grumbled. "We're splitting that trip up next year."

His chuckle vibrated in his chest as he ran his hands up my back, tugging me closer. "It wasn't *that* bad. The drive to Flagstaff was just as long. We can leave the horses in the trailer, right? They can sleep there and be fine."

As if on cue, I heard the lock to the trailer being opened and the squeak of the hinge. Wyatt raised his brow at me, that sexy grin raising one corner of his lips, which I promptly kissed.

"I texted Cash when you were napping as we crossed the border." I gave him a wink and pulled away from him.

"I was not napping," he protested, following me.

We both rounded the trailer, coming face to face with Cash. It was almost midnight, and he looked completely out of place in his flannel sleep pants stuffed into his boots. He yawned, opening the separator to Hook, giving him a pat on the neck.

"I hope we didn't wake you." I leaned against the trailer, folding my arms across my chest. From the corner of my eye, I saw Wyatt's arm above my head as he mimicked my lean. His body heat radiated into my back. I couldn't help but lean into him.

"Nope." Cash shook his head. "Were we in bed? Sure." He glanced at us, shrugging his shoulders. "But not asleep."

"Thank you for coming to help. I'm so sore." Pushing myself off the trailer, I stretched my arms again. "Never." I twisted and glared at Wyatt. "Ever." I twisted again. "Spending fourteen hours in the car again."

"Hey," Wyatt started. "It worked on paper."

Cash let out a laugh. "It always works on paper." He pulled on Hook's reins and led him from the trailer, his hooves hitting with a hard clink. "Get to bed. I got your boys."

"You don't want to see my gold buckle?" I asked, the tired tone I had seconds ago gone with the idea of showing my trainer who helped me get here my buckle. "It's just right here. I'll go get—ah!"

Wyatt hoisted me in the air, flinging me over his shoulder. "Night Cash! See you in the morning!"

Cash's laugh echoed as Wyatt began to carry me to the bunkhouse. I used his back to prop up my elbow, resting my chin in my palm, shaking my head as Wyatt took longer strides than necessary.

"You know all my things are in the truck, right?"

"I have extra toothbrushes and oversized T-shirts that will look amazing on you. We can unpack in the morning." He squeezed my thigh. "Your boots, hats and all the things are safe."

"The keys are still in the cab."

"Cash will move the truck, because believe it or not, I texted him too. While *you* were napping." He took a step and climbed, and I flinched, grasping onto his shirt as the ground got further and further away. I wasn't one to be afraid of heights, but watching the world get smaller as he climbed the steps made my heart rate pick up. *Just please don't drop me.*

"I was not napping." I laughed, knowing full well we both were napping at some point. "You can put me down."

He shifted but kept a firm hand on me as he dug through his pants pocket. He fumbled with some keys, and then we were inside his small bunkhouse apartment. He took the few strides to his bed and tossed me down. I landed with a soft bounce, a giggle escaping as he climbed over me. This man made me giggle more than I liked to admit. Giggling was annoying and probably my least favorite thing to hear—yet with him, I was constantly giggling.

He rubbed his nose against mine. "There. You're down."

"Jerk." I hit his shoulder playfully. "Pro tip: don't climb stairs with someone over your shoulder. That was slightly terrifying." My body fluttered as his baby blues bore into me, landing directly on my lips.

"I had you." He kissed the tip of my nose and pushed himself off the bed. "I'll get you a toothbrush and shirt."

Grabbing his collar, I pulled him back down to me. He rolled on his back, his legs dangling off the edge of the bed, lifting his arm to let me cuddle up into his side, where I fit perfectly. We were exhausted from the car ride, both of us sore from sitting for so long, our minds just as drained. Closing my eyes, I felt my breath slow, and as I listened to his heart beat, thump, thump, thumping against my ear...I felt myself begin to drift.

It wasn't long until he let out a sigh, placing a kiss on the top of my head. "If I don't get up, I'll fall asleep like this."

I hummed into him. "Fine. But don't blame me if I'm asleep when you get back."

Wyatt squeezed me closer before getting up, and this time I let him. I turned on my side and watched as he dug through his drawer, tossing me a T-shirt, and then disappeared into the bathroom. I heard the shower turn on, and suddenly I was very, very awake.

I gave him a few moments before I undressed, leaving my clothes in a pile at the foot of the bed, not hesitating even once before slowly opening the door to the bathroom and joining him in the shower. We stayed there until the water ran cold and our fingers were wrinkled, taking the time to explore every inch that we could.

Wyatt sat across my couch from me with his focus completely on the episode of *Once Upon a Time*, the pizza, sushi, burgers—basically everything I asked for—sitting on my coffee table. I asked him not to make a big deal of my birthday. It was never something I celebrated as a kid, so when he showed up with bags of takeout food, a vase of flowers, and a soft "Happy birthday, gorgeous," I never felt more celebrated, more loved—more seen.

And he was way too far away from me.

The entire time he watched as Emma and Hook danced together in the past, I watched him. The itch to reach out for him tingled into my fingers. The man had touched me in so many ways; his tongue had licked basically every inch of my body. He learned how to make my body ignite in ways I never knew possible—but we had yet to go any further. We were the definition of a slow burn...and the want was growing stronger. I wanted him.

The other night when we got home, for a moment I thought it was going to happen when he crawled over me, then the shower—I was sure he would make the move then. I could feel—and see—how much he wanted me, but he wouldn't take it further than just touching and kissing. Even when I bent on my knees in front of him, taking his entire length in my hand, he made sure I knew I didn't have to do it—I didn't have to do anything I didn't want to. I showed him exactly how much I wanted it, but the moment the shower was done, we simply went to bed. If he didn't make a move soon, I would.

Heaving a sigh, I pushed myself off the couch, knowing exactly how the episode ended—with Hook and Emma finally admitting their love for each other—and knowing exactly how I wanted our night to end, I suddenly felt very parched. Filling my cup to the brim with water, I chugged it down, hoping the cold water would chill the heat that boiled in me. It did not. I could hear Emma say her line, *You traded your ship for me?* Then Hook: *Aye,* and for the first time since discovering that show and rooting for Emma and Hook to be together, I rolled my eyes.

I could hear the show end as I quickly chugged another glass of water, drowning out the monologue of love with my heavy gulps. The now-empty glass clinked on the counter, and before I could make the decision to go and jump my boyfriend, I felt his arms wrap around my waist, pulling me into him. I didn't even hear the TV turn off, or his footsteps come behind me, but suddenly it didn't matter. He made my decision for me.

I hummed. "You read my mind, just what I wanted."

"A hug?" He kissed my temple.

"You," I answered.

I leaned my head on his shoulder and inhaled, my hands running along his forearms, holding him tighter, loving the small chuckle he let out.

"I know I already said this,"—he began to sway us—"but happy birthday."

"I hope the night isn't over yet," I admitted, twisting to face him. He kissed me the instant my lips became available to him, and I moaned into him, loving the taste as his tongue began to dance with mine. "Please tell me," I whispered against him, placing my forehead against his, "I can finally have you tonight."

"Quinn...," he replied, pulling away slightly.

"I want more than touching," I began to beg. "I want more than teasing. I want all of you, Wyatt. Please." I lifted my head. "For my birthday."

"Pulling the birthday card, huh?" He raised a brow, and I laughed, giving him another chaste kiss. He let out a soft groan. "You have no idea—"

"Oh, I do. I have an idea. I'm done waiting, Wyatt."

"I don't—"

"Don't what?" I asked, cutting him off, my hands sliding down his chest. "Don't want this?" *Me?*

His eyes flashed with concern. "Fuck no, Quinn, I don't think you know how much I want you."

"Then why are we waiting?" I breathed, meeting his gaze.

His lips parted. "I've wanted you for so long, probably since you first turned me down, but—" His forehead fell to my shoulder, but once he lifted his head and his eyes hit mine, a deep breath left my lungs. He bit his bottom lip and searched me. "You have no idea how much I love hearing all the sounds you make when I touch you or the way you shiver under my tongue. It's been absolute torture not being inside you. But Quinn, you're more than sex, and I couldn't rush it. I didn't want you to think that's all I wanted when it came to you."

"I don't think that. In case you haven't figured it out yet, you're all I think about. I love the sounds *you* make, too. I love the way you taste on *my* tongue." I grinned at him, seeing his cheeks blush when I used his own words. "Wyatt, please—I want you to make love to me."

Make love to me.

He inhaled. "I don't think I've ever made love before," he admitted, his voice deep and heavy, causing an electric jolt to pass through my body.

"Then let me be your first." I reached for him, my own voice shivering as I watched him melt.

Wyatt lifted me off the ground with ease, and I gasped. He moved, taking each step slowly as he made his way to my bedroom. It wasn't quick and frantic like I expected it to be; it was slow and steady, each move orchestrated as we climbed the stairs, almost as if we had practiced this. My hands started to get needy as they trailed all over his neck, tracing his veins down to his shoulders. Giving in to him, I kissed where my fingers just were, loving the soft groan that came from him as he kicked my door open. Gently, he set me on my bed, his hands moving from my ass to my hips, slipping his fingers under my shirt, the tickle driving me insane.

"You better not be teasing me," I said breathlessly. "You've teased me so much; I can't take it anymore."

"I've done more than tease." He grinned, his voice heavy with need, lifting my shirt to kiss my stomach. I shivered. "I've kissed you here." He kissed my hip. "And here." He kissed my navel. "And here..." His fingers trailed down my shorts, skimming over the seam of my center.

"I want so much more." I moaned, wanting to feel him literally everywhere.

"I'll give you everything, Quinn."

"I've told you," I whispered, reaching down for him, my fingers threading through his hair. "All I want is you."

"I'm yours." He slipped his hand under my back, lifting me to a sitting position. He raised my arms and slowly pulled my shirt over my head. I had been naked in front of him before, but this just felt different. I was bare in more ways than one, and his breath hitched as he raised his hands to my neck. "Fuck..." he growled, his eyes roaming my bare skin. "I'll never get used to seeing you like this. So fucking sexy."

"And you..." I began to play with the hem of his own shirt, tickling his abs the same way he teased me. Once his chest was bare, I arched my back and studied him. If anyone was fucking sexy in this room, it was him, and he was mine to feel. "I'll never get used to touching you. I love it when you shiver under my fingers." Lightly, I trailed my fingers down his chest with my gaze following, taking the time to trace every defined line that graced his body.

"Quinn," he breathed, lifting my chin with his thumb and forefinger. "I love you," he hushed, a shake to his voice.

I paused my fingers, held my breath, and met his gaze. Nothing was more certain than this.

"I love you." I had absolutely no hesitation, no shake to my own voice. I was sure. "I love you."

Grasping the nape of his neck, I pressed into him. A breath left his lungs, and when he kissed me, the pull to him was so much stronger than it had ever been. No more waiting, no more wanting—all that was left was me and Wyatt...and I never would have imagined it was him to make me feel this way.

"You're mine?" I asked, kissing him softly.

He nodded, whispering, "Yours" against my lips over and over until we both were trembling, completely out of breath, and still so immersed in each other.

THIRTY-FOUR

Wyatt

I TRAILED MY KNUCKLE up and down Quinn's bare shoulder. I wanted to wake her up, but couldn't bring myself to do so. I knew the minute she woke, we'd banter about something. It could range from anything, really. The water being too cold in the shower, the massive amounts of boots she was about to pull out of her closet—again—or the fact that I cuddled a little too hard last night. The longer she slept, the longer I could get away with just watching her—like a creep.

Okay, she had to wake up.

I kissed her shoulder, lifting my knuckles. "Quinn, baby," I whispered against her skin. "Time to wake up."

She hummed, scooting closer to me. A moan escaped me as my fingers trailed to her waist, pinching her hip slightly. Bickering over boots suddenly became the last thing on my mind. Last night, we made love for the first time; we fell asleep only to wake a few hours later to savor everything all over again. I would never get enough of her. Never understood why she had finally chosen me.

"Wake up," I said again, my fingers sliding lower.

She inhaled, exhaling a soft sigh once my fingers began trailing down her navel.

"We have a lot to do today," I cooed. "Breakfast, Abi wants to have lunch with us, we need to start planning our next leg...but first—" I kissed her neck.

"Wyatt," she mumbled, her eyes still closed. "I'm sleeping."

"From what I can tell,"—I began to move my finger in a slow circle, feeling her wither against me—"you're wide awake."

She rolled to her back, wrapping an arm around my shoulders. "You mentioned breakfast." Her voice was breathy. I could tell she was trying to ignore my touch, but I was winning this battle.

"After." I took over, knowing exactly how to touch her.

I never spent this much time wanting to learn about a woman's body, and I wanted to know everything about Quinn. I never woke up multiple times with the same woman, and I couldn't wait to wake up every morning next to her. I never found myself wanting as much as I did with her, and I wanted *everything*.

I never found myself wanting to give myself fully to a woman before, and with Quinn...I wanted to give her all of me.

As soon as her body calmed, she finally opened her eyes, the desire still lingering there behind the green specks. Her lips twisted into a sleepy, sexy smile. "I was promised breakfast."

I chuckled. "Breakfast."

"Shower first?" Quinn smiled.

"Sounds perfect." I kissed her, but before I could deepen it, she shot up—the blankets flying off the bed entirely—and rushed into the bathroom. Without even a second thought, I ran after her.

Abi's gasp startled me as I rounded the corner of the stable, completely stopping me in my tracks. I stiffened, looking at her, trying to read her, but having no luck—which was weird because normally I could read my sister like an open book. She stood there, her eyes wide, her jaw dropped as she stared at me, her hand flying to her chest. Then it hit me—she was gonna throw a joke.

"Oh my gosh," she said, her voice dripping with sarcasm. My shoulders instantly loosened. "It's Wyatt...without Quinn!"

I glowered at my sister. "Oh my gosh," I mimicked her tone. "It's Abi...without Cash!"

She grinned. "Joke's on you. He's in the arena." She tossed her thumb over her shoulder, and one glance behind her proved her right. I saw Cash leaning up against the gate, watching a client run drills. "But seriously, where's Quinn? You two have been glued at the hip since the wedding."

"She'll be by for her training block. She's currently packing for the weekend, and I don't need to be surrounded by all her boots again. Plus—I figured I've been skipping work too much."

A ping from my pocket pulled my attention away from Abi for a moment. I twisted on my heel to head to my side of the stables.

Hawkins

> **Group chat still alive?**

Sam

> **Depends on Hartwell.**

Me

> Still alive.

"I haven't touched Rusty's stall yet. He made a mess with his water bucket, so…" Abi trailed the O. "Have fun cleaning that up."

"I'll do all the stalls, sis." I gave her a wink and shoved my phone back into my pocket. "I see a few new horses?" I glanced up and down the stalls, seeing some that were free a few days ago now occupied. Who knew that when I suggested this, it would really take off and become Abi's new passion? Oh, wait—she knew. Abi loved these stables more than she loved me, only second place to Stetson and Cash.

"Yeah," she mused, "and this one is pregnant. Owner said maybe a few more weeks. They didn't have room for a foal."

"And we do?"

"How many acres do we have?" She raised a brow, giving me a *come on, you dumbass* look. Of course, we had room for one more horse.

"Okay, true." I shook my head. "I take it you're gonna try to buy the foal?"

"Damn straight." She grinned. "Of course, once it's able to be away from mama. I'm thinking Poppy's first birthday present."

"She's nine months, and you're gonna up her parents and get her a pony for her first birthday?" I chuckled at my sister, opening up the gate to Rusty's stall. I was greeted by a shit ton of wet hay.

"I'll talk to Rhett first." She leaned her arms over the gate.

I looked up at her with a single brow raised. "You weren't kidding about this stall."

"He had fun. I think Hook is becoming a bad influence on him."

I peered across the stall to the black gelding that was already watching my every move. I narrowed my eyes at him, and he just gave me a head nod and a huff.

"You're next." I pointed at him.

A few more pings came from my pocket, and once again I dug my phone out.

Hawkins

Just wondering what your schedule looks like the next couple of weeks.

Me

Committees need names?

Hawkins

Not that I know of. You've been with Compton. We wanted to see if our schedules match. Sam and I are partnered up for the next month or two.

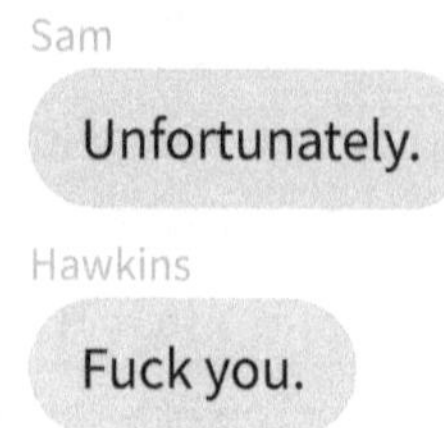

I listed the cities Quinn and I would be at over the next few weeks and shot them off to the group. August was jam-packed, probably more so than July was, and I honestly couldn't wait for the break in September when it was just Quinn and me. She'd be training more for the NFR since she was well on her way there, and I would watch in wonder and then make sure she knew just how wonderful she was.

"You said Quinn was packing?" Abi asked right as I shoved my phone back into my pocket, reaching for my gloves and pitchfork.

"Yeah, we leave next weekend. We'll be gone for a stretch this time."

"Is any of this helping you in the announcer field?"

I shrugged. "Not really, but you know that's not the reason for it."

"I know I just..." She paused and pushed herself off the gate, hitting the ground with a thud. "Wanted to ask."

"Don't want me on payroll anymore, huh?" I teased.

"How many times do I have to tell you I love you being here? It's refreshing to see you like this."

I narrowed my gaze at her. "Like what?"

"Happy," she said, her eyes hardening on mine. "Like yourself again."

"Happy," I parroted with a huff. "It was always going to be with her, the second she walked back into my life." I caught my sister's gaze and gave her a smirk. "Told you I wouldn't mess this up."

She raised a brow. "I can see you and Quinn traveling together, you know. You announcing, her racing—all the way to the NFR. She's good for you."

She's the best damn thing that ever happened to me.

"I love her." My voice broke as I whispered the words. It wasn't like telling Cash and Lach I was feeling more—this was Abi. My sister, who knew everything there was to know about me and then some. And the look in her eye, the gleam that hid there, told me she already knew.

Abi's lips formed a small smile. "Never thought I'd hear you say that. But I'm glad it's her. You two took a hot minute, but you're perfect for each other."

"Wyatt!" Lachlan's voice echoed through the stables, his stern owner's voice front and center, until it changed. "Abi?"

"He says my name like it's sour and yours all soft and sweet." I gestured to the hall opening, keeping my voice low so only Abi would hear.

"He's still making up for the 'put your big girl pants on' comment."

"That was over a year ago."

"Exactly. I'm holding a grudge." She spun on her heel. "We're here, Lach," she called.

Lachlan rounded the corner. "The architect is here; this is your meeting, Wyatt, so...let's go."

I dropped the pitchfork and glanced at the disgusting stall, then at the gelding. "Don't make a mess while I'm gone." I rubbed my palms together and turned to Abi. "Let's go." I parroted, basically jumping out of the stall, grabbing Abi by the shoulders to push her out of the stables with me.

THIRTY-FIVE

Quinn

MONTANA WAS BEAUTIFUL. I'D almost forgotten how beautiful it really was. I hadn't been back since I moved in January, since I packed up my entire life and started over in Alpine Ridge, but nothing compared to these mountains.

The past months since my birthday, Wyatt and I had been all over the country, hitting any circuit we could, keeping my rank solid. Tennessee, Alabama, Oklahoma, Texas...we'd been almost everywhere. I even joked it was a new goal to hit rodeos outside of the United States. Australia had some pretty amazing rodeos, and the Calgary rodeo had always been a bucket list item of mine—even if I was just attending. Wyatt's response to my new goal: "We'll make it happen, baby." He sealed his promise with a kiss.

And now back in Montana—one of the last stops before we slowed down for the fall and trained harder for the National Finals

Rodeo coming up in December—seeing everything that we had done, that I had done, that goal didn't seem so far off.

We could do it.

I could do it.

I took a deep breath, taking in the crisp autumn air, and grinned.

"I do love it here." I sighed.

I heard the trailer door squeak open right before I felt Wyatt's lips on my cheek.

"It is gorgeous," he agreed. "And I think Hook knows where we are. He's bouncing."

Leaning back and craning my neck into the trailer, I finally registered the clanging on the trailer floor. Hook was indeed dancing.

"My family home isn't too far away. He can sense it, probably. Home."

Wyatt stepped into the trailer, opening the separator and unlatching Hook. "We should stop and say hi to your"—he caught my gaze—"old stable. You know the one you used to work at."

I shook my head. "Nice catch."

I swallowed. I've heard from my dad on a constant basis—we texted and called weekly—but my mom...I hadn't heard or seen her since I told her off. Even Dad kept her out of the conversation. She had to be here somewhere; this was one of the biggest rodeos in Montana. But I kept my focus and wouldn't seek her out. There wasn't any point. I was here to win and get closer to the NFR—not for a family reunion.

"We won't have time anyway. After tonight, we're back on the road. Three more rides after this and then back home." I slipped my arms around his waist as he tried to step out of the trailer, making it physically impossible for him and Hook to move forward.

"Do your parents know you're here?" he asked gracefully, most likely not wanting to strike a nerve.

Wyatt was that person—my person—that I could talk about anything with, but the topic of my parents never seemed to stick. He respected that aspect, and I loved that he did. My life had been a lot easier since I stopped worrying about what my mother was thinking, doing, or where she would be. Hell—when I booked this rodeo, I knew very well that she was going to be here. But it didn't stop me. I wanted to ride in this arena again, and nothing was going to take the feeling away.

I nodded. "My dad does, yeah. If he told my mom, that's a separate story." I rested my chin on his chest. "She has to be here, though. Miss Rodeo Montana is, and she comes with Kelly."

He raised a brow.

"It doesn't matter. I'm still taking home the biggest check."

He grinned, leaning in to kiss me. I'd lost count of how many kisses we shared, how many times he's made my knees weak with just his lips, but each one was still just as perfect.

"I'll go get checked in," I said softly.

"And I'll saddle Hook. I'm going turquoise. Please tell me you brought the shirt Abi got you."

"The satin one?" I begrudgingly let him go. "I did. It's in the garment bag for tonight, steamed and ready—unless your hat box crushed it." I gave him a wink and before he could respond, I jumped from the trailer and jogged with a skip in my step—literally—to the check-in booth.

Once I had my number and was ready to go, I spun on my heel. We had a few hours before the event actually began, and I planned to spend those hours with Wyatt. One of the reasons why I picked this rodeo was for the fair that accompanied it. I wanted to get an overpriced churro. I wanted to buy him another hat from a local vendor. I wanted to play stupid carnival games and win an oversized stuffed animal. I wanted to walk hand in hand with him, showing him one of my favorite things about my home state before we both got busy with the chaos of the rodeo. I couldn't wait to whisk him away, kiss him against a tree, tell him I loved him, do all the things a couple would do. We'd been together for four months and still had yet to go on an official first date. I wanted tonight to be that.

But the moment I rounded the corner, that vision vanished.

I took a deep breath and reminded myself of what I told Wyatt just a few minutes before. *It doesn't matter*—and here she was, her arm linked with my dad's, talking to Wyatt as if they were old friends.

Wyatt met my gaze, and his smile widened. I closed the gap between us, forcing that hurt down and focusing on the baby blues I was headed towards.

"There she is!" My dad called, slipping his arms from my mother's grasp to wrap me in an all-consuming hug. "Good to see you, pumpkin."

"Hi, Dad." I leaned into him. "I didn't think you would be here."

"Both of my girls here; how could I not come? And I finally got to meet the famous Wyatt we've heard so much about." He let me go, taking a step back to slap Wyatt on the shoulder, forcing him forward with how hard my dad hit him. "You got yourself a good one, Quinn."

"I didn't think you were dating," my mother finally said, her tone blank.

"Since June? Right, Quinn?" Wyatt looked at me, his brow furrowed.

I nodded. "Yeah. You knew, Mom. It was at Reno."

She raised her chin and gave a slight *hmm*. "Oh yes, glad to see you're still together then. He must be a bigger help than you thought."

"No, ma'am," Wyatt answered for me, sticking his fingers in his Wrangler pockets. "I just saddle the horse."

She gave him a tight-lipped smile. "I'm sure you do more than that."

"Helen, leave him be. He was saddling up her horse when we got here. Which one is this? Charming?" Dad turned to Hook, who gave him a side eye as his ears tilted back.

"This asshole is Hook." Wyatt reached up to scratch behind his ears, automatically easing the tension in him.

"Excuse me?" Mom snapped, her eyes flaring wide as she looked at Wyatt.

"He may be an asshole"—I gave Hook a pat on his nose—"but he's great. He pulls in amazing times." I added, ignoring Mom's comment.

"The horse is only as good as the rider. They're a team." Wyatt met my gaze. "And Quinn—barrel racing's princess, right? She's worked hard to get here. So have her boys."

"It's really been wonderful watching you, pumpkin. I can't wait to see you in action tonight." Dad gave me a smile.

"Yes, well." Mom took a step forward. "I'll be with Kelly and the girls. Chelsea won Montana this year, did you hear that, Quinn? So, she's following Kelly closely to America, learning everything to get there herself. Kelly is a shoo-in this NFR to take America."

"That's great." I faked excitement.

"Well." She sighed, keeping her eyes on me as her hand gripped my dad's forearm. "We'd better go help her get ready and everything. Lance."

"Good luck out there, pumpkin. We'll be cheering for you." Dad gave me another hug, kissing my temple before Mom swept him away from us. I watched until they turned the corner and vanished, and then the breath left my lungs.

"What were they talking to you about before I came up?" I turned to Wyatt.

"Me, mainly. Your dad knew who I was. He was asking about Rhett and Lachlan, too." He looked out over the crowd. "They just asked a bunch of questions. I'm kinda surprised they didn't stick around longer once you got here. They just...left." He raised his arm towards them.

"That's normal." I shrugged a shoulder. "I'm glad they didn't stay longer, honestly. Now..." I leaned into him, placing my hands on his chest. "There's a carnival, and I would very much like to take you—"

"Hartwell!" A loud call broke me off, and I turned, seeing Hawkins run up. "Oh, hey, Quinn..." He stopped once he got to us, completely out of breath, placing his hands on his knees. "Sorry,"—he raised a finger—"gimme a minute."

I held back a chuckle and looked up at Wyatt, who also seemed like he was trying hard not to laugh at his friend.

"You good, man?" Wyatt chuckled, watching his friend heave breath after breath like he just ran a triathlon he didn't train for.

"Yep. Just ran around the entire arena looking for you. If I didn't run into Lance, I wouldn't have found you so fast." Hawkins stood. "Sam's sick—like dying sick."

"What?" Wyatt asked, his voice raising higher than even he probably intended. "Is he okay? What's wrong?"

"Yeah, he'll be fine, but he caught the flu somehow—he can't announce."

"You got the show right? You've done it." Wyatt wrapped his arm around my shoulder.

"Fuck no," Hawkins croaked. "This is a two...three...man job, and without Sam, we would be drowning. I'm just glad you're here. Archie agreed to let you fill in."

Wyatt furrowed his brow. "Wait. What?"

Hawkins formed a tight smile and nodded.

My jaw dropped, quickly spreading into a wide smile. On one hand, I wanted to spend all the time I could with him. On the other hand, I knew how badly he wanted to be back in that announcer box. I saw him on the Fourth; I saw the passion he carried in his entire body. He had to jump on this. He had to get his ass in that box with Hawkins and prepare—yet he was a statue.

"Wyatt..." I said softly, reining in my own excitement for him, pulling on his arm.

"You're serious?" Wyatt asked, his fingers pressing into my shoulder. "He's the guy—"

"Yeah, I know." Hawkins laughed. "But seriously, man. He's agreed to it, and we need you. Come on."

He turned to me, letting out a shaky exhale. "Quinn…"

"Go." I pushed his shoulder.

"Just…hold on a minute," He turned back to Hawkins. "Give me a sec."

Hawkins nodded. "Just a sec. We got a lot to go over."

Wyatt pulled me to the other side of the trailer and held onto my shoulders, dropping his head between his arms.

"Why are you stressing?" I asked him, leaning down to try to look at his face.

"Archie is the guy I sent to the hospital a year ago. To have him say it's okay for me to be in there—this could get me back in the box." He hushed, his voice almost breaking.

"Then why"—I took his face in my palms and raised him up to look at me—"are you stressing? Go. This is huge. Imagine you announcing my ride again, imagine the excitement you'll bring to the entire crowd. Wyatt…" I held his gaze. "I want to hear your voice over the speaker. Go."

He smiled, and I felt his body begin to hum with energy. Almost like a switch flipped, he was ready to give me what I wanted. "I fucking love you."

"I love you, but go." I kissed him, deeper than I planned, before pushing him away. "He's coming, Hawk," I shouted, not once taking my eyes off Wyatt.

His smile grew, then he moved, opening the back door of the truck. He plopped his hat on his head, gave me one last kiss, then ran off with Hawkins to the announcer booth.

I folded my arms and watched him, biting my lip. We had more than tonight for a date. We had so much time.

All the time in the world.

THIRTY-SIX

Wyatt

WHEN I SAW ARCHIE, I gave him my winning smile and shook his hand, thanking him over and over again for the opportunity to step in for Sam. He smiled back, telling me right off the bat, without even a hello, that if I did anything uncalled for, I'd be out. I chuckled, promising him my best behavior as he sat down next to Hawkins and me. We began to go over the sheets, and this close, I noticed his nose was now slightly skewed to the left—something that my punch most likely created. This was the moment I needed to get my career back together...get my life back on the right track. I had to watch my every move, not just let loose like I loved to do behind the mic. I had to say things he wanted to hear. I had to keep it civil...and get back on this man's good side.

Watch what you say. Only things he wants to hear.

And then it started, and the three of us pulled it off without a hitch.

I was back.

The best part of the entire night was watching Quinn from this view.

The camera angles were perfect. They captured her just as she took off, getting the best shot of her rounding each barrel. The hardest part was not jumping up after her run to wrap her in my arms and kiss her. She beat the top time for the night, and I couldn't see anyone else knocking her down. The camera followed her to the back dirt, the satin of her new shirt shining from the lights.

"You're dying right now, aren't you?" Hawkins asked in a whisper, leaning over so only I could hear.

"You have no idea," I replied.

Archie drew us back to the racers, and the three of us built the hype for the bulls. When the event ended, we thanked our sponsors, the crowd, and the great state of Montana. As soon as the lights dimmed, all three of us let out an exasperated sigh. I lifted my hat to run my hand through my hair, the adrenaline of being back behind a microphone pumping through me. The Fourth of July rodeo was great—but it was nothing compared to being back here.

And I couldn't wait to get to Quinn, scoop her up, and tell her everything.

"Damn, man," Hawkins cheered. "That was a show. Now if you don't mind...I'm meeting a girl." He looked between Archie and me, giving us a stupid grin before leaving us both in the booth. I chuckled at my friend and turned back to Archie.

"Thanks, Archie, this uh...this meant a lot."

"Gotta say, Hartwell," Archie drawled. "When Hawk said you were here, I wasn't too thrilled." He tapped the side of his nose.

"I was shocked you agreed. This is my first time back since—"

"Yeah, I haven't made that easy for you, huh? Guess I should apologize for that." He leaned back in his seat. Archie was about my age, maybe a little older. Tall and lean, with dark brown hair and deep brown eyes. He was known for his looks and his voice. Not only was he the head of the Wyoming committee—but he was sought out for his abilities. If I hadn't punched him a year ago, he probably would have been a decent guy to get to know. Made my shot of getting to the NFR all that easier.

"It's actually been a really great year. Sure, I've missed this, but I'll get back at it in no time." I tapped on the desk, the pile of papers sliding when I lifted my finger.

"We've all been watching you, you know." He gave me a coy grin. "Hawkins has been telling us about how you're cleaning up your act—no more bar fights in your future."

I chuckled. "No, Arch. That was a..." I looked over him and tapped the side of my nose with my thumb, mimicking his gesture from earlier. "One-time thing. Just—don't insult my girl anymore."

He barked out a laugh. "Your girl? Compton? Yeah, Hawkins told me you were helping her out. I almost didn't believe it. But then I saw you at a few rodeos, hell, even at Reno after they turned down your name. You've been sticking by her like a magnet."

I smirked, the thought of Quinn waiting for me making my heart swell. "Yeah, she's great."

"Closing up the booth, guys." A head popped in the box. "Make sure you have everything and lock up."

Archie and I gave him a nod, and we both stood, grabbing what was left of the papers to make sure everything was in order before we shut down the booth. Archie shut the door behind us, locking it and giving the keys a jingle.

"It's gotta be your game. I know you, man." He slapped my shoulder.

"Game?" I repeated. "There's no game. I just want to get back in the box. This is where I belong, seeing everything from right in that seat—it's what I was meant to do. Traveling with Quinn, helping her out when she needed someone, helped me get here. If I weren't with her, who would you have called to cover for Sam on short notice?"

"Yeah, that's right. We got lucky. Just...whatever you're doing, keep doing it, and I'll make sure your name gets back on committees. Keep her around for a bit longer, okay? She's good for your image, and it's helping her out too."

"We're helping each other."

He raised his brow and winked. "Sure you are. Keep it up. Great show tonight."

"You too. See you around." I replied, still keeping my façade.

Archie gave me a nod, his gaze traveling behind me. A quick shake of his head and a wave of his hand, he turned and left. I had this in the bag. Archie said it himself, they were watching, they were noticing—maybe I didn't screw up as bad as I thought.

Making a mental note to thank Sam for getting sick— and also to get well—I spun on my heel, ready to see Quinn and feel her in my arms. I hated not being there after her ride, but this was almost better. We both had reasons to be buzzed and energized. We were both flying high, and I couldn't wait to see it in her eyes. Couldn't wait to just be near her.

Was it too early to propose? Would she even say yes if I asked? I chuckled, trying to imagine exactly what she would say. I could see her eye roll, the way she would slap my shoulder, but she'd let me take her in my arms and kiss her over and over again until she told me, *Come on, Hartwell, we have more than tonight—remember?*

"Wyatt? I knew that was your voice."

A hand touched my forearm, pulling me from my daydream and right into the gaze of Miss Rodeo Montana.

"Kelly." I smiled. "Miss Rodeo Montana in the flesh."

She grinned, "For a few more months, and then it'll be Miss Rodeo America," she said, her tone pompous.

"That's right. NFR bound."

I looked her up and down, noticing all the details about her. Her blonde hair was stiff and sprayed to perfection, even after riding her horse around the arena. Her crown sat a tiny bit askew on top of her hat, and her makeup was a tad overdone. She was gorgeous, there was no doubt about that, and there was a week that felt so long ago that maybe she could have been more—there was a spark between us, but I knew who was waiting for me back at the trailer.

"You too, I hear. Helen tells me you've been traveling with her daughter."

I raised my brow, feeling the heat rise in my cheeks. "Yeah, Quinn and I—"

"Helen says you've been helping her with her horses."

I scoffed. "Yeah, something like that."

"I gotta tell ya,"—she took a step closer—"it was good to hear your voice again over that speaker. Brought back memories. So many memories."

"Yeah, well..." I reached up and fixed the crown on her hat, leveling it out. "I'm kinda hard to forget." I brushed a piece of her hair that had managed to get out of place over her shoulder.

"You are. I've been hoping I'd see you at more events." She took another step, closing the inches between us. "But I'm just glad you're here tonight. I can't tell you how much I missed you. You've been on my mind since last year. And Wyatt..." She said my name breathlessly, her gaze dropping to my lips.

She leaned in, her eyes fluttering closed.

What...the...fuck?

"Whoa." I grabbed her shoulders, stopping her. "What are you doing?"

"Kissing you." She sighed as her hands began to trail up my chest. "I remember the way you tas—"

"I'm with Quinn," I cut her off. "As in she's my girlfriend, and I'm very much her boyfriend. I'm flattered, but no."

"Girlfriend?" She slumped her shoulders and stepped back. "Wyatt Hartwell has a girlfriend?"

I nodded, "Yes, one that I'm madly in love with. You should have known that; she's your coach's daughter."

"She said it wasn't very serious." Kelly pouted, folding her arms across her chest.

"I was legit thinking about asking her to marry me before you came up."

Kelly laughed. "You? Getting married? That's funny." She exhaled. "Well, fine then—maybe you are a little forgettable. See ya around, maybe." She huffed before she turned, giving her hips a shake.

She passed me, bumping into my shoulder, and for a moment I stood stone still, trying to replay it all in my head. *Did that really just happen? Did she really try to make a move on me? Was she expecting me to rise to the challenge and pretend like there was no one waiting for me?* I could feel a knot form in my stomach, because yeah—once upon a time—I would have. But now I couldn't even fathom the idea. I blinked and forced myself to laugh, taking it for what it was and how much I had actually changed. If only Abi could see me now.

Once I made it back to the trailer, I noticed Hook was already unsaddled and ready to go. I gave him a quick pat and locked up. Quinn was in the driver's seat, so I climbed in and leaned over to kiss her cheek, the entire last twenty minutes with Kelly disappearing once my lips touched her skin. This woman right here could make anything disappear. The knot faded, and the thrill began to creep back up again. I had so much I wanted to tell her, and I wasn't sure where to start.

"God," I said, finally breaking the silence of the truck, reaching out to touch her jawline. "Tonight was one for the books, don't you think?"

"I think..." Her voice was heavy as she took a deep breath. "You need to get out of the truck." She turned and looked at me, all life drained from her face as her eyes began to glaze over with tears.

I flinched.

"What? Why?" I asked, pulling my arm back.

"Get. Out."

THIRTY-SEVEN

Quinn

I WAS AN IDIOT.

Words I probably weren't meant to hear rang through my head.

Helping her helped me.

If I weren't here with her, who would you call to fill in for Sam?

I'm kinda hard to forget...

After my ride, I had one person I wanted to see. I could watch the bulls from the announcer's stand, and I didn't care how the night ended just as long as I was with him. I couldn't get to him fast enough. But of course, I got stopped by a reporter whom I talked to for a moment before graciously declining any more press. I got stopped by a few fans, throwing me for a loop when they asked for photos. And finally, I got stopped by my mother.

She gave me a lackluster hug, said something I didn't pay attention to, and then I left her standing there with her jaw to the floor when I pulled away, my body aching for Wyatt's arms around me, not hers. The rodeo was over, the crowd was dispersing, the lights were dimming, and the one person I wanted to be with seemed farther and farther away.

Until he was right there.

And I heard him talking.

Helping her helped me.

If I wasn't with her...

Then...Kelly came up.

I'm kinda hard to forget.

The moment I saw him brush her hair off her shoulder, the gleam in her eye told me everything. I knew that move. How many times had he done that to me right before he kissed my neck? How many times did he use that voice right before he touched me?

Every piece began to come together.

Coming to the rodeos.

The fun, flirty banter.

Making sure my mother wasn't going to be here...that was more for his gain.

All of this—everything we had been through in the last couple of months—was all a play.

He played me.

Wyatt Hartwell made me think he wasn't the man I thought he was, made me think he...

Sliding the heel of my palm over my forehead, I blocked everything out—even the loud voices in my head telling me how messed up this whole thing was, that I was a complete idiot.

Somehow, I made it back to my truck.

And the entire world froze. Time literally stopped until I felt his lips against my cheek. The ice that had surrounded me wanted so badly to melt, but I couldn't let it. I couldn't let him keep winning at whatever he was doing. I wanted to look into his eyes. I wanted to pretend it was all in my head...but all I could hear was him telling Archie that helping me helped him. All I could imagine was him kissing Kelly after I finally turned away. And when I finally looked into his eyes, pushing back the tears, the only thing I saw was all the lies he told me to get here.

"Wait...why?" I heard the surprise in his voice as he shifted in the seat next to me.

"Get. Out." I repeated, not exactly knowing how to form the words I wanted to say. I could feel my blood beginning to boil. I would snap at any minute if he didn't just leave me alone...

"Quinn."

"Helping her..." I finally croaked out. "Helped me get here. If I weren't with *her*." I turned to look at him, and I finally let a tear fall. "That's all I was to you?"

"I'm confused—"

"I heard you. With Archie. With—" I swallowed, not even being able to choke out her name. "How long were you going to play me for?" My head was swimming, everything was just so loud. I wanted to scream everything at him all at once, if only the words would form.

"Play you...? Quinn, I did—"

"I'm not stupid, Wyatt. Well, maybe I was falling for you, but I'm normally not stupid." My head snapped away from him, eyes sealing shut as I tried to contain every thought in my head with my palms. "Just get out."

"No, Quinn, talk to me. What's going on?" he asked calmly, leaning over the console, his hand lightly touching my forearm.

I ripped it away from him. "You won't get out? Fine, I will." My body moved of its own volition, grasping the handle and yanking it so hard I'm shocked it didn't come off. And then my feet were on the ground, and I was slamming the door behind me.

"Quinn!" he called. I looked up to see him jog around the front of the car. "What the hell is going on!?"

"I came to see you after my ride," I began. "I heard your voice the entire time. *Your voice* got me through my ride! I just wanted to be with you so bad, I came—"

"Hold on. You're mad I wasn't there after your ride? I had to make sure everything was set and cleaned up. You knew I'd com—"

"I passed talking to reporters. I ran past fans," I cut him off, my voice getting harder with each word. "And!" I finally screamed. "I think I told my mom I'd call her later. All to get to you, and what do I hear? What do I see?"

His eyes darkened, his brows pinched. "I'm not sure. Care to enlighten me, Quinn?" His voice rose, his own confusion turning into anger behind his eyes. "Because once I closed down with Archie, I had a one-track mind to get to you."

"Oh, bull shit. I *heard* you, Wyatt." Narrowing my eyes, I took a deep breath, trying my hardest to calm the storm that was brewing in me. It didn't work. "'Helping her helped me.' 'If I wasn't here with her, who would you have called?' 'I'm kinda hard to forget.'" I glowered at him, my jaw beginning to shake. "I heard every word. I saw you with Kelly."

"Fuck," he muttered under his breath, dropping his chin as he removed his hat to run his hand through his hair.

"Yeah. Fuck. So again, how long were you going to play me for? How long were you going to let this go?"

"I wasn't playing you. Damn, Quinn; I love you." His eyes softened as he took a step closer. "You know I do. Kelly was coming on to *me*."

I flinched and took a step back. "I don't believe you. I saw you! I know all the moves you pulled on her!" I screamed, flinging my arm up, gesturing to where he stood with Kelly. "Everything I heard back there, everything I saw, only proved that what I used to think about you was right. I'm just a pawn to you, aren't I? This was all for your own gain. I bet..." my voice began to shake harder, "the only reason why you were so kind to check the schedule for Miss Rodeo Montana wasn't to make sure I was ok, but to make sure you wouldn't get caught. I never pegged you for a cheater—"

"I'm not! Please, listen to what you're saying. I checked her schedule so your mother wouldn't bring you down."

"Save it," I blared. "You've been caught. Wyatt. Hate to tell you, but you've been caught."

"Fuck, Quinn. You're taking this all out of context. If you'd just listen to me, I was going to tell you everythi—"

"When? Once you get your shot to announce at the NFR? Lord knows I would have been able to help you get there. Or sooner? Put me out of my misery and dump me sooner. How long were you going to string me along?"

"You keep asking that, but you don't believe my answer?" He was yelling now, his voice close to echoing off the stadium walls.

"Like I said, I heard and saw everything—"

"So, you saw me turn Kelly down? You saw me tell her I was in love with you? You heard me say I was seriously considering asking you to marry me when I saw you? You saw and heard all that then, right?!" he shouted, his arms flying out to his sides, anger radiating off of him.

And I...laughed.

"Marry you!? Wyatt, we've been dating—no, I can't call it that—we've been sleeping together—" I paused, another thing sliding into my memory. "Not even *that* for only four months! I can't say dating because we haven't been on an actual date yet. I can't say sleeping together because you barely gave in to my advances a month ago!" Another puzzle piece snapped into place. "That's why you wouldn't sleep with me, isn't it? Not because you didn't want to *rush* it, not because you didn't want to show me I was more, but because you knew you I was never going to stick. You didn't want to get too serious and really screw me over. At least you had that decency until *I* practically seduced you. God dammit, this is so messed up. I'm such an idiot." I covered my forehead with my hands, my boots coming into focus.

I heard his shaky breaths, each one shorter than the last. Then, the tips of his boots came into my view. The warmth of his hands covered my wrists, and he pulled them away from my face. I looked up, meeting his gaze. His eyes were calm, his breath finally steady as he studied me for longer than he had a right to.

Another tactic.

I bit the inside of my lip, tasting blood.

"Listen to what you're saying. If you please, just stop overreacting and let me explain everything—"

"No," I snapped at him, yanking my wrists from his grasp, the stupid comment filtering through my senses. "You don't need to explain anything. You won, Wyatt Hartwell. You played me, and you played me well. I'm done. With you. With this. All of it. Fuck. You."

He huffed, and his glare darkened, the calm that was there mere seconds ago gone. "Do you wanna know why I punched Archie in the first place? Why I lost my reputation—why no one, for almost an entire year, would hire me?"

Taking five steps away from him, I crossed my arms, my heartbeat vibrating in my chest.

He took two steps closer. "Last October, he was talking shit about you"—he pointed at me—"to other riders and announcers. Saying how 'that Compton girl' couldn't have gone as far as she did with the type of injury she had. That you were using your dad's name to gain access. That you must be sleeping with the judges in order to get shorter times. That you were a piece of meat for anyone to take, and he'd gladly welcome the fun and make sure you got a good score—just as long as you'd sleep with him, too." His eyes were heavy and solid on me. His jaw clenched. "Do you really think I'd do to you what he was accusing you of? What I defended you for?"

I puffed a breath of air through my lips, my shoulders slumping.

My vision turned red, and suddenly, every single word he said only fueled his lie.

My voice shook. "You have no idea how much I want to believe you."

"Then believe me. Why would I do that? Why would I chase you and want you only to do *this* to you? You know me, Quinn. Come on." His tone faltered, a hint of sincerity filling each void.

But even still...

I didn't know which words to believe.

I shook my head, dropping my chin only to see a tear fall to the dirt. "No. I don't think I do. We're done. This is done. Get your bag out of my truck and leave me alone."

"Then what?" he asked, raising his hands only to slap his thighs.

I shrugged. "I don't care what you do. I'm sure Kelly will be happy to help you out. Hell, you're a Hartwell. You can make it back to Alpine Ridge no problem. Just..." I waved him off, ready to be done with this entire thing—forget it even happened. Forget the entire year if I could. "Leave me alone."

I climbed in my truck, my hands firm on the wheel. Wyatt stared at me through the windshield for a moment before he dropped his head, came to the side of the truck, and grabbed his bag. The moment the door closed, I started the engine...and left him there, not even looking in the rearview mirror at the giant mistake I just made.

Thirty-Eight

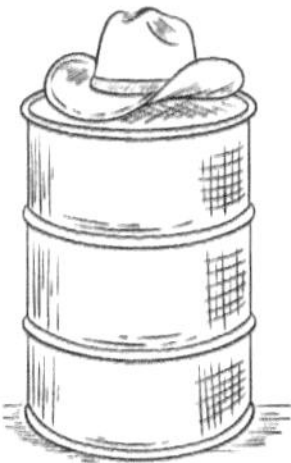

Wyatt

> I'm sorry. I can't explain if you don't let me. Please call me.

> I love you.

THREE WEEKS.

It had been three weeks since Quinn left me at that rodeo. Three long weeks since I had to catch a flight home and beg Cash to come pick me up at two in the morning. Three fucking weeks of absolute misery.

And the worst part—I saw her every day.

She'd come to train. She'd come to ride. She'd come to spend time with Abi and Kyla.

And even though I was right in front of her the entire time, she wouldn't even look at me. Or if she did, it was as if she saw through me. Like I wasn't even there.

It was so fucking hard to try to smile. Try to be...normal.

The only good news I had gotten this week was that—*yay, please note sarcasm*—my name was picked for a few rodeos. Four rodeos contacted me since Montana. And each time my phone buzzed in my pocket, I prayed it was Quinn, only to have my heart fall when it wasn't her. I, of course, put on a happy voice, agreed to the jobs, and travel with my friends—and that's exactly how I found myself standing in the middle of my bunkhouse apartment, surrounded by every pair of boots I owned.

I had my hands on my hips, each pair staring me down as if to call me out. They were just screaming at me that I was the idiot here, that I was the one who fucked things up, and now I had to live with it. Live without her.

I just wished she would talk to me. I just wanted to hear her voice and see her smile. I just wanted her.

"God dammit," I glowered, heaving a sigh and kicking a boot over. It landed with a soft thump.

The doorknob to the bunkhouse rattled, opening seconds later to let in the crisp fall air. Abi stepped over the threshold, followed quickly by Stetson, both carrying baskets of eggs. Abi gave me a quick smile before she began to make herself at home in the kitchen. She filled the fridge with the eggs from the coop and let out a soft groan when she saw the last batch she had put there untouched.

"I hope we're going to make omelets soon," she muttered under her breath, yet still loud enough for me to hear.

"Hey Uncle Wy—whoa." Stetson stopped in his tracks, his eyes going wide as he took in the sight of my living room.

"Hey, bud," I responded, folding my arms over my chest before turning back to the boots.

Okay, his reaction was valid. It was more than my boots. It was also my hats, and every button-down shirt I owned. But only the boots were screaming at me.

"What...are you doing?" Abi asked, coming up behind me.

I looked down at my baby sister. "Packing."

"For?"

"I got jobs," I replied duly.

"Like rodeo jobs!?" Stetson called as he plopped on the sofa.

I gave him a soft smile. "Yeah, bud. Rodeo jobs."

"And that requires your entire closet to be out in the living room...why?" Abi trailed off, tilting her head as she looked over at me.

I scrunched my nose. I didn't even like the detail I was about to give her. But—and I hate this saying, too—it is what it is. "Well, I'll be gone for a bit, traveling with Sam and Hawk since they are in the same cities half the time. So"—I waved my hand over the clothes—"I wanted to see all my options."

Abi raised an eyebrow. "See your options? By laying them all out on your floor?"

I shrugged. "It's something Quinn does."

She raised her head, her eyes never leaving me. "Ah, that makes sense."

"What makes sense?"

"Nothing." She used her hip to bump mine. "When do you leave?"

"Friday. I'll be back in November."

"November?" Her voice rose in stunned question.

"You'll miss Halloween?" Stetson asked, his brow furrowing.

I nodded. "Yeah, sorry, bud. I mean, what's the point of staying here? I have committees wanting me, I need to get back there, and this is the way to do it."

"What's the point of staying here?" Abi repeated.

I met her gaze and waited. And waited...and waited.

"You can say it." I groaned, dropping my arms and bending to pick up the first pair of boots I saw. Snakeskin, not good for a rodeo. I tossed them behind the couch, hearing them hit the wood floor with a loud bang. "I know you want to."

"There are a lot of points in staying here. You're just being an idiot."

"I know."

"At least you can admit it."

I heaved a sigh. "I'm assuming she told you everything," I asked, toneless, vapid...drained.

She gave me a soft nod. "I was just waiting for you to come tell me everything." She folded her arms.

I knew why I didn't—and even looking at her now, I stuck by it. Abi was my catch-all. She was there no matter what, just like I am for her. She's seen me at my worst, I've seen her at her lowest, but we are always there for one another. I knew if I went to her and cried on her shoulder instead of on my pillow, she would have wrapped an arm around my shoulder and let me have my time. But...

"You're Quinn's friend, and she most likely needed you more than I did," I admitted, taking a deep breath once the words were out in the open. "Plus, it's not like I haven't been through a girl ghosting me before."

Abi rolled her eyes, letting out an annoyed huff. "Not like this, you haven't." She folded her arms and added, "I wouldn't choose sides, you know."

I furrowed my brow. "So, all those years I hated Cash because of what he did to you—"

"Were the dumbest years of your life because he was your friend too, but that's beside the point." She waved her hand in the air. "Listen." Grabbing my sleeve, she yanked me to the couch. We both sank down next to Stetson. I wrapped my arm around her and pulled her close to me. She snuggled close but gave my knee a hard slap.

Stetson laughed, then settled into his mom's other side. "Quinn doesn't know what to think. She had this whole image of you in her head, and you completely erased that. You—I don't know—became yourself in front of her. Everyone saw how different you were. Don't think you became designated babysitter just because you're good with babies. Do you know how nervous Kyla was to leave Poppy with you? I had to talk her into letting you babysit that first night, and then Kyla admitted you were the baby whisperer, you even took on the nickname—"

"Where are you going with this?" I raised a brow, cutting her off.

"You're different than you were one year ago, and I think a lot of that was due to Quinn."

"All of it was."

"Well, not *all* of it, but eighty-nine percent of it. The other eleven percent was you trying to prove to her the kind of guy you really are."

"And see how well that turned out?"

"Uncle Wyatt." Stetson leaned forward. "She loves you."

"She does. She's just..." Abi sighed, her hand giving my knee another squeeze.

"Pissed."

"Very," Abi said, her voice to the fact. "She saw someone so different than who she thought she was getting, and she fell in love. But now, she thinks she's been fooled; she thinks she's been lied to this entire time. She thinks she lost her best friend. She gets that the entire fight was blown out of proportion, she gets she went down a rabbit hole, but to her—it's valid. I see where she's coming from.

After seeing who she thought you were—going after girls, rumors flying around about you, useless and lazy—"

"Yup, I get it." I ran my hand down my face.

"—and then having you do everything the exact opposite of what she thought was true, things you said hurt. They proved to her that she was right about you all along."

"I can't even tell you what was said. I don't remember."

That was a half lie. The entire fight played over and over in my head. All I could hear was her telling me *it's over, it's over...*

"Well, she does, and it's gonna take her some time, but I think"—she nudged me—"if you give her that time and don't run away for a month...you'll find your way back to each other."

"Did she tell you about Kelly?" I asked solemnly, my eyes focusing on anything but Abi.

"She..." She dragged out the word. "Did."

"I didn't—"

"I know. I know. You wouldn't. You may have been a player, Wyatt, but you were never one to cheat or break a girl's heart. Quinn doesn't know you like that. She saw you with an old flame, one who her mother tried to manipulate you with, one who, if I remember correctly, you said could have been something—"

"That was before—" I started to interrupt her, but she raised her hand to stop me.

"She doesn't know that. All she knows is that you never really committed to anyone. She's wondering why she's different."

"She's different in every way. I love her. I've never felt this before." I licked my lips and inhaled through my nose, my chest rising. I held it one...two...three...then let it out. "I just need to give her space," I said, hating the way those words tasted as I uttered them. "I can't see myself falling in love with anyone else, but"—I squeezed Abi's shoulder, and hoisted myself off the couch—"I need to get back on my feet."

"There's no way to convince you to stay, huh?"

I shook my head. "No. Not unless you can promise that if I show up at Quinn's house, she won't slam the door in my face."

Abi bit her lip, but stayed silent.

"She would. I know because I tried. She's not answering my texts, she's not looking at me when we're in the stables, she's ignoring me completely when she stays for dinner—she has probably fallen out of love with me."

"She hasn't."

Ignoring Abi, I shook my head and looked at my boots. "I just need to go on this trip. I need to announce, and I need to figure it all out."

"What about the meetings that you and Lach have been having? What's that all about?"

"My two hundred and fifty acres."

"And?"

"I'm still going through with my plan. Even if she doesn't want it, I don't need it. She does."

Abi gave me a soft smile. Standing, she rubbed her hands on her thighs before wrapping her arms around my waist. "Just promise me you'll give her time. Don't give up on her yet. Despite what you think, I don't think she's given up on you."

I hugged my sister, pulling her into me. "Thanks for the encouragement, but..." I put my chin on her head. "I'm pretty sure she has."

Two Weeks Later

I fucking miss her.

THIRTY-NINE

Quinn

"ANOTHER AMAZING RUN FROM Quinn Compton and her horse, Charming!" The female announcer's voice called over the speakers. I wished it were Wyatt's. "This girl has been in the top standings for weeks now. If she dips, she goes back up—it really has been a whirlwind to watch her."

"Especially after the injury she had that knocked her out for a lot of last year, but looking at her now, you wouldn't even be able to tell."

I did recognize that voice. That was Sam. And I wished it were Wyatt's voice instead.

I constantly had to remind myself I was furious. That he hurt me in more ways than one.

This was by far the worst breakup I had ever been through. Not only had I lost my boyfriend—but I lost my best friend.

After I left him at the arena, I went straight to the hotel and crawled under the covers, breaking down the moment my head hit the pillow—and I cried myself to sleep. I woke up the next morning, washed my face, and tried to carry on. I couldn't stop now; I couldn't let this break me worse than my injury had. But with every step I took, each minute that passed, my heart ached for him. I still looked for him after every ride for a kiss. I would still reach for him in the middle of the night, only to feel a cold, empty bed. I wanted him with me.

I told myself it would be better once I was home. And then I got to Alpine Ridge, and it got worse. He was at the stables working. He was at dinner. He was at The Steel. He was in my text messages. He was...everywhere.

Unable to hold it in any longer, I finally told Abi everything. She listened and let me cry on her front porch, holding my hand the entire time for comfort. She didn't defend her brother or judge my outbursts; she was just there. Abi comforted me, something I wasn't quite used to. I never had anyone to talk to like this, no one to hold me when I cried.

But the worst part of this entire thing? She confirmed that the reason why Wyatt wasn't in any committees was that he did, in fact, punch a guy for talking about me. He defended me when he knew I wanted nothing to do with him, and she knew that he would do it again in a heartbeat. That stung in a different way, a way I couldn't explain. I didn't exactly know how to take the fact that he punched a guy in my honor, either; should I be angry at him or swoon? Did I thank him for stopping rumors, or did I tell him it was overkill and I could handle myself on my own? Abi's advice was to let it ride—that it would all come to fruition on its own, but that didn't seem right either.

None of this felt right.

"I don't think he knows what he really said, and he probably doesn't see what happened with Kelly the way you do. He can't see how hurtful it was for you. You're the first person he's ever truly loved this way," she said as she squeezed me against her. *"I think you both need time. I'm not giving up on either of you, and you shouldn't either."*

But half of me felt like I already had.

The idea that this was all a ruse was louder than any voice in my head telling me to give him another chance.

I couldn't look at him without getting mad or feeling like he used me in some way. He would still laugh with Cash or be with my boys, always giving Hook a peppermint. He would blow raspberries with Poppy and swing her around, cooing that he loved her giggle. And then he would meet my gaze and go right back to what he was doing as if it didn't matter. He was acting like nothing happened, so I tried my hardest to act the same. It was all an act, all a game at this point, and isn't that exactly what I accused him of—playing a game? And now I felt like I was playing one, too. I hated it. This was all new territory for me, and I wasn't sure how this feeling was going to fade...so I did the only thing I could think to do.

Ride.

I booked every single weekend in October, getting down to the wire for the NFR. And even though I was doing this—taking care of all travel accommodations and my boys on my own—not a day went by that I didn't wish Wyatt was here with me. And every time that wish popped into my head, I would snuff it out and go through the motions, trying to enjoy my last ride for a few weeks.

"What a ride, Compton. I'm sure if Hartwell knew you'd be here, he would have taken this job over the other." Sam came up to me as I latched Charming to the trailer and started undressing him piece by piece. He leaned up against my trailer like Wyatt would. Except Wyatt would be moving, working two steps ahead of me, not just watching.

I ignored him as best I could. "Yeah, well,"—I shrugged—"glad to hear he's working."

"Oh man, it's like he never left. It's been great."

I gave him a nod and smile, convincing myself I was glad Wyatt had moved on so quickly—further proof it was all a ruse. Further proof I had to get over this. I had to focus and just forget Wyatt Hartwell even held a piece of my heart at one point.

Back at the hotel, I read. Since any episode of *Once Upon a Time* would make me miss him, I had finally let Abi convince me to join the Smutty Grannies book club, and this month was a dark romance that had gone viral. It wasn't exactly my cup of tea, but I still snuggled into the warm hotel bed and let it take my mind off everything.

That is, until my phone buzzed on the nightstand.

Mom.

I ignored it; the book was getting too good to bring that back up.

I could really only deal with so much.

She called again the next morning while I was brushing my teeth. And again, once I hit the road to the next rodeo. And again, as soon as I pulled up to the Nova Luna Stable. And when my pocket began to vibrate as I was settling my boys, I couldn't take it anymore.

"Shit, you'd think she'd give up," I shouted at no one as I slammed Hook's stall closed. The door rattled, and I flinched and looked at the now-loose metal latch. "Dammit."

"Don't worry." I heard his voice from behind me, and instantly, my body froze. I slowly turned and saw him, reminding myself to breathe. "I'll fix it later."

Wyatt stood in Rusty's stall, his baby-blue eyes focused on me, a brush in hand, his damn hat on backwards with his hair sticking out at different angles, his voice just as perfect as I remembered.

I huffed out a breath of air.

Not worth it.

"Thanks," I replied, leaving the stable without another word.

The next day, the latch was fixed.

FORTY

Wyatt

"HE'S THE MILLLL-ION DOLLAR bull rider." My lips rubbed against the microphone, and I forced myself back to give the crowd a clear voice. "He's the one that everyone has been watching, the one that is well on his way to the NFR in just two weeks, the one who always, always"—I tapped on the screen, and the music blared to life. Jon Bon Jovi's *It's My Life*, filled the stadium as the crowd cheered—"gives you a show. Oakes Ashford riding" —I looked down at my notes—"Wild Honey!"

Who the hell names a bull *Wild Honey*?

Furrowing my brow, I finished Ashford's ride with the same enthusiasm, the same spark that I had before. He definitely gave a show, leaping from the bull and waving his arms to the crowd, and they went wild. Oakes pulled in an eighty-nine to lead the night, and he was the first rider, followed by seven more for Wyoming's last rodeo of the year, before every cowboy and cowgirl headed to the National Finals Rodeo.

Ever since I had gotten back in the announcing world, I had been behind the microphone at multiple rodeos—each one reminding me how much I loved and missed doing this. That part of me that I had been missing for a year was making its way back into my life, and there was no denying it. I still had it. Once that mic turned on, it was as if no time had passed. The year I missed didn't exist. My passion for this was still there. I still loved it just as much as I did before my fist connected with a nose.

But the other part...the part that was stronger...hated that I was here without her. That she wasn't going to be the one I saw right after closing the booth, that she wasn't going to be the one I was going home with...that we weren't doing this together.

It was hard enough seeing her at the ranch. Being out with Sam and Hawkins the entire month of October was a good break, but when I got back home and my eyes instantly connected with hers, the rush of the rodeos didn't seem so important. She was smiling, she was riding, she was always going—she was moving on so fast. The least I could do was attempt to show her I was moving on as well, even though it hurt like hell to do so.

So I did the only thing I could think to do.

Announce.

I flicked the light off in the booth at the same time I felt the buzz in my pocket. I locked the door and pulled out my cell.

Lachlan

Everything is set. The blueprints look great.

Me

Perfect. Thanks, man.

Lachlan

It really does look fantastic. I'll send you a pic. For the one who wanted no responsibilities, this sure is a lot.

Me

It's worth it.

Lachlan

She sure is.

My cousin, a hopeless romantic at heart.

I pocketed my phone, feeling a smile tug at my face at the thought of how this had played out. It may not be ideal, but it was going to happen anyway. She may not want me the way I want her anymore, but if I could be her friend again...I'd take that.

"Hartwell!"

I spun on my heel, right in time to see Archie come bounding up. I knew he was here, and if I was being honest, he was the last person I wanted to see tonight. Not after our last interaction, but I gave him a welcoming smile. I knew he played a part in getting me back in the game, so I forced myself to play nice. *Remember Hartwell, only things he'd want to hear.*

"Hey Archie," I said, putting on my best voice.

"Great show tonight," he cheered.

"Thanks, man." My stomach twisted. I wasn't used to this anymore, but I could still feel my chest swell with the praise.

"Half expected to see Compton here with you. Where is your girl?" He caught up to me, slightly out of breath with that same stupid, cocky grin on his face.

I inhaled, holding the air in my lungs.

"She uh"—I let out a breath of air—"she's doing her own thing. Probably prepping for the NFR."

"She's top spot, I saw. Can't believe it. Well—ha, no, I can. You two sure did help each other out, didn't you?"

I stopped and flinched, feeling the zing of anger run up my spine. The last time we spoke, it took everything in me to play the part and roll with it, tell him all the things he wanted to hear to help get my career back on track. And at the time...it worked. But now...it took everything in me not to punch him again. That would only put me right back to where I started.

"What?"

Archie answered with a laugh.

I raised a single brow, turning to face him. "Do you remember why I punched you in the first place?"

He chuckled, his thumb reaching up to touch the side of his nose. "Yeah, I do. Laughable now, really—"

"Why is it laughable?"

"Don't be an ass, Hartwell."

My eyes widened as my eyebrows rose, and I suddenly didn't give two shits about what he wanted to hear. Playing the part lasted all but three minutes. Why play a part when I could be the man Quinn helped me become?

I took a deep breath, feeling my shoulders rise and fall as I released the tension that had been building since Archie called my name.

"You think she used me to get to where she is, and that I used her to get back in the booth?" I used my thumb to point behind my shoulder.

Archie furrowed his brow. "Come on. That was your game—"

"I was never playing a game. You're the ass who was assuming the worst from someone you didn't even know. If you ask me, you kinda deserved that punch. She didn't need me or anyone else to get to where she is now. That happened all on her own. And me...well,"—I shrugged—"I'm not sure what miracle got me back here, or if you had any part to play in it, but I can tell you it wasn't because I was using her. She's too strong to be thrown around like that. She would have had my ass handed to me. Now that I think of it, she almost did. We helped each other sure—but not in the ways you're accusing us of." Shoving my hands in my pockets, I took a step towards him.

"You really expect me to believe you settled down with her? That she picked you—"

"I do. She did. You know we're together—" I clenched my teeth. "We *were* together, and Arch—I'll never stop defending her, even though she doesn't particularly want to be near me right now, which I also have you to thank for, in a way." I yanked my hand out of my pocket and gestured to him, palm up, before shoving it back in my pocket. "I won't punch you again, but just...have a bit more respect. Stop talking about my girl."

Archie raised a brow. "You're serious?"

"I've figured a lot of things out within the last year—including how to be a tad bit serious from time to time. So yeah...don't talk about my girl."

His lips parted as he held my stare, then after a few moments of pregnant silence, he finally said, "Got it. I won't be at the NFR but...congratulate her for me, yeah?"

I gave him a wry smile, which he returned in kind before leaving me for the crowd that was waiting for him. I bit the inside of my bottom lip, ignoring the sting that somehow had found its way into my chest. If only Quinn were here—she'd not only congratulate me on not breaking more than his nose this time, but she'd kiss me and tell me how amazing the show was, helping me erase the last ten minutes, allowing me to melt into her. If only...

If only.

But she wasn't...

So...I did the only thing I could do.

I took that step forward and tried to move on.

FORTY-ONE

Quinn

I PUSHED MY SHIRTS to the side, attempting to see everything I owned in my closet instead of sprawled out everywhere. My boots were too shaded, but I knew what they looked like. My belts were all mixed, but I could pick them apart. My shirts needed to be steamed before I did anything else, but I could remember what I paired them with. My head was a jumbled mess as I tried to keep this new system organized. At least it was my head that was a mess and not my condo. Abi was on her way to help me pack, but until then, I still had to wrap my head around what I was packing for.

The National Finals Rodeo.

I made it.

I was NFR-bound.

And I left in two days.

Two weeks, ten rounds...

This was the big one, and I thought *now* was a good time to change my routine.

Squatting down, I pulled out a pair of boots—brown with turquoise accents—and reached up to grab the satin shirt at the same time. The shirt fell from the hanger, landing directly on my head, the satin sliding off my hair with that static sound everyone loves. I could feel my hair standing on end. I stood and attempted to pat it down.

"Good lord," I mumbled, laughing at myself.

My phone buzzed in my pocket, the vibration rattling through me. Without looking, I swiped and held it to my ear.

"Abi, please tell me you're on your way. You're going to lose it when you see me." I laughed. "It's like I touched one of the electric balls you see at a science museum."

"Quinn?"

That wasn't Abi's cheerful voice. I closed my eyes tight, banged the edge of my phone on my forehead, and looked to see who had called me. Dammit—I should have checked before I answered.

"Hi, Mom," I grumbled.

I heard her inhale. "I've been trying to reach you."

"Yeah, I..." I shook my head. *I've been avoiding you at all costs.* "I've been busy."

"I see."

She grew silent, and the space between her and me seemed too thick even through the cellular world.

She cleared her throat. "So, I talked to your dad."

I nodded, even though she couldn't see me. "About?"

"You."

"Me?"

"Your dad was a little upset with me after we saw you last."

"That was months ago," I said flatly.

"Yes..." She trailed off, then let out a sigh. "He brought it to my attention that I haven't been the best support to you through the years."

"You haven't."

"I just..."

"Mom, I really don't want to have this conversation." I plopped on the edge of my bed.

"I do," she snapped. "I've been trying to call you for weeks now, and I finally got you on the phone."

"Did you ever think I wasn't answering for a reason?"

"Well, you've been *busy*, but I knew you would have to answer eventually."

"I thought you were Abi. I wouldn't have answered if I saw it was you. Mom, I really am busy. I'm packing and—"

"Quinn, I'm trying here," she said harshly, the same shout from my childhood, which only made my stomach churn.

"Are you, Mom? Or are you trying to make yourself feel better?" I asked, the tension finally snapping in me.

"I just wanted to connect with you somehow. You didn't want that."

"I didn't want to do pageants." I raised my arm in the air, pretending to release all the frustration. "I didn't want to be a rodeo queen. I wanted to work. I wanted a horse. I wanted to race—but that wasn't enough for you to be proud of me."

"Quinn, I show you I'm proud of you in other ways."

"Like?" I asked, the annoyance spreading through me.

Silence.

"I asked you before I moved, and you didn't answer."

Again, she was silent.

I inhaled. "Your silence is loud, Mom." I exhaled.

"It's not that I'm *not* proud of you," she said softly. "I just wish you had chosen what we wanted for you."

"That's just it—what you wanted. Not what I wanted. You have no idea how much I love racing. How much I love this world I'm a part of. I'm good at it, great even. I'm going to the NFR—did you see that?"

"Your dad may have mentioned it," she muttered.

"I'm packing right now. I'm looking at my closet full of shirts and boots and hats, and I have to convince you that this is what I'm supposed to be doing." I ran my hand through my hair, still feeling the static that clung to me. "*This* is what I'm supposed to be doing," I repeated.

"I..." I could hear her swallow. "I know. I can see you."

"Then why don't you tell me that? When you see me at an event, it's because you're there with your rodeo queen, and you make sure I know they are carrying the flags. You were more interested in Wyatt than the score I got one night. Everyone is always more important than me. Everyone has always been more important than me."

"Quinn I—"

"Mom." I stopped her. "Reno. I told you what I really needed from you...and here we are, months later, and I'm saying the same thing. I don't think this is an easy thing that a phone call can fix. It's not going to get better overnight."

"I want to try to make it better."

Slowly, I closed my eyes. "Mom—" I breathed, feeling the tears swell in my eyes. This is what I wanted, what I needed. I wanted my mom's acceptance more than anything—and yet... "I don't know if you can make it better."

"I can try."

A knock on my front door snapped me out of the melancholy that was building in my chest. I sniffed, let a few tears fall on their own, and stood.

"Maybe you can, but you can't start now. I still need space." Another knock forced my feet to move. "Abi's here. She's helping me pack for the NFR and then maybe after...we can try to work on our relationship, but for right now..." I slowly walked down my stairs, seeing the blonde of Abi's hair through the glass. "I can't."

"I'll be at the NFR. With Ke—" She stopped herself. "I'll look for you, okay?"

Nodding, I grasped the door handle. "I gotta go, Mom."

I heard her tsk. "Okay, we will try."

Then she hung up before I could say anything else. I shoved my phone back in my pocket and used my thumb to wipe at the tears under my eyes. I sniffed again, took a deep breath, and put on my best smile for my friend. Abi was becoming close to me—enough that I knew I could talk to her, but she didn't know about this. The only person who knew about this was...

And I couldn't call him now, could I?

One more calming breath was all I needed, and then I swung the door open.

"Abi—you are very late—" I froze, seeing not Abi, but finding myself staring at the man I wanted so badly to see—but never wanted to see again.

Wyatt Hartwell raised his gaze and gave me a small, sorrowful grin.

And I...

Slammed the door in his face.

FORTY-TWO

Wyatt

I FLUNG MY FOOT forward, stopping her door before she could slam it shut. *Fuck*—that hurt. Sucking air in through my teeth, I ignored the sting. I was wearing boots, but damn, she flung that door hard.

"Quinn, please—" I started, leaning against the door frame to poke my head through the small crack. "I know I'm the last person you want to see right now, but I just need twenty minutes. I have something for you, and then I'll leave, and..." I closed my eyes and groaned, the pain shooting up through my foot. Is this what Cash felt on a daily basis? "Quinn?" I mumbled.

I felt the pressure on the door loosen, and it swung open, revealing her gorgeous face. *Damn.* I didn't know exactly how much I missed her face until it was right in front of me. She was flushed, a tint of pink glossed the ridge of her cheekbone, and those emerald eyes I loved more than anything were wet. Weariness lined her features, and I had to fight the urge to pull her to me, wanting to take whatever was causing that look away. Remembering why I came here in the first place, I tightened my grip on the cardboard tube I held at my side.

"Just give me twenty minutes."

She twisted, no doubt looking at the clock that hung behind the door. "You've got fifteen." Then, she stepped aside and let me through. Abi had told me she was packing for the NFR and that in twenty minutes she'd show up and kick my ass out...but by the state of her house, and the lack of boots, she couldn't be packing.

"Your house..." I began, taking the steps through the living room into the kitchen, dropping the tube on the counter.

"What about it?" Quinn rounded the other side of the island, her arms folded across her chest, her eyes anywhere but on me.

"Abi said you were packing?" I raised a brow.

"I am."

"Where are your boots? Your hats? Belts? Shirts?"

"In the closet," she said, raising her eyebrows and looking at me like I was the crazy one for asking. "You now have thirteen minutes, Hartwell."

I cleared my throat. "Right—yeah, okay." I popped the top off the cardboard tube. "I've been working on something, and I want to show you. This isn't set in stone; no groundbreaking has happened...but..." I pulled the large paper from the tube and carefully rolled it out on the counter. "I just—wanted you to see it all."

The blueprints that I had been mulling over for months sat in front of me, showing off a new barn and stable that would fit up to twenty horses. Behind the stable was a fenced-in pasture that connected to another small building that could be used for vet visits, bathing, and grooming needs—anything a retired horse would need to live a comfortable life. Above the drawing of the front of the barn was written in block white letters *Once Upon a Rescue.*

The room went silent, and even though I knew she was taking it all in, I also knew my minutes were flying by. I bit my lip, waiting for her to talk first. The pink tint in her cheeks deepened, and she finally let out a heavy breath.

"Wyatt, what is this?"

"Yours," I said softly, sliding the blueprints to face her. "I figured out what the best thing to do with my two hundred and fifty acres was, so over the past couple of months, Lachlan, Rhett, and I found the perfect piece of land that's not a part of the cow fields, close enough to the main house and barn that it's not secluded, but it has its own space. We marked it, and then we met with an architect. We thought twenty horses would be a good start, but the land is big enough that you can always add to it, and I can buy more land from my brother or cousin if you need more space." I pointed to the pasture space on the print, then slid the first sheet over slightly to show off the aerial view of Hartwell Hills. The red line drew out the acreage and had a small barn sticker where we thought it would make most sense.

"More space...Wyatt..." She placed her hand on the paper, her fingers tracing the lines. "Once Upon a—"

"That's a placeholder," I cut in. "Of course, we can change the name to whatever you want, and like I said...this doesn't need to be built any time soon. I figured you wanted a few more years in the rodeo, but...I wanted to have everything ready to go so when *you* are ready...we can make it happen fast."

"You're..." She swallowed, and her gaze finally rose to meet mine. "Going to build a horse sanctuary on the ranch?"

"Not just any sanctuary, Quinn. Your sanctuary. I don't want or need these two hundred and fifty acres. But you..." I decided to be bold, reaching out and placing my fingers over hers. "You could take them and make them brilliant."

"I can't take them from you," she whispered, her fingers starting to intertwine with mine.

"You won't be. I'm giving them to you. Or we can simply add your name to the deed if you would rather."

She inhaled and glanced down, her eyes searching the blueprints. I watched her face the entire time, desperately wanting to know what was going through her mind. Her brow pinched, a sigh left her lips, and she once again met my gaze. A small hint of anger flashed behind her eyes...and my stomach dropped.

"If this is to make me forgive you—" She pulled her hand away quickly.

"I was working on this well before I fucked everything up," I admitted, keeping my hand right where it was, hoping she'd take it again. "This was always the plan. I wanted to give it to you at Christmas, but Abi told me your lease was ending soon. I got nervous you would be leaving after the NFR, and...well." I shrugged. "I couldn't wait until then. Quinn, I..." I stopped, placing both my hands on the counter and lowering my chin.

My mind flashed to the bar when Quinn first kissed me, the way she said she had prepared an entire speech, and the moment she saw me, it was lost. I said that her kiss told me everything, but in this moment, I couldn't kiss her to tell her exactly what was going through my mind. I had the words—they just wouldn't form. I needed them to—I needed her to know.

Swallowing the lump in my throat, I raised my chin. "I never meant to hurt you. It kills me to see you every day knowing I'll never be able to hold you or kiss you again...just *have* you again. The first moment I saw you, I knew. Even after you turned me down so many times...I knew you were it for me. You were the one who was going to change my life. And fuck, Quinn—you did. I found myself wanting to be better, wanting so much more than I had, as long as you were there, too. And then...I fucked it up. I can't tell you how many times I tried to forget about you, but I couldn't...I can't. I'll never be able to move on from you. I hate that I hurt you. I hate that it's taken me this long to find the words to say, and believe it or not, these are not the words I practiced." I paused briefly, catching the little smirk on her lips before she dipped her chin. "But I need you to know you were never a play. I need you to know that Kelly—" My throat closed, and I tried to force myself to keep speaking, but nothing came out, not even a sound.

"That..." she squeaked. "I may have overreacted. That's nothing. Abi...she..." she stammered and then waved her hand in the air as if to erase everything. "It's not important."

"I hate that I let it happen. I never meant to hurt you," I raised my gaze, meeting her eyes. "You were never a game. You were more...*are* more than that. You're my everything; you'll always be my everything—and I will never stop loving you, even though you've stopped loving me."

"Wyatt..." she whispered, her hands morphing into fists.

"It's okay. I didn't come here to win you back; I came here to tell you that and give you these—which I did. So." I pushed myself off the counter and looked at the clock on the oven, letting a breath out through my lips. "I believe my fifteen minutes are up. I'll respect your boundaries and give you the space. I'll stop chasing." I wiped my hands in front of me, erasing everything that had happened since that night in The Steel when I first approached her. That felt like so long ago, but now with her in front of me...I couldn't help but have some hope. Maybe, just maybe, we could be friends again. I just had to stop chasing.

A slight shock flashed across her face. "I'm not moving," she said quickly, catching me completely off guard. "I signed another year, paid in full." She picked at her fingernails. "And I'm going to talk to Jeff about buying the place."

I felt the corner of my lips tug up. "That's great." I took a few steps back, telling myself the further I got from her, the less likely she was to hear my heartbeat. It was pounding, echoing through my chest and most likely this room. If I didn't leave, I never would. I gave in to the smile. "I'm proud of you," I added, loving the small gasp that came from her. "And glad you'll be sticking around. I'm sure Hook would miss me."

She chuckled and licked her lips. "Yeah...he would."

Would she?

"I'll just..." I pointed behind me to the front door.

"You don't need these?" she asked, her hands gliding across the blueprints.

I shook my head. "No, they're yours. It is your sanctuary, after all." Slowly, not wanting to leave just yet but knowing I had to, I made my way to her front door, only to twist and take one more look at her. "We're all going to the NFR, by the way. All ten days. Cash made sure we all got tickets to support you, but..." I hesitated, suddenly shy as her green gaze bore into me. "I'll stay out of the way and just cheer you on from the stands. I can't wait to see you take it all. I know you will."

Quinn, who was still frozen in place in front of the blueprints, took a deep breath in, her shoulders raising.

"But"—I waved my hand at the pristine living room—"you should pull all your boots out though; I tried it, and hey"—I winked—"It really helps you be able to see everything."

And right before I shut the door behind me, I heard her soft laugh.

FORTY-THREE

Quinn

"ROUND ONE," CASH MUSED as he scratched Hook behind his ears.

"Round one," I repeated, slipping my phone into the small saddlebag.

"You ready?" He raised a brow, craning his neck to see me.

"Yes," I said positively, giving him a sure nod.

I had this in the bag.

Probably.

I would be lying if I said there wasn't a small flutter of nerves in my stomach. I was top in the nation for earnings. I was predicted to come out if not first, then second or third, and I had a lot of eyes on me. I had been to the NFR as an attendee before, watching from the stands, so I knew exactly how many people were out there. I knew how big the arena floor was, and I knew they were all watching me. I think if I weren't nervous, that would be more of a problem.

I had already seen the rodeo queens, which meant I had already caught a glimpse of my mom. Even though I tried to brush it off and ignore the fact that she was here, the small wave and smile she gave me told me one thing—she was starting to try. So, I smiled back and gave her a wave. It was the sweet little kiss she blew me with her fingers that threw me for a loop. So much so that I blew her a little one right back.

"Just remember—" Cash started with his routine trainer points. Not too loose, not too stiff. Don't cut the corners too close...blah...blah...blah.

I let him ramble, pretty much knowing his entire speech by heart. I was just happy he was here. I listened as best I could, giving Hook more focus than Cash. I tightened his saddle by a millimeter, turned the stirrup, ran my hand along his coat as I walked behind him, and once I reached his nose, I dug in my pocket for the peppermint that I had begun to carry with me. I offered it to him, loving the way his furry lips felt against my palm, and I kissed his snout.

That's when I heard it.

That familiar laugh that never left my mind.

I glanced up, my vision catching Wyatt like a bee to honey.

The noise of the entire arena faded, and all I heard was his laugh as he joked with announcers, his hands moving as he spoke, his eyes gleaming with pure joy, handsome as ever in his Wrangler jeans and T-shirt. I held on to Hook's reins a little tighter.

When he showed up at my house, the last thing I expected was for him to hand me my dream on a piece of paper. I expected a *'please take me back'* move—not *'here's two hundred and fifty acres, you're my everything'*. Those three words stuck with me more than the numerous *I love you's* he's given me before. I had never been someone's *everything*, and I was his. When he left, I stood frozen, studying the blueprints, wishing he had stayed a little longer—and when Abi showed up five minutes later, she had that knowing look on her face. The first thing I told her was "*I love him.*" She simply smiled and said, "*Yeah, you do.*"

What I wouldn't give to have him next to me. All it would take was one shout of his name, and I knew he would come running. But no—there was time. There was more time. I had a ride to get to, and he was obviously caught up in something that made him happy. It could wait. It really...really could wait.

Right? It could. What did he always say...we had more than—

"Quinn?"

My attention flew back to Cash. "Hmm?" I hummed.

"You listening to me?"

"Yes," I lied.

"Then tell me exactly what I said." He folded his arms and waited.

I heaved a sigh. "Not too loose, not too tight. Make sure you round the barrels and keep your toe in. Make sure you're not cutting those corners. Use your spurs. Hook's fast, but he's only as fast as you make him. Don't pay attention to the clock...just focus on your horse and the dirt in the air." I mimicked his light Southern accent, something I knew drove him crazy. "Oh, and I'm living vicariously through you, so make sure you make me proud."

If he raised his brow any higher, it would disappear under his hat.

I gave him a cheeky smile. "You *are* living vicariously through me? Right?"

"That's not what I said at all."

"At least part of it was."

"I stopped talking when I saw you looking at Wyatt. I got to 'don't cut the corners too tight' before I noticed you weren't even paying attention."

My eyes widened. "Oh. Well, it's not like I haven't heard your speech before."

Cash huffed. "You good?"

I nodded. "I'm great."

I couldn't even try to hide it. I was semi-gawking, and he caught me. As if on instinct, my eyes darted to Wyatt, then quickly back to Cash.

"Do I need to get him over here?"

Yes.

"Nope." I popped the P, turning to fiddle with something on Hook's saddle, lowering my gaze. "My focus is here." I patted his coat.

"I know; you're always focused. Saddle up, get him warmed up, and then put on a show. I'll be in the crowd with Abi and Stet. We'll scream so loud, you'll be able to hear us."

I gave a soft chuckle, slipping my boot into the stirrup and hoisting myself up into the saddle. "I'll make sure to listen for it." I looked down at my trainer, the person who first showed me support in this crazy ass journey of mine. "Round one."

He cocked a grin. "Round one. See you after."

I nodded and lifted my gaze one last time to Wyatt.

Except that time he was looking right at me.

Our eyes locked.

Even from a distance, I saw his lips twitch before he broke the contact, returning to whatever conversation he was having, that bright smile filling the darkness of the arena.

Without a second thought, I kicked Hook into a trot. I closed my eyes tight, willing my brain to focus on anything other than Wyatt Hartwell.

I saw the dirt in the Hartwell arena, Stetson helping me with the barrels—Wyatt sitting on the gate with his boots locked in the bars.

You belong on the dirt, don't you? Watching you ride...you fit right in with the Hartwells. It's about time we make it official.

I envisioned the rodeo in Flagstaff, a huge win for me, beating out a girl whom I had no qualms with until—Wyatt.

Oh, right—it's your love I have to earn.

Dammit. I stopped Hook and breathed, Wyatt's voice now filling my head.

Come on, Quinn. There's only one girl I want to chase right now...

Tell me I'm not making this up—tell me this means more for you...

The only reason why I'm spectacular, Quinn, is because I'm wanted and loved by you...

We have more than tonight...

We had all the time in the world.

I pulled Hook into the corral and kicked him into a gallop, starting to run in circles to keep up with my mind. No matter how hard I tried to concentrate on the ride, all I could remember were bits and pieces of the last year with him. Wyatt showing up at my door with food and drinks. Wyatt sitting next to me, enduring episode after episode of my silly favorite show. Wyatt lifting me into his arms after every ride. Wyatt listening to me when I needed someone to talk to about my life, and then not dwelling on the negative aspects of it, making sure I knew I was important. Wyatt's lips on mine for the very first time. Wyatt's warm comfort as I fell asleep. Wyatt—always chasing...

I was his everything...and he...

He was mine.

"Racers!" The shout pulled me from my spiral. A man wearing a headset and holding a clipboard began shouting off the order of riders. "As soon as the rider in front of you is done, you get your horse up to the gate—waste no time, that clock starts ticking the second your horse's hooves hit the dirt."

Third. I was third.

Meaning...I was out of time.

And I really didn't want to wait until later.

I twisted, reaching for the saddlebag, slipping my phone free. A text may not be the best way to get his attention, but for now, it was my only option. The thought of me screaming his name on top of a barrel flashed through for a second before the more reasonable thought hit. The first rider broke through the gate, the announcers sending the crowd wild.

I pulled up our text thread, one I'd been ignoring for months now. I saw his last message *I love you*, and a gasp of hope left my lungs.

My thumbs shaking, I typed...

> You're mine, too. Maybe it's time I start chasing you?   Me

The blue line above the text began to creep across the screen. Hook bounced his feet, jolting my body from side to side.

"Okay, okay—it's us." I locked the screen, praying the message was delivered, and slipped my phone back into the bag.

The second rider flew past me, her time being shouted at a sixteen point eight.

Okay... I took a deep breath. *He'll see it. I'll get to him. I got this in the bag.*

"Quinn Compton from Bozeman, Montana, has been one to watch this year, and tonight she's riding Hook—"

I blocked out the announcer's voice and kicked Hook into full speed heading left, watching as that first barrel got closer and closer. Hook knew what to do, and without my guidance, he turned.

"That's it," I muttered, rounding it and gaining more speed for that second barrel. Clean turn, not too loose, not too tight. "One more." I breathed.

Hook took over, his speed matching that of a jet plane as he galloped, rounding the barrel and flying back to the gate. My sense of hearing came flooding back once I heard the crowd scream, and I could swear I heard Cash louder than anyone, just like he promised. I loosened my shoulders and let out a loud laugh, not even caring what my time was. *I just rode in the NFR. I couldn't care less if I rode the next nine rounds—I did this. Me.* And then, all I wanted was to be in his arms. All I had to do was get Hook in the corral—he'd be fine there to cool down—then find him. I'd chase him.

My time came flying over the speakers, followed by another cheer, but Hook was already in the corral, and I was already dismounting, my boots moving on their own towards the man I so desperately wanted to see.

But they didn't have to move me far because, of course, there he was—shoulders moving up and down as he caught his breath, his hat skewed to the side, his phone in his hand while his other was curled into a fist at his side, those perfect baby blues hyper-focused on me.

"You heard your time, right?" he asked, still catching his breath, his hand holding his phone pointing towards the ceiling.

I shook my head. "My mind is a bit preoccupied at the moment."

"Eleven point two."

"I really don't care about that." I walked to him, my heart beginning to race.

"I'm pretty sure you just broke an all-time record, and they're still screaming about it—the girl after you hasn't even gone yet. You just blew everything out of the water with that time."

I shrugged a single shoulder. "I had somewhere I needed to be." I was inches away from him. I could see the tint to his cheeks from running, the specks of blue that floated in his eyes.

"Where's that?"

I grinned. "You know where. If you didn't know, you wouldn't be here right now."

He inhaled, closing the last inch between us. "I'm so sorry, Quinn—"

"You have nothing to be sorry for." I cut him off. "I'm sorry. I'm so sorry. I didn't listen to you, and I should have told you days ago, weeks ago...months ago...that I'm sorry. That I miss you. You said I'm your everything..."

"Everything," he parroted in a soft flutter.

"I never fell out of love. I never got over you. I want you to always chase me. I want you every minute of every day. I love you. I love you..." My hands found the nape of his neck, pulling him to me, and our lips finally—*finally*—met.

How I didn't kiss this man for the past couple of months was beyond me; everything was in this kiss. Every word, every thought, every emotion we could possibly hold was right here between us.

He broke the kiss at the same time as he raised his hand to remove my hat, then removed his own, dropping them with a thump on the ground. I pressed my forehead to his, humming and breathing him in.

"You have no idea how much I love you," he said, so only I could hear. "I never want to make you feel that way again. I want you to know just how perfect you are; please, let me try to be everything for you."

"Wyatt," I breathed as I pulled away from him. "You already are."

His shoulders dropped as relief flooded through him, his eyes swelling with tears that were beginning to form.

I pinched my brow, my lips twisting into a tiny grin. "Don't go all soft on me now, Hartwell." Lifting my thumb, I swiped a tear from the corner of his eye.

He laughed, dropping his chin for a beat, and when he looked at me with that quirky, sexy grin on his face, I fell as hard as I possibly could, "Come on, Compton. You're the one who turned me soft."

"Mmm." I scrunched my nose. "As long as it doesn't stop you from chasing."

His eyes darkened, and his gaze fell to my lips. He kissed me, a sweet butterfly kiss that sent shivers through my entire soul. "I'll never...ever stop chasing you."

"Good." I played with the hair at the nape of his neck. "I'll never stop chasing you, either, because Wyatt"—I traced his chin with my finger, bringing his lips to mine—"we have all the time in the world."

EPILOGUE

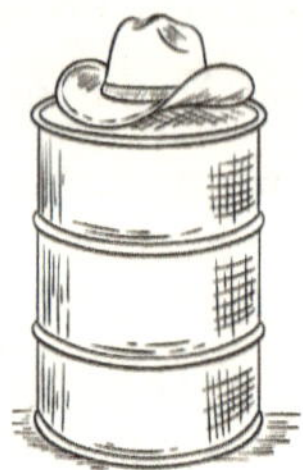

Wyatt

Two Years Later

Lachlan

He had this planned. You'd think he have it on him!

Me

I didn't want to lose it. I thought I was putting it somewhere safe.

Lachlan

I don't even know what to say to that.

Cash

My bet is it's in Hook's saddlebag.

Me

Nah, she would have seen me slip it in there and then got suspicious.

Grace

We're looking.

Abi

Are you sure you don't have it?

Me

Yes. I can't find it anywhere. It's almost her event...I kinda need that for this to work.

Rhett

Lachlan found it! It was in Beckett's diaper bag...he's on the way!

Seeing my cousin race up to me calmed every nerve in my body, but when he tossed that small black box at me—and I caught it—a whole new set of nerves took shape.

"Don't"—Lachlan pointed at me—"lose it."

I waved it in the air and spun on my heel. I had exactly ten minutes to get back to the box, grab the microphone, and then race to the complete opposite end of the arena.

It was round one of the National Finals Rodeo...and not only was Quinn the first barrel racer on the sheet, but I was finally announcing. I had already planned on popping the question this year, but when I found out we'd both be in the arena at the same time, a Wyatt Hartwell Stupid Plan was set in motion. And I was grateful enough to have a lot of people in my corner in order to pull this off.

The past two years had been absolute chaos, blending perfectly with pure bliss. Almost every weekend, Quinn and I were on the road, bouncing from rodeo to rodeo. Rusty joined us on the adventures, adding the third horse to the mix with Hook still pining for as much attention as he could get. Sometimes we were in different cities the same night, but most of the time we were at the same event—me behind the mic and her earning as much as she could to get back to the NFR. She won her first year, setting a new record that no one has been able to break, but last year she didn't—meaning this year she was even more determined to reclaim her title.

But after the busy weekends, we always wound up back at home. I officially moved into her place—well, our place after we bought it together—and when we weren't planning our trips, we were working on the sanctuary. She kept the name Once Upon a Rescue despite my telling her it was just a placeholder for her real name, but she would smile and say it reminded her of us. Speaking of which—we finished *Once Upon a Time*, but moved on to *The Office, Schitt's Creek, Outlander, Doctor Who*, and she finally got me to watch *The Princess Bride. Once Upon a Time* was still our go-to, though—we rewatched it at least once already.

Checking my watch, I opened the door to the box and grabbed the mic that was waiting for me off the table. T-minus five minutes. I passed Hawkins and Sam, both of them shouting a 'go get her' at the top of their lungs, and was stopped by Lance and Helen Compton on my way to the other side for a good luck hug. Helen promised me she'd be waiting for us, making sure to tell me exactly where we could find her after.

Quinn's relationship with her parents—yes, parents, after her father came to the realization that he held a part of the blame—had gotten better over the past few years, but there was still a lot of work to do. They met with a family therapist, and slowly the trust started to form. I sat with Quinn and held her hand, supporting her the only way I knew how. There were good days, and then something would be said, and both parties would get upset. I'd simply remind Quinn that it was baby steps—and I was amazed at her progress with her mother. The fights, when they happened, never lasted long.

I opened the gate, weaving through the crowd, and I caught the pickup men placing the last barrel. The large screen overhead showed a slow-motion video of Quinn rounding a barrel with fancy wording over it, getting the crowd excited for her event.

Which I was announcing for.

I flipped the mic on and brought it to my lips.

"And now we have the top ten cowgirls in the arena with us tonight to show us their skills and tell those barrels who's boss." I lowered the mic and exhaled through my lips, waiting for my partner to reply.

The plan was simple. I'd announce from here, he'd announce from the box, acting like we were right next to each other the entire time. I just didn't account for A) being completely out of breath, and B) any noise the mic would pick up that was around me. I brushed those thoughts aside. I knew Quinn—she wasn't going to pay attention to what I was saying anyway.

After my partner finished his bit, I lifted the mic back up. "And we're starting with Quinn Compton from Alpine Ridge, Idaho. She's riding her spitfire, Hook. She's been training and working hard to get here, her third year in a row to reclaim her title of World Champ, and I'm sure that she's gonna take it all back—"

I watched as Hook burst from the gate, Quinn's turquoise shirt brighter than anything else in the arena. She had the perfect form as she rounded the first barrel, her hair flying behind her, and then the second barrel, taking the corner a little too tight, but not hard enough to knock it over, then the last barrel.

She rounded it, and I moved, turning off the mic so my partner could finish her ride. Hook was fast—I just had to move faster. My boots hit the dirt, slipping just slightly, but I made it to the barrel and climbed until I was standing on it. I heard whoops from the crowd and saw myself on the screen overhead. Quinn was still moving, but suddenly she halted, stopping Hook right before they ran into the now closed gate. Hook reared up and turned, and once all four of his hooves were back on the dirt, I raised the mic and flicked it back on.

"Hey, Compton," I said, my voice now booming through the entire speakers, louder than before.

Quinn settled Hook, then she faced me, and I swear...I saw her smile from here.

"You look like you belong on this dirt." I heard the shake in my voice.

Quinn kicked Hook forward, closing the gap between us. She looked around the arena, piecing the puzzle together. Once she got closer to me, I jumped from the barrel, and she dismounted Hook. We closed the gap, her breath just as heavy as mine. We were inches apart. I smiled, meeting her emerald eyes and telling myself I couldn't kiss her just yet, then I held up the small box, opening it to reveal the square-cut diamond with turquoise jewels surrounding it.

"How about we make it official? Will you marry me?" I said in the mic—and the crowd screamed.

Her gaze went to the ring, to me, back to the ring, and finally back to me. Her entire body began to bounce, buzzing with what I could only assume was adrenaline and excitement. She bit her lip, but her smile still grew, and when she threw her arms around my neck, we both lost balance and fell to the ground, the dirt flying up in all directions around us.

"Yes, Wyatt," Quinn whispered into my ear so only I could hear. "Yes, yes, yes."

I dropped the mic, its sound resonating throughout the arena. I raised her face to me, loving the way the flush spread across her cheeks. Her lips were slightly parted, perfectly kissable. And before anyone could make us get off the dirt—I did just that. I kissed my fiancée.

Acknowledgements

This book holds a special place in my soul. When I was done with *Never Left You* I wasn't sure how I was going to enter the world of Hartwell Hills again, especially writing a trope I didn't really care for (hi reformed playboy). I was still listening to every negative thing my own mind was telling me and I was scared of my computer, to say the least. It wasn't until I wrote something in-between *NLY* and *Fool For You* where I found my love for writing again and then Wyatt's story just...poured out. I have never had a story comes so easily before. I had so much *fun* writing this book. It brought me so much joy every time I sat down. I giggled, I swooned and I fell in love with Wyatt and Quinn.

But that doesn't mean I did this on my own. Quite the opposite really.

My husband and kiddos thank you for dealing with me yet again writing, revising, rereading, editing and ignoring every single household chore for fifty-five days while I spent my entire start of 2025 in Hartwell Hills. I felt the love and support you gave me, and it means the world

Jessee, I love you. You listened to every voice message, you talked me through every scene, you let me send you daily word count screenshots, and you read the messy first draft and encouraged me in every way I need. Without you—I would have quit when I was low. Without you—Wyatt wouldn't be as amazing as he is. You're my best friend and a huge part of my journey. I love you and can't wait to hug you again!

Tessa, you took this chapter by chapter, you squealed and loved it as much as I did. The way you have latched on to my characters, you help me bring them to life and love them...I'm not sure you know how much that means to me. You will always get the messy, you will always get the notes, you will always get my vague voice messages. You always give me to courage to keep going.

Kate, your support means more than you know. Meeting you in person, wrapping my arms around you, was a highlight of 2025. I look up to you in so many ways, you have a fire in you that no one will ever put out—just like Quinn—and I admire it and strive to be like you! I love you and all the encouragement you've given me!

Kayla, the best PA an indie author could ask for. Thank you SO MUCH for taking some of those daunting tasks that I hate and avoid to help me become a little more organized. Thank you for looking out for my mental health and being there for me! I couldn't have done this without you!

My writing group—Grayson, MJ, India, Cindy and Jessee. Thanks for listening to me complain and then love it and then complain and love it again. You guys have been a saving grace and still put up with me for some reason!

My betas—Beth, Kayla, Meghan, Sydney, Cait and Quin. With your feedback, I was able to make this the best it could be! Thank you for loving them!

My street team! YOU made this book release fun for me! Thank you for your support, your excitement and you love for me and my craft! I truly have the best team in the world, and I can't thank you enough!

My amazing editors, Allie and Elaine. Your help and comments (especially the unhinged ones) built my confidence and helped me make this my best work. I am so grateful for you and loved working with both of you!

To those in the rodeo world who have helped me make this as accurate as I could and who have answered my random questions. Elizabeth, Alex, and Lindsey—thank you for putting up with me!

To the artists who have given the most perfect pieces. Melody giving me the most amazing cover. Erika giving me the character art of my dreams. Grayson bringing one of my favorite scenes to life in the best way. Kloe giving Wyatt an edge and making Quinn absolutely stunning. Valerie giving me an art piece I'd never thought I see come to fruition. Each peace means so much to me and each time I look at them, joy radiates through me. I can never get enough of my characters, and each of you bring them with your own flair.

This one may seem weird—but I have to add it. Each book had a movie that was playing in the background while I edited. For *SLM* it was *National Treasure, NLY* was *Twisters...FFY...KPop Demon Hunters*. So...thanks Rumi and Jinu (insert embarrassing laugh) for the company while editing!

As always, I'm forgetting someone. So many people encouraged me through this and I hope you know how much you are loved!

And you—the readers! The ones who allow me to take you to a new place, thank you for your love and support! Until the next book!

With love – Stefanie

Also by Stefanie K Steck

Standalones

All Because of Elowin

Under the Marble Sky

Moments of Us Series

That Right Moment

That Next Moment

That First Moment

Hartwell Hills Series

Somebody Like Me

Never Left You

Fool For You

About the Author

Stefanie K Steck is a romance writer, full-time dental assistant, Army wife, mom of three crazy kids and curator of a small zoo. She currently lives in Utah and has recently found joy in camping. In the little spare time she has, you can find her reading, writing, cuddling her favorite Guinea pig, Nugget, or rewatching the *Back to the Future Trilogy* or the *Marvel Cinematic Universe (The Infinity Saga* obviously)...again...or obsessing over *Twisters...er...*she means *KPop Demon Hunters.*

Follow her on Instagram @authorstefanieksteck
www.stefanieksteckbooks.com